In tribulations

In tribulations:

50 years of Russian marriage

Georgiy Ulchenko

Copyright © 2019 Georgiy Ulchenko. All rights reserved.

ISBN: 978-1-0972-8016-2

For my sister: rest in peace

Simple Soviet people read a lot - or drank a lot. Some managed to combine one with another in a big way that strike imagination.
ALEXANDER BALOD

Contents

Title 2
Copyright 3
Dedication 4
Opening Quote 5
Chapter 1. She's a bastard 7
Chapter 2. The youth and the love
during the war. 27
Chapter 3. The wrong start of the marriage 63
Chapter 4. The old love returns 97
Chapter 5. Fly up to fall 118
Chapter 6. Living people with dead souls 151
Chapter 7. On the way of madness 171
Chapter 8. The desperate assassin 200
Chapter 9. The end of the road 222

Georgiy Ulchenko

Chapter 1. She's a bastard

For eighty-five years, they called me Eugenia Nicole. Earlier I was Gina, Gena, and Genie as you like. I was not so lucky to be born at a time when people still respected traditional family relationships. My misfortune was born at once with me because I had no father's name in the birth certificate. In our short street where we lived at the edge of the Marina Grove, in Moscow, they did not forgive this fact nor mother neither daughter. Fatherless is a social status that has burned the stigma on my sensitive soul. A wound of the stigma was sad and bleeding, and it is impossible to have an easy character with such a wound, isn't it?

Here we go with my mother straight the center of Moscow to her workplace – the hotel "National", where she works as a parlormaid. It's a summer morning, sidewalks has washed, passers-by hurry up to their job sites. On the cobblestone pavement cars are rustling with tires, everyone is beeping and honking to other. In the middle of the intersection on the narrow Tverskaya Street there stands a uniformed traffic cop on the pedestal, he has white gauntlets on his hands and brandishes a stripy baton to and fro. What a beautiful scene!

My mother drags me forward, tugging at my hand, but I twiddle my head, looking at the traffic cop, who is astonishing among ordinary people, and I want so much that he becomes my dad. My heart freezes with delight when I imagine as he comes home, throws a striped baton at the entrance, removes his white gauntlets and neatly puts them on the chest of drawers, hugs me, kisses my mother, and our happy family goes to lunch together.

I saw such a scene in the friend families more than once and always fatally envied them. I was jealous of them so much and wished something would happen to their father, maybe he will left them at worst. Moreover, if such occasion have happened, I was the first in a crowd of teenagers to scoff at our ex-friend, teasing her with a "divorcee," as if husband had left her, not her mother.

This misfortune persecuted me right along my life. Every my girlfriend had FATHER, everyone around us knew it and saw him, finally, she had a record in the birth certificate, therefor she was a legal citizen of a great country. However, about the country I did not care. Here, on my street, on one side of which stood six two-story log houses with walk-in yards, and on the other - there was an embankment of the old ring railway, every dog knew that I had no father, he did not leave us, and never did not come.

This gaping emptiness of the half of my existence brought me multiple misfortune. I even could not ask my mother to tell me about my father, because she long ago has forbidden me to mention about him. When I still broke the ban, my mother punished me, and often - beat, so the desire to stir up my mother's past have disappeared.

No matter how I refused to go, we finally got to hotel and passing through the vestibule on the way to my mother floor, we visited the buffet.

"Hello, Ann, you son Nick sling one's hook again, did not care Genie?" asked the barmaid Mary, an old friend of my mother. "There's no one to leave you with at home, poor baby!" - She tells me with a lisp, but I do not like it, especially, when I feel a hint at my birth on the wrong side of the blanket.

Suddenly I have blushed and cried out evilly and obstinately: "It's not your business, bitch, my mother takes care of me, I do not need to be leaved anywhere and I'll be always together with my mother!"

After shouting, I picked up and rushed out. I felt that I had said superfluous things and very bad words. I understood that offended this woman, who was always kind, felt sorry for me and called me a poor orphan, because of this feeling, I was angry with both her and myself. I was young, awkward and stupid.

Such bad words I recently heard from the neighbor who quarrel with my mother in the shared kitchen, a gathering of six housewives; clashes were inevitable due to the population pressure, the harmful character of people and general disorder of life. One of them has trouble with his job; the other one has trouble with a family. Yesterday Stalin said that it is necessary to tighten their belts, because Ukraine is sabotaging the delivery of grain yield to the state bins, thus everyone must think how much rise the price of bread due to these Ukrainians, a murrain on their! Tomorrow they must pay for electricity and gas, but wages have still not issued, as a result, no matter how many reasons may be, one way out for you is to let off steam by attacking the bestially your neighbors, so that they become ill as well as you are.

Subsequently the steam came out, the time healed the caused traumas, there was nowhere to go, therefore all together discussed again the product of industrialization - a new factory that swallowed a nearby coppice and came close almost to their yards: now because of it, there will not be mushroom and berries so close and conveniently near the house. In addition, the neighbors regularly and with pleasure put each other in the swim of the great construction of a miracle underground railway with an unusual name "Metro". They waited, when the stations will lined up next to them and the first train would come to their outskirts of the capital. They also talked about the new Avenue of Peace, which had already begun to be built from Kalanchevka corner to Ostankino settlement and goes now straight to the All-Union Agricultural Exhibition was opened recently. Each of them wanted to see what the hell miracles represents the Exhibition, but for various reasons they did not get there.

Locals did not care for perpetual workers - for Ukrainian peasants, who would really begin to die (a murrain on their!) six months later. The iron hand of Soviet Union took their by the throat and squeezed out the bread – basis of their life and even took life itself. Muscovites did not know that the notorious Komsomol brigades in the construction of the metro were squads of prisoners, the same peasants with workers and other intellectual fungus. Prisoners put in jail not because they were guilty of something, but because of the nature of socialist production invented by the Bolsheviks, which based on slave labor of prisoners. Locals did not think about why the life of Muscovites is much better than that of the inhabitants of the completely vast country, but they perceived it with understanding, because they live in the Capital!

Meanwhile, Mary shook her head regretfully when her friend Ann asked to forgive daughter and sweared that she would flog this bastard girl then she does not beat her lips, and gently chided Ann: "You should not do this her because you must know what it's the misfortune to be bastard. I know it as my mother brought me into the world without husband, but your son has grown up, he is a big helper for you, he works and is self-supporting, be gentle with Genie, it is easy than to be in feud."

Ann made a face like a smile, stopped the conversation and hurried to catch up me.

However, I was already on the sixth floor, above one where my mother works. I was sheltered in the hall behind big armchairs between the columns and caves with palm trees and believed that I was not visible. Nevertheless, my mother did not thought so. She went to the governing woman, who mutely pointed out the place where I have hid, went to the columns, but changed her mind and went back to her workplace, leaving me to think my poignant thought.

I did not want to mourn further because no one offended me here where are many massive men with gross briefcases and beautiful women in vivid attires, although they not paid attention to me. Among them were some good-looking men who spoke weird language and mostly gave me sweets and ice cream, stroked my head, pronouncing something like "baby", or "kinder", or else somewhat. Here I was so thrilled of them that forgot my troubles, I felt happy with these men, moreover I dreamed that one of them would suddenly say he is my father, would take me away with him, and another life would come to me.

However, people dispersed on their businesses, leaving their keys with woman on duty who they called a strange word, like a hiss, but with some kind of breathing in the voice as "hostess". I understood that this word is not in Russian, but I felt it is a good word, respectful to the attendant. From good word, I was immediately returned to a bad word, which I suddenly and unexpectedly for myself shouted to Mary.

"I will go to ask her to forgive me," I decided, and slowly began to descend the stairs, pondering what good words I can exchange for forgiveness, or maybe more interesting things, for example, a candy or maybe, even a cake.

"Eclair - what a beautiful thing, and when you eat it - you can bite off your fingers," I thought, creeping up to the buffet. Mary was not in place: the morning hours of work had already expired, for the break the barmaid went into the back room, where she did not let me in for some unknown reasons, no matter how I invoked her. This time I decided that circumstances allow me to enter: there is no one to ask, but I have to implement my decision, especially if the encouragement can be much higher than the moral loss.

I got to the door of the pantry and heard strange sounds outside the door, which seemed me similar as I heard when Steve the electrician visited my mother to repair a loudspeaker, and they put me out the room. Later mother have told Mary that she paid for the wiring in kind by own nature, because she spent money to Nick's new shirt, when he went to work the first time. I know what money is: I saw paper rubles and saw coins–kopecks, but what the "nature" is I do not know, because I did not found it nowhere. I was ashamed to ask, because after that my mother had an unusual happy even gentle look when she gave tea for Steve.

Quietly opening the door, I was distinctly heard clear words, uttered, albeit in a whisper, but deafening me in the silence of the pantry room.

"Darling, it feels incredible when you press me, do not feel sorry for her, I'm yours," Mary whose faces were not visible whispered by a sweet voice. She laid on the bed under a man who knelt face to her. He held her hips tightly with his hands and swung them back and forth so much that the bed swayed and creaked. I immediately guessed why the sound was so familiar - it is simply the bed!

Suddenly I felt ashamed, but not because I was peeking, but because my mother could do such with Steve. Moreover I was scared that I would be caught peeping, so I closed the door and ran to my mother's site.

I did not want to share my life's observations with my mother because she did not like when I began to meditate, analyze and compare, she said that such thoughts would not lead to a happy end if I poke my nose into people's business. I just ran around the richly furnished rooms and helped my mother clean up, straightening the curtains, moving the chairs, bettering the huge cushions, which are heavy even to lift, but falling into their downy abyss and lying around was a complete pleasure. Although you can get a slap on the head, easily, but it was worth it!

"I go to Ms. Masha," - suddenly I have remembered my decision to apologize her, and dodging my mother's hand, quickly jumped from step to step. At the buffet, Mary was already standing at the counter, wiping the glass with a clean linen towel. Her face was as peaceful as my mother's one, when Steve had come, so I conclude it was not necessary to apologize at all.

"Ms. Masha, did you pay this man in kind by your nature, didn't you? Do you have no rubles?" I asked the barmaid and with horror realized that I again have said the vulgarism, which I unable to understand.

Mary is slowly blushing, and I was about to run away, but she surprisingly laughed with a ringing, happy voice without any menace. Mary laughed until she began to weep, did not stop her the my mother's arrival, she waved her hand to me, splashed her hands, swayed back and forth, bursting into laughter, and then took the biggest eclair and handed it to me, making a gesture off herself, as if saying "run already from here, while I'm kind". In addition, until I was running through the vestibule, I heard again a whoop of laughter of both my mother and Mary.

"Well, let them have fun," I thought, licking the cream from the cake. "They are decent."

This thought raised my mood, because everything turned out so well for me this morning, no one punished me for insolence and everybody around me is cheerful and friendly. It was possible to come back and dream up how to spend time further in this luxury and to be lost in reverie about things I do not have, for the time being, but one day everything will be in my life.

Sometime later, I returned to hall and approaching the buffet, I heard what mother talk to Mary. They had good-natured speaking about me, but some words were, as it seems to me, not enough good.

"All in all, she is fatherless," lamented Mary. "No rigidity at all, your husband might have it, but you have no husband in home. You are able to contract with someone, aren't you, Ann?"

My mother was silent for a while, so my heart even stopped in this moment: right now, she will say that she will have husband, he will become my father, and we will have everything, like other families.

"Well, it does not work for me with the men," she said, "always married men are clinging to me, but I cannot resist. Anyway, my time has passed, I think. Nick is already sixteen, and I ask, what is the man who wants grown-up son? Moreover, Nick will not accept anybody, because he knows his father and keeps company with him. His father looks like a madcap drunkard, but always tell Nick good words. He does not send him out of the house; does not give his wife to mistreat him."

"Listen, Ann, is her father not returned to Poland yet?" Mary asked, "Maybe, you both will go to acquaint Genie with him, and then it'll be all right, you know."

This talk damp my spirits right away. I didn't even understand what kind of father they was talking about. Life seemed unfair to me: the most valuable things in it are distributed unequally. Someone has everything, but I have nothing. I thought about it and dropped my tears, standing behind the column and not seeing that my mother noticed my presence, gave Mary a sign to keep silent, and they both approached me. Looking at their sympathetic faces, I completely turned on the waterworks, buried my face into mother's apron and shook with sobs.

While I was not yet ten years old, I perceived my sufferings as punishment for my fault, that I did not know, but others around me knew this one and constantly punished me for it. I thought about my unsettled life somewhere in the nook and every time came to the same conclusion: my fault originated from the fact that no one knows who my father is, but when I find him, the attitude to me will certainly change.

I wanted to know who my father is, but also I was afraid of it, because he could be like Alec's father, which is big, dirty and always drunk. On the other hand, he could be as Georgie's father from a neighboring yard, who beat his wife and five his children, especially beat Georgie as an elder, because he always rushed to protect his mother and smaller children. Most often, it happened so that the father was exhausted already on him, so he always walked in colored bruises, but everybody respected him in our street, because he was brave and he had a father like everyone, notwithstanding he has his own drawbacks.

I was sure that I could bear both the beatings and the terrible look of my father, if only I had him, then I could tell anyone in the yard who has offended me: "I'll tell Daddy that he'll kick your ass, you'll know it!" However, there was no father, even in absentia, I knew about this for a long time, when two years ago my mother have taken me to school and have showed the head teacher my birth certificate, which was ran a pen through the line "Father". The head teacher immediately took note me as a potentially dangerous element for the process of Bolshevik upbringing and did not miss the opportunity to find fault with and without reason.

Years passed, life changed, and when the academic year begin, I spent time in my mother's work site only on weekends. In mid-October the weather was still not cold, there was dry and clear days. On Saturday, for a long time I walked along the paths of public gardens around the city center, raking dry fallen leaves, moving from one square to another and basking in the rays of a calm but not fiery sun, until finally I reached the hotel.

I was surprised by the pandemonium near the entrance to the hotel. Some of the trucks were unloading, others drove off and drove up, the heavers carried things to the hotel, and some men walked among them, speaking a language similar to English. We began to learn English at school, but language I heard here was different, with some growling sounds and some vowels was stretched right up to the howling, although our English teacher – old woman with pre-revolutionary experience did not teach us like this.

Quickly slipped between the heavers and strangers, I ran up the wide staircase to the mother's site. There was quiet and calm in it, as usual at this time.

"Mam!" I cried when I have seen my mother coming out of the room. "What are they loading in the entrance? I saw strange men I have not seen before now."

"Quiet, you," my mother hissed, "why you shout like in the forest? They are the Americans who came here to have an embassy in the hotel, two floors higher. A week later the ambassador will come, his surname is as strange as a bird, either Kenar or Kennan. We are forced to gather there and will clean up what these Americans will bring disorder."

We went up to the floor, where pieces of furniture was moved in and out; things were brought in and carried out. Everybody was busy and worked hard, even a cat who lived here in silence and peace for many years, scampered amongst the heavers and slipped between their feet without stopping, otherwise it would have heard the selective berate of the tired heavers as big as a barn who had pronounced a curse to cat and all cat's relatives to the seventh tribe.

My mother immediately joined the work: parlormaids went to the rooms after the heavers and immediately began to clean it up after they left. I was left alone and immediately I felt sad in this busy bustle. I found a place near the window just opposite the entrance from the stairwell, where the governing woman usually sat, but now her place was free. On the top of the bureau was the newspaper Pravda, the back number of this year summer. A big article, which caught my eye, was about mysterious television that will stand to the service of socialism. Probably, it is a soldier, who will serve and protect our Soviet homeland. This spring I was accepted into the pioneers, i.e. I became a member of the organization for children, such as scouts, but established for the communist upbringing of the younger generation, so I became an expert on the political situation and knew about capitalism and socialism, but now it was not interesting.

When I have sat back comfortable, I began to watch the stout American man, who directed everyone: the heavers, parlormaids, and his staff, while managing funnily puffed a long, thick and brown cigarette, the sweetish bitter smell of which tickled my nostrils. This man with a cigarette was like a rock in a turbulent flow, about which the waves of workers scurrying along the corridor were breaking. I was so carried away by this spectacle that I did not notice the tall, broad-shouldered, middle-aged man that began to gain flesh. The man was dark-eyed, bald, with the remains of curly brown hair.

"Tell me, please," he ask me. I was bemused by such politeness. People never asked me in adult-like manner, and this man immediately seemed engaging. "Whom I can contact with at the American Embassy?"

The pronunciation of the bald-headed man has kind of lisp; he put the accent in the wrong place. I had already seen such people in the hotel, my mother said that they were "psheks" i.e. poles, persons from Poland, adding at the same time "yours compatriots", although never explained why she calls them my compatriots.

"Sir, listen to me, please!" I answered politely, but with dignity. "There's an American walking around with a big cigarette, he must be the most important person here, so you can ask him."

"Thank you for your advice, but it's not a cigarette, it's a cigar, they smoke such cigars in America," the tall Pole said, then politely bowed to me as an adult, rummaged in his pocket, took out the keys, unhooked the keychain in the form of Little Red Riding Hood in large wooden shoes and handed it to me.

"Please take this little present, little pretty Lady," he said with a courteous smile, "maybe we'll meet again when you grow up, but now let me bow out."

He went to meet an American with a cigar, briefly talked with him and then left with an active American lady, who had a stack of papers in her hands. Going around the corner, he waved me in farewell and disappeared, but suddenly I felt so sad and lonely, as if I had lost something familiar and dear for myself.

When mother's working shift was over, we went together to a tram that was going from the Bolshoi Theater to the Tower Street. On the way, my mother noticed that I have a new toy and asked where I got it. Apropos of nothing, I lied, saying that I have found it in the Alexander Garden, where a lot of people walk. Why I lied, I do not understand until now, because if I should tell the truth, my life could change in the most wonderful way, but it was happened and my life is that as it is.

Later a ghost appeared in my life. The ghost was my own grandfather Nicander, who will be died in the end of thirties in Moscow. Grandfather was a gypsy baron, who in his youth overlived in Moscow restaurants after a long journey with a nomadic camp. Where and how he met the shirtmaker Mary, my grandmother, nobody told me about this, but the meeting with him left in my heart new bleeding wound.

One summer day, when I was returning with friends from the cinema "Uranus", where for the first time in Moscow they showed a movie with a young pretty singer Claudia Shulzhenko, my mother said, "I've been waiting for you, get ready and let's go to see my father."

Mother's words took me by surprise. "What's going on?" it flited through my mind, "my mother shared a life only with me, but at once mother disclosed unheard-of father."

Worst of all there was my naivety but I sincerely considered my mother was more pitied than I was, because my mother have no father too, as I thought, and her life was already over without happiness. As it happened, I was wrong and severely wrong! My mother has her FATHER!

This fact destroyed in my mind of a teenage girl the whole creation, where I graded everybody by priorities depending on the availability of such things as the harmonious family life, food and stuff in plenty, and last but not list, the presence of the father. My mother and me in this creation were neighbors with each other, were sharing the confusion of life, and now my mother moved several steps higher than me, of course, because she had a FATHER.

With difficulty, I got used to a new situation for myself, and I could only babble: "Ah, well, this your father, where did he come from?"

My mother was not paying attention to my feelings and she quickly explained what from which. "Your grandfather is a gypsy; he was the most important in the camp, gypsies called him the baron in Gypsy language." He met my mother in the year eighteen and eighty-six, when a Moscow gypsy choir was created on the basis of their camp, and they sang and dance in a circus on the Colored Boulevard. Then my father and mother were married at Church of the Exaltation of the Holy Cross of the Lord at the Yama schools, behind the Tver outpost, immediately after it was consecrated by Overlord Ioannicos. Soon I was born. Well..." she hesitated, seeing how white I was; my lips trembled and tears rolled from my eyes as beads. "Hey you, girl! Do not be silly, there's nothing terrible that I did not tell you before. You were too young and my dad all the time nomadized after the Civil war, until Bolsheviks began to collect gypsies in collective farms. Now he is completely useless, he is strongly sick with the mental illness."

We went on shanks's pony, then went by tram to the station, took a suburban train and after half an hour got off the train on the outskirts of the Petrovsko-Razumovskoye village, which was located far out of the capital center, but in the ensuing year it will become part of Moscow. We crossed the highway without going into the village, then crossed another railway branch and went along the path through a pine forest. The tall, slender pine trees stood sparsely, so the sun was illuminated the tree crowns and the thin shrubs under them with soft warm light and tickled my nose. I sneezed several times, took a deep breath and felt the pleasant aroma of tar melting under the sun.

I was in a state of euphoria. I liked this place, and wanted to walk incessantly through the midday forest, but suddenly we went to the edge of a wood and I saw a yellow two-story building at the foot of the hill with a large courtyard surrounded by a high metal fence. Unusual people, men and women, walked about the yard all alone, each in his direction. All of them were garbed in suits like those in the sanatorium whom were shown in the newsreel before the movie show beginning. Here and there in the grass were sitting groups of several people in ordinary clothes, and among them - one in a suit. Everyone had some tense faces, as if people together experienced one common big trouble.

I yanked my mother's sleeve softly to draw her attention and asked, "Mam, what are these men standing along the fence, why they do not look like the others?"

My mother seemed to wake up from her thoughts; she looked around, sighed and answered: "They are warders, daughter. It is their duty that the psychos do not run away."

The word "psycho" was familiar to me, among pupils of my school this was one of the common abusive words. It was not perceived as the worst, but it was rather unpleasant, because one of the "psychos" named Sonny lived in our street. He was odd man out, but was kind and did not take offense when he was teased. When street boys beat him with sticks or threw stones, he cried like a defenseless and lonely child. I felt sorry for him, but I did not dare to show this, and in the crowd of teenagers, I teased Sonny but in my heart, I felt contempt for myself.

Here was a whole sanatorium of the "psychos", no one insulted them, all behaved quietly and calmly, but many guards along the fence escalated a strange sense of discomfort, and I could not get rid of it while we were there. My emotions was gradually settled until we approached the gate. Mother spoke quietly with the gatekeeper, and we were let into the yard. I was scared now, suddenly the guards will come to me and will understand that I am odd man out too; they will call me "psycho" and take into of the big yellow house.

However, we approached the high porch, and nothing special happened. The guards still stayed near the fence, the patients, as I named the "psychos", were still pacing back and forth, and a nurse in a white coat accompanied by a tall, stately man, whose old age was shown only by uncertain gait and wrinkled skin, came towards us. His eyes were dark and glittering, like a young man has, and his hair was little touched by snow, only on the temples.

The nurse said approaching us "Hello, Ann! Today the Baron had a disease attack, so you must try not to worry him, and do not take him long. I'll be nearby."

"Very well, we are quick," answered my mother, and, addressing her father, she spoke softly, with such warmth that I never felt in my life with regard to myself. "Hello, Dad, how do you feel? Let's sit down on the grass; I will lay down a blanket."

With the help of his daughter, the old gypsy sank to the blanket and looked at me searchingly. I blushed for no reason and confused, till he said something to my mother in an unknowable language. She answered him somewhat incomprehensive too, and translated me, "Grandpa said that you grew up and became a beautiful girl. It's in gypsy," she explained in response to my puzzled look. "I also know how to speak a little, but I have forgotten language, I have not spoken for a long time."

"Genie!" Nicander told to me in an unexpectedly young and warm voice. "Your mam probably did not tell you about my existence. Sorry, in my seventy-four years I see you only the second time. Well, how do you like your grandfather? Although, what's here to like, life has passed, I have left you nothing, sitting in the jail, who am I for you?"

Grandfather's voice began to grow with hysterical intonations appeared in him, he even got up and began to gesticulate animatedly. One of the guards noticed grandfather's behavior; he moved away from the fence and hurried to us. Mother, who probably more than once saw the result of such development of events, began to ask her father not to be angry, to calm down, and not to attract attention to himself. I was quite frightened and moved away from grandfather, but he, shouting curses against his enemies who planted him in jail, jumped up and, ran to the fence ridiculously jumping on the twisting legs.

On the left and right sides whistles of security guards were heard, three of them went towards the running Nicander, and the rest ones began to gather other patients to the entrance of the building, driving them with sticks like geese. It might look ridiculous, and the next time I would have laughed, but now I watched in horror as two guards grabbed my grandfather by the hands, forced him to kneel down, and the third one beat him up with a stick in his head, on shoulders and on the back.

The grandfather shouted something, and then hung his head. When the guards dragged him into the building, I saw that his face was cyanotic, and he wheezed dropping foam from his mouth. Mother grabbed my hand into her hand and picked up with the other hand the supplies from the ground twisted it in the blanket, and dragged it to the porch, shouting on the run: "Do not beat him, he's sick, you must see how bad he is!"

However, the sturdy guards already stopped beating Nicander, who was drooping in their hands, and they just dragged him along the grass, then up the stairs, until disappeared behind the doors of the yellow building. We also approached the door, which was closed, because every "psycho" already had been driven to their rooms, there was no one left in the yard, except for confused relatives, who has unsuccessfully visited their patients.

Mother knocked on the door. The little window in the middle of the door was opened, and the face of the nurse that brought us grandfather appeared.

"Anya," she said, "give me quickly what you brought here until the guards come, otherwise they'll take everything away. When he and the around situation will calm down I'll give this him later, I'll feed him and everything will be glorious."

It was evident that the nurse had a special regard to my grandfather, but my mother did not care for it. She has been coming here for seven years, since her father was the first time sent here for the cure as "the wrong Gypsy." Nicander did not accept "the attention" to him of the Bolshevik Party, which at the end of the twenties of the last century adopted directive on tying the Roma to a settled way of life. In that time, several gypsies agreed to work in agriculture cooperatives or in the industrial company, someone of gypsies simply deceived the government, receiving start-up money of 500-1000 rubles, and went off, but few of them, like Nicander, understood that "landing on the ground" will be the end for Rome people; they began a slashing criticism of the government and tried to appeal to the international community. The last ones were attacked by the repressive apparatus of the Bolshevik regime; some were deported to Siberia and Central Asia together with the camps, others were shot as enemies of the soviet people, and for the most dangerous leaders, as baron Nicander was, officials found a permanent shelter in a psychiatric hospital, because were physicians who served the government in the way to put the diagnosis, which needed the officials, and they not tormented with remorse.

In fact, the diagnosis of Nicander was a rarely defined at that time form of thromboembolism, caused by atherosclerosis of the carotid arteries. In this disease, thrombus that formed in the arteries moved along the bloodstream and enter the vessels of the brain, and it led to ischemia of some separate parts. Until the clot dissipated, the area of the brain without oxygen supply gradually died off, and when the full blood flow restored there were consequences that could be mistaken for schizophrenia: the person reacted inadequately to stimuli, raved, and was easily excited, sometimes suddenly lost consciousness.

Without going into the clinic, the prison physician diagnosed him with schizophrenia that was approved by the chekist investigative department; because the old gypsy was already well-known human rights activist and diplomats were regularly interested in his condition. Time passed, but there was no changes for the better in his condition, and the gypsy baron did not receive treatment for his illness, the food in the hospital was meager and not enough high-calorie, and the delivery of food from relatives were stolen by the guards.

A few months later, in the winter, mother were informed that her father still took advantage of the guards and fled the hospital, till he was running with mighty force towards Moscow, and no one could to capture him. The large blood clot completely blocked one of his brain's hemispheres, which deprived the entire body of sensitivity. Nicander fled, not understanding the road like a mighty elk through bushes and coppices, until he fell into a pit near the railway. The doctor who was performing the autopsy and found the blood clot told the mother that his brain was already dead by that time, but how great is the gypsy craving for freedom, that he continued to run away from his executioners even when he was dead!

Mother was sad when came from the funeral, but she was not too grieved. I met her in the courtyard and realized that I can talk with her.

"You buried your grandfather, right?" I asked.

"Yes, daughter, I do not have a father now, although, of course, he was not anyway; he was wandering, then he was in prison or in the hospital. It's good that the hospital has buried him, it has a cemetery behind the yellow house, near a wood. You know, there are so many people buried there, I don't understand where they have been housed in that hospital?" the mother thoughtfully told me about what she had seen, as if again experiencing this day. "The most important thing is that most of the crosses did not have inscriptions on it, thus a person has left, and they never know who lived and when he died."

"Well, Mam, after all Steve have made you a table," I objected, but my mother picked it up. "It's really good, now they'll know who is laying in the ground, what was his name, when he was born, when he died, for him is the Kingdom of heaven. Well, daughter, call our neighbors, we'll remember my father, and do not forget Steve."

"Mam, you'll tell me about your grandfather, because I do not know anything about him," I asked my mother, but she took objection. "There is no time, daughter, now neighbors will come, and what I'll tell you when I saw him myself several times in my life, and my mother did not tell me anything, because she died a long time ago, but you, Genie, must silent about my father!" Mother made strict eyes, and I froze in perplexity.

"Why not," I exclaimed in desperation, "he's your father, and I'm his granddaughter, I look like him! Do you remember how I have danced as a gypsy girl on the anniversary of October revolution? You did not tell me anything then."

I also wanted to add that it was a great happiness to know your father, but my mother abruptly cut me off. "Remember this, my girl, our people do not like gypsies! You know, they called gypsies as prowlers, "horse thieves", beggars, but God forbid does anyone know that you have a gypsy grandfather! This will not be forgiven you, because you are the fatherless and wants to be ahead of everyone in school, moreover you are the leader in the pioneer squad."

My mother was so hotheaded that it became clear to me; for many years of her life, she had to relive it all, and she wants to protect me from a similar fate. Well, I decided that I will keep silent, but I could not know what is it to live forever in fear that someone will recognize a gypsy in you and immediately everyone will be persecuting you for any reason. I must tell farewell to good life, farewell to dreams, ahead of me there are heartache and empty dreams about another, happier life.

In the late thirties, when I finished the seven-year school, life was again on the rise. I was an honors pupil, an active member of the Komsomol, a well-known sportsman among the schools of the district; I had no equal on the ski run, even many guys lagged behind.

The old story with my gypsy grandfather, that upset my nerves for several years and made me shudder when I spoke about the gypsies, gradually fell into the background. I have blossomed enough, became a beautiful girl with a goodly body and a small oval face with white, thin and clean skin; I had big dark brown eyes wrapped in thick eyelashes, inherited from the grandfather-gypsy. A long, thick plait of curly dark brown hair lay freely on the lush breasts, perhaps it was too large for the young girl, but the set of my shoulders and a svelte figure gave nice proportions, forcing young and experienced men to turn around.

The danger from the grandfather-gypsy and the insulting children's state of fatherlessness was also forgotten, and I did not bother that my mother, having crossed the half-century line, was working in the hotel as a cleaning lady, not as a parlormaid. I told myself that the country was already different; life became the other, now everything depends only on you, and how do you use opportunities that the soviet country provided to children it is your choice. Enemies of the working class were mostly exterminated, industry rose, collective farmers reaped heavy crops; it was only necessary to make the new generation of people to be smart and beautiful, like everything countrywide.

Approaching my courtyard, I watched as children from the three neighboring houses play lapta game, a sort of the hardball. I also loved this game and was among the best in the street, but for some time now, I was not so often got into the game, because many players felt on their backs ball hit by my hand. I went around players along the edge of the courtyard and met my brother, standing under a tree near the table, where domino players usually gathered.

He was exploring a grey-yellow slip in his hands. "Hello, Nick, why are you have gone so early from work?" I asked my brother.

I loved my elder brother, who replaced me the father in many ways, especially in to keep the family and in protection from courtyard bully. After three years in Army, Nick worked in the electric factory, he was in honor list and thought how to continue his education, but decided that he must teach his sister at first, and then think about himself.

"You see, Genie, the call-up paper has come to me, they are calling me to the army again," my brother Nick replied sadly and gave me the slip. In this slip was written that it is the order for Nickolas Shaman to arrive in the military registration point in three days with documents and a one-day packed meal. My brother's last name was from his father, and my name was invented by the name of our grandfather.

"Nick, it will be soon, on Sunday," I explained in perplexity, "what is the stupidity, they will not give a pause for the rest before the army?"

"There's no time to rest, Genie, there are much enemies around us, we must strengthen our war effort," Nick repeated me the words of official propaganda and mused inwardly why they call him to the army. Perhaps, he guess there was a shortage of soldiers in Poland, where to our troops entered under the Molotov-Ribbentrop Pact, maybe the fighting continues again in the Far East, but his reflections was such far from the truth, as the government of his native country, which recruited him to the army, was far from him.

I wanted to please my brother. "I have got a referral to the pedagogic courses, in ten months I'll graduate courses and will become the elementary school teacher," I told my brother. "Well, Nick, you will be in the army for a long time, but what we will doing without you?"

I remembered how my brother has been going to the fixed-term military service in the first time; the room where we all three lived, has become empty without him and we have missed him, but in the courtyard local punks treated me kindly, without ceremony, but without bullying because Nick before leaving strictly ordered the local leader Serge "Does not hurt my sister! I'll be back and you will answer me if anything will happen."

This covenant acted flawlessly all three years, while Nick was in the army, but with him our life would be both more fun, and easier, and, most importantly, more reliable.

"It's good," said Nick about my courses, "that you settled yours affairs, you will finish the courses, will go to work, and will help our mother. Listen me, do not leave her, she's our only one."

He spoke as if he is leaving us forever, and the chill went down my spine ostensibly the icy wind burst into our small cozy courtyard.

"Did you already tell our mother?" I asked, shrugging my shoulders from the chill.

"What's wrong with you, are you frozen?" Nick appreciated this gesture in his own way, "yes, the summer is ending, please, come home. Mother already knew about me, she collects the goods for me on the road and sent me to the store, I'll go at last."

He left me, and for a long time I looked where he had disappeared, trying to remember his silhouette in the distance. An anxiety took the soul, gradually leading to the numbness of the hands and feet, so that I could not move. Something was changing in my life, and I was in my heart sure that these changes were not for the better.

At that time, the mother came into the yard with a tall, burly man in a stylish suit and a broad-brimmed hat. They approached me; the man took off his hat and I saw his bald spot. Something familiar flashed in his features, but when he said, "Przepraszam, panienka!" I immediately remembered this man, who had given me a trinket in the form of the Little Red Riding Hood.

"Eugenia," my mother said with worry, "get acquainted, this is your father."

"Daddy?" I babbled, getting my breath from the unexpected news, my eyes filled with tears, my lips quivered, and when my knees buckled, I sat down on the bench. "Well, where have you been all this time?" I exclaimed and suddenly rushed to his neck.

I cried like an offended little girl, embracing the most precious thing I only had in my life. "I knew, I knew," I repeated, swallowing my tears, "I knew that you are, but where have you been until now?"

"Come with me, Genie, I'll explain to you everything," father said and looked at my mother. She nodded in agreement, and we went.

"My name is Felix Vabia, I'm a Pole," my father began his story as we walked along the railroad tracks towards Avenue of Peace. "In the early twenties, I had come to the Soviet Union to be employed at the factory, because life in Poland has deteriorated, and we were out of work. In Russia the NEP led to high growth in economics, well, you know what new economic policy means, don't you?"

"Yes," I nodded, looking with adoration at the features of my freshly found father. "We learned it at school. Lenin invented NEP."

"That's right, Lenin did it," the father said approvingly, "and he was not mistaken, because life in Russia had risen so much for three next years. I left my family in Poland, in the house of my mother-in-law, and went to Moscow. Here I stayed at the National Hotel, where I met your mother. We got together and lived for several months, before my family arrived. We parted with your mother and I have not seen her until today; I moved to an apartment, which I rented near an electrical plant, where I work now. Believe me; I did not know about your birth, otherwise you would have been with me.

"Genie, when I came to the hotel, you remember it, I wanted to get a job in the American embassy." I nodded silently, took out a keychain from my pocket and showed it with a smile.

"At that time there were no job in embassy for me," my father continued, "and I continued to work at a plant, and I worked there all this time, was even a party secretary of the factory workshop. Later life got better, and I was about to return to Poland, but recently soviet troops occupied Poland, dividing it in half with the Germans."

"No, we did not occupy Poland," I with fervor interrupted him, "because we freed Slavic brothers from the capitalist yoke, did not let the Germans go further to our borders."

Propagandistic enthusiasm of the Komsomol activist visibly upset Felix, but he did not argue; he already knew how propaganda could deceive people. This was especially noticeable in the United States, where the media were indeed accessible to everyone and penetrated into each house, media didn't leave people alone at work, on the street, at home, so people thought and acted almost as propaganda forced them to do. The same happened in Germany where the fascist leadership made organization and strict order in all areas of life, including propaganda. Everyone should listen to the report of the leader, everyone should go to the meeting, everyone should march in the ranks, and everyone should even think about the same thing, so, nobody couldn't fall out of the well-organized system of the totalitarian regime.

"Yes, the Red Army "liberated" my village," he said me, "so I came to take my mother to Moscow, but it turned out that neighbors took her to the West, when they fled from the "liberators" into German territory, and I lost her traces. Poland disappeared from the map of the world. So I decided to fly from here by plane to England, and then to America. That's it."

He paused for a moment and then continued:" I'll be an American. You must know that you have two more brothers, one is older, another is younger than you, and two younger sisters. They will all live with me in America."

"Listen, when I found out about you," my father added, "I immediately wanted to take you to America. Let's go with me, please! Soon in Europe it will be very hot, a great war is beginning, we will be in safe in the United States."

"Nick was again taken for compulsory military service," I inappropriately remarked and explained, "This is my brother, and he will go to the army the day after tomorrow."

"Yes, the mobilization is in full swing, you need to run away, let's go with us, daughter," my father called me daughter for the first time. Because of this word my heart began to beat like a sparrow in a cage, I did not want to part with my unexpected father, but I don't forgot my brother's words.

"I cannot leave my mother to be in the solitude," I said sternly, "especially if there will be a war. I will go to defend my homeland. I can shoot and bandage up the wounds," I boasted with pleasure. Father's face was grimaced because of my last words.

"The war is not for girls, your mother will not be lost without you and your brother will return sooner or later, but we'll both go to America, is it right, Genie?" father ingratiatingly asked, however, already without some enthusiasm, because the current impulse of the soul couldn't overshadow the part of past life and stable family and life ties. The fate gave the father too little time for the meeting with his daughter.

Talking about our life, we approached the tram stop, from which tram went to the hotel near the exhibition of achievements. While we were waiting the tram, I completely recovered from shock caused by the appearance of my father, and a new, fresh wave surged up in me giving a rush of energy and enthusiasm, so I suddenly said, "Well, we don't need these idle talk about war and America, because now I know that I have a real father. Anyway, you have not lived with us all this time, and further you will not live with us, because you have your own family. Let's say goodbye, I will not leave my mother anyway, I'll be with her until my brother will come back, and then we'll decide. You will write letters to me when you come to your home in America, this is my response to your offer, we'll write letters to each other."

The last thought was pleasing to me therefore I turned to my father and made him promise to write letters, and then I kissed him goodbye and went to home.

Felix Wabia was so upset with this happening, that he did not even stop his daughter, did not try to detain her, to continue even this little bit of their unexpected meeting. I did not go, but flew, like on wings. Everything in my life took its place, everything was developing as it should, and from this harmony the soul flew to heaven, and sang, and rang with happiness there, in the high blue sky.

I thought that everything would be fine, but perhaps this was again the grimace of my fate, which gave me a long life, but did not let me enjoy even brief moments of the happiness. Suddenly a "Black Maria" swept through the road, and I thought, "Why in the daytime?" We already knew that at night these dark signs of trouble could come to any house in town, even in our short street it once took the whole family and little children too. I was not afraid that it would come to us, but when I saw "Black Maria", I felt a danger that it brought with itself.

The creaking of the brakes behind me made me turn around. At the tram stop, a group of three in civilian clothes persons assaulted upon him, bound his arms, and blindfolded him before dragging him into gaping blackness of the open doors of the wagon. It was quiet around, rare passers-by rushed away from this place, and I seemed paralyzed. I wanted to run to my father, call for help, do something, but could not move. Before my eyes, the doors closed, and the "Black Maria" with the roaring engine quickly disappeared behind the next turn. Life is broken, it'll never start again.

In addition, in the fortieth year when I graduated from the Moscow Karl Liebknecht Teachers Institution and already worked with first-graders in my native school, one more event happened. My brother Nick was captured in the Finnish "Winter" war. After the end of the war and repatriation of my brother, the Soviet government has identified him as a defector like every prisoners of war; the court sentenced him to eight years in labor camps with subsequent exile, and his was sent to Siberia. It was another blow for me, and both two blows were more painful for me than childhood fears or nuisance with family relations; because it was aimed not in the past, but in the future, in which there will be nothing, neither study at the university, nor good work with high salary, and even nor good marriage, because nobody will take my with such a brother and with such a father.

At the end of the year, the district police officer visited us. Such respected man not every day came to our home, so my mother set the table, as it should. Officer ate, drank, talked about trivia, but in a leisurely talk he did not forget to allude to my grandfather Nicander whom the authorities did not like, and my brother Nick, who, after his imprisonment, had to stay for the same period in exile in Central Asia, and then he was leading up to my father, who was sentenced to ten years of camps without the right to correspond with. It was suspiciously for me how they knew that I was his daughter.

Mother, as she could, explained officer, "My life was too bumpy and I gave birth to the daughter from a Pole, but nobody has known he'll become the enemy of the people. Who should be responsible for this?" Mother asked him. Then she added, "If the special service found out everything about the girl, it means that it works very well."

To this the officer said, "We know better how to work, we are fighting with spies, and many enemies have been exposed, I mean in every yard and even in every family there are prisoners, traitors, enemies of the people, who fought against our revolution, but now because of their bad status their relatives have no life at home. You must thank to Comrade Stalin, who said that the son does not answer for his father. As well as the daughter."

"Do you understand the hint, Ann?" The officer looked pointedly at the mother. "Listen, they could take away your daughter's job because of her father, couldn't they? Yes, they could. I don't understand at all, how can you trust them, these Poles. Look, Genie, you will have trouble with this father, you must forget him and never reminisce. Otherwise, they will come for you from there!" He raised his finger pointedly at the ceiling.

After the sentence for my brother, I was ready for everything worst that could fall into my lot, but I did not think I could lose my job. If this happens, could I help mother, as I promised my brother?

"Comrade Lieutenant, I have no father, you can check the certificate of birth which has no the father's name in it." I reported to the officer with the severe voice. "You can inform your commander that I'm true soviet man, and I will not betray my Motherland," I said, looking straight into the eyes of the officer.

The policeman looked at me with doubt and pity, as if he thought that the girl would lose herself with these prisoners-relatives, but he did not say anything. Maybe he was already used to see how everybody renounce their relatives, who were imprisoned as enemies of the people, or he may be thought, "You are bitch, that you so easily abandoned your father."

Whatever he had in his mind, but he reported to the commander about work he did. Since then no one reminded me of my father or brother anymore, this case gradually went into oblivion. The girl's life again began to increase; I was joined the Komsomol and appointed as the senior pioneer leader, I had enough money for life, even for fashionable clothes, there were fans around me. I began to dream of a happy life again, in my ideal life there will be a good husband, several children, a favorite work and all that is needed in the house.

My mother was happy for her daughter, but she warned me that this joy would not last long. She remembered the gypsy habits that she had acquired in her youth when she was visiting her father in the gipsy camp so she conjured and read the cards, and often cards showed us that troubles would come and not alone. Perhaps either something will again happen our family or I will be punished because of my brother, father and grandfather, but maybe something worst will happen.

The premonitions did not deceive my mother.

Chapter 2. The Youth and the Love during the War

I was eighteen when I directly from girlhood got into the hard tangled time of the war. I received a signal about a new turn of life, like every fellow citizen, with the voice of newscaster Levitan, soviet radio announcer, which broadcasted of every loudspeaker. I went to my mother's work site after the end of exams in Russian language and literature among high school students, where I, a young teacher, was invited to help the examination board, and then I could be going on my first teacher's vacation.

In the tram of the new model, there was spacious and few people, as usual on Sunday, however, people were some bewildered. They whispered quietly to each other, and when the tram approached the Bolshoi Theater, I noticed that near the loudspeaker, whose horns was sticking out in all directions, a large crowd gathered, but people kept coming.

I jumped off the footboard and went to the crowd. Before I could open my mouth to ask the guy in the plaid cap what was happening and why people gathered there, the loudspeaker suddenly hissed, and the loud voice of the announcer began to say terrible things, due to which the heart began to beat extremely in my chest and then fell somewhere down and hided maybe in the heels.

"War? War... War!" Everybody together breathed out this word, but each in its own manner, the crowd began to speak up into different voices, discussing the news, someone shushed neighbors, trying to listen to the end, but finally everything was clear. Those who were older, who served and who had fought, their wives and widows, they knew what the misfortune came to their home. They fell in sorrow, bent over and carried this heavy burden, preparing for unprecedented trials. Those who are younger, especially the boys-pre-conscripts, squared their shoulders, puffed out their breasts, and their eyes was burned.

"We'll kick ass the Germans to get them away from our land," shouted they with enthusiasm, "we'll throw out them beyond the border line and we will beat them in Germany, on their territory." They reasoned among themselves in such way, and they immediately decided that it was necessary to go to the military enlistment office and ask to send them to the Army until it was too late, because it may be that the regular units of the heroic Red Army will complete a victorious war without them.

I rushed to my mother's hotel to inform the unexpected news, because could not immediately assess their influence on my life and was waiting for mother's reaction. She already knew everything and in hopeless sat among her colleagues, not knowing what to do next, and not having orders from the direction. She knew well what the war did with her life, and she foresaw the disaster, but worse than the three previous wars had brought.

"You know, Genie, what kind of grief is war?" my mother decided to pour out her daughter's soul, "I was young and was already getting ready to get married, when the Tsar and the Japan emperor began to make war. They took away my betrothed and killed him in the marshes near the Russian city of Port Arthur, which is in China, and how to live after that, no one asked me, no one said anything."

She further told her daughter in tears, "So I was neither a wife and nor a soldier's widow, I was waiting for him and thought maybe it was the mistake, maybe my betrothed have been in the prison or in the hospital, but he still will return to me and our life will be nice. Then I was completely grieved when an old soldier came from China, he told me how my falcon was fighting, how he had been dying among other heroes like him. It was hard for me to survive these years, I barely managed to get out of the hard illness, which happened just because of the bitter sorrow, but I have survived, have recovered and again have met a man, it was Nick's father Timothy Shaman. For a long time I take his measure, beat him around the bush, and in the autumn of the fourteenth year we decided to get married, but the war again intervened us!"

The mother also told me that Timothy had been fighting the imperialist from the beginning to the end of war; he rotted in trenches on all fronts and met her only at the end of the sixteenth year, when, he was released for a short stay in his native place after being wounded and treated in the hospital.

During those two short weeks, they had time to marry and conceive the son Nick, they was in abyss of hopelessness due to the near collapse of the world and swore, that they will always be together, no matter what happens. Further Timothy disappeared from my mother's life as if he had been swept away by the wave that was making by the First World War, then the war already come to naught, the revolution was kindled and the civil war began to swirl across Russia. There were rare letters from her husband from the west or the east, or from the south, but in his letters was not a hint of that oath to which they had once tied themselves.

"In my heart I believed, that he was not mine and he will leave me soon," my mother sighed and continued, "Timothy returned with his young wife, she was somewhere from Ukraine, she was a cover girl and literate not like me, and he, the beastly bastard, hung on to her. She was much younger because I was over thirty at that time, Nick was three years, and I did not have my own man and eventually I do not have now. Things had come to a pretty pass, and one day I grabbed Nick in an armful, rushed to Timothy and his wife, and said, "You deprived me of life, take this bastard and I'll go to drown oneself.

"Naturally I was not drowned, I was crestfallen but I didn't go mad. I changed my mind, took Nick back and began to live on. My little son such a piglet, during a short time, when he lived in father's house, used to them and did not want to leave, I took him away barely. Since, Nick had a good relationship with his father, and Timothy's wife never said him bad words. You can see, daughter, what means the war in my life. You, girl, must get married, but there's a massacre ahead of you, that will decimate many men, whom will you stay with?"

I felt frightened as if I had lost something dear to myself that still have not met in my way. Thus, the war will take away my future life, which I set up in dreams for many years to come. What will remain for me in return?

"Nothing, nothing will remain," lamented my mother as if she heard her daughter's thoughts, and I could not understand what my mother was scared of, because in the movies and newsreels they showed war that was not very scary and sometimes was even ridiculous, in which the Red Army necessarily gained a victory.

"Maybe someone will not be lucky," I reflected, listening to my mother, "someone will be injured and someone will be killed, but that war will not last long, may be within a month or two the war will end, and a good life will begin again."

I consoled myself in this way, but could not believe my thoughts, because around me, everybody was worried, my mother was desperate, and her words took into my heart. Anyway, the war went to us from border, and it was necessary to put up with it somehow.

The time has come, and we, the residents of Moscow, were driven to dig anti-tank ditches at distant approaches to the capital, bombings began in the city, and the way of life began to differ from the pre-war. However, all this was on the wave of patriotic enthusiasm, people says, we will defend the capital, we will not surrender to the enemy, if the war is on we must put up with difficulties, so for the time being the war was perceived as harmless enough.

Late autumn, when half of the country was handed over to the fascist, and the front came to the gates of the "white-stone" Moscow, factories and plants were basically evacuated, and in our school a front-line hospital was placed with so many wounded that I realized that the most gloomy forebodings were justified. Than my mother and I went to evacuation and was quartered in a private home in a small village in Mordovia, which was remembered to me only by high snowdrifts, burning frosts and the strange accent of locals speak. I taught Russian the local and evacuated children, and this provided resources to live together with my mother.

When the Germans were repulsed from the capital, and it became clear that Moscow would not be surrendered, we returned and continued to live, but not by the peaceful life, in a completely different way, and the longer the war lasted, the more it seemed to me that there would not be return to the past life. My brother sent us a letter saying that he was not allowed to go to the front, though even the enemies of the people were given a chance to spill his blood for his native country in the penal battalion, but he, as a former prisoner of war, is kept in special custody and not allowed to fight. I felt very bad, nevertheless the summer was green, the sun was shining, and my youth went on.

I was not telling anyone about the disappointment that I felt of the war, especially of its beginning, it was my secret experience, which may not divided into two or three persons, because I knew that nobody will understand me or maybe they will laugh at me. Everybody live through the same events in own way, because one has his own plans, and other one hopes for a favorable outcome of events: where one finds peace and joy for himself, the other must suffer and be disappointed.

In the summer, when classes at school were over, and the children went on vacation, I had time to think about my fate. Here, in the rear, among women and children, while men are at war, I cannot be useful to the country and find my destiny, because the real events where the history is taking place and where the people are rushing, passed me by. It seemed to me that the war was the main event of my life, and if I did not take part in it, my further life might not turn out.

My conclusion is one: I cannot overcome the strength of fate; I must submit and be where the fate of the country was decided, and mine too of course. Having seized a free day, I went to the military enlistment office and asked to go to the front. As an educated and physically developed girl, I was sent first to study at an air photogrammetric school to study all the photographic processes that are necessary in aviation, and, most importantly, made me the decipherer of photos taken by scouts from planes. The essence of this profession is simple - it is important to recognize ground targets according of their contours, individual elements and location, where the desired target is located, to distinguish it from a false goal, to consider it even under a layer of disguise. I was a common soldier, I did it work and even not bad, that's why I was released from the courses ahead of schedule, and already in the winter in early 1943 I was sent to the rear Bashkir town of Davlekanovo, to the regiment as part of the air division, which stood under formation before being sent to the front.

I began to like such war. I was placed with five other girls in the hut of a local worker of a bakery near the training base of the regiment. Although

Georgiy Ulchenko

life was severe and sometimes ascetic, a regular schedule, a good ration and the environment of a large number of young people, especially officers - recent graduates of military schools, created a sense of peaceful life, which had place for both recreation and entertainment, and it was possible to dream about a better future.

Anxiety in the soul created service duties, when it was necessary to keep watch at the headquarters all day long, but most of all I was afraid to be the watchman in the sentry. Girls were appointed as sentry to the warehouses with food and clothing, to the training base and yard outbuildings, for two-shift night posts, from which the sentry was removed in the afternoon. The guys, unlike us, guarded the airfield, military equipment and ammunition around the clock, but in the frosty and windy weather, in the dead of night for me there was no difference. Try to stay on open air two hours in the dark, around no one, the light bulb barely illuminates the object, and what's happening around it, you cannot see anything. You look and look into the dark, your eyes get tired, you stop being afraid, you lean against the wall, and you'll just fall asleep standing up. Although, being on post you must not sleep, it is categorically forbidden!

On one of these nights, when the spring was already ringing with a drizzle during the day, and at night the puddles froze and crunched under my feet with ice glass, there was my third shift, that is, I went the third time to replace my friend for two hours. I was already tired of walking around the warehouse yard, and I sat down on a box of sand by the fire shield, and fell asleep inadvertently.

I woke up because someone grabbed me from behind, squeezing my torso and hands at the same time.

"Well, this is the end," the thought flashed through my head, "but I will not give it up, you'll remember me, you shit."

The last words I already said out loud; I crushed down the raider to the back, flattening him by the weight of my whole body. The grip of an unknown person weakened for a second, that I turned in his arms face to face and pushed him hard from me.

I must say that over the years of skiing, I so pumped up the muscles, that by their strength could easily compete with the guys. Especially I liked to "shove" the boy, that is, to push him with all my forces from me, and he rolled with a head, such force was this push. At school, this reception was well known to me, and when I said, "Now I'll "shove" you!", then the guys who likes to paw over the girls immediately fell behind.

The reception also worked this time. I caught a falling rifle and prepared to pierce the intruder with a bayonet, as he yelled, "What do you do, soldier, you asleep on duty, and try to kill her boss with the bayonet, stop it now! At attention, bitch, fuck you!"

It was the guard's chief, my platoon leader, senior lieutenant Kuroyedov. He was not taken to the front because of a wound that was received on Khalkin-Gol in Mongolia, because of which one leg was shorter than the other was, and even a special heel on the boot could not compensate for this defect. This, as well as the fact that he had to rule the unit of the girls, greatly depressed the experienced warrior, so he did not miss the opportunity to direct his anger at his subordinates.

"So, soldier", he began to bend his fingers, "You slept – the first, sat on the post – the second, left the weapons from hands – the third, you'll have five days for each violation, total you have fifteen days under arrest. When you finish off your shift, then I'll find a place for you in the guardhouse chamber."

The rest of the night, I spent in confusion and tense anticipation of the denouement. When changed from the post, I went to the barracks, handed over the weapons and ammunition to the duty officer, and went to report to the company commander. He met me unfriendly, he already knew about the violation in the guard, therefore, without saying too much, he called the soldier on duty to the company, handed him a note on the arrest and ordered him to hand over private Nikandrov, i.e. me, to the guardhouse.

The soldier on duty received a trilinear rifle in the armory room, charged it and ordered, "Private Nikandrov, to the guardhouse, forward march!"

Without a belt, in an overcoat dangling on the body, with hands laid behind my back, like real prisoner, I walked through the whole garrison to the guardhouse. The shame was terrible! Earlier I saw how the guys were led to the "guard", but it looked somehow natural: the guys were put due to drinking, like a civilian in the police for fifteen days, however I was sentenced for violation in the guard, due to non-fulfillment of the combat mission, as the ultimate traitor.

The spring day turned out to be sunny, slush flowed from roofs, the feet squelched through puddles, here and there on the sunny side was faded green grass, which was already broke through the ground, but I did not care about this. It seemed to me that all those who met me, looked at me with condemnation and contempt, I was afraid to raise my eyes, thus I wandered under the gun until we reached the guardhouse.

The soldier on duty handed me over to senior lieutenant Kuroyedov by the book of the arrested, and returned to the barracks himself. Kuroyedov, the chief of the guard, arranged a humiliating search procedure for me, forced me to turn my pockets, he stripped me to the underwear, examined everything, saw if there were any tobacco, sharp objects, then he took off my waist belt and, allowing me to dress, locked the cell door on the bolt.

Left alone, I burst into tears. I was filled with fear, shame and anger, my humiliation was immeasurable. When I finished crying, I realized that I am alive and well, so I quickly coped with myself and began to dress. In the middle of the chamber was a table with benches on either side. I sat down on the edge of the bench, waiting for what would happen next. Some time passed, and nerves, stretched to the limit, have weakened, it came indifference and apathy. I wanted to eat, and as specially, someone near the door on the other side made the noise, the window cut in the door, opened, the soldier who was ordered to accompany the arrested, where they works, held out a bowl in the window and said, "Nikandrov, Genie, take lunch!"

It was the soldier of our company, Sandy, a great master of evasion from service even in the days of the war times, and he went to the guard not to the post, where the cold, lack of sleep, responsibility, but went as the soldier to accompany the arrested, he slept through the night in the warm room, and now he loitered near the food things. I did not like him, but now he seemed almost native.

"Sandy, how are the guys there, what are they talking about", - I asked, taking a bowl of soup, "and what should I do, what sort of order is here for me?"

Sandy explained in a nutshell that I would be working from morning till afternoon to clean snow, or to clean up the public convenience in the sentry's yard, or, at best, they would take me to work in the headquarters, and after lunch, I must be learning the army regulations and training marching. There was nothing new in this menu for me, I was only confused by one thing - to clean up the public convenience, however in wintertime, when everything was frozen and was not smell I could endure it. It's a pity that time behind the bars was very slow, there was no clocks here, but you could not ask "what time is it", because no one was allowed to talk to the sentry, and there was no one else in my chamber, men sat in the next one.

Thus, I stayed here for two days. I was taken to a nearby grocery storehouse to work - picking carrots, beets, potatoes. The work was not difficult and ordinary, about the arrest was reminiscent only the presence of an armed convoy soldier and jokes of my friends who also worked side by side with me. Then on the third day, the guardhouse was checked by the division commander, who was recently appointed to complete the formation of the unit, its equipment, and to lead people to the front with the active army.

Lieutenant-colonel Vladimir Smirnov was born somewhere near Voronezh, he was thin, slim, his hair was black as pitch, and his eyes blue, even blue, he wore a mustache in the form of a thin strip above his upper lip. Smirnov sewed the service uniform according to his own style: it was the same in color and a set of elements, like the others, but was taken to the body in the right places, and was added in others places, always clean and ironed, that's why it looked special unlike the others.

In tribulations

The exterior of the dandy did not interfere him, who at that time was only 26 years old, to be a dashing pilot and desperate shirt in combat. He had already shot down nine planes in battle with the Finns and at the beginning of the Patriotic War and a series of high awards could hardly fit on his chest. Smirnov took the air division after his wound near Kharkov, when his regiment defended our retreating troops from complete destruction by massive raids of Nazi aircraft. In heavy air battles lasted day and night, he had lost virtually all the regiment's fighting strength, and himself had been wounded in the leg, he burned in the plane, but was able to land on our side of the front and for a long time got to the hospital.

The female part of the division was simply fascinated by its division commander, who in return did not miss the opportunity to take advantage of this attention. all over the division there were rumors that he slept with one girl or the other, they attributed to him superfluous and something that was hard to believe, so I, although treated these rumors with understanding, but did not really believe in it, because that everything was happening before my eyes, and it was clear for me what was, but what was not or what attributed him by people's rumor.

And now, when the sun turned in the direction of the guardhouse and shone into the barred window of my chamber, flashing glares on the table and on the pages of the military statute that I memorized by heart, suddenly I heard the screams, "Stand at attention!", "The guard's chief - to the exit!", then sounded a loud report from the guard's chief, and steps began to approach my chamber. Someone from the upper authorities first walked to the sentry, and then the procession went to the guardhouse. The bolt clicked and the door was opened. I was ready for the arrival of the boss, stood at attention, and the division commander came into the chamber.

He stopped in bewilderment, because in the middle of a long chamber near a wide table stood a charming girl with long oblique and dark shining eyes in a tunic without a belt. Strands of curly hair, knocking out of the hair, glowed in the sun, surrounding my head with a shining halo.

"Who locked this Madonna in a cage?" Smirnov with displeasure asked his chief of staff. The chief of staff looked at the engineer, to whom was subordinated ground aviation technical services, including the decipherers, and the engineer, sensing the annoyance in the commander's voice, decided to soften the situation.

"This is soldier Nikandrov; she fell asleep on the guard post," he explained, "company chief has been planted her for fifteen days."

The commander of the division grunted, turned sharply, and began to read his rules to subordinates.

"Who is foolish enough to put the girl in a cage for fifteen days? Yes, you have no conscience! Or you have already forgotten that it is doubly hard for women in war, but you are still mocking them!" The commander was almost shouting, but, restraining himself, sharply changed his tone. "Well, now! That girl, what is her name", - "Nikandrov," prompted the engineer, "yes, Nikandrov, you release her, send her to the location, and tell me how you organized the guard service. Come on, carry out!"

Everyone left, and the door remained open. Then came the sentry, the door closed again, and everything seemed to me some kind of dream. However, the dream is terrible but the Lord is full of charity. An hour later, the duty soldier came and took me to the barracks. Thus ended my first and last imprisonment in life.

I was glad to see my girlfriends and for a few days just told everyone about the case in the guardhouse, about the arrest, about the "guard" and about my happy release. In the end, the girls were tired of my stories, and they began teasing me with my words, for example, screamed sarcastically how I hugged with Kuroyedov, and how the division commander fell in love with me, then I shut up and did not spread more about myself.

Spring gradually superseded the winter, the snow had completely disappeared, and bushes grew along the fences of the military cantonment. I was again put on the guard post, guarding the same warehouses with food; again, there was a third shift. There was dark quiet night, without a breeze, some lights flashed on the distant airfield, and preparations for the morning flights began. From there came the voices, the noise of the engines of the machines servicing the flights, the usual combat training was going on. I was not bored this night, I did not want to sleep, spring aroused the soul and body, I wanted to relax, dream about my future life, about the grooms, when suddenly on the edge of the post, near the precipice, a figure of a man blurred in the wrong light of lanterns has appeared. The figure seemed huge, it silently approached the fence, and I waited in a daze what will happen next.

All articles of the military statute, which are applied in this case, flew out of my head, and I just could murmur quietly, "Freeze!" The sound of my trembling voice, so repulsive with its timidity, angered me, and I immediately remembered everything I had to do and loudly shouted in a rude "male" voice, "Stop, who's coming!"

The figure silently, not responding to the cry of the sentry, approached the fence and was already beginning to squeeze between the rows of barbed wire, as I cried out again, already confidently and spitefully, "Stop, I'll shoot!"

Then I shot in the air, as I was taught in numerous exercises. The figure froze, then transported between the rows of wire; unknown person stood up to the full height and became to look like the commander of our platoon Kuroyedov, who came to check how the sentries are serving. Today he was not the chief of the guard, and I should not obey him as a sentry, so I immediately decided to show who the boss is now. "Lie down, face down,"

I commanded, contemptuously pointing at the place with the tip of the bayonet.

Kuroyedov screamed, "You, bitch, what do you do, soldier Nikandrov! What means your words "face down"? I'm your boss, mother-fucker; I've come to check you!" He tried to climb through the second row of the fence, not executing the sentry's command, but I shot a second time, aiming in the direction of my commander, not at him, but above and rather far off.

Upon hearing the whistle of a bullet, Kuroyedov rushed face down onto the wet earth. He did not stop shouting, "I'll remember this case! Whom you raised your hand on, soldier! When you'll change from your shift, then we'll see who the boss is!"

In this time a detachment of reinforcements, headed by the chief of the guard, was already running to the sound of the shot. I cheerfully reported that I had detained an unknown person who had violated the border of the guard post, but not saying that I had recognize my platoon commander. The soldiers of the strengthened detachment pulled Kuroyedov from the mud, and the guard's chief, the commander of a neighboring platoon, immediately recognized his comrade.

"Nikandrov, did you not recognize your commander?" he ask me. "You could have killed him like an infiltrator!"

"He must not get through the guard post," I answered with a grudge in my voice. "I warned him, as it is required by the statute, but who is he - the commander or not, it is not recorded in the articles of the military statute, he trespassed the guard post".

"Ah, well, yes, that's right," the head of the guard quickly find the right decision, "you, man, excuse me," he turned to Kuroyedov, "I have to detain you as an infiltrator."

Then the strengthened detachment headed by the guard's chief, moved the "infiltrator" to the guardhouse. The rest of the night, I spent as a holiday. It was a joy that I taught a lesson "that old beast," by whom was Kuroyedov for our girls, and dreamed that I'll be stimulated in acknowledgement of vigilance in performance of duty. Then between the girls, I will be the best, and the division commander may be turned his attention back to me, but not as it was in the guardhouse.

Thus it would be, but my fate is strangely twisting, and for every good day it gave me ten days which not so good, frequently bad and sometimes frankly lousy. I can say that no one can resist fate; you can discuss this yourself when you find out how it was.

When the division commander called out some successful fighter pilots and me too to announce us gratitude, several girls and I sat in the garden pavilion near the division headquarters. We exchanged impressions, gleefully spoke and laughed. When Lieutenant-Colonel Smirnov have heard our voices, he came to us. Everyone jumped up, they shouted "At attention!", and he, relaxed by the girl's environment, sat between one more girlfriend and me, and he began to joke with us and to say compliments. The girls grew bolder; they asked him when our division would be at the front, they were already tired of studying and preparing. Our commander chided girls that there was no need to rush to where the blood and fire were, the high commander knew our mission and prepared us for a big offensive, which would be either in late spring, or in the summer.

Having talked like this, he jokingly embraced one girlfriend and me around the waist and pressed us together one to other, saying, "Goodbye, I must go." Suddenly my girlfriend screamed, and he let us go. He saw with bewilderment that a bloodstain was spreading on my friend's chest, and the bloody blade of a penknife that I always carried with me, using as a manicure set for nail care, sticks out from my pocket. The joy of Smirnov was suddenly replaced by anger, he pushed me away, ordered me to hand over the knife as a nonservice weapon, sent my girlfriend to the paramedics, and promised me if the wound was severe, he will punish me with the rigor of wartime.

Fortunately, the wound was shallow, the blade slid along the rib and cut only the surface of the skin, no one punished anyone, but it caused me to feel so depressed from which I could only get out before as I went to the front.

At the end of spring the division, where I served, was thrown into the Central Front in the Kursk Region. Conversations about the offensive acquired the character of practical training, and all officers and soldiers lived and worked in suspense of terrible events. Everyone remembered the victorious battle at Stalingrad, wanted to continue to beat the enemy, so Nazi had to give up so that he would roll from our land to his lousy Germany.

The planes of the division flew daily to the rear of the enemy with reconnaissance missions, photographed a lot, and we, the decipherers, had a lot of work. Particularly we were loaded from the division headquarters, every day after flights from there, one of the staff officers came and demanded at any time of the day and night to give information on the decipherment of objects on the reconnaissance terrain. The nerves of the girls-decipherers were at the limit, they were falling down due to fatigue, but our work just grew with the introduction of a new service uniform and shoulder boards, it was necessary to photograph the officers on identity card.

One of these days, I have already finished deciphering the next batch of photographs, the staff officer just left my place and went to the division headquarters, but someone knocked on the door again. The Second lieutenant came in; he was young, his face looks like a girl's, evidently, he

In tribulations

just started to shave, but he was already such a brazen one. He said, "I need a photo on identity card, I'm still there without shoulder boards."

"Comrade second lieutenant, I'm busy," I answer with politeness. "Now the flights will run out, I must prepare soluble material for the photo processing, develop the films and printing photos, and then decipher photos until dark; I ask you, come tomorrow morning, okay?"

"It is wrong answer, Comrade Soldier," the young lieutenant said with enraged voice. He flushed; it was evident that he did not feel confident at the service due to his small rank, so he demanded respect for himself from the girl. "I'm an officer, I order you to take a picture on me right now!"

I was dumbfounded by such impudence. All the officers were normal, they were polite, when they came to the decipherer girls, the pilots brought chocolate, the aircraft servicemen brought condensed milk, the re-enlistments sergeants dragged the stew, everyone tried to be courteous, and everyone was respectful in response to any comments by the girls. However, this one flew off the handle!

I wanted to call the platoon commander, who was in the next house, but he went into the room of the photo service, attracted by loud voices. "What's the buzz, but there is no battle royal?" he asked cheerfully, stepping over the doorstep and pulling back the blackout curtain of the laboratory, "what kind of trouble have you, Second lieutenant, why did you shout so loud?'

"Comrade Senior Lieutenant, I came to be photographed on identity card, but she does not want to," the Second Lieutenant began to explain, but the platoon commander interrupted him.

"What is your name, Comrade Second Lieutenant," my commander asked severely, in practice well knowing that if you start a conversation with finding out the name of a junior by rank or position, he automatically gets on your hook and stops resisting.

"Second Lieutenant Buchenko," the young officer reported, and covered his face with a shamefaced blush. I looked at him, and for some reason I blushed too.

The commander looked at him, then at me, shrugged his shoulders and asked, "Genie, what is it with your work turns out, come on, Nina will replace you, and you'll rest. When you'll have to decrypt, you'll return, eh? She will also "shoot" by camera this eagle. Is it work?"

The commander was kind, he believed that war was ten times harder for the girls than for men, so, as far as possible, he did not bother us with discipline and tried to create all conditions for normal life. The girls paid him a boundless sisterly love, tried not to let him down, and in every case, they came to him for help, because he was always on their side.

"Well, commander," I answer him, "you mustn't do this, why should girls worry about my work? I'll do everything myself, and if Comrade

Second Lieutenant Buchenko will smoke with half an hour, I'll take a picture of him." I spoke and from the corner of my eye, I noticed that the younger man was also pleased with this outcome.

Smoke break of Buchenko ended more quickly than in half an hour, about ten minutes later he went into the laboratory, politely asking me for permission to attend, while I prepare the solutions. Thus, we talked through the wall, because I "conjured" the photographic solutions in the other room, but this just helped us get rid of unwanted restraint.

We acquainted, and I found out that his name was Anatoly. "You can call me just Tolly," he said. Second Lieutenant Buchenko Anatoly arrived to the division after the reserve regiment, where communication specialists were trained in new equipment and communications in combat conditions, in its turn they was sent to the reserve regiment after the end of the Kharkov communications school, which was located already in evacuation. He was born in the Stavropol region, in the Kuban Cossack family. Later his father worked in Central Asia as land-surveyor until the war, and he was one of the most respected people in this district. He said that he graduated from school nearly "excellent", and he was almost one of the first in the school, also he has received the Morse code at the fastest speed, from all this I concluded, in short, he is the braggart.

However, when I put a huge camera in the middle of the room and began to set it up, Tolly became completely shy and began to respect me, because I am the simple girl and I can also do such complicated things, and my face is nice, and my body is strong, since I so easy managed the heavy apparatus.

In the spring of 1943, my life began to take on new colors, a bright and happy life streak followed, and the war no longer seems so terrible and cruel. Fans constantly circled around the decipherer girls. They were different, from the simple soldier to the division commander, who became a colonel in that time, but about him, they continued to compose legends about his amorous adventures.

Many girls could not resist the courtship of Vladimir Smirnov, but none of them stayed with him for long, because he was accustomed to easy victories, he did not consider those who slept with him, to be worthy of him who was an order bearer and a great commander. One day the commander of the front demanded from him urgent information about the position of Nazi troops on the front, where, according to the intelligence data, the movement of enemy forces was observed. The pilots "ironed" the area by airplanes, almost "on the belly", photographed kilometers of film, and the decipherers delay the results because of much volume of work. The dissatisfied division commander had to go to the photo lab himself.

The colonel was ready to disperse the negligent "photo ladies", but known to him girl who he had freed from the guardhouse in Davlekanovo, appeared from the darkness of the photo laboratory. "Yes, it is me,' I thought when his emotions showed that he remembered my dark eyes and thick hair, similar to the gypsy ones, but my face is white, not gypsy at all.

"Eugenia," the commander called me by name and said, "what's going on here; you are detaining us everyone, the staff of the front are yanking us by cord, the result is needed urgently, right now, and what are you doing?"

"I do my work, comrade commander," I replied with dignity, as if dismissing all reproaches, "have already identified every goals, which are over there, in the pictures on the table, and two more goals I could disassemble only in these pictures." Then I lifted the photos in both hands, while the large breasts heaved airily after my hands, swayed a couple of times and stopped. I looked that Vladimir gasped.

"What kind of girl is sitting here, in the dark," he probably thought, "I am not a commander, if I do not see her and do not know. Disorder."

He immediately decided to win my favor, by all means, without doubting that the victory would be easy, as always he did. He began to frequent to the photo lab, and everybody in the division began to talk that he had laid eyes on Gina Nikandrov and was about to drag her to his bed, but time was passing, and no result was seen.

"What does it turn out for us," Smirnov blamed me at one of the visits, "I'm wholehearted with you, but you seem to be avoiding me; you don't love me or you have someone else. I saw how you go with some Second Lieutenant; if it is true I'll drive out him in the penal battalion."

"Volodya, do not be angry with me, I do not go around with anyone, I just have a lot of work," I answered, horrified that he'll imprison somebody because of me. "My mother brought me up in such manner that I cannot give me up to a man, if he does not marry me. You can do with me what do you want, but I cannot be your fancy lady."

"And I'll do it now, here I'm the master over all of you," Vladimir said got angry and grabbed me in an armful, dragged me to the trestle bed. I tried to break free from Smirnov's hands, but he was wiry and tenacious, did his job, despite resistance. Then I told him with the voice that was squeezed with excitement and physical tension, "Let me go now, otherwise I'll "shove" you!"

However, Smirnov was not up to it, he stubbornly continued to struggle me, not noticing how my hands tensed; I rested my hands on his chest and pushed him sharply. From surprise, Vladimir flew far to the wall and fell under the photo camera, and I stood over him in the middle of the room, hot and ready for further struggle.

"Well done, you pushed me along," instead of getting angry, he suddenly laughed. "I was good to you, but you shoved me. It is your upbringing, isn't it, Miss Genie?"

"Do not dismiss your hands." I answered with difficulty, calming my breath, "You are my commander, but not a king, and not God. If I treat you well, then you must respect me, you may not fuck me, moreover you will not take me by force; I'll die, but I'll not give me up to you."

"Don't worry, Genie," Vladimir changed the anger to mercy, "I've done it due to me love to you, but what I've done, I'm sorry, the devil made me do it, because you are very nice for me. Since you are so touch-me-not, we'll be preparing for the wedding, you'll marry me after the offensive." Since then, Vladimir was not so rude, removed his hands out of me, and was gallant and courteous, like a gentleman from the French novel.

On May holidays, the division commander arranged a holiday for his staff, where the girls were invited from all the service units. I came too. We walked in a miraculously preserved school building, which survived both our retreat in the forty-first, and the protracted battles of the forty-second, when the village passed from hand to hand. The guerrillas also did not touch the school during the short occupation, when the Nazi commandant's office was here, but its worst days had passed it by when the rapid offensive of our troops was here, and they was mercilessly exterminating the Nazi and everything where they hid.

Entering the hall where there were tables at the corners, and in the middle of the room some pairs was already dancing a slow waltz, I looked for Vladimir's eyes and, not finding it at once, went along the wall in search of my girlfriends. I was having fun, my soul filled with some kind of special enthusiasm, I wanted to run somewhere, find my beloved and dance with him until I'll fall from fatigue. At that time the dance was over, the couples began to disperse to their desks, when suddenly the hall filled by cheerful and prankish music - the orchestra started to play "The gypsy dance". I could not restrain myself, as if I had been pushed to the middle of the hall. I pulled a handkerchief out of my breast pocket, waving it up on the way, so that it would be more convenient for them to accompany the dance, and rushed in a circle, began to stomp with heels and to spin the toes of the shoes by the rhythm of the music.

Everybody around me turned to me, stepped away from center, making a wider circle , and I flew around, waving a handkerchief like a real gypsy shawl, trying to dangle a short skirt, also I shook my shoulders and breast; it led guys standing around the center to the real delight. Everyone clapped his hands to the beat of the music, whistled and shouted, and a minute later everyone was stomping their feet, portraying a gypsy dance. I had blushed due to dancing, and I danced, forgetting about everything, when nearby me suddenly appeared Volodya Smirnov. He grabbed me by the waist and we whirled in a dance although it was completely different one, not "The gypsy dance".

Trying to outshout the music, Vladimir said with admiration, "Well, you, Genie, is my absolutely gypsy girl, your dance is simply remarkable, I did not yet see such dance. You're my talent. After the war, when the victory will be ours, you'll dance with my help in the best ensembles!"

Then I was rushing on the waves of dance and my love, I just wanted one thing, that this evening never ends and lasts all my life. We walked for a long time, until night. The Nazi, who usually arranged shelling and bombing on our holidays, this time was not particularly active, it seems that the preparations for the offensive were thoroughly conducted, and no one dared to open his disposition ahead of time. After that, Vladimir, having checked up the duty shift in a division and having received reports from chiefs of services, has gone to spend me. This evening we swore to be faithful to each other and decided to play a wedding after the offensive.

Soon the combat fighting began at every parts of the front, troops moved west, but the Nazi, still not weak, fiercely resisted, inflicting damage to the Soviet army. Death mowed to the right and to the left, not knowing who is the simple soldier or the general. In one of the fights behind the front line, the division commander Smirnov disappeared without a trace. The pilots reported that his plane fell behind the German trenches, but did not explode for some reason, probably the fuel was over, but was the commander alive or dead no one could say. It's true that at war no one did grieve for a long time, so the new commander took the division, and the battles was continuing harder than ever.

Only I was grieved alone like no other, because I lost the closest person, my fiancé, about which no one has guessed. So, with fights, in the works of military and bitter grief I moved along with the division to the west. In this dark and sad strip of life, the only consolation for me was this dear young man, Tolly Buchenko. We had friendly relations, although someone said that he was seen in the company of the windiest women from the flight canteen. His adventures did not interest me, because I had not yet forgotten my Vladimir, and with Tolly I just got in the mood; he came occasionally to talk, in a walk he composed all sorts of cute stupid things, in which I did not believe as well as half of his news, and never pawed over me.

Nevertheless, sadness remained bitter. Every good thing that fell out in my life, necessarily collapsed, disappeared somewhere, which caused me suffering and in return it brought me grief and disappointment. I decided that it is impossible to resist a cruel fate; I had to accept everything as it is, had to life with my hurt and no longer hope for the best. However, on occasion, when there will be a bright strip in my life, I'll take advantage of it, come what may.

At the end of the war, when in the spring air of Germany through the smell of fires and explosions, through the rumble of engines and the cannonade of explosions, the smell of Victory broke through, it was clear that this long nightmare, which brought most unfortunate events for more than half world, was about to end. When the war was over, I was seized by the rise of all feelings, I thought that happy peaceful days will come, there will be joy again, there will be warmth and comfort in my home, there will be more love and fulfilled desires.

With this feeling, I returned from Berlin to Moscow on the eve of the Victory Parade on Red Square. The capital appeared to me as a peaceful city, well-groomed and washed, almost untouched by war. My mother still worked in the hotel, the courtyard of our house was green with thick grass, because nobody had trample it - the youth fought, and the kids had not yet grown up to play lapta.

I went again to the hotel to see my mother, but the times have changed, I was not even allowed to enter the foyer. Steep-haired guys in identical suits were strolling at the doors, and inside, where they could be seen through the windows-showcases.

"Uncle Basil," I said to an acquainted porter who greeted the incoming foreigners with a reverence, "I wish your health, why didn't they let me see my mother?"

"Gina, is that you?" the porter was surprised. "Well, you, the girl, became absolutely adult. You did not come here for a long time, where you were all this time, is it really in war?"

"Of course, I went as far as Berlin, I signed the Reichstag wall," I could not resist and boasted to the old man, "but how can I see my mother?"

"It's good, Gina, that you've stayed alive, the war exterminated much people," complained Uncle Basil. "You see, at the war my son became a cripple, and now, without a leg, he is not a breadwinner for me."

I immediately stopped to boast. Where can I go with my joy, when the troubles due to this war are around us? However, the old doorman is visibly accustomed to the misfortune, and the son was still alive while so many people were killed. He did not start to complain me about fate, but simply sent the cleaner of the hall to summon Ann to her daughter.

"You wait, girl, your mother will come soon, she was called her, but you cannot go inside, it is such order now. Foreigners are "isolated" from our people," with pride, he said this word, which he heard from his boss. "They are invited to the Victory Parade, there are diplomats all kind of sorts here, honorable guests, the military men, and I say - all the world and his wife, but our plain folks are not allowed in. That's what I'm talkin' about."

After the conversation, I waited for the mother, then we quickly talked, because it needed to escape to the workplace - the order was strict, almost as military, if you are a little bit aside then to you will be recorded the absenteeism, and next step is that you will already go to the court . I was amazed by such rigor order, but I did not condemn the discipline, I only sympathized with my mother, who would be sixty next year, and it was not easy to tolerate her such serious procedures.

Saying goodbye to my mother, I went to the tram to go home, but then decided after so many years of war it would be better to take the metro. I liked the Moscow metro because at great depths you enter an escalator in beautiful vestibules, it's clean around, the festive lighting is here, everything creates the feeling that you are in the palace. But in Berlin, where I was at one of the local subway stations, when water was already pumped out, there was the dark shallow dungeon in it, such as a cellar in the village, it had the poor decoration, it was so simple as the platform of a suburban train, in a word, no comparison to Moscow one.

I drove to Krasnoselskaya station, got off the metro, walked along Rusakovskaya Street to the railway bridge. After passing under the bridge, turned left into my street, went into the yard and sat down to rest at a table in the garden house. It seemed to me that post-war Moscow had changed in something, especially in the center, it had become more businesslike, people had become fussy, hurrying somewhere, almost running, outrunning each other. Nevertheless, here, in our yard, you could relax your soul, gain strength to resist a cruel life, hide from problems and worries. Everything was the same as before the war here, it was quiet and cozy, and it seemed, it will always be so.

I couldn't know that plans for the reconstruction of Moscow are already ripening in the jungles of bureaucratic offices, in accordance with these plans in twenty years there will be no place here for our house and all the other houses on this street - their place will be occupied by a growing large factory. Further, in another thirty years the factory will be plundered, bankrupted, privatized at a low price and its territory will be sold for the construction of a new elite residential area.

All this will be later, in a future unknown to me, but for the time being I have watched with interest as a guy, who was young and did not yet have time to go to war, tore off the flowers of lilac for his girl, as young as himself. I suddenly understood that in my twenty-two I look like the old women sitting at the entrance, watching the youth and quietly condemning it.

"Well, what is happening to me," I snapped myself, "life is just beginning, and I will have everything, give me some time." Immediately the next day I went to get a job.

The choice was not great, either to go again to teach youngsters to my native school and painfully try to regain a sense of peaceful pre-war life, or start all over again, using the knowledge and skills gained during the war years. Moreover, my front-line commander of the girls-decipherers platoon, who was retired already in the forty-fourth after a severe wound, invited me to his work; he served in the MGB agency and needed a good photographer in his department. (MGB - rus. Ministry of state security)

I chose the second because in civilian life it was not as usual as at the

Georgiy Ulchenko

front in the last few years, and there were not around comrades of arms, and maybe it caused I wanted to be again where discipline is, where severe events experience people on strength, where you can still feel the breath of war. My decision also maybe cause I did not find a place in a peaceful life, could not get used to civil procedures, did not know where to put myself when free time came.

I became a photographer in the department of one of the offices of this notorious institution, which was mysterious for me, but I did not really want to know what was happening around in other departments and offices. I just came every day to work, I did everything was included in my official duties, I did everything correct and clear, like a machine, but this work did not evoke neither emotion, nor the desire for change, and neither fatigue nor satisfaction. I had to work mostly alone because the secrecy was very strict, every day I copied and multiplied dozens of documents, images was showed up innumerable photos in the vessels for solutions. These documents was carried away by silent performers into the darkness of the long corridors where I was forbidden to enter.

However, this mode of work suits me perfectly, because the soul was numb in anticipation of changes that were about to come, if not today, then tomorrow for sure. Something told me that everything would change; moreover, my life must change!

I saw how some girl arrange their own destiny, who was either absolutely sleazy or ugly and debilitated girls, on which the guys should not look no way. It didn't matter, because fate smiled at them, they married good guys, front-line soldiers, with arms and legs, even non-drinkers, well, I didn't understand, where were their heads, when they were going to get married?

It was nonsense situation, I was fine girl, but men avoid me. May be in my daze I looked like a snow queen, cold and inaccessible, although from inside I was burning the fire of unfulfilled hopes and desires. Men prefer simpler girls, but I with my education and beauty put myself as high as a prize that no one can get it, if you touch it, immediately your hands would be beaten!

In addition, everyone knows that I work in such a place, where you could not do foolish tricks, wrong man would be find and imprisoned easy. What kind of marriage can you talking about!

Due to this in half a year I was languished again, something didn't add up in my life , but I cannot change position because I had neither forces, nor desire. After work evenings I was sitting with my mother in the room, she also grieved over the fact that her daughter is so unlucky, didn't fit into life. Her daughter has passed the Great War already, she had enough lived years and she should know what and how, but something does not work, hard life distorted her girl.

One time in the fall, we sat at the table and wrote a letter to Nick, who was released ahead of schedule in the honor of victory and send into exile in Kyrgyzstan, to the cattle breeding collective farm near the lake Issyk-Kul. Then a neighbor knocked on the door, she called my mother and they whispered about something behind the door, then mother came in and said with a smile, "Gina, what a friend Anatoly you have? You pretended to be meek but found the officer for yourself, didn't you?"

"Who told you that it is about me, Mom?" I asked indignantly, but suddenly stopped. "Where he is? Tell me is he coming here?"

I rushed to the door and saw that there was such a painfully familiar Tolly in the corridor. I hugged him tightly, kissed him several times, but, frightened of my own fervor, I stepped back from him and then noticed that neighbors were pouring out of the rooms and were watching with pleasure, how this prude hug the neck of an officer in front of all honest people. That's what she is, Genie, fine goings on! Now they would be talking something about, someone immediately remembered that my mother gave birth to me without a husband and I had grown up without paternal guardianship, as a result, that's where the debauchery comes from!

"Hello, citizens," greeted the Airforce Lieutenant, "Eugenia and I used to beat the Nazi enemy together, we reached Berlin, we served in one division, and now I've come to Moscow to study, so I went to visit her."

Anatoly spoke with a soft southern accent, and the letter "g" pronounced with aspiration. The neighbors decided that he is khokhol, and he is very fast, but will he really take our Genie to himself? (Khokhol – rus. Ukrainian)

Then in the kitchen tables were moved together, everyone was exhibiting what he had, and the clou was the food and a bottle of cognac brought by Anatoly. We sat until late at night. I could not wait for everyone to disperse, but the people have come, praised the leader of the nation and socialism, our invincible army and its soldiers, and pitied the dead and the crippled. Everyone drank either together or individually, and ate everything was on his plate. We broke up after midnight, when Anatoly also got a load-on. He told the people sitting at the table how heroically his division fought, and the impression was that he was the commander of the division himself, and only he accomplished all the feats. I listened to his stories, in which, often there was no truth to that, and I thought: He's still the same braggart as he was, and the war did not teach him anything," I thought so, but I felt sympathy for him as a close person with whom I had been bound a significant part of my life. I touched his hand, inviting to eat or drink with her, and this touch burned, causing the blood to flow to the normally white cheeks.

Mother watched me and did not recognize me. She understood that a turning point had come in our destiny, and then everything would go differently. I had warned her about this when we talked "about life", i said that the time will come and we will have to part, and everyone will go their own way, but it was somehow vague, maybe it will, or maybe not, but now the changes have come with rapid force, sweeping away the established manner of our joint coexistence.

Now I was melting from the feeling of Tolly's close shoulder, who suddenly become my own and almost a dear, whether it was a wrong feeling, or so it was in fact, I did not want to understand, I wanted to extend this moment, that this feeling will be always in my life.

Anatoly has now become like a part of our family, he came after classes, and sometimes he was left to spend the night after long sit-rounds. He slept on the Nick's bed, in the morning he washed and shaved with Nick's razor, this made us more united, however, time passed, and our relations have not advanced beyond conversations and memories about our front friends. We often hugged, when the mother left the room, shyly kissing, but when parting on the staircase, the embrace grew hotter, and the kisses - more and more long. There have been a parting after that, the longing of the soul and the body did not find a natural solution, which caused me even greater suffering than in the absence of all this. Eventually I made up my mind.

Before the New Year, I went to Maria, a long-time mother's friend with whom they had worked together for a long time at the hotel, and subtly hinted that my mother had not seen her for a long time, they could meet together. I said, "Mrs. Mary, you would invite my mother to her home on the New Year's holidays and you'll have a good time together." Mary hade liked this idea, she invited my mother to her, but my mother accustomed to sitting at home with her daughter, and now - with Tolly and she did not immediately agree. Mary and I persuaded her for a long time, and finally she was persuaded. Then I began to prepare my own celebration.

I have not told Anatoly until now, I doubted whether I was doing the right thing, I found out slowly whether he had any plans for a festive night, and it turned out that we could spend the New Year night together, for the first time alone with each other. Moreover, it frightened me as if I had not gone through the front, and was still a schoolgirl, who was to have a first date. Nevertheless, the desire to get close to Anatoly was overcome all my fears, and I decided whatever happens, I invited him to my home for the celebration of the New Year.

He came without any second thought, thinking that as usual my mother with us will be bored for the night, but everything was not so as he could imagine. "Gina, where is the mother?" Tolly asked warily, not finding my mother in the room or in the kitchen. He even looked for her in the water closet, just in case, but there was no my mother either. "Where your mother went, soon we should be sit at the table."

"And we, Tolly boy, are alone with you, we will celebrate the New Year together," I answered with a playfulness in my voice, and a nervous tremor ran through my body in anticipation of someone unfamiliar feeling, but such a welcome one.

"Genie, yes, I'm yours," he gasped with tenderness, came up to me, hugged me and already wanted to kiss, but I escaped from his hands.

"Do not rush," I commanded, "what a smart one, we have all night ahead of us. We'll have time to kiss again and again."

I slowly finished laying the table, arranged everything so as not to go again to the kitchen, where each time I was met by interested views of neighbors, and they invited Tolly to the table. We drank one glass of wine for the past year, which seemed to us both the best in life: there was Victory in the Great War, here the war was over, we were alive and met, and there was a whole life ahead. Such a year, in my opinion, cost ten previous ones, which hadn't half of such happy days that we lived in this one. Anatoly agreed with me, but looked a little nervous, too excited, he was joking the wrong thing and did not eat much, but this excitement was mutual for us.

I turned on the loudspeaker, there was passing some slow music in it. "Let's dance," I suggested to Tolly.

He immediately agreed. He was a good dancer, he knew how and loved to dance, and besides, he was impatient to hug me now, to cling to me, to feel how everything in him rises to meet my body, he becomes ten times stronger and I was with him. The dance did not last long. Tolly stopped, began to kiss my lips, eyes, ears, hair, he pressed himself to me, and so I felt his hardened flesh. I answered him with kisses, and tried to move away from this aggressive offensive, but Tolly kept closer and moved me to the bed.

We sat on the edge of the cot next to each other, Tolly with one hand pressed me to him, trying to grab my chest, and the other hand began to stroke me between the thighs, thrusting his hand deeper. I took my breath away by such pressure and tried to free myself from Tolly's hands, but my hands became weak, and he was so hot, so dear, that in a trembling voice I said, "Well, enough to sit, come on, put out the light, undress - and go to bed."

With all the accumulated life experience, in matters of sexual relations I was a complete nerd. I did not know, and never took an interest in, unlike all my school friends, what is it between our legs, how it works, what each thing mean, and most importantly how it should be used. Moreover, with friends at the front, I did not talk about relationships with men, and when they began to tell how they meet men, what they do to them, I got up and went off not to listen to them and not to blush. It always seemed to me that on my face there was too much lively interest in such conversations, and for not to show this, I avoided them and deserved the completely unfair glory of prude and arrogant woman.

Now it has happened to me, for the first time I accepted a man, and I absolutely don't understand what really we did. Tolly, as he could, reassured me, explaining in a nutshell the structure of mine and his genitals, gleaned from his own experience, from the stories of comrades and the atlas of the human anatomy that he found in the library of the school. After the explanation I felt ashamed that I did not know, such elementary things and Anatoly seemed so clever that a great deal of respect was added to my love, which for the woman also serves as a source of passion.

This New Year night I remember all my life in detail, much of what was hidden from the mind in the fog of passion, I thought out in years, much of it I began to understand only with the advent of experience, after frequent repetitions of these voluptuous exercises. I was not ashamed of a single moment of that night, I was not ashamed even for did it out of wedlock and that fact I was a profane in such delicate matter seems to only have played in my favor. Maybe it was these moments in our life together that did not allow me to give up my Tolly, when he became a finished alcoholic, and even when he lost the remnants of the male vigor.

But then, in a successful post-war year, I was at the peak of happiness, all that I dreamed of for many war years, which I so eagerly desired to receive from life, came to me at once, it dizzied me and carried away into a new and joyful world. My Tolly came to us more often, the meetings were more and more prolonged, now the mother tried to leave us alone, knowing that the young people were getting along. In the spring, when Easter passed, Anatoly was solemn when he came to our house; he brought flowers and a whole string bag of different delicate foods and a few bottles of vodka from a commercial store.

"Mrs. Ann, madam," he said to my mother in a constrained voice that did not match the resolute expression of his gentle face, and then he cleared his throat and exclaimed, "Mom!" Mother shuddered and understood that the decisive moment of our relationship had come, her legs went limp, she looked for a chair near her, but, not finding it, she leaned on the table by her hands. She turned her frightened eyes to Anatoly, then to me, and I cunningly chuckled at her. At first mother could not catch the meaning of the phrase, which the young man began vigorously and floridly. "Mom, let me express all the feelings that I feel for your daughter, and in this connection, I ask you to give me the hand of Eugenia, and I hope, I won her heart already!" - Anatoly said, standing at attention as on the parade and holding a bouquet of flowers before him, which prevented the mother from seeing the expression on his face.

When Tolly had finished his short speech, he handed the future mother-in-law a bouquet and stepped back next to me. The mother recovered quickly because her doubts and worries about will I get married or not were ended. Now her Genie will be under control, and mother is guaranteed a happy old age next to the young. She wanted to take an icon from the wall, but was frightened of doing harm to a military man, because neighbors, who already watched them through the door slot, could inform the state security organs. Mother approached us, kissed me first, then the groom, briefly made the sign of the cross over us, and said, "God bless you, live together the long life in love and peace!"

Then we quickly laid the table, invited guests to celebrate such a significant event, all around there was a revival and joy. Tolly has already stopped being nervous and has relaxed, he joked a lot, told funny stories from the life and study of the students of the military courses, where he was retrained. I rushed from room to kitchen and back, like clockwork, so soon everything was ready, and the guests sat at the table.

There were a lot of vodka at the table, and the contingent was mostly female, although it was customary for the war to do everything on a par with men, even to drink vodka, but in our case women with men was not equal, so Tolly had to be the man one for all. He drank one drink after another, not missing even one, not skipping toasts and he drank for every wish of happiness, until he got drunk that he couldn't walk on his own two feet. He could neither move his tongue, nor stand up by himself from the table; finally, he slid off his chair and crawled to the middle of the room on all fours.

The guests were amused by this "way out" of the groom, they at first thought that this was such a joke on the part of this ridiculous lieutenant, but when he staggered to his feet with utterly insane expression on his face, with necktie that was moved on the side, and with a shirt that got out of trousers, everybody realized that the young man was as drunk as a lord.

Tolly surveyed everyone with an unseeing glance and muttered, "What, dastards, why are you sitting here, get out from here! Eh, I'll now fuck of all of you, I'll crush you like lice! Come on, come on, get out to hell, motherfucker! You are fucken dogs, go out, I said!"

The people gasped. Yes, here in their settlement, things do happen but locals punished such idiots for lesser fault words, they beat him so that there was no healthy place on the motherfucker, but now at once he come with such fatal words, and who is he - some sort of stranger, even if he wooed to Genie.

Two men who were sitting closer began to move to the edge of the table to teach the villain, but I jumped up, rushed to Tolly, intercept them from him and shouted with fury, "Do not touch him, please, It's not like he said, it the vodka said, he said it not from evil!" I pushed the already approached man off and I asked plaintively, "Well, dear neighbor, you have never seen a drunk indeed, forgive him for me, please, I beg you very much."

While I screamed, my mother got up and came to my rescue. Mother was respected here, although she was simple women, but she had a solid essence, she loved and knew how to stand up for justice. Mother stood up beside the young ones, bowed to the guests and said, "Do not blame me, neighbors, everything happens, you had time to have fun - now it's time to come home. Thank you for coming, celebrating the betrothal, you may go in peace. "And with that," she pointed at Tolly, who, seeing the mother's reverence, smiled foolishly and tried to bow, but fell to the floor, "we'll take measures. Now he's already ours," she concluded sadly.

The guests began to come out, cautiously bypassing Tolly lying on the floor, who was already sleeping in the baby's sleep, snoring and mourning in a dream, and my mother with me cleaned from the table, trying not to look at each other. I was terribly ashamed of for the beloved's escapade before my mother, but I could not even think that he could do this, and my mother was in sorrow because her poor daughter also got the same drunkard as many women in the district, although he is wearing form of an Airforce officer.

From that day, my mother Ann ceased to respect her son-in-law, but she did not discourage me from marrying him, she was convinced that everyone in this world is ruled by destiny and a simple person does not have enough strength to resist it. If you will go against fate, then it will grind you to powder before you'll see that you are doing wrong. It is better not to have a tiger by the tail, let it comes what may. Mother hoped that may be the military service would restrain him, it would not let him becomes decisively an inveterate drunkard. Therefore, with mutual silence women put things in order in the room, in the middle of which Tolly lay around like a corpse.

The next morning he sobered up and was horrified at what he had done when I approached him with reproach. Tolly began to apologize, that he overestimated his potential, he went over the edge with the rams, but he justified himself by the fact that everybody is drinking and it is happened they drink too much, he will not do it any more, he loves me and he will not drink vodka in any way. My mother nodded in agreement, but she thought such a case has occurred with him more than once. She thought, "Uh-huh, he will drink ever, either with Genie, or without her, because it is customary in native people to drink about any reason, in joy and in sorrow, when it is necessary and when it is not possible, at birth case and on deathbed." Then mother asked him out loud,"why had you shouted on people as they are dogs? You had no bad thing from them."

"Ah, Mom, I do not remember this, my head is weak," the son-in-law explained openly, "it became after my concussion, at the beginning of the forty-fifth, when the Nazi airplanes have done air raid to our airfield, already on the pre-war German border. That time the bomb hit my radio station and exploded; the devices took over all the fractions of bomb, only one hit me, right here."

He pointed to the right breast, and then held out his hand to the chair on which was thrown into his military jacket, his fingers found the lapel, pulled him over, and Ann saw that the Red Star Order was concaved in the center as if it was broken by something.

"I was so lucky that the splinter was aimed to the Order, otherwise all would be lost, I had could die now!" Tolly said with a happy expression." Almost the whole of my platoon has decimated, but I had no scratches on me, only a bruise was on my tits, and my ribs ached."

Mather shook her head and thought, "what did youngsters experience in the war, so Gina talked almost nothing about the front, evidently she have known sorrow. Thank God, both are alive, not injured, and his contusion will someday pass."

We cleaned up, washed and ventilated the room, and then we sat down to tea. Gradually the hot tea warmed my weary soul and tense body after yesterday event, which became an obvious lesson to me. I was looking at Tolly, who was sipping tea from the saucer, and trying to understand if it was just an unfortunate episode from a long and happy life or it's sign of trouble. I thought, "On the one hand, everybody has drunk here, both men and women, there were fights and stabbing, and no one considered that vodka was such a strong impediment to life. On the other hand, some man has finally ruined oneself by drink some man has been died. Worse still, the women who suffered so much evil from their man-drunkards became drunkards somebody had become crippled or had killed their husbands."

Nothing resembled the recent events in Tolly's face, only a slight pallor of his skin showed the weakness of his stomach. He recovered a little from the booze and again spun a yarn about that or about this, exasperating us by his chatter. That day I could not imagine even for a second that for twenty years later this joker turned into a silence bugbear whose tongue would not be able to untie even a large volume of alcohol poured into him. I did not understand until the end of my life, I could not find the moment when this substitution took place, and alcohol overcame Anatoly finally.

My greatest misfortune was that through my life the destiny has given me variants exactly when the choice had already been made, and it was impossible to change nothing. This went on for a lifetime, only in the youth the options appear more often than in old age, but I could take advantage of none of these chances. Is it my fault or the destiny play with my life, it's impossible to understand, but I did not want to understand, because I knew for sure that whatever I did, everything turned against me, that means that I am the one to blame for everything.

After the marriage offer was made, we applied to the registrar, and two

Georgiy Ulchenko

months later, we were to have a wedding. The term of training of Anatoly was ending, but it'll be only in three months, and now it was necessary him to be in time to come to the military unit with a young wife. In addition, for week before the wedding that the father of Tolly, Captain Igor Buchenko, the battalion commander of the Guards mortars named simply "Katyusha" was returning from the war against Japan. It was already the third victorious war of Igor, who by that time had been forty-five years old, and he was glad of gift that his only son had given him, so he did not go directly to home in Central Asia, but decided to make a detour and visit his son's wedding.

On the eve of the arrival of the future father-in-law, I was sitting in the room and waiting for Tolly from his classes. The unpleasant incident at the engagement was already forgotten, I was enough glad of my groom, he willingly helped me and my mother in the household to cook something, clean up, go to the store, even he was taking out the trash that for most men was an unbearable work. I was worried only that he could not repair anything in the house, he could not screw a light bulb; he could neither saw off a board nor nail it. Tolly was not easy to do simple work, everything came out improperly, but I held on my mind reasonably that the time will come when we will live in own home, and he will learn everything.

There was a knock at the door and a neighbor told me, "Genie, in the courtyard, there is somebody there," she choked with excitement, "there's a general at the car, he's very important person, the whole yard has gathered to look at him. He has a star on his chest; he is the Hero of the Soviet Union, that's how it is!"

"Well, Zina-girl," I responded, not very interested in what was happening, "why do I need your general? I do not a girl who looks for man."

"Hey, look at her, you know, Genie-girl, I have not come for show," Zina was indignant, "on the contrary he has arrived for you and order me to bring him petty officer Nikandrov Eugenia who lives in this house».

"What did he says, the petty officer?" I began to interest in it. I ran to the window and looked out onto the street. At the sidewalk stood a black car, similar to those in which the members of the government go, and next to it stood a driver in flight uniform leaning on the fender.

"And who can it be," I thought, choosing in the wardrobe the best dress. "A lot of pilots received the "Hero star" during the war, but none of my acquaintances happened to be a Hero." I quickly ran down the stairs to the yard, ran a few steps towards the crowd that gathered near the table, but suddenly a chill ran down my back, my knees got weak and my eyes welled up tears. It was he, no doubt, in the circle of my neighbors was Vladimir Smirnov, such a native, but long time ago buried and almost forgotten by me.

It turns out that nothing forgotten at all. I always thought of him as alive, only he left me and did not come back, that's all. Moreover, for me he did not become over the years a stranger, although I'm already a married woman. Timidly I was shuffling my feet awkwardly then I took a step towards Vladimir, who at that time was talking with the surrounding residents of the nearest houses.

He did not notice me, carried away by the conversation, but now he turned his head, and I froze again. He did not notice me, carried away by the conversation, but now he turned his head and I stood still again. Smirnov made a move towards to me, and people moved away. In front of me stood all gray-haired man, whose pale face did not at all disfigured scar, he had thin mustache and blue gleamed eyes.

The Air Force Lieutenant General's jacket was sitting on his shapely body like a glove, and the little star of the Hero gleamed in the rays of the sun above the wide stripe full of award's ribbons of different colors. I pulled myself up, straightened up like in ranks, but then came to my senses and walked by light steps to the military man. He smiled broadly at me, and I finally recognized him, my Volodya, with whom I was so unfairly separated by fate.

"Hello, Genie, hello, dear," Smirnov said and grabbed me. He whirled round in circles with me in his arms and then told people before him, "Hey, clear the runway, we take off!"

My heart was broken of happiness and anguish. Of the happiness because we are together again, but of anguish because I have already been given to another. I began to break free from Smirnov's hands, to beg him to stop. He took it as a sign that I was dizzy, put me next to him, put arm around my waist and suggested, "Let's go into the house or somewhere else, we need to talk."

Warmly saying goodbye to the residents of the house, Smirnov followed me, and I pointed out the way to him. While people dispersed they whispered among themselves surprised by this turn of events, "Genie have already a lieutenant and now comes a real general else. Hey, Genie, well done, who told she is touch-me-not, she don't blunder away her chance!

I led Smirnov fast into the entrance, the second door of which went out onto the street, hugged him tightly, kissed her hotly on the lips so his cap flew to the floor and with the words, "Wait me here, I'll be right now," I ran home.

Smirnov leaned on the banister in perplexity, touched his lips burning from the kiss and thought that he did not know this new Gina who was very different from that naive and strict young lady from the photo lab. At that time, I wrote such note to my mother, "I'll be late, it is need to do something", and left it in the middle of the table in a prominent place and returned to Smirnov. He was waiting for me there, and I silently pulled him by the sleeve to the exit to the street where the car was standing.

Coming out of the entrance, I said, "Volodya, I do not want to talk at home, I need to tell you a lot, but soon the mother will come, and everything," and without a word, I waved my hand somehow indefinably.

We got into the car, and Vladimir asked me, "Where shall we go, Gina?" I answered, "At National Hotel," and the chauffeur who drove the car, which allocated by the commandant's office to Smirnov as a general and a Hero, nodded his head, unfolded the car and sent it to the right under the bridge along Rusakovskaya Street.

For a while, we drove in silence. I held my Volodya by the hand, gathering strength to survive this day and not die from the confusion of feelings, and Smirnov was intrigued by such a continuation of the meeting and could not understand out how to behave with this new Eugenia.

While the silence lasted, the car slipped through the Boulevard Ring and drove down Gorky Street to the hotel. Everything was familiar to me in the hotel and my companion followed me through the back door to the counter in the corner of the hall. Fortunately, today Mary was on duty, an old friend of my mother, not young, but still beautiful and so alone. While the General come to the buffet, she took a good posture going to flirt, but her fervor was frozen by me.

"Mrs. Mary, he is with me," I said quietly not to attract anyone's attention, "talk to who is on duty today, let she give me a backup number for tonight, therefore I'll be your debtor."

"Yes, I do it for you, you'll be in deluxe suite, I promise," Maria said cheerfully, no less than Smirnov surprised by my unexpected appearance here with the gentleman, who is a General!

She ran to the reception desk, briefly talked, and returned, carrying the key to the room, "Dancing, girl, I did it as I said. My friend on duty always has the best at hand. Until eleven, it's all yours."

Having bought cognac, champagne, fruit and sweets in the buffet, Smirnov followed me up to the second floor. The two-room suite was quiet, cozy and solemn. I took the food from Smirnov's hands, spread them on the table and, turning to him with my face, put my hands on his shoulders. Our eyes met, lips converged in a kiss, and the bodies moved towards each other, as if trying to merge into one.

We were seized with some kind of madness, clothes was scattered all over the room, while we reached the bed, and in bed we proved to be capable of something that we had never noticed before at least I am. We hugged tightly and parted away, changed the poses and positions of the bodies, we had orgasm and then again attacked each other like two insatiable hawks, and, finally, tired and quieted down in exhaustion. Sometime later, I was the first to wake up from oblivion, because although

I gave myself to Volodya with all the dedication of a loving soul, but inside me there was a part of the sober mind that demanded everything to be put in its place. Throwing on our bodies a large terry towels, we sat down at the table and pounced on the provisions. After drinking and swallowing some fruit, I decided it was time to explain myself.

"Volodya, dear, I have buried you back then, at forty-three," I began with the most important thing. "Forgive me, if you can, I did not wait for you, my falcon."

My eyes filled with tears, I shuddered in sobs, and Smirnov, as he could, consoled me. "Well, I'm here, with you, alive and healthy," he inspired me, stroking my hair, "we love each other very much, but what did you say that you did not wait?"

However, I burst into tears more than ever and could not put in a word, because my lips did not obey. Volodya poured me more champagne, then, changing his mind, splashed half a glass of cognac. "Drink, you will be easier," he ordered, gradually guessing what caused in his darling such changes, which led them to this strange and passionate meeting.

I brought the glass to my mouth and, taking breath from sobbing, slowly, with small sips, began to drink cognac. While the cognac in the glass was reduced, it became warmer and calmer, and at the end, I became so indifferent to what would happen later that I even laughed with a drunken laugh.

"You're late, darling," I told Volodya unexpectedly in a sober and reasonable voice, "Your plane has flown, zing! Then I stayed on the shore, alone. Now no longer alone, I was picked up. Are you remember, that some Second Lieutenant was in the communication company, he always carried on a love affair with cook women. It was a moment when he was on duty in the officers' canteen; he got drunk thus, you expelled him out of duty. Well, do you remember?"

The division commander is not obliged to remember all his lieutenants, except maybe the pilots, but not some dirty piffling platoon commander, but Smirnov remembered Anatoly Buchenko very well. Such impudent, drunk like a pig, spewed right in the kitchen between the pots and pans, in the holy of holies, where food was prepared for all the officers of the division, and moreover he cussed out so that Smirnov had not heard such words before that day. If it were not in the rear, but at the front, he would be in the military tribunal. Yet then, after the guardhouse, he kept a low profile, repented at the Komsomol meeting of division officers, even shed a tear, in a word, behaved not as a real man does. Nevertheless, she chose him!

"Ah, I had no choice," I continued as if reading his thoughts, "I was sitting like a cuckoo, all the time alone and alone. At first, I waited you for a long time, and then decided that at the front to be lonely is even more convenient, less excitement and unnecessary conversations, but after the war, I somehow did not fit into a peaceful life. The younger girls were already picking up the guys, the elders and that like me - already married, but I did not have anything to do with them. Then he appeared here, in Moscow, and began the retraining. You know how it happens, at first I was glad that the familiar front-line pal came, and then I got used to it because he was next to me, after an opportunity had happened I began to sleep with him in to get intimate finally."

I thought for a moment, as if imagining all the things, I was talking about, and trying to assess whether I had acted correctly. "He asked me to marry him and I agreed. There will be a wedding in a month," I added, not daring to look into Smirnov's eyes, who wanted to interrupt me not to hear those terrible words for him and he wanted to listen to the very end to understand how far they are from each other. His blood was boiling with indignation that his woman, whom he had been thinking about while the Great War and while returning from China after the Japanese war, his woman he wanted to marry now, belongs to another man. Someone should answer him for such a shame and resentment, but, in my words, it seemed that no one is to blame; it is the natural order of life.

"Life, life! The devil knows what a life it is!" he snarled. Smirnov jumped up, wrapped in a towel, as if in a felt cloak, ran through the room back and forth, sat down again, but could not calm down. Then he poured himself a glass of cognac, drank it in a gulp, bit with candy, and somehow immediately became weaker. What did he want? How much time has passed, the war was over, he did not give any news, that's the result. All this swirled in his mind, putting a point in their relationship, but cognac running through the veins have warmed the body and revived his interest in life.

"Well, Gina, now I came here and want to marry you; as you decide, so it will be," he said calmly and judiciously, "because you are not yet married, give the resignation to your lieutenant and that's all."

"I cannot do this, Volodya," I answered, "How I will look into eyes of mother, neighbors, what will people say? Already people judged me that I still have the ready groom but I take a boyfriend and go with him. They will say that I want your big stars, you have it more than enough." I nodded at the general's jacket, which was lying around the threshold. These arguments seemed to me correct, but Vladimir had a completely different opinion.

"But we can be together. Right now you gave it to me too, like to him," he retorted." We have long been in love with each other, and I was the first who made you offer, it was when the war was still in full swing!"

"Willing or not, he's my first man," I stood on my ground, "if I had obeyed to you then at the war, maybe now everything could be different, but now, I'm sorry, you're already the second. You will not forgive me that I was not a virgin when you would marry me, you, males, always do so."

"I am not like others male", started to boil Smirnov, "everyone wants to get his wife virgin, I will survive it, although, of course, it's a pity that I was late. Nevertheless, you could understand I'm still a general, older than you, you'll have better life with me. I'll take care of you, just live and please me."

"Well, you said it and began to bargain for me, this is male's nature," I perked up, sensing that I already drunk. "Come on, we will not waste time in vain, we have only a couple of hours left, let's go into bed. I will probably become pregnant by you today because my periods will go soon. I'll gift you a son or daughter, be sure!"

I playfully wagged my finger at him. Volodya having heard the word "son" jumped on the bed then bounced out depicting "Lezginka dance". He rushed to the bed with a cry, "You will name your son Ruslan to find Lyudmila!" began to kiss me from all sides.

We continued the love games again till we exhausted and calmed and then we lay still in bed, pouring cognac and champagne, eating grapes with sweets and remembering some moments of our life.

"Remember, Volodya, how did you bring me the flowers from the airfield?" I said thoughtfully. "You told me that you collected them in a parking near the refueling of the second Squadron of the Kursk Regiment."

"Of course, I remember, there were big yellow "Snapdragon" flowers in it, they were all the same. Probably, it was not necessary to give you yellow flowers because this leads to parting as it turned out."

"But you don't know the main thing," I continued, already noticeably agitated, "I came there after you disappeared when our airfield had been heavily bombed. Therefore, when I got there, there was a huge scorched funnel on the place of refueling, and no flowers there anymore. It was like a sign that you were no longer there, not even a trace left of you. Then I cried so much, I thought I'll be crazy. However, nothing happened, I've been went through the war and now I'm fucking with you.

I grinned sadly, but Volodya stopped me indignantly, "Well, Gina, do not say so, I'll be in Moscow a month, as soon as you change your mind, let me know, you know how. But now let's kiss as if we just met and we are fine."

We were happy with our closeness so we did not immediately hear how in the back room there was a knock at the door. A voice of Mary's friend could be heard from behind the door, "Eugenia, well, how are you there, it's time for you, it's almost eleven, and soon the customers will appear get ready!" She forced us to hurry up, knowing well from experience that no one left the room in time, if not to remind. "It's time," I whispered to Vladimir, and we began to gather.

We left the hotel very calm, everything was decided between us, everyone went his own way, both literally and figuratively. Smirnov went by car to the commandant's hotel, and I took the subway and half an hour later, I approached the house. I walked, hardly moving my legs, from not only fatigue, but also more from reluctance to see any of my relatives and friends. I prayed to God that there would be no one at home, for instance, Tolly would not come today and mother would stay with her friend, but all in vain. Everybody was assembled at home looking at me with fear, because I was disheveled, with dark circles under the extinct eyes, but alive and unharmed.

"We really did not know what to think," my mother began to say. "People said that you was taken away on a car, it did not seem like "Black Maria", and the real general accompanied you. What's wrong, Genie, tell me, please."

"Do not worry, Mom, this is my job," I said with a hoarse chilled voice, coming up with something on the run and reluctantly dropping words, "you don't need to know. I'm tired today, I want to sleep, come on, Mom, make me a bed but you, Tolly, forgive me, you'll come tomorrow."

This explanation, apparently, suited everyone. When Tolly left us and my mother and I was calmed down each in own places, I mentally again and again experienced a meeting with Vladimir, alternately, I excited by the recollection of acute moments, then bursted into tears because of the awkward life which gave me everything opposite to my dreams. You see, only three months have passed before the appearance of Smirnov, but everything not going so well. Moreover, everything went bad.

Later I was angry with the general-pilot because he was away all this time and I could not understand why he not find me earlier, and why he came uninvited today? I twisted and turned in my bed whole night and fell asleep just before morning, and so my mother, hearing sighs and sobbing, feeling something amiss, but did not show me that.

Nevertheless, in the morning I woke up in a good mood and, as if nothing had happened, went to work, leaving my mother in complete perplexity. My mother also went to work, where Mrs. Mary was waiting her to share her observations with my mother in a feminine way.

This point I don't like to remember at all. Mother, having returned from work, managed to arrange me a tremendous bashing before the arrival of Tolly. She said, "It isn't only shame in the workplace, but the whole hotel already knows about you, everyone saw this Air Force General in the courtyard, and when they will inform Anatoly that his future wife is a whore and a General's harlot, he will immediately throw you. However, here no one will pick you up any more, you'll be like me, your mother, you will be lonely along the life, you're a carrion. I raised you up not for shame, I refused everything need to myself, I forced Nick to work so you had an extra piece of bread and butter, but what you did with us!"

As I could, I reassured my mother saying that there was nothing like that, it was just a front-line comrade was coming, but Tolly should not know about him, I'll marry Tolly because I was probably already pregnant. My mother sat down on a chair, but she did not worry me anymore, she was imbued with my position and, having changed her anger to mercy, from that moment she became affectionate and agreeable to me.

We got married as it was agreed. Tolly's father, Yegor Buchenko, was a tall bony and noisy Kuban Cossack, smoked by the Mongol winds and the Asian sun, even his shaved skull was brown and gleamed dimly in the rays of the summer sun. according to custom he kissed everyone, was cheerful, courteous to the matchmaker, and I was already prepared that the elder Buchenko, as Anatoly told me about their customs, would start giving presents to Bride and groom, but not this time. Unceremoniously examining his daughter-in-law from all sides he grunted in displeasure but said nothing and only noticed to his son, "Let's go to smoke, son, there's something to talk about."

I hurried after them imperceptibly opening the door to the stairwell. Descending on the creaking steps Yegor exhorted his son by bass voice, not worrying that anyone overhear him. "What are you, Tolly, son, you're a disgrace to our family, you shit," he did not hesitate to say, "You got in touch with some gypsy bastard. Are they Muscovite really? She is like a male, she is broader in the shoulders than you, although her boobs are bigger then pails."

Tolly answered something to his father in a muffled voice, they descended lower and now I didn't hear nothing. I froze at the door neither alive nor dead. "What is being done?" I thought, with difficulty restraining sobbing, "Occasionally something good will fall out in life but one goat will come and spoil everything."

I understood that his father could persuade son not to marry, and I could not believe in it because Tolly and me can be separated only if we'll die. I have not yet told the groom that I am expecting a child, and now, maybe, I will not have to say anything.

It was necessary urgently to think what it is possible to undertake but quietly, do not noise. I had to prevent his father to persuade the son in any way. I swore in the hearts by dirty, front-line, long-forgotten words, and rushed into the yard. Men stood near the gazebo, the elder, apparently, suggested something to the younger one, and the latter, standing with a guilty look, seemed to justify himself, but did not yield. I hurried to the aid of my fiancé.

"Mr. Yegor, mother urgently calls Tolly to the kitchen," I began to say first thing that occurred to me, "let him go and later you will continue the conversation."

"Well, you've already been harnessed your ass to the kitchen, lout," the old soldier said, "you're going to clean up floors here; you're doing the women's job! I raised you not for this, fucking your soul! Well, you will come; I will arrange it to you."

Yegor threw the cigarette and began to triturate it heatedly by the sole of the chrome boot. He did not look at me and was silent, so I decided to start the conversation first. "Mr. Yegor, why are you set against of me?" my voice was trembling, but I was on a straight path. "Why are you repelling Tolly from me? We are going not to the necking party, we'll have a wedding in a week, did you forget? And further, you said that I am gypsy, well, even if I am a gypsy, you think I'm not a person already, don't you?"

"And you're not person," Yegor retorted. "You're a woman, and place in the kitchen is yours but not of my son! Surely, you specially thought up that he should leave, but you must know I do not love you and I will not Yegor if I cannot persuade Anatoly. We have so much girls in the Kuban, do not kiss you, they are not like you, and they are good housewives, they are cultural and polite, they do not sais any words will in defiance of either her elders or her husband! Moreover, what you told me? Whom you are going to teach, chick!"

I was already beside myself with despair, it seemed that everything is lost, it was necessary to reverse decisively the course of the talks and I decided to speak plainly. "Do not waste your nerves here," I said threateningly to Yegor. "I became pregnant of your son a month and a half ago, if he refuses me I'll go to the political department, they are able to wake up his consciousness, you do not know me yet!"

Yegor retreated in perplexity, looked at my figure, trying to find at least some signs of an unexpected pregnancy. "He's already got it, yobbo," he said, immediately lowering his tone. He did not like political "workers" still in the civil life, and in this war his simple homegrown views on life, society and power often led to conflicts with commissars and political instructors "Do not scare me, girl, they have been already scaring me, you better tell me how you caught him so cleverly."

Here seeing that the preponderance on my side I allowed myself to go on the offensive. "Father, you got the wrong idea about me because I was virgin through the whole war," I approached him closely and whispered fiercely in Yegor's face. "I repelled all the males, you do not understand how I was waiting for my fiancé, and I made love with him only when he made a proposal to me," I said, adding a little fib in the last sentence.

Yegor, dumbfounded by such pressure, took a step to the side, turned away from me and began to strike the flint of the cigarette lighter. It turned out that this bitch overlaid his boy on all sides like a wolf hunter. Paying tribute to the way I skillfully have dealt with his loser, he did not find for me neither understanding nor love, well, he did not like me, it happens sometimes. "But it was necessary to put up with what had become. One way or another," he thought, "she would spoil the fate of my son, so let him suffer with love than without love."

"All right, Eugenia, let it be," Yegor agreed, inhaling deeply the tobacco smoke, "I will not hinder you, but you must know you're not worthy of Anatoly, he's an eagle, but you're fucken hen."

He spat at my feet, heading for the entrance. He did not spend the night with us, stayed all week in the barracks, where he was billeted by the commandant's office along with other soldiers and officers who on their way home from the army came to look at the capital. At the wedding, which we celebrated at the restaurant of the "National" hotel, where mothers gave everything cheaply as its own worker, Yegor sat darker than the cloud, almost not drank and did not sit until the end, he said good-bye to the bride and groom in the middle of the action and went by train to Central Asia.

Georgiy Ulchenko

Chapter 3. The wrong start of the marriage

From Moscow, Anatoly was sent to serve in Poland, in a large "capital" garrison, where the command of a newly formed group of occupying troops was located. In winter a boy we wait was born, we gave him the name Ruslan, the same as famous personage of Pushkin's poem has. We also decided that the girl must be called Lyudmila, so that everything would be like that of a great poet. I loved reading Pushkin from the time when I have been a teacher; his poems seemed to me melodic songs that have a simple and clear meaning, not so as these modern poets did among whom I especially did not like Mayakovski. All these stairs-lines were annoying for me, they did not let me penetrate the meaning of his poems, the melody of his verses was not perceived by me, naturally, and I cannot read his poetry without this!

However, in secret, the main thing for me was how Vladimir said hugging me that I should name my first-born by Ruslan thus he would know that this is his son. Ruslan and Lyudmila, it's gorgeous and sublime, so I talked to my husband, and he did not mind, because he did not care what was Pushkin writing. The name though rare, but Russian, no one will laugh, moreover, for him the main thing is not the name, but the fact that his son was born.

Anatoly was so proud of the birth of the son, his heir, that he had "wetting down" celebrations of this event with everyone in succession, with friends and acquaintances and simply with amateurs to drink paying nothing. When he brought his wife from the hospital, he had to start new paternal duties, but he could not stop yet, he was ready to pour vodka to anyone who would say a few warm words to his son and he himself did not miss this opportunity to drink.

Naturally, there always were fans to drink at someone else's expense, so Anatoly almost every night come home drunk. Sometimes he was carried home by stronger drinking companions, and to my reproaches that I literally drowned in diapers, cooking and cleaning, that he was not helping me at all, looked away and swore that it was the last time, and he would no longer drink.

In the evenings, waiting for this drunk to crawl home, every day I was nervous imagining some trouble, it was winter, and although it was softer than in Moscow, the frost was sufficient to make freeze to death if drunk Tolly fell down on the road. I imagined that Tolly have wandered anywhere and come to some young women and will stay with her, but what can I do without him with a small child? I had to be nervous all the time, my irritation grew day by day, and I began to be afraid that milk might disappear. But nature rewarded me with an excellent mother's tool, milk poured from large breasts with a plentiful flow so I gave away what Ruslan did not suck to two more young mothers who did not have enough milk.

I could not anymore be in constant suspense and when Tolly came once again drunk, I arranged him a great beating. I cried, screamed, scolded him by dirty words, and when he was rude to me, I grabbed a stick for mixing the laundry in the tank and hit him with this stick. This turn of things immediately sobered Anatoly; he grabbed a stick, tossed it away and swung at me. Now, as if the devil pushed me, I jumped toward to him and with force "shoved" him on the chest. Tolly flew as bullet to the exit from the kitchen and hitting his head on the doorpost; in fervor he wanted to jump on me but suddenly went limp and fell silent in unconsciousness.

I got very frightened, started to cry, splashed water on Tolly, pressed him to me and he shuddered, turned his senseless eyes, saw me, smiled faintly and said: "Ah, Gina...", then he abated and at once was snoring in a dream.

After this night Tolly settled down, joked that wife have directed his brains to the right way and our life went more fun. Youth and health gave us the opportunity to love each other the way we wanted. We used this opportunity while I was breastfeeding and could not get pregnant; at least that's what folk medicine claimed. Anatoly helped me in everything and I blossomed having felt help, grew prettier and more attractive for my husband. He never left me a step, we everywhere appeared together - he, the child, and I and we didn't need anyone else.

However, less than a year later I became pregnant again although I continued to feed Ruslan. I hurried to say this to my husband and he was delighted.

"So, we'll wait for Lyudmila," he embraced me, "you're my darling but what about your health, after all, little time has passed since the birth?"

"Nonsense, it's all right, I'm still an ex-sportswoman," I answered thoughtfully, "but now I'll have to manage with two small children, and this scares me. The boy is already on his feet and I cannot leave him alone for a minute, but what can I do when the girl appears?"

In the fact that it will be a girl, we did not doubt at all, must be Lyudmila that's all.

"And I'll help you," Tolly assured me, "after the birth of my son I went crazy but now everything is all right, we can manage together, and my queue in a nursery-garden will be by spring. Ruslan will be in kindergarten during the day and you'll be with the single baby."

We agreed on that and life continued in peace and harmony. A new year has come, then other holidays took place, both the day of the Soviet Army on February 23 and the Women's Day on March 8, but my husband has been restrained, drank a little, he was beside me and did not go anywhere, only from home to the work and backward. Lieutenant Buchenko did his work well, he was already hinted that he will be promoted, so my husband and I made plans and dreamed about how we would live the four of us and how our destiny will develop.

However, in the middle of the spring came tribulation. It happened second time of my life that I never want to remember, but whatever you say, the turn of our life began from this moment and to this time where we are today. I knew that only he, my husband, was to blame for everything, it was he who led our joint life to such an outcome, but I could not blame the weak-hearted Anatoly, it's like accusing the grass for that it grows, or blaming the birds for what they sing. My miserable destiny is to blame that everything went wrong, but I reconciled with it long time ago. Moreover, I made a lot of mistakes too, at least that later I admitted to Tolly in love affair with Vladimir, it was a momentary mental breakdown, but how much this changed our destiny.

On that terrible day I did my housework, I cooked dinner and set the tank with bed linen to boil on the stove as always at the end of the working week. Our son Ruslan could not yet speak but he pronounced the word "mama" boldly and distinctly and the rest words were the same as "dih!" i.e. "this"; he said "dih!" and pointed to something he wants. He was playing in the room occasionally running to me into the kitchen to show what he had done there. At that unfortunate moment a neighbor knocked on the door, she often came as it usually happens for a pinch of salt, and we had the opportunity to talk, exchange news and that was for us more than newspapers, radio and television.

I opened the door and wanted to invite my neighbor to the house but she refused. "Gina, excuse me, here's the thing," the neighbor was visibly nervous, "your hubby is lying near the next house on the path; he is drunk as a skunk. Run and take him away, and I'll run too."

Ruslan appeared in the doorway of the room, who was smiling to this woman, but in embarrassment, he hid behind the door. I was stunned by this news and went to the kitchen to check the linen; I adjusted the lid and went back to the door. Quickly putting on the sweatshirt I rushed to the opposite house, rounded it and saw that my husband was lying against the wall, and around him, the children danced and teased him, saying, "You are drunk, you are drunk!"

Seeing his wife, Anatoly made a stern face, as far as it was possible to create on a drunken face and began to threaten her with a finger. This gesture was so inappropriate that he immediately roused me and I slapped him in the face, his head reclined back, and he hit his head against the wall.

Feeling pain from a double blow Tolly made an offended face and began to whimper, but I did not listen it, picked him up like a wounded soldier and dragged him into the house.

At this time, little Ruslan, taking advantage of the absence of his mother, slipped into the kitchen and immediately headed for the stove. I never let him get close to it so without me he wanted to see what was happening in the tank where everything boils and gurgles.

Ruslan looked back at the door, pulled the heavy stool closer to the stove and climbed on it. Although he began to walk very early at the age of nine, but was still unsteady on his feet, and here, on a stool, it was so high that his knees began to tremble. He grabbed a stick sticking out of the laundry tank but could not restrain himself because the stick reached for his hand, lifting the lid. Falling to the floor Ruslan pulled a stick out of the laundry tank and it began to sway on the cooker, tilting it to the very edge...

Dragging Tolly into the house I suddenly heard from the kitchen a thud of the falling of a heavy object, a splash of water and a wild scream of a baby. I threw my husband in a fright in the doorway, flew into the kitchen and saw a terrible picture, my child was wet and lying on the floor and steam rose from his body as well as from the soapy water spilled from the tank that was lying beside a boy. I ran to the child in horror, grabbed him in my arms, but he could not scream anymore, he wriggled in my arms and become bluish from stress, soundlessly opening and closing his mouth. Time for me became frozen. I did not faint, but I could not budge, I stood and clutch child to me, time seemed like an eternity and I did not hear anything, did not see and did not understand anything. I came to myself from the voice of my husband, who immediately sobered from the picture he saw.

"Gina, let's get a sheet," he said and shook me; "we need take Ruslan to the medical unit quickly. Where do we have the sheets?" Now he didn't wait for an answer and decided to act himself, seeing that I was ready to faint.

Anatoly took the child from me, wrapped it in two sheets and rushed headlong into the medical unit, shouting on the run to neighbor from the next house to look after his wife. I came out of the house staggering and, supported by a neighbor, wandered to the medical unit. My head did not understand anything, the body shook, the hands trembled, it made me weak in the knees and only one thought was beating in my head, "I did not save my son, damn Tolly, what will be now, how I will tell Vladimir about this?"

Anatoly in the medical unit was met the head of the medical service who ordered him to accompany the staff of ambulance which sent the child to the nearest district hospital where there was a burn department. Anatoly was shaking with a hangover, the car's movement made him pain, and he kept asking himself why he had such a disaster if everything in his life was so good.

However, he really was scared when Ruslan was taken to the hospital and he was examined by an elderly lieutenant colonel. He only shook his head doubtfully and ordered the nurse, "Give him anesthetic!" Tolly was not so scared even at the front. He realized that nothing would save his Ruslan, his firstborn, when he was born Tolly almost went mad with happiness and now he had the opportunity to go crazy with grief. He did not understand how everything happened; he bowed his head, when he was told that he might traveling by car to the location of the unit because there would be no help from him here.

At home, no one met him as usual, he went to the kitchen without undressing, and saw me sitting on a stool. Around on the wet floor lay bedclothes, and the empty tank lay here. The picture as his son fell under the boiling water flashed before Anatoly and he was terrified.

"Where were you, bitch?" he whispered, bending over me and grabbing by my throat. My head jerked back and forth and my face stopped opposite his face. Anatoly, seeing in my eyes an endless hatred, suddenly remembered all clearly, how I dragged him home and how our son was boiled. He was seized with a cowardly tremor because of which his knees buckled and he breathless. He let me go and knelt beside me. Grabbing me with his hands, he sobbed, at first deafly, restraining himself, then in a loud voice, and I became tremble in his hands too.

"Forgive me, forgive me," he repeated, as if in unconsciousness, "I'm to blame, I'm to blame, forgive."

Thus, we sobbed a long time until a neighbor came to help us clean up and at least somehow encourage the grieving parents. We did not go to bed that night, we did not talk much, without looking at each other, and the next morning when Anatoly came to the office, the duty officer told him that they called from the hospital and asked to take the child's corpse.

"And whose corpse, what child," asked the officer on duty who had come in the evening and did not know what had happened. "Mine," Anatoly muttered briefly and went for the car.

Ruslan was buried in the military cemetery next to the soldiers, his little coffin was carried by the father himself and Tolly himself put it in the grave. I seemed to have grown old for a hundred years, I was barely dragged after him on naughty legs and thought only about what I should do now, whether I could forgive Anatoly, how much myself it is to blame, what I should do now with the unborn baby that needed to be bear another six months. I was afraid that a new child could not be in safety, and I myself was marked by a seal of suffering, because of which my relatives always would be in bad luck and everyone sees this seal on me, condemns me and never does not want to have anything to do with me.

Feeling again and again the death of my son, I first blamed only Anatoly, who behaved like a pig for his family and for me. A drunk and dirty hog, that's for sure. Although, when I imagined how sweet his face with a delicate skin was, I was conscious that he was not like a hog. Such a vile piggy-wiggy which spoiled everything his hands touched and did not understand his guilt, the meaning of his actions did not reach him and he didn't understand that he could spoil life to relatives around him. Now I knew that part of the blame for the death of my son is mine. It was necessary to lock the boy in the room, take him to a neighbor, finally, come up with something else, but do not throw him alone. You see, how could I do right choice when my life was fully abnormal due to the drunkenness of my husband! The constant stress of my husband's tricks and my family affairs, which I had to manage alone, created some confusion in my head.

"Maybe I went crazy already, like my grandfather," I asked myself the same question, "maybe it's hereditary?" I had no answer, but over the years, my own guilt did not become either more obvious or more painful. It was just theoretically possible to do something, but in practice, everything went wrong, and the son was killed by us.

I remember the gray and dull days, which passed in that spring after my son's death. I did not know whether there was a sun in the sky or rain, but the melancholy that seized me painted the world in all shades of gray. I did not sleep with Tolly all these days; I just did not notice him. I was already tired of crying for my son and seemed to be frozen in a state of numbness, not noticing anything around. Tolly tried several times to get me out of this state, but I did not answer him. This lasted for several days, and I cannot remember how much days, sometimes it seems to me like an eternity, and sometimes - only a few hours. One day, something in me was bursting like an abscess and I imagined everything again that was on the day our boy died, and I began to cry. At first, tears flowed little by little, then I began to shout loudly, then I long cried and beat my head against the wall, until my husband came and found me during this exercises.

Anatoly grabbed me by the waist, dragged me away from the wall, but I resisted and fought against him, as if not understanding who grabbed me, then I tired and calmed down. Tolly put me on the bed, stroked my head, and I slowly lifted my head, fixed on him eerie black eyes without pupils, which burned with dead fire on the limy white face, then I slowly said, " Do you know what you've done, you fool? What have you done, you are dirty brute?"

"Gina! Oh, Gina, do not say so, I did not want to do it," Tolly blurted, frightened of my terrible, insane appearance.

"You knew," I continued, "you asshole, you knew that he is not your son and you have builded this case. Yes, it's not your son," I exclaimed in response to his puzzled look, "He is the son of Vladimir Smirnov, our division commander."

"Gina, you're crazy, he died in 1943!" my husband indignantly objected, "why are you saying such nonsense, I'm guilty, of course, but my son is mine!"

"No, you fucking fool! Remember, the General had come to us," I reminded that strange case, "yes, it was Smirnov, Lieutenant-General, and Hero of the Soviet Union. Yes, I had fucked with him that day and immediately became pregnant. With you I did not become pregnant, but with him at just one day! Because he is a male!"

"And do not touch me," I cried when Anatoly reaches hand out to my face, as if trying to close my mouth to not hear this monstrous confession, "I'm not longer your wife, I hate you!"

Actually, after that our life turned into hell. Tolly went on the booze completely; he stopped to come to the military service, drinking vodka every day and night until he was seized by delirium tremens. In delirium, he shouted his son's name, cried and roared, then threw himself at me with his fists, chased after me through rooms and in the courtyard. I hid from him among neighbors, finally came a commandant's patrol caused by neighbors and took him to the guardhouse.

At the guardhouse, Anatoly in awful agony was coming out of the booze, he tore his clothes, groaned terribly or bitterly sobbed, he terrified the sentries, which was changed every two hours, and they had to watch this dramatics. A sometimes he was visited by a doctor, with the help of sentries he tried to give Anatoly some medications, but prisoner kicked him, swung his arms, trying to hit the vague blurred silhouettes of his tormentors, but he did not allow to pour poison into his mouth, clenched his teeth and turned his face away.

The command of the group of troops already knew what had happened. The situation was ambiguous. On the one hand, there was a grief matter that was understandable to severe front-line soldiers because of its weight and its injustice, it's normal to die a soldier at the battle by an enemy bullet, but it's not normal to die the newborn and furthermore, to die healthy without a visible reason - this is extremely abnormal. On the other hand, the officer drank vodka, rudely violated discipline, and brought himself to the delirium state, sits in the guardhouse like the final drunkard. Such actions are not forgiven for officers. The commanders decided with the sub commander for political affairs; they have considered and decided that for violation of discipline, it is necessary to punish, but they had taken into account difficult family circumstances and gave lieutenant the opportunity to make remedy the situation by his successes in military service, and then they will look at. For one violation nobody can punished twice, the charter does not allow, so the punishment was limited to guardhouse.

After spent ten days in guardhouse Anatoly he became thin, emaciated and overgrown with bristles, finally he appeared at home in such a form. The evening began. I was waiting for him with impatience and fear. I was afraid that I hate my husband so much that I cannot even look at his facade, I wanted either to die before he appears, or he not to appear at all. Now he came home.

Anatoly slowly hesitantly opened the door to the house and saw me standing in the hallway. The first thing that caught his eye was the noticeable waist thickening, which the pinafore could not hide. All the words, feigned and useless, which he prepared for me sitting for days on the "guard", suddenly took a back seat. He had felt that our relationship are changed a lot, and we need to find some new words so that the living together continues. However, there was no word; there was emptiness into us. He stood for a while in the hallway then shrugged his drooping shoulders and slowly, shuffling his feet like an old man, came into the room.

I watched him go; his stooped figure was like a wordless request for forgiveness, so expressive that I was filled by pity. After all, we were left alone, the same dear, as before, we will have one more child, his child, I need to live on and live with him, and we need to accept this, understand and forgive each other.

"Let's go, Tolly, to wash you up," I said hoarsely, going into the bathroom, "I am going to rub your back, you became too dirty."

Anatoly breathed out cheerfully and fussed about, he quickly brought a towel and clean underwear, and the heater was already hot and the water in it was almost boiling. I rubbed not only his back to him, but everything else, both up to the waist and below, his body was so close and dear for me that I washed him with water and my tears. Tolly in my hands felt that many days of fatigue, pity, guilt and hatred to me were gradually disappearing, and in the body, an excitement was growing even sharper than before. Somehow washing away foam and not even wiping off, Tolly picked me up and leaving a wet trace carried me to the bedroom.

We hardly slept that night. Embrace and coition were alternated by stormy scenes of delight and reconciliation, we shed tears into each other, remembering the first-born, gave the floor to support each other in life, always remember what happened, and not blame each other but always be together doing everything that it not happen hereinafter.

Only I have been as good as my word, not Anatoly. You cannot doubt he quickly forgot his guilt, partly because of the lightness of the character, partly because of his inability to deeply and for a long time to experience the same feelings, but the wife's confession of treason he remembered firmly. Anyway, soon he began to hang out with friends long playing preference, Russian card game, or playing billiards, and did not miss any opportunities to arrange a drinking party in occasion and without it, and I spent many evenings alone until the time came to give birth.

The girl was born on a warm September evening at the end of Indian summer. She was not named Lyudmila, so as not to invite disaster as it became with Ruslan, and we gave her name Helen, or if you want Helly, Lena, Nell, Nelda, Nelly.

Tolly was not too happy about the birth of his daughter, he still remembered how it happened with his first child, so he cautiously celebrated the birth of his daughter in a circle of colleagues and continued his usual way of life, occasionally helping me in my household chores.

Nothing changed neither after Anatoly was transferred to Riga, where their son Yegor, named for his grandfather, was born, nor after their Air force division was relocated at the Polar circle in a small border village of Alakurtti. Anatoly sent our children and me for a couple of months to his muscovite mother-in-law in order to prepare for our arrival the adequate living conditions.

My mother Ann greeted her daughter in an unfriendly manner. For four years of family life her daughter had so many things that it would be enough for others in whole life, but she does not care. She is like her grandfather, never repent. Wise Ann sincerely believed that wife is always to blame for the family troubles, she must strengthen the bonds of marriage, she must keep the hearth, and she must watch the children. However, her Genie could not!

Nevertheless, in the long midnight conversations between mother and me, when the children tired after the day's running were fast asleep, my mother gradually realized that not everything here depended on me, although a substantial part of the blame laid on me of course. The son-in-law from the stories of her daughter looked like stupid, capricious and selfish child besides without the necessary brakes. You can add his constant drunkenness and this picture become black at all.

"Look at my life, Gina," the agitated mother addressed to me confidingly, "I am not a husband's wife, I have the only two children who grew up always in poverty, in hard working and without needed care, I did not see high days until you have stood up on your feet. Yes, you know what it means to be with your man in bed, he's yours, everything in him is familiar by the every lines and folds, everything is beloved but what will you do without this? Someone maybe comes, today one, tomorrow another, no one will remain for a long, because you have two kids and you must give to drink and feed him, everybody like to live at other people expense, but what you will have from this? Do you really think that it's better to be alone?"

Mother raged raising her voice, but she stopped, seeing my son Yegor stirred in her sleep, and she continued in a whisper but with the same passion, which was caused by her experience. "I'm rather old, I'll soon be seventy, I really cannot help you because I cannot catch up with these desperados. You know you have to work, you will give the children to the kindergarten, but how they will be without their mother. You know what was with the first; do you want it happened with others?"

She touch my bleeding wound. "Mom, what about me? What will happen to all us when he became a complete alcoholic?" I almost yelled to mother. I imagined Tolly lying in the corridor in a puddle of his own vomit, and I felt sorry for myself even more and I said, "What will I do if he would be expelled from the army, because he's already been expelled from the Academy, because he had an ulcer from drinking."

"And you, my daughter, do not be afraid of what else is not there," my mother instructed, "but you must be afraid of what you did not do. After all, much depends on you, my daughter. When he will have been got a hangover, you will start talking about the fact that he's not right, with a hangover every man repents surely, here you can take him in and do with him what do you want. Let him swear that it is the last time. Then every time he drinks, he will be to blame for breaking the oath; you could trim him carefully in this way. And you must go with him together to the picnics, you would not give him to drink a lot, you could arrange so that he'll skips one pony of vodka or more, you would distract him with dances and talks, so he could drink less. In other side, you could try to limit him of cash, to check his salary whether he completely brought it to home and where he concealed some money. You could also hide money from him so he did not find it and did not steal it to booze, and if he needs let him ask you much. You'll see changes soon because man is very obnoxiously to beg money, maybe, he will drink still less."

My mother in her abstracts told me everything she heard from her happier neighbors, who had husband even if he is a drunkard. Spouses often argued with each other, mostly because of drunkenness and because of money, sometimes they fought, but then they put up with and continued to live together because divorce at that time was a rarity.

Thus in everyday conversations with my mother and in the distance from Anatoly I gradually got used to the idea that I would have to live with a drunkard all my life, and I gained experience how to live and manage my life.

However, like every woman, I could not tell my mother the entire truth mother about how my husband was kicked out of the academy. Probably I did not know every detail, I just could guess a lot about it. I wanted to present to my mother the case so that he himself is to blame, or rather his drinking, which has led to an ulcer and, consequently, to the exclusion from the academy by health reasons. In fact, everything was much more

Georgiy Ulchenko

difficult and even sadder, but cause and effect has swapped places.

It was the end of the reign of the "father of all peoples" Stalin when in remote republics especially in Central Asia the national "establishment" began to steal up to the seats of state power. Formerly the state power at a high level in the union republics was exercised by those who have been sent here from other regions of the country remote to indigenous cities and villages. The "leader" was wary and did not trust local representatives of national minorities. Local wealthy surviving during the Civil and Patriotic War and their sons gradually moved to the helm of power, beginning with the lower managerial post and simply "bread" posts, where they have enriched, have gained weight and simply have bought dominion over their compatriots.

To his misfortune my father-in-law Yegor Buchenko was a bad politician, he did not have close acquaintances with local clans and firmly believed in the inviolability of order built by Stalin and the system of state power. He was not a great administrative boss, but he held a significant position as the chief land-manager of one of the largest regions in the heart of Central Asia. Every piece of agricultural land here are worth its weight in gold and the decisions of all land disputes in these arid places depended on him.

Yegor was known both old and young in that region, the petitioners with considerable gifts came every day to his house outside the city, but not everyone was accepted by the chief land-manager. Yegor was an avid hunter. Time to time he saddled horse, collected the whole pack of dogs and went to the desert to hunt gazelles and jerboas. He had twelve heads of big dogs, not counting dogs of undersized breeds, who lived in his house behind a high clay fence around the yard He could spend the night somewhere at the sand-dune, he could drive into some village and make a great feast there at a friend's house or he could throw his horse and dogs at a distant neighbor and visited one of his paramours for all night long. The unregulated working day, the respectful position of the "essential person" and the patronage of old comrades who settled in Central Asia after the war against the Basmachi, local participants in the resistance against the Soviet regime, gave Yegor the opportunity to live a free way of life, rather than he had turned into an ordinary clerk and sat around from the beginning of the working day to its end.

It happened on one of the days of the hot Asian summer in the middle of the twentieth century when Yegor leisurely drove up to the house on horseback after a successful hunt.

Dogs were swirled around the horse intimidating one another and jumping to the saddlebow, where skins of hunted gazelles were fastened, trying to disrupt them from there. The horse shuddered at the pain caused by the claws of the dogs, swaying aside. Yegor by steady hand restrained the horse and calmed the dogs; he was pleased with his prey and answered the greetings of his neighbors with dignity.

Approaching the gate Yegor gave a command to the dogs and they jumped through the fence right onto the roof of his house. He jumped off the horse, fastened a halter on the pillar sticking out at the top of one of the gate sash, and went into the wicket to open the gate. Suddenly, from behind the gate, some people pounced on him, knocked off him to the ground and began to tie his hands. Sensing danger, dogs rushed at the offenders of the owner, began to tear clothes with teeth and to bite their hands and feet. Out of the yard could be heard abusive language, screams and moans, until a commander's voice sounded over this dump. This voice was familiar Yegor from the time when their horse-drawn troops had been advancing in the direction of the whites troops on the battlefields of the Civil War. Head of the regional department of the NKVD Petrov shouted, "Yegor, stop the dogs, and you, soldiers, let him go, I told you, it's need to do more carefully!"

Yegor was already well crushed with bruises and traces of blood on his face, his jacket was torn; he took a breath and ordered the dogs to get out. The men stood around Yegor, holding their rifles at the ready. Petrov stepped forward and said, "Do not be offended, Yegor, these fighters overdid, they are still young and poorly trained. But the paper about you came to us; you got into a great fracas, it turns out you are the enemy of the people."

"Well done, Sam," Yegor said indignantly. "We've gone through whole Civilian war with you, I went through three wars for my Motherland, did not betray or desert, I am here for many years! You know that I am not enemy, fuck you!"

"Fuck you too," Petrov raised his voice. "It's not the position like you have now so that can fuck others. Well now, will you go or we tie your hands?"

Then surrounded by NKVD security guards with rifles at the ready Yegor Buchenko went across the city under the gaze of neighbors, friends and acquaintances as if he was the worst criminal. Someone looked at him condemning, someone - with sympathy but anyone shouted curses. And all around it was clear Yegor was burned away and he will not come back again. Therefore, his enemies could have fun and pour out their hatred at him even by cries but friends kept quiet thinking about how this arrest of Yegor could threatened them.

In the dungeons of the NKVD, the conversation was not long. Details were not explained to Yegor, objections were also not taken into account, so he was charged with betrayal of the Motherland, judge gave him eight years of imprisonment followed by exile and sent him to the colony of the strict regime near Makhachkala the capital of the Autonomous Republic

Dagestan.

Therefore, in the early fifties of the twentieth century Yegor Buchenko was imprisoned for a long time, as it seemed to everyone, to his friends, relatives, and especially his enemies. The ricochet of his arrest struck his family, which had now one person, his patient wife Anna, and it struck his son too, who was far from him and who had been turned out from the second year of correspondence faculty of the political academy.

Anna moved to the city of Derbent, in order to be closer to her husband she rented a room of an Azerbaijani family in one of the mahalls as they called the part of a residential area in the old part of the city. She had no working experience even for a single day in her life; she always "worked" as her husband's wife, sat at home and looked after her husband and her household.

She did not become a "Soviet worker" even now. At that moment her skill to sew acquired from her mother in early youth, came in handy to replenish their income. Anna began accepting orders from local fashionmongers who liked blouses, skirts and dresses made of crepe-georgette, silk, taffeta, organza, chiffon and brocade. The sewing machine in Anna's room worked without ceasing all-day while Yegor and other prisoners built a gas-pump station in the field at the foothills of the Caucasus Mountains. The women she dressed up were married to wealthy people, so the money earned by her was enough for her life and for making transfers to her husband every month, and she stock up money for a rainy day too.

Here I the daughter-in-law of the old Yegor, in early spring got a message from my husband, in which he ordered me to take away children and to go to his long-term residence at the far Arctic Circle. We did not gather for long, bought tickets for the Moscow-Murmansk train to Kandalaksha station, and I left my mother in mid-March.

"Well, Mom, I'll go on further to suffer because of my Tolly," I sighed and told my mother about the letter I had received. "Let's get ready for the journey."

"Yes, my daughter, you will have a lot of suitcases," mother reasoned, gathering the children's things together, "but it's probably half the trouble. I'm worried about your son Yegor who cannot be left alone for a second. Many suitcases with winter things will not allow you to budge while waiting at the station. Well, I'll look after him here, at Moscow station, but when you'll change a train in Kandalaksha and will wait for a suburban train to the village where your husband serves, you'll be alone with two children all day. Of course, on the train he could not be leave unattended because he immediately could run away to the next compartment or climb to the upper shelves where due to the young age he can easily fall. Then, look, daughter, he will start to play his games to stick to passengers passing through the railway carriage, for which they can get a slap from some drunken man. Protect them, daughter, especially look after Yegor! You must remember how it has happened with Nelly in Jurmala near Riga the capital of Latvia!

My mother reminded me of one of the pranks of a baby again. We have a clever boy, nimble and tenacious; he could get out of any situation himself, although he was only two. However, that time he just did something incredible!

Once my husband's co-workers gathered to feast on the veranda of our Finnish house on the Jurmala seashore in the district of Riga, where we lived with three other young families. Neighbors came from neighboring houses too; they brought home cooking dishes, taking children with them. It became noisy, fun, and as soon as they were heated with alcohol, songs and dances began immediately.

The summer evening is long; especially it is here in the Baltics. It was already late when the children, having played enough with each other and running from the room to the room and around the house, gradually calmed down, settled in different ways, someone fell asleep but some older one took a book to read or to see drawings, younger kids whimpered and pestered to their mother to go home. suddenly my son Yegor jumped into the veranda, waving his hands as if he invite us to follow him, but he could not get to me through the table and points to the door, shouting "There!" and running away again. He returned to us again and again, and his eyes were full with fear, he stomped his feet, waved me up by the hand, but he could not tell about because he knew only a few words. Now it dawned on me because I remembered that Yegor had started to chase after his older sister Nelly, maybe something had happened to her.

I jumped out from the table into a wide corridor next to the veranda, which was like a storeroom for every family. There they kept household equipment, work clothes, stocks of cereals and other non-perishable products and household goods, as well as the water reserves created by men that their wives do not go to the water pump every day.

I found Nelly in one zinc tub full of water. She tried desperately to grab the edge of the bathtub, but she could not do it because she was lying on her back across the tub, her legs were sticking out and she could not figure out how to drag them into the bathtub. The girl had already swallowed water, but continued to fight for life though without much success.

I screamed in horror and rushed to the bathtub, I grabbed my daughter and pressed her to me, began shaking to release the water out of her. Frightened by what had happened, Nelly was even more fearful of my actions, she began to break free and shouted louder than I shout. The whole company ran to the call of our cries. Tolly wrest daughter from my hands and began to calm the girl, who was only crying and pointing at Yegor with her finger. Here already everyone paid attention to him.

"What's wrong, baby," I cried to my daughter, "How had you got into in the bathtub?"

"Hey, how did you end up here, what did you do?" the guests in surprise clamored vying with each other; they were seriously puzzled by what they saw.

"Mom, I did not want to do this, it's him at all," Nelly said crying and she pointed to Yegor. Culprit sidled aside people to hide from his mother, but he was caught and placed in a circle in front of her.

"He took my doll," the girl continued to complain, "but I wanted to get it back, she's mine. He took it from me, but I did not give it away. Then he bitten me for tummy, right here, and I fell into the bathtub." Then she pulled up the dress to show the place of the bite. Indeed, Yegor's teeth were imprinted on the belly of the child with a red double arc. The amazed adults fell silent, suddenly sobering up; they imagined that if mother had not come to help her daughter at the right moment, it would hard to revive her away.

I looked perplexedly at the guests, then flushed with anger and slapped Yegor on the ass. Feeling that his mother would not terminate the execution soon, he immediately screamed but not by much pain, he wanted to protect in this way his soft place from unnecessary beatings. He had used this theatrical staging earlier, and here in the presence of so many spectators success was guaranteed.

Every guest started talking to me saying that I did not touch the boy because he warned us, he did not want to drown his sister and there was nothing for me to do but to wipe off the snots out of the little boy and to take him and his sister to sleep. The fun party came to naught on the spur of the moment. Guests was full of impressions about what they saw, they came home worrying about their children, who were left unattended.

Leaving my friends to clean from the table, I went up to the nursery and sat down on Yegor's bed. He was already asleep, he was unwashed and traces of tears were on his dirty cheeks, but with a smile he moved his fingers and whispered in his sleep evidently justifying himself before his mother. Right now, I felt sorry for my youngest kid because I beat him in vain. Children play and it's normal, but Nell could have fallen into the water either because Yegor had bitten her or because she is so clumsy and she could fall herself.

Nelly was also sleeping. On her face froze the expression of resentment, which did not leave her from a young age until today. I am a mother and I did not like this facial expression. It seemed to me that I gave birth to unhappier creature than I am, and it was unfair. It turns out that I presented my daughter with unhappy life from the very birth, while it did not make any easier my life. What awaited in life the heirs of my unfortunate destiny?

Over time, it became clear to me who fully inherited my misfortunes. Of course, this is not Yegor Jr. He wandered through the world but it was clear that he liked it, and he did not very upset with the confusions in his family. It would seem he is not a desperate optimist, he treated easily to what prevented him in life, to his mistakes, stupidities and misses because he understand that all bad things will pass away, but the good things will remain. Maybe it's because he's a Cancer by the horoscope and can wait out bad times in his shell, he also can retreat to move forward. Contrariwise, I'm Leo although the difference in birthdays with my son was less than a week, in critical situations I had a hard time. He had the iron will same as I had, and he felt how to evade the blows of fate, to survive, not to break, but I was bent and broken every time when happened tribulation, because I could not resist fate.

My daughter Helen inherited all my stock of misfortunes. She has naught character; I would say she had no character at all. Nothing that happened to her, both good and bad, leaved positive emotions in her soul but only negative ones. When she had met a good guy, he was unsuitable because he needs something bad of her, otherwise he would not have approached her. If he earns good money, he can lose it, someone can rob him or he can simply spend it on something useless, that is, money will all go to waste.

In addition, if would she be promoted at work that it's bad too, because she could overlook something or somebody would steal in the workplace but everybody could think that she did it, and moreover, fellow worker could work badly and they would blame her, because she is responsible for it. Especially, when she go to the store, it's just flour for her. If she bought a good thing, somebody will be jealous, but if anything worse was chosen they would say that she is awkward, cannot dress like people. In general, her life was like a series of unfortunate events.

It was my little psych consult, but the reality immediately made me aware a real dose of tribulations, which wait for me now. The days when we served in Poland or on the Riga seashore even if they were marked by various misfortune, seemed to me a paradise when we arrived in the Arctic region. The wild northern nature is not like the lovely landscapes of the central strip. To go crazy, you only need a long polar night, which is pretty depressing by its bottomless darkness, and the continuous polar day when you do not know whether to go to bed or you have to get up. In addition, you dispirited of your distance from civilization for many hundreds of kilometers and from all benefits of civilization too. All previously said was enough to plunge me into a deep depression, which was aggravated by Anatoly, because he did not change his way of life even in such wild place.

The Senior Lieutenant Buchenko was almost a complete alcoholic and they sent him here to get rid of him with a guarantee; they threw him on a higher position to the cold North and put him on the Maj.'s post as the chief of the inner service department of the fighter aviation division. This fact greatly raised him in his own eyes. He began to drink even less for a while not to disturb dissected stomach, a large piece of which had been cut off during surgery to remove the ulcer of the duodenum. He had an ulcer for a long time and he healed it with varying success. Especially he liked the method of cauterization, when it was necessary to drink a small glass of vodka on an empty stomach then he would have felt better, either because the cauterization really helped or most likely because alcohol was quickly absorbed into the blood and had intoxicated the brain.

He had to go to surgery when he was still in Riga. One day Anatoly was called by the chief of staff. "Listen, Senior Lieutenant," the chief of staff said it and stopped as if hesitating because he remembered well what had done this dashing young man at the guardhouse when his son died. Nevertheless, after a pause he spoke again, "Do you know what my security officer reported me? What about your father?"

Tolly's hamstring have shook right away. His mother wrote him recently that his father was imprisoned for anti-Soviet activities, but he did not report to anyone because he thought that it was so far from here in Central Asia. He was wrong; they would have got him anywhere.

Seeing that the Senior Lieutenant turned pale and was silent, the chief of staff regarded this in his own way. He said, "Yes, it seems to me I am the first who have to tell you about this. Your father have been imprisoned recently, the article of the law is for anti-Soviet activities and terrorism. At least they gave him a minimum term of imprisonment only eight years although article provides for the death penalty; it seems he did not do much. Well, do not get so upset," he noted with concern, seeing that eyes of his subordinate were already rolling up and his knees trembled like in the cold.

The chief of staff continued, "Don't worry, son, your father is alive, God blessed, he'll finish his term and they let him out. Now about you. A letter about your dad came from the Academy; they ordered to consider the expediency of your further education. You see, it's happened that you are now the son of the enemy of the people, they do not say that outright, but anyway there we have a command to kick you out of the academy. It makes sense to do that not to spoil the biography; we offer you one variant about what I was consulted with our chief doctor. He says that you have an ulcer, so you have to cut it off, and we'll write to the academy that we ask them to dismiss our officer for health reasons because of the operation on the ulcer. How do you like this option, Tolly?"

The chief of staff spoke softly in a fatherly way, but Tolly hardly understood anything from fear. However, the main thing he had understood, he thought, "they kick me out - it is the first, I have to cut the ulcer - it's the second, and the third, it will not be recorded about my father anywhere." Thanking the commander for his care, Anatoly went to the head of the medical department and next day he came to hospital to do the operation.

The spring of the 53rd found us in the Arctic region at the new duty station, when died the "Great Leader". His death had estimated the price for many things in our life. When I was arrived to my Tolly with the children, I told my husband how I had been going to Stalin's funeral. I was nearly crushed there and I almost froze my legs although I was in felt boots with footcloths, because the frost was hard and I had to jam together almost five hours motionless among other people, they stood body to body that it was impossible to get out of the crowd.

Tolly didn't care about it because he was afraid of Stalin and understood that his fellows were not better. Especially Beria was with his terrible eyeglasses. He did not tell me about his father because I should not know this if he does not have such note in his a biography. Nevertheless, in the soul Anatoly hoped that with the appointment of the new ruler something would change in the fate of his father.

It happened at the end of the year; Yegor Buchenko was pardoned and released. It was not a rehabilitation but we should thank own communist party for the fact that he was released alive, but elder Yegor thanked destiny for being alive. He settled with his wife in Derbent but did no longer want to go to the civil service, remembering the lesson that his "friends" taught him in Central Asia. Yegor had been engaging in bookbinding. Since then, he used to walk or ride "on the goat" how he named his old motorcycle made by the town Kovrov plant, then he used to ride on the bus, when he had broken his motorcycle under the wheels of a truck, across the mountains of Dagestan from one end of the republic to another seizing neighboring areas. He carried a heavy sack behind his back with paper, glue, cast-iron press, sharp cutter and other tools for making office books for remote mountain collective farms. At that time his wife Anna was sitting at home waiting for him with earnings, but she did not lose time and continued to sew for local women.

The days of the northern garrison are harsh and monotonous. The changes occurred only during the furlough when you could briefly leave for the "life place", where there is a civilization, normal living conditions, culture and just warmly and cozily. Such a moment came for me when for the first time with my husband we went to rest in a sanatorium.

Anatoly after the operation to remove duodenal ulcers had to get a permit for a sanatorium to him to heal his entrails, and at the time, the head of the divisional medical service had only a family permit. Tolly categorically did not want to take me with him, so he decided to cancel the tour or at least postpone the vacation from May to winter when there will be single trips, but the doctor-in-chief insisted.

The experienced colonel knew what young officers were doing when they came to sanatorium without wives, then waitresses and nurses were in great demand of them and in their spare time they played a preference game and drunk a lot of vodka. This Senior Lieutenant he already had on a note when he before the operation went alone to a sanatorium to treat an ulcer, he brought a reprimand from the head of the sanatorium for gross violation of the daily regime. Although he told on the officer's trial of honor that he was late for dinner once and the other time he did not come to the enema, they did not believed him because in his certificate of treatment at the sanatorium it was specifically said that he was in a sanatorium in a drunken state. Indirectly his violation also struck the head of the medical service who had to must be responsible to the division commander for this young man. It is better; if his wife would restrained him there then it will do without women, cards and vodka. There is nothing to do; Tolly had to take his wife with him. At home, he played a whole play with me as a spectator, with the plot "a caring husband knocked out from bad commanders a ticket to a sanatorium for his wife."

"Gina, get ready, we are going to go to a sanatorium," he shouted from the doorway returning from service on a frosty March evening.

"What do you say the sanatorium?" I asked because I was dumbfounded, mentally figuring out one of the options for explaining, he is either drunk or he is mocking me, and I told him, "I have not yet ready and we have no places to leave our children, now I need to go to ask my neighbor to look after them."

"Don't worry, Gina, I'm serious, we're going," he smiled broadly, "but not today, of course, it'll be in May."

"Really, then, I have time for collecting things," I concluded, "but why did you decide to take me with you? Previously, you somehow managed it yourself."

"You also need the medical treatment after the polar night," explained Tolly with the importance of the specialist, "I did my best to persuade every doctor to get you a permit!"

I was surprised at husband's concern but still appreciated his efforts with dignity, few of the young officers and their wives went to the sanatorium by the family permit, family trips were mostly given to the leadership of the headquarters of the division or to the commanders of the regiments, and after all - to a simple senior lieutenant. Willy-nilly I was permeated with respect for my husband although certain suspicions remains. Whatever it was I could not confirm or deny my doubts so I gladly began to prepare for my first visit to the wide world.

Two months passed quickly. During this time, I was able to persuade my mother to take a vacation and to sit with her two little grandchildren while my husband and I will be at the sanatorium. It was not easy - to get the tired old woman to take on a heavy load of responsibility for my children but I begged my mother as if it was my last chance to fix problems in our family life. Finally, my mother agreed.

Then I ran around all the modistes in our small village and ordered several new dresses, skirts and blouses. I was going to buy a swimsuit and shoes in Moscow where we will stop for a few days. The rest of the time, I was in high spirits, which was passed on to the children. They were delighted that they would be alone with their grandmother, without their father and mother, and it will be so good there! Even the fact that I kept telling them that they would have to obey my grandmother, be careful and obedient children, did not cloud their joy.

In the sanatorium, everything also began as in a fairy tale. I did not know that such luxurious places exist in the army. There was an antediluvian mansion with columns among a pine grove in the foothills of the Caucasus, we settled here on the second floor. A spacious double room with all the amenities, which we did not have in our home in a polar settlement, a gigantic dining room with high ceilings and windows from all sides, all this fascinated me and reminded me of my childhood I spent at the National Hotel.

After we were settled I started to undergo procedures, and the nurses was engaged by me, the first one wrapped me in the mud with a canvas cover; others watered me under the water from a hose with a big head or made enemas with a decoction of herbs. At first, I was embarrassed by the nakedness of the intimate places, open to the local staff, among which not all were women, but then I even felt some excitement. My strong young body exhausted by the harsh winter, lack of sunshine and tedious homework was quickly gained strength from the accepted procedures, from abundant food and from a steady state of rest.

I was so filled with energy that I was ready to pounce on my husband and rape him with all the fury of prolonged abstinence because behind us we had a long journey on the train, we had been staying at home with my mother and children together and I feared to make love with my husband in an unfamiliar place. Up to this point, my sexual feelings have been frozen, but now I had the comfortable condition and I rested, it was time to do something enjoyable to myself with my husband.

The time was after dinner when the sanatorium was immersed in peace and sleep, it was so-called "dead hour". All around was a calm and transparent silence, through which outside the window you could hear the birds cheerfully echoing in the trees, and sometimes you heard a creak of footsteps on the gravel tracks of one of the technical staff, and inside the hull muffled voices came from those who could not sleep.

I got out of bed and stretched all over. Suddenly, in the lower abdomen something shrank right up to the pain, then burst, and poured into my underpants. Well, you have to understand me, I had wanted to make love with my husband just before, but then, as ill luck would have it, and the periods came.

Now the procedures should also be set aside for a few days, and I'll not go to the mountains on a tourist route as well as I could not even think about a trip on the sea coast. Tolly had come, when I was in the toilet to make myself the tampon from the gauze and cotton wool. He had gone to the library and brought a few books, which we would have read until the end of the term.

"Genie, where are you, here I am," he informed me so loudly that I flinched with surprise, "I brought books, come here to read it."

Tolly from the young years was a book reader although the read, as I noticed, did not leave obvious traces in his brain. He did not remember the book titles he read, neither the heroes of the narrative nor the plot. Sometimes he remembered certain episodes that he liked or did not like, and he talked about them, but it looked like an incongruous anecdote, just as unfunny and just as vulgar. Now Tolly was interested not in books but me, his wife Eugenia, or rather my body, which attracted him with his hot flesh and energy of excitement. Apparently, communication with the librarian, a young and handsome lady who clearly was not averse to having an affair with him, excited him greatly, and he wanted to enjoy.

"Hey, there you are, where you hid," said Anatoly in a sour voice, in which there was already a note of impatience, "what were you doing there, are you washing up?"

I stood before him in my underpants, and he began to throw off his clothes, stroking my body with one hand and trying to kiss. I slightly pulled away looking at his bulging panties with regret, and said, "Cool it, Tolly, I have periods today. It is impossible to me."

"Well, how come it, so much time we had no sex, why these periods had not passed then?" he asked stupidly and his lips twisted in offended tone.

"You will order food in the dining room," I quipped because I was uneasy about my condition too, "but here the nature is, everything comes in its time. Suffer a little, soon the periods will pass, and we will have everything."

"Why do I have to endure?" Tolly outraged, "you always have something wrong, when I want you - you cannot, or your head hurts and something else. I'm tired of everything, I'll go to get drunk, and you will sit alone here with your periods."

Then he left me, slamming the door on the farewell. A hollow blow in dead silence deafened me. My legs weakened, and I had fallen down on the

In tribulations

carpet. This bastard spoiled everything again! I did not cry because there was no grudge, I hated him because he does not understand my female nature, but he sees in me only a device, sometimes the washing machine, more often the cooking machine and anytime, the machine for sexual intercourse. He does not care how hard it is for me to raise two children practically alone, because my husband leaves in the morning and comes late in the evening, always drunk, but how I live as a person, what my interests are in life, how he can help me, about this he never stuttered. Nevertheless, I must give him a meal on his first demand, provide him with clean and ironed clothes, cut off his toenails, and most importantly, fuck him at any time when he requires it. Behold right here, lie down and spread legs!

I did not like it because I am also a person, so he must treat me like a human. I hardly got up, and rubbed my numb back, than I began to gather for dinner. Menstrual flow was much more plentiful than ever; however, I did not panic, believing that the climate change and the medical procedures were the cause of it. After putting myself in order, I went to the dining room, but I had supper without an appetite just that the food do not waste, and then I returned to the room.

There was no Tolly here. Thinking about where he might be, I went to the pavilion where men played dominoes, then to the outlet from the sanatorium to the store where they sold wine, after that I went back to the main building and at the end, I went to the cinema where some old film was shown. My husband's tracks seemed to be dissolved. I was afraid to ask someone so that it would not think we had a quarrel because I already noticed how the local girls looked at Tolly, if I have turned away then they are already here. I had no choice and I went to the room to sit and to wait.

I had to wait long. The footsteps under the windows had already died down, the bolts on the entrance doors had thundered, probably doors had been closed until the morning, somewhere in the distance, and the horns of locomotives could be heard, usually not audible during the day. I felt anxious. The bottom of my stomach was sick, my legs were swollen and ceased to bend, my thoughts were bad, then were worse and then disappeared at all. It'll be alright if he just got drunk, but he might get under a train, local Caucasians could slaughter him, but what else I can think? There, next to the mountains was a deep gorge, if you are falling down into it then you will be flying for an hour, and no one would have gathered you bones! Where is this lousy ass?

I waited a long time and fell asleep. Somewhere far beyond midnight below me at the entrance there was a knock at the door, loud screams, swearing, the ringing of broken glass, and then Tolly, drunk like a monkey, burst into the door. The duty receptionist followed him with a squealer, screaming and yelling. I stood up and tried somehow calmed the poor woman, who was indignant most of all because of this drunkard waked her and he startled her strongly. Then I escorted the receptionist out the door. Here I approached her husband, who was standing in the middle of the room and loudly resented that an old woman had not let him in, put my hands on hips and began to examine him.

Tolly was dressed in light pants, on the knees of which were the greenish-dirty traces of grass and earth, and in the white T-shirt, which was smeared with lipstick on the shoulders and chest. The neck was black by fresh hickeys, and through the unbuttoned fly it could be seen the soiled men's briefs. Tolly finished shouting and seemed to wake up. He looked around, checked his clothes, then looked at me with dull crazy eyes and held out to me the two figs to my nose.

"Did you see this?" he twisted the figs before my eyes, "you did not fuck me, so there were some who did not refuse! I spit on you, do not scare me! You are a whore yourself because you had fucked the general, but you are still pressing on my conscience! Fuck off, bitch!"

He swung at me but could not keep his balance and fell down the carpet in the middle of the room. A minute later, he was snoring like a whole barracks of soldiers. I was frightened by husband's behavior and I was startled by his words and shabby appearance, and most important I was startled by the dissonance of this low and vulgar scene with the coziness and luxury of the surrounding interior. I was very worried and because of it I felt that something was finally breaking down at the bottom of my stomach, and blood poured from inside down me onto the carpet. I shrieked and fell down next to my husband to be fainted.

We would have been lying so until the morning while the husband, having sobered the next morning, would not find the bloodless corpse of his wife, but the vigilant receptionist did not leave our room but overheard standing behind the door. Right after my cry, she burst into the room and rushed to me thinking that this drunkard had killed his wife, but then she saw the blood between my legs. She picked me up and dragged my feet up to the chair, so that my ass was above my head. Then she tucked the tampon between my legs to block the blood and rushed down to the phone.

I regained consciousness in the infirmary. In the room, there was no one apart from me and I heard no voices beyond the room too. Tell me what normal people can do in the infirmary, if they had come to rest and gain strength and health. It's only I who could be here with my unlucky fate. Remembering step by step the events of the past day, I groped for the tampon between the legs, looked around to see if there was any blood and calmed down at last. As it appears I'll be living, but I did not know how to live after such a shame. Another thing what I can do with Tolly, it was also unclear.

After leaving the medical unit, I had to crawl almost on my knees before the head of the sanatorium, so that he would not expel Anatoly for violating the regime and wrote nothing to the division commander. The pain of bleeding and the pain of humiliation have since merged for me into one and were tightly connected with the tricks of my husband, although when he sobered up he was also lying at my feet, tearfully asked for forgiveness, told me about two our children and about our shared responsibility to care them. I looked at him and knew he did not think about kids, when he fidgeted on the grass with some whore, but sooner or later, I had to forgive him, although the recreation was spoiled completely.

In the Far North, without the right amount of sun, without fresh fruit and vegetables, on porridges and flour dishes children wane during the winter, are often sick, although they mostly stay at home under the supervision of the mother and do not go to any kindergartens. The climate is not suitable, in one word. Our children were no exception. I was especially worried about the little Yegor, whose sore throats were accompanied by very high temperature, fever, delirium, but recovery was long and not always successful. Therefore, the next summer the whole family gathered to the south to the shores of the Caspian Sea, to the Dagestan city of Derbent, where the elder Yegor settled after he was released due to an amnesty from the strict regime colony.

They traveled long and hard. First, we got on the local "cuckoo train" from the border to Kandalaksha, where we stayed for a day, waiting for the train to Moscow. Yegor Jr. was weak from his illness and he had immediately shaken up on the train and began to spew, he had become more weakened and mostly lay. Next two days we went to Moscow, and now Nelly was added to Yegor.

In Moscow, we stayed with my mother, and she immediately started scolding me for I pulled children at younger age into a dirty southern city, moreover, populated by representatives of national minorities, in abbreviated form, "natmin". I was disgusted by such a manifestation of chauvinism from my mother, but I did not say anything, because I also did not like the "natmin", although I could not really explain the reason for my hostility, maybe because I did not know their customs and beliefs, and frankly saying, did not want to know. We are Russians, when we do not know much or know nothing, we do not like it or this do not exist for us at all. Anyway, I stood my ground, the southern sun, the sea air, the abundance of vegetables and fruits will lift the children to their feet. Mother could not but agree with me, however, she was afraid that from infections that are walking among not very clean people, children will pick up some virus and they will get sick even more.

"For the local children there is nothing dangerous in Derbent, but your children lived in sterile purity, among the white snow and severe frost," she persuaded me, "they were not sick in your tundra except tonsillitis, but there they'll have dirt and unsanitary conditions anywhere, the water is dirty in the sea, there's nowhere to wash, well, Is this for the comfort?

"Nothing, somehow it'll be," I was hoping for the Russian traditional "possibly", "I'll look after them, and I suppose they will not get sick."

Further, there were two more days of a way from Moscow to Derbent, and I thought, that children would not sustain a way. Tolly was in the best situation. He did not think to help the children, so he left the children for me and went to the dining car. There he spent an hour or two eating and drinking without care, then, having returned drunk, fell asleep. In the same time, I ran around the platforms during frequent stops in search of decently cooked food, consulted train conductors what I can take and what I does not, but the children I left alone sick and helpless, tried to entertain themselves in their own way. Nelly was not waiting for her mother will come, she gave a shit in the middle of the compartment and sat next to a pile crying from the stench and waiting for punishment. Yegor urinated on the curtains in the corridor, he competing with the neighbor's boy which of them will urinate higher. They urinated and laughed running from one window to another, and the adults shout at them calling for their parents and the train conductors.

I cleaned the compartment and paid the train conductors to wash the curtains and windows, and then I began to feed the children, crying from impotent rage. The only thing that consoles me was the healthy kind of children. As soon as the train passed Rostov-on-Don, they seemed to be replaced. Yegor rose firmly to his feet, he ceased to vomit and revived, and he began to be naughty so as always. Nelly also became more alive, she did not lay further, but sat and walked around the car, telling my about her impressions.

It was hot in Derbent. Asphalt melted in the rays of the sun and floated underfoot, the meager greens of the parks were covered with yellowish dust from the shell rock, from which every footway consisted here. The houses were made of the seashell rock blocks, the sidewalks and pavements in the old part of the city were covered by the paving stone of shell rock, from which fences, gates, the city wall, and the old fortress of Naryn-Kala were built. A chopped mixture of the seashells covered pedestrian paths of parks, squares and boulevards, and the dunes at the seashore consisted of seashells too.

Every day from ten in the morning until three o'clock in the afternoon, I sat with the children on the beach. Sometimes we were joined by a husband who went more shopping on points where natural local wines were sold with the quality superior to anything he had tasted before. Anatoly easily get acquainted with local men, treated them heartily, they answered him the same, so by the evening he had hardly crawled to the house, thus I had to go shopping, to cook meals for everybody, cared the children, in short, this was my recreation.

At home, if you can call "home" two rooms in a typical Azerbaijani house that his parents used to rent from the owner of the house, only Anna, Tolly's mother was with us. Yegor was away. He recently found a job as a independent handicraftsman, forging a bindery business, which he studied on a three-month course after an amnesty. Now he traveled along the distant auls "on the goat" - by the old motorcycle, producing office books for various documentation in each individual collective farm and aul. He would be in Saturday.

He returned when he was expected. We went out to the courtyard to meet him by the whole family. Yegor led a motorcycle into the yard, put it in the pantry and greeted everyone. He pleased with attention to himself and he washed his hands under the washstand, which he had recently attached to the grapevine. Her naked twisted stem from the middle of the yard rose to the level of the second floor and there branches already expanded in all directions with leaves and bunches of juicy grapes.

Yegor went to his wife, embraced her and turned to his daughter-in-law. He looked me around to recognize me, but did not recognize me. In front of him there was a shapely slender woman dressed in a silk dress, freely fitting figure. The light colored tone of the fabric only emphasized the light tan, which I managed to gain for the week, and the bright red lips that do not need lipstick. Yes, I made an impression on him, because my dark, almost black eyes, in which it was impossible to distinguish between pupils, seemed to be piercing Yegor through, and a thick dark chestnut braid lay freely on a tall, lush breast. I was much taller than his wife was, so Yegor retreated a little to gaze me full-length from head to foot and he thought, "Calf muscles are fleshy, but other parts are good. Where I was that I did not considered her before. Look now, how it blossomed like a bud. Then she was such a unpresentable a soldier woman, but now she walks like a peafowl, as if she's swimming. I'll be checking her whether she make love on the side. Certainly, she is not a pair for Tolly. Although he has a nice face, but he is not strong enough for such a woman, not like me. Well, let's see."

He kissed everyone, especially he hugged me, but when I had been felt his tobacco fumes, my back tensed and I recoiled from him.

"You, my daughter, forgive me the old," he said, "that I am smoked so much. Because of my work, I had never have time to smoke thus I never release a cigarette from my mouth. Moreover, we have such a tobacco, the spirit from him goes to the whole district."

"Hey, old man, you were never apologizing to me, although I tolerate your smoke all the time," my mother-in-law Anna was offended, jealously glancing at her stately daughter-in-law.

"Drop it! You are accustomed to me, Annika, it is not the news for you, and you will suffer me further," Yegor snapped carelessly. "Well, let's go, we'll eat what God sent."

Then again, there was a rest at the sea and household cares of the house, during which I was noticing on myself the gaze of the father-in-law. I am remembering how he did wrong to me before the wedding, called me with dirty names, considered me unworthy of my husband, but now he's looking like a wolf, which hunting on big game. Well, nothing was happened, I will have to endure till Monday when he will go again to the mountains and I cannot be afraid to walk around the house.

Next day, Yegor as usual went to the bazaar to create a stock for a week. I also needed to go to the bazar and I had to go together with the father-in-law. On the way, I was surprised that everybody welcomed Yegor. Every old man or young man and even the children, shouted from afar: "Mr. Yegor, salaam aleikum!" He politely, but with dignity was lifting the visor of his octagonal cap-of-stalin and answered everyone "Salam".

It was also on the bazar where all the traders knew him, everyone shouted, "Mr. Yegor, come to me, I have the best and freshest goods today, and I am not deceiving you!"

In response to this, he went around and paid attention to everyone, tried vegetables and fruits, inspected meat from all sides, in a word, behaved like a real habitué of the bazaar. In the bazaar through the crowd, children were scurrying and they carried water directly in buckets. They shouted "Soo, soo," which meant "water," and for only five cents poured water into a common mug.

Yegor was choosing food for me too. He pushed me in my side showing a fruit worth the attention, and he slightly embraced me at the waist that I gave a way to the porters, then we collided in the crowd by the hips, which made me shudder every time, and I was trying to move away. But there were a lot of people in the bazaar and I sometimes had to cuddle so closely to him that I could feel through his blouse the fat-free bones and iron muscles.

"Tolly's hands would be weaker," I had evaluated the father-in-law when he was carrying two bags of food in each hand on the way back. He walked easily, carrying his back straight, his shaved head rose high above the crowd on a long wrinkled neck. "Well, he is a real Cossack," I thought, and finally forgave him for my past grievances. The only thing that deteriorated him was the almost complete absence of teeth in his mouth. By a lucky chance, he had two teeth on each side, top and bottom, located directly above each other, so he could have something to bite or gnaw out. He lisped funny, but he spoke legibly and clearly.

"Well, why are you looking at those teeth," Yegor said with annoyance, noticing how I looked into his mouth, "they've been knocked out halfway with a buttstock and half I lost from scurvy last spring. The colony is not the dance floor, as our deputy commander for political affairs said.

Thus talking, we gradually got home. By that time we talked enough, I was fascinated by Yegor, and he no longer seemed to me that old rascal who wanted to divorce me with Tolly. For his part, Yegor had been still looking at me and realized that his frail and shortsighted son had a real woman. Moreover, he will not be able to give this diamond a real frame, and she will suffer with this son of a bitch! This woman is simple but reasonable, she has a character and education, she respects the elders, at last, she has two big tits, and how does this simpleton handle it? Here an iron horse is needed," Yegor thought, "to plow deeply and without a break."

He surreptitiously looked at my lush but firm breasts, which remained beautifully shaped even after I had fattened three children; he appreciated my broad but taut ass, which bulged under a thin dress. "Wow, yes, she's good," Yegor thought, admiring me, "she walks as if she writes and then crosses out. One time - there, one time - here, oh, my God, I really cannot keep myself, what can I do now? I will find a chance and she will be mine!" after half an hour we reached the house and was imbued with mutual sympathy, but I had my heart in the right place, and he as it turned out, had his mind in the gutter.

The next Sunday we went to the sea with the whole family. Yegor Jr. was sunbathing without panties and he became black, now he was not at all different from the local boys. He had already learned a few Azerbaijani words and he was amusingly inserted them into the conversation, although he did not speak confidently in Russian. On the contrary, Nelly a fat and shy baby girl, always sat alone, pouring a sand, molded out of it cakes and then destroyed them. She sat in silent until she was asked.

Mother-in-law Anna remained sitting in a dress, in which she came to the sea, only burying her bare feet in the sand or walking along the coastal strip and sometimes she wetted her feet in the rolling wave of the surf. Elder Yegor came to the beach in his everyday underwear.

"Well, what are you doing, Dad," I said in confusion, "you could said Tolly, he has some spare swimming trunks, he would gave you."

"I don't care," Yegor, countered turning up his panties so that they looked like swimming trunks, "I feel good. It's you, young, you are used to wearing modern clothes, and we - in the old-fashioned way, in everyday clothes."

Suddenly, he broke off not having finished. I took off my dress over my head and stayed in a black satin swimsuit. The brassiere caps completely closed the breasts, but the material was thin and through it protruded sticking up nipples. My panties were as deep as Yegor's, but panties was tightly wrapped around my ass, and a thick pubis appeared sharply ahead.

"Wow, she's completely naked, foolish woman," Yegor stammered, "what can I do, oh, I cannot keep it!" He lay down on his stomach and began to bury himself in the sand. His son Anatoly undressed to his underpants and took out melting, he put one foot in the armhole and fastened the second armhole to the other side of the thigh. Then he took off his panties and stayed in the narrow swimming trunks, in which his manhood could hardly fit.

"Shit! And he's there," Yegor has already turned blue due to shame, "What kind of rag is that on it? He pictured it here, as if he had full swimming shorts of goods, he is able to show himself, my son!" We bathed and sunbathed the whole day, our family dined here with supplies, which we took from the house. Tolly and I played also with the youth in volleyball; the kids practically did not get out of the water. The father-in-law seized the moment, when Tolly went with the volleyball players to drink a beer on the other end of the beach, and his wife Anna fell asleep under a beach umbrella, and he sat down beside me.

"You amaze me, Gina," he said in a soft voice, "such a voluptuous woman, big and strong, and asleep only with my Tolly. Do you ever have lovers?"

"Never, father, how can you say such a thing, are you fool enough to tell about this Tolly also, aren't you?" I was embarrassed by surprise, "I am an honest woman, and I do not need others."

"That what you have is enough for you, don't you?" said Yegor, who in his own way regarded embarrassment of a daughter-in-law, "is he strong in making love? Only it seems to me that Tolly is not enough for you. Look, you're such a luxuriant!"

Saying this, Yegor grabbed his daughter-in-law for the breast, once again marveling at the fact that his large palm barely covered only its top, it was such a voluminous.

"What are you doing, you bastard," catching my breath I hissed in face of my father-in-law, "You're old ruffian! Once Tolly will come, I'll tell him everything and also Mrs. Anna."

"Well, Annika knows without you that I'm a male dog," Yegor admitted, "but you do not have to disturb Tolly. He's weak, that's why my son is even closer to me and for him I'll tear off the head of any. Do not quarrel me with him. Let's agree. We'll make love, but you will tell my son nothing. You don't lose anything."

"You are really a male dog! Incredibly how you could offer the daughter-in-law such a thing!" I said and stood up trembling with anger and resentment, "you should be ashamed! Remember, it should never happen again, otherwise I'll tell Tolly!"

"All right, all right, calm down," Yegor replied in frustration, "I joked, I wanted to check you out. But if you change your mind, then let me know,

I'm here and always ready!"

Then he turned a somersault over a low coastal dune and dived into the oncoming wave. He came up to the surface far from the shore, but this did not already delight me. I froze in frustrated feelings, rightly believing that this old goat would poison the end of the vacation for me. I wanted to stay with the children after Anatoly left to work, but now it was already impossible.

It took some time and I got used to the northern life gradually. On weekdays on long winter evenings, when electricity was turned off at 10 p.m., the neighbors was gathered at someone's house by the light of a kerosene lamp. Wives conducted conversations, discussing in detail the scanty village news, exchanging recipes for dishes, patterns of dresses and embroidery designs, and their husbands sat until late playing the preference for half a penny per whist. For the holidays, the women with the children went all together to see how their husbands paraded under the battle banner, and then all together arranged cheerful banquet. Anatoly's vacations were always in the summer, because he was on his own in making a list of vacations, so our family every summer rested either in a sanatorium or in the Caspian beach.

Well-adjusted life even brought Tolly to state close to normal, he was no different from other drinkers at least in the service. Moreover, he knew his business and did it perfectly, so when he was promoted to the rank of major by the age of thirty-four, he was appointed to lieutenant-colonel position. He became the head of the personnel department of the aviation division. Thus, it would continue until his pension but anything good not lasts for long. Then leader of the Soviet Union Khrushchev had wanted to make the army reduction with one scratch of the fountain pen. In addition, those unfortunate "one million and two hundred", namely, how many soldiers and officers were planned to be dismissed, will have been left their service place in the summer of 1960 to nowhere.

In one of the spring days of that unhappy year, the head of the human resources department Anatoly Buchenko was, as usual, full of work. The dismissal of the officers passed to the final stage, it was necessary to urgently fill the files for those who retire or those who went without a pension, others could to be ensured by transfer to vacant posts in other aviation formations and to go on retraining and further service in the new missile forces.

Then a long-distance telephone call was made in Anatoly's office. He did not hurry to answer the phone, dissatisfied he is being distracted; just now, he was working on the personal file of his old friend, with whom he was in the final period of the war in Germany, and then they broke up and met again here in the North. The hot-tempered and dashing pilot Michael Krasnukhin needed a half a year before retirement, and Anatoly was ready to help a friend, considering long friendship and frequent joint drinking over many years.

In the Krasnukhin personal file there was a note that he had been on retraining to a new type of Mig-17 fighter in the settlement of Gryazi near Lipetsk for nine months. According to the existing provision on calculating the length of service, this deprived him of even those northern "one year for one and a half years" that were given to each officer, not to mention the "one year for two years" for the pilots of jet vehicles. Anatoly thought about how to remove this record or concoct some additional paper that would allow saving preferential years of service for his comrade for these unfortunate nine months.

However, the phone buzzer called him again. "They are too persistent today," Anatoly determine. From recent times, they called from the cadre department of the military district, urging him to hasten preparing the personal files, because of the near deadline for the report to higher commander about the destruction of the next combat unit. Therefore, he did not hurry to answer, knowing that this call would lead to just an unnecessary hassle. Although, on the other hand, someday this call could touch himself, because he did not intend to retire and asked his friend in the central apparatus of the Air Force to find him a place more decently.

However, they called now from another place and it concerned Anatoly himself. The representative of the main headquarters of the missile forces offered him to head the personnel department of the missile army, which was being formed somewhere beyond the Urals. The deadline was minimal; there was a lot of work to be done on the bare ground. It was needed to create all the necessary structures and work out all the documentation while simultaneously looking for personnel for vacant positions. Eventually, his position will correspond to the rank of general with all the useful and pleasant followed circumstances. The decision must be given for the day, and by eleven the next day they waited for an answer. This proposal was so unexpected that Anatoly was dumbfounded, he mumbled something like that, "Yes sir! I'll think about it," but the body trembled with the inexpressible sweetness of the pie offered to him and the tremendous responsibility, which will make him choke.

Tolly came home sober, he was silent, thoughtful, before dinner he often went out on the porch to smoke, and it was so intriguing that I could not stand it and asked, "Hey, Tolly, how are you, you got sick now, didn't you?" I began to speak from afar, "maybe I will pour you a hundred grams?"

Anatoly replied after a pause made for importance, although he wanted to drink immediately, "Come on, we'll eat and talk at one."

Till eating he overturning a couple of glasses of vodka then Tolly sensed determination and told me about the proposal, which was made to him. I was a real wife of an officer and immediately appreciated the grandeur of the future position of my husband. I already wanted to speak nearly that, "come on, you must agree, you still think, why?", but I stopped on time, rightly leaving him the right to decide.

I thought a little and decided to change the topic of the conversation for the time being, "did you decide anything with the length of service of Mick?" I touched on a painful topic, "will he be able to get a retirement pension?"

"Do not doubt it because I owe him my life. You remember how we had been catching fugitive convicts in the hills, and they almost killed my group and me too. Mick had come to us on the "Studebaker" with his men; if he did not have time to come then I would not be sitting with you now. He showed me then his leather raglan, there was about fifteen, no, seventeen bullet holes in the skirt of the raglan, how he survived I do not know."

After the pause he added, "Well, for him, I already thought of what needs to be done. I will compose the order by the Air Force headquarter that for six months he had preferential years "one year for two years", because the flight program for re-training had lasted six months, and for this time they flew for more than seventy hours. Here's the "one year for two years", which give us missed half a year and a pension to Mick."

"You can write an order for the Air Force, but who will sign it to you?" I said with doubt. I interested in the details of the case, because I was friends with Maria, Krasnukhin wife. "Although, the signature can be any, but how will you act with the seal?"

"It's Mick's business. He said that he had the right petit man near the chief of the Air Force headquarter, which would seal. Difficulties arose to me with Abdulla," Tolly continued, sharing with me the complexities of his work. He passed the whole war and after the war he, the asshole, quit the army and went to the civil life. Some months later, when he realized that there was low wages for him in a civil life, he entered the military school, where he, a front-line soldier, was taken even though he was already more than twenty-three years old. I see now that without the year, when he walked on a civil life, he does not get twenty-five years length of military service. We'll have to do something to get rid of these records about the fact that he quit and came to the army again. I'll write to him that he was taken to the military school directly from the unit, then he will have a pension.

"Well, you'll do it!" I endorsed his actions with admiring, realizing that now my support is needed for my husband, "look, it is dangerous, someone could catch you on forgery."

"Well, don't worry! Who is looking at these details now?" Anatoly waved his hand, as if erasing doubts, "I have all three copies of personal files. Everywhere there will be identical records, I'll do everything with the utmost discretion. Gina, that's what I wanted to talk about," he returned to the most urgent topic, which concerned himself personally. I froze, anticipating the outcome, which would be very unprofitable for me.

"Well, I do not want to go to these missiles, for the life of me!" he continued, making a convincing expression on his face, "I'm a major now, I'll be chained to the oar for the fifteen years until I would become a general, during this time anything can happen. Imagine, what happened if I cannot cope right now? They called me for new occupation, but it's hard for me to do business now and here. There, beyond Ural mountains, they do not have now anything at all," he told and made round eyes, as if he horrified by this desert, in which he is to lay a blossoming garden, "nothing, you know!" I will need to do all this from scratch; here it is not long to break the neck. You remember, beyond the Urals there is no land for us, as one well-known political leader said! No I'm not going! I tell you a secret thing that a trustworthy comrade has promised me that we will be invited to the group of Soviet occupation troops in Germany. I'll have a captain's post in the regiment, it is a decrease for my military rank, but after three or four years I'll go to a new position in the aviation corps headquarter and I will have a rank of the lieutenant-colonel."

I froze in confusion. At first I wanted to persuade Tolly to go to the missile troops, but this impulse was overcame by the prospect of going to Germany, where, according to rumors, people are so well provided that they accumulate enough money and things for the rest days of life. Weighed in the mind the vague general future of my husband somewhere beyond the Urals and the real welfare here in the center of Europe, in a country that we defeated a short time ago, I came to the conclusion that with husband's drunkenness and his indecisiveness in military service, it is better to agree to a transfer to Germany, since he is so confident in his comrade.

I went to Moscow as before, with two children who had grown up, until Anatoly will get an apartment at a new duty station in the regiment of communication in a small German village somewhere near Berlin. This time I had to live in my aunt's apartment, because it's been two years since my mother left the world, and our room was taken by the state, and it did not come in handy with my family. I greatly had regretted when it happened, and I had been cursing Tolly, who did not agree to live alone while I looked after my mother till her death. If the room would be left for us then it would be possible not to go to Germany, but to claim a place of service in the capital as having housing there, or just live anytime in own habitation, and not disturb the rich relatives who had never loved my mother and me also.

In Moscow while the children were frolicking in the courtyard of the

"Stalinist" post-war house on Mira Avenue, I cooked dinner and dreamed about how first tapestries, then carpets, will appear in Germany, then we will buy porcelain, for example, the service "Madonna" or "Hunters", undoubtedly crystal and Czech glass, a bunch of all fashionable clothes, and then, closer to departure, we will need to buy furniture, a bedroom set, necessarily, a sideboard, a hall furniture and a soft corner. In our future apartment, which we will get in the Union with no doubt, when we transfer from Germany, it will be very nice and cozy. The end of my life seemed to me well fed and provided, but in my desires, as usual, I did not take into account one well-known and very negative factor.

Georgiy Ulchenko

Chapter 4. The old love returns

Upon my arrival in Germany, it immediately became clear to me what I missed in my thoughts on the best share. Anatoly, who met us at the railway station in Wünsdorf, was quite rumpled, as if he had drunk vodka for several days. Moreover, at home in a two-room section of a Finnish house, where he brought in a few beds from the military goods yard, bedside tables, cupboards, chairs and tables, there was many empty bottles of local vodka called "Korn" and cheap beer in dust and debris. I wanted to buy something for home in a garrison store, but Anatoly after a pause said that there were only a hundred German marks left, it was a residue of money, by which we had to live three next days to the payday.

It was a dastardly blow. I lived in Moscow for four months with children and I did not make unnecessary expenses because we were with little money when we left the North. Moreover, at this time, he could save money, which should not have been spent on home, on food, or on clothes, but he drank and spent it all to the last penny.

"What are you doing, you insatiable," I hissed at my husband, muffling my voice so that the neighbors would not hear behind the plywood walls. "I did not come here with you, so that you could prepare everything for our arrival and accumulate some money, because children need to dress for school, winter is coming soon, but what you had done?"

I was beside myself with rage and grabbed the broom that came under my arm; I began to groom my husband, shouting curses at him. It was not painful, but Tolly was frightened by my fury and the pressure with which I chastised him. Earlier I was more patient, and skirmishes over money, which he drunk, arose time after time, but I somehow restrained myself. Now, when it was clear that my dreams of satiety and material well-being in Germany ended, I became enraged in earnest.

"Eugenia, well, okay, wait," Tolly grabbed and tore the broom from my hands, "you know it happened so. A neighbor, who lives up two houses away, a front-line soldier like me, the deputy chief of staff of the regiment Major Barabash, he is also without a family, well, we have drunk with him a little, do not be angry, I'll get an exchange tomorrow, we'll have money."

The "exchange" was a part of the salary in Soviet rubles, which could be exchanged for marks and use up here in Germany. The rest of the ruble salary was accumulated in the account in the Soviet Union and it was possible to receive only after arriving at home. Thus, the government artificially reduced the purchasing power of Soviet people who was sent to serve in the Group of Soviet Forces in Germany, so that they could not take all the available luxury goods from here to their native places.

I cried with anger because everything from the very beginning goes not as I had dreamed, but I took myself in hand and said, "Money, when you get it, you'll bring to me all, for a penny. Now without my permission, you cannot buy even a single bottle. Did you understand what I said?"

"Yes, that's all, I understand, I'll give it all to you," Tolly answered with relief because he was glad of the end of the scandal. "Everything will be fine, well; I'll run to the service. And about the store - it is located near the checkpoint, on the left from enter there are food, on the right are household goods, and on the reverse side are manufactured goods."

Anatoly ran to the service, and while cleaning the apartment I thought about why I permitted my mother to persuade myself to continue this endless nightmare. He did not change, no way, scoundrel! There is no deterrent for him, but I also lost control. Now I needed to follow his every step so that money would be in my pocket, and I'll be giving him the booze strictly according to my plan, and maybe I'll be buying it myself in order to know how much does it cost.

While the apartment was cleaned, dinner was cooked, and the children returned from the street, telling what interesting things they had seen in the new place, I had a detailed plan, how I would hold the husband in my hands. God forbid he'll try to hide from me at least a pfennig, I know what I'll do him. I was strong enough to beat his drunken face, and then he would have explained his chief where he got bruises.

With this plan, our joint life began in Germany. I struggled with the addiction of my husband as best I could, but he was drinking a substantial part of his salary, and we should buy food for money of an exchange, instead of postponing it to purchase goods. Somehow, I was able to buy tapestries while other housewives and wives were already dragging into the house such carpets as "Russian beauty", "Roses", "Deers", "Bears" and others. Money was sorely lacking, but Anatoly did not care. Often in the evenings, I had to run along the path leading to the official territory to pick him up, when he lay drunk on the side of the path, and take him home until the entire garrison saw him in this kind.

Then I took a new step. I found out who was Tolly's most frequent drinking companion, I came to everyone, talked with their wives and with them, persuaded them not to agree to drink with him, because they all drank at his expense, preferring to carry their money to the family. If the conversations did not help, I threatened that I would go to the political department to bring them to light, and, ultimately, the Tolly's circle of drinking companions significantly narrowed.

He came home sober, and he did not like it. His organism, accustomed to alcohol, demanded its portion of vodka, and the large intervals between the boozes made him angry and irritable, especially he stood ill when his children frolicked in the next room. He suddenly went into the kid's room to show children his disapproval and asked one single question, "What's the matter?" he asked the subdued children, frightening them with incomprehensibility and pointlessness of the question.

Especially younger Yegor was afraid of him because he even was not ten. He tried to understand what his father wanted him to do and did not understand. Yegor Jr. did not have any matters, he just frolicked with his sister and was happy with life, and then he was asked about an incomprehensible "matter" and was demanded to explain what it means. Because of it, he began to shake from fear and cry, squealing like a battered puppy.

His kind of form was even more irritating to his father, and he asked his son, "Well, what's the matter?" again and again he asked the same question, obviously, referring to a change in the mood of children in connection with his questions, but he could not explain the essence of his question to himself or others. The brain, already decently treated with a pesticide called "vodka," could not properly analyze what was happening, and could not form more or less connected thoughts that were appropriate to the moment.

Anatoly felt himself normal only in the office, where everything was familiar to the last comma, and there was no need to strain the extinct brain to make a commander's decree or to check if the travel precept was filled correctly. He used for communicating with his colleagues and commander some phrases from the military regulations, "Yes, sir!", "No, sir!", "I am!" and a few obscene words. His tongue was untied when he took the first two hundred grams to drink. Then he could speculate about women, although his sexual appetite to them was drastically reduced due to drunkenness, and about official affairs, especially he liked to talk about bosses, which, he believed, could not live without his help. For one he compiled the necessary document, he taught the other how to walk the combat step correctly, for third he helped with the transfer to a good place, and the fourth man simply cannot organize a guard service without Anatoly. Listening to him, everybody would understand that only he has real weight in the regiment, and all others are lazy, stupid and craven.

In truth, no one believed in his drunken delirium, otherwise, someone had already informed about his talking and the authorities would have found the levers of influence and the opportunity to eat a drunken major with giblets. He had regular drinking partners, they were verified, not accidental persons, and they will not tell about him anything superfluous. Nevertheless, I heard rumors that my hubby sometimes told too much or criticized the superiors, but in Germany, it was very simple, if they will find out, then you will fly out from here into the Soviet Union in twenty-four hours. Such a result was not in my plans. Just now, I began to save money for decent things, we just started to buy carpets and crystal, and all this could collapse from one crooked word of my Tolly.

Now I started hammering into Tolly's head every day and every hour the thought that he should be silent in a drunken state, that he may not talk anything superfluous because it threatens consequences not only to him, but also to the whole family. If Anatoly wants me, Eugenia Nicole Buchenko, to live with him even further, he must forget about talking in his drunk form, keep quiet or talk only about wenches. The work I have done to develop a conditioned reflex has borne fruit because Tolly had fallen silent. He was always laconic, but now, if he was drunk, he either had been responding only to direct questions addressed to him, or commanded: "Pour!", when there was a delay and his glass was empty.

Overall, he became a bad drinking companion. Our people are so brought up that when they have drunk they want to talk. On the contrary, when there is nothing to talk with him, why do you need to drink with him? It is clear that his former drinking companions turned aside Tolly, inviting him only to common feast, when there was a lot of different people. It was my turn to be surprised because my hubby one day is sober, two days, then a week or two; it became strange for me, but in my heart grew a quiet joy when Tolly stopped drinking. Because of it, I lost control and was punished by the psychological trauma when he got drunk again.

One day he came from the office sober and morose as always, I let him eat and went to visit our neighbor to discuss everyday affairs. When I returned an hour later, my hubby was still sitting at the table, but he was completely drunk. He sat and guiltily smiled and was silent, as usual, but on the table amid barely touched food there was a big bottle of vodka, which had been containing already less than half the liquid.

"What the heck," I waved my hands, "you already like drinking alone, a fucking alcoholic! Why you do not eat, a scabby dog? You're completely drunk, how did you do this, Tolly? Now eat it, come on!" I was not merely frightened by this spectacle, but also outraged to the limit. It turns out that I cannot be left him alone, even for a minute, because he will immediately get drunk. This new grade of my husband puzzled me. In spite of my struggle against his booze, he will still come up with something that I cannot foresee. I sat opposite the husband and began to examine it, as if I had first seen it. At that time he, smiling drunkenly, poked a fork into the potato and could not hit the mark. It amused him more and more, and he began to laugh wildly like a mad, poking fork already in the air towards the potatoes as if showing his wife what a potato is naughty.

I hardly recovered from this case. "You, mother-fucker, why did you giggle?" I turned to him and told, "There's nothing to do, right? You're drunk like a dirty dog and you're laughing at me, you bastard. Well, I'll show you, you'll get it from me."

Now it was Tolly's turn to be surprised. "Why are you shouting at all," he asked, hardly moving his tongue, "I was not somewhere with my friends, I had drunk at home, now I sit and say nothing to you, I do not touch anyone. What's wrong with that?"

"At home it's better," he added after a pause, "I do not need to pour anybody and do not need to give a drink to anyone. Great savings!"

This conclusion struck me even more. Notice, in order to muddy his brain by vodka, he acquired a strange prudence. Although, on the other hand, he is right, if he cannot be without vodka, then let it be at home without freeloaders, without witnesses, if he will have got drunk here, then he has the bed next to him, he don't need to go far. I once again took an investigating look at my husband, but did not find anything new or interesting in him; he was the same drunkard, only he became some kind of innovator. Well, God is his judge!

I left my husband sitting at the table and went out into the yard to pick up a few radishes and onions for the children for dinner on a small garden bed, that I had digged up in the spring. I stood by the willow, which in the twilight overhanging bent branches over the water surface of the canal flowing into the nearest lake, I watched as the ends of the twigs plunged into the water and the wind led them to draw the water surface with intricate patterns.

This kind of picture calmed down my soul, instilled confidence that nothing terrible, in general, did not happen. My husband drank before he will drink further. This fact does not depend on me. Now it will only be easier to manage the process, it is not necessary to run anywhere and to look for him drunk in cuvettes, nobody will beat his face when he is drunk, moreover, there is no need to share vodka with anyone, and this substantially reduces costs. Well then, my husband will be under supervision, and I'll accumulate more money, it will be possible to buy more things before the time comes to be transferred to the Union.

I sighed with relief and looked around, was there anyone nearby who could see me in a moment of confusion. There was no one nearby, the willow still dipped its branches into the dark water of the canal, the place was quiet and calm, everything seemed to tell me, that now everything is in my hands, his tempestuous and wide drunken frenzy has ended. There came the era of "controlled madness". I could not get my husband out of vodka for almost twenty years of living together, so let this harmful habit go into the framework, the limits of which I will determine myself. This is a delicate work, an uneasy and previously uncertain psychological burden for me, but the most important thing is a heavy responsibility, when I keep in my hands not only the behavior of my loved one, but his health and life.

"I will cope," I thought with hope, "I will do everything so that we live happily ever after, I will not let anyone prevent me. Tolly will walk on the line for the rest of his life, and will not go anywhere. Tolly can drink without limits, no matter, because he cannot drink more than one bottle right off, but our money will be safe and everything will be fine."

Certainly, the need for money was growing constantly. The daughter Helen finished eight years school, but there were no high schools in the group of troops. To some great boss the idea hit the head to close the graduation classes in schools, and it was forbidden to keep beside parents the seventeen and eighteen years old children. According to the authorities, when they had graduated the school, they continue to live with parents, get a job, and then get married, in a word, they multiply the civilian population of military garrisons, but this generates a housing problem and the problem of employment. Moreover, someone would like to become related to the locals, especially girls want to marry the Germans, but the authorities did not trust them, although they were socialists, but all the same, for Russians they remained Germans, "Fritzes", fascists who were not killed yet. In addition, our soldiers had a great temptation to see how the ex-babies are blossomed into pretty girls, and it is already close to sin.

Therefore, the unfortunate graduates of the eighth class went to their relatives in the Soviet Union, if they are lucky, and the rest went to several boarding schools for children, whose parents continue their service abroad.

"Really, like poor orphans," I was indignant, but whether you want it or not, Nelly had to be sent to Saratov, where there was one such boarding school. For the maintenance in the boarding school the payment of 50 rubles monthly was established, it was the decent money at those times, when the majority of the people had a salary of 70 rubles.

Moreover, we could send her a parcel of twenty rubles cost once a month and not more often, because more frequent shipment had not allowed by the rules, set for employees abroad. Besides, our family lost her ration, which was given to every child up to fourteen years old, and this ration had such products that were much more expensive in the local store than in the Union. It is the extra expenses, but I had to manage a household to keep within the salary and still to save money for the future, and I did what I can do.

One day in winter, when we were still serving in the garrison near Berlin, the phone rang in the room. A voice from somewhere from afar ordered me, "Apartment Buchenko? Now you will speak with the army headquarters."

After that, Vladimir Smirnov's familiar voice sounded in the receiver, "Eugenia Nicole, do you understand with whom you are speaking?" - He minted, clicking on the word "understand."

A hot wave running through my body caused a shiver of my knees and

Georgiy Ulchenko

made my head dizzy. He found me here, this desperate devil! But how are we going to talk, when every telephone operator on the line listen to the conversation and be sure to spread the news all over the garrison, if she hear anything worthy of hearing.

"Yes, I understand," I answered Vladimir, and I really enjoyed this conversation. Probably, he came to Germany and wanted to meet me.

"Here is a parcel, which transported from the Union, please, meet a person in an hour at the station from the Berlin side of the platform. Do you know this place?"

"Yes, I know," I said disappointedly, thinking that I had made a mistake. On this spot officers were often met, who moved from one garrison to another and at the same time delivered the parcels. This "mail" worked properly, only it was necessary to walk through the half town to the railway station.

"Be ready to be absent from home until the evening," Vladimir said meaningfully. "Do you understand?"

Of course, everything was clear to me. He's came to me. From Wünsdorf, where the army headquarters was located, it was about a half hour drive to our village, so we will soon meet. I quickly gathered, wrote a note to my husband that I went to Berlin for shopping and will be late at night, grabbed my purse and left the house.

The Finnish house we lived was on the edge of the garrison. Behind the house along the canal passed barbed wire, it was connected at right angle with a netting fence, which separated the garrison from the road. Across from our house at the very edge of the fence, the cunning people cut a hole in the grid, and everyone used it as a gate, not to bypass from half a kilometer to the checkpoint. The local commandant's office regularly tightened the hole with a wire to prevent the violation of the access regime, but people were far from the concerns of the commandant's office, so the wire could not stand on the fence for more than one day. Through the hole women went to the store, schoolchildren fled to the neighboring garrison where school was, in the morning they went there and after lunch they returned, on weekends officers went to visit the neighboring gaststätte, the local beerhouse, they came out in the daytime and crawled back in the night.

I climbed hardly through the hole because the wire was clinging of my coat. I'm a big woman, therefore the size of the hole is too tight for me. I unhooked my coat, crossed the bridge over the canal and went along the street, which fully justified its name, Birch Alley. On both sides of the alley grew tall old birches, which were no less than fifty years old. Here and there, the broad stumps of cut trees protruded out of the earth, they died of old age or perished during the war. No one planted new trees, and it always surprised me, but the Germans were neat and pedantic, they cared for their town like for their yards, but they did not hurry to update trees for some reason.

Now I did not see anything wrong with this. I slowly walked along the street, admiring the birches covered with fluffy white frost, even snow cover on stumps caused only positive emotions.

I reached the center of the village and turned the corner to an alley that ran from the shore of the lake to the railway. The people were few, the gloomy winter day with a dank wind dispersed everyone to their homes, and that's good for me. On the road, I did not meet any of the garrison women, and when I turned left to the station and went along Goethe's alley, I tried to walk on the right side behind the bushes, that nobody could see me. Fortunately, because of this weather no one dared to leave the garrison, so I came to the station square and boldly went to the north side of the platform.

At the end of the square, I noticed a commander's jeep, of which a tall military man get out and went to my side. I stopped, looked around, but no one was here, and I hurried to meet him. It really was Volodya, stately and attractive as before, especially in the greatcoat, which sat on it tightly without a single wrinkle. I stopped at a step from Vladimir and silently looked into his eyes; he just nodded without a word to show that I should join him over the corner.

After I turned to the next street, I heard the rumbling of the car from behind and quickly ran to the car. Only I began to sit in the back seat, as strong hands dragged me into the car, and Volodya put me next to him, hugged me and began to kiss. I tried to free myself, by mimicry showing that the driver saw everything, but he only waved his hand, showing that the driver did not count, and we merged into a kiss. My legs weakened, it suddenly became hot, and I hung my hands around Vladimir's neck.

"How long have you been gone," I whispered to him between kisses, "I missed you."

"I knew about this and tried to come," answered Volodya breathing heavily and shouted to the chauffeur, "go to the alley along which we arrived, and turn not to the right but to the left, and drive to the end, there I will say."

We continued to kiss, breathing of the native smell of each other, and we were getting more and more excited. Five minutes later the car slowed down at the end of the alley, and the driver, a young soldier, who was uncomfortable by such a scene in the car, cautiously asked, "Comrade General, where will we go next?"

"Come to that two-story building with a canopy, look there."

"Yes, sir," the chauffeur answered, and we drove up to the resort hotel, which worked regardless of the season all year round. There was sunbathing, swimming, boating and yachting in the summer and in the winter the main occupation was the ice yachting. The lake was more than a mile long, and ice on it was smooth, so the snow was blown from it into the coastal thickets of reed, and it was pleasant and safe to drive by the ice yacht on the lake surface. The main thing here was a casino, which worked at full load regardless of the season, so the Berlin playboys had been visiting this hot spot with an enviable regularity.

Vladimir threw off his greatcoat, took off his fur cap and took out the pilot's leather raglan without the epaulettes from the seat, in which he flew still during the war.

"We need to disguise ourselves a bit that the Germans do not worry that they are dealing with the Russian general," Vladimir joked, "otherwise they first go to the Stasi to report about us."

Vladimir told the driver that he drove the car behind the house and waited for him, and left him twenty marks to dine in a gaststätte and to buy himself tobacco. We got out of the car and went to the hotel. I looked around. I have never been here, although this place was a stone's throw away from the garrison. When my husband and I rode a boat on the lake, the inscription "Casino" on the roof of the building was visible from afar, but I could not think that I would ever visit here. Snow on the site around the hotel was cleaned up to the very edge of the water. Boats and yachts were not on the pier, but on the mirror ice, which was blackening right up to the horizon, stood abreast several ice yacht, the rear ice-skate of which was chained to the yellow metal frame.

The receptionist came out from behind the counter to meet this strange couple, a tall slender man with a military deportment, in raglan and chrome boots, and a woman dressed simply as if she had jumped out of the house to a nearby store, but she had an attractive kind of beauty. Vladimir in good German with a small accent ordered him room until the evening, to bring wine and fruit in the room and not to disturb. Paying for the order and receiving the keys, we went to the second floor to our room, and the porter stayed to give instructions to the staff.

"Gina, will we wait until we bring the wine?" Vladimir asked cautiously, knowing how much his beloved does not like to hurry up in love affairs, but I pulled him to me by the tail of the unbuttoned raglan, and he lost his balance by surprise. We fell to the bed with a loud scream, and immediately began to kiss each other, touch each other, remembering favorite body, gradually throwing off our excess clothes. Finally, we stayed au naturel, and looked like a sandwich that lay by butter down, the swarthy and hairy Vladimir was on top, and I was downstairs white as fresh butter.

Vladimir lightly pushed apart my knees kissing me, and we merged in a love dance. My sexual intercourse with my husband was infrequent because of his constant drunkenness, so I quickly got into a state of ecstasy, the movements became strong and sharp. Volodya sensed this and realized that the completion is close. With shouts and groans, we made several more movements and fell off, falling off each from other.

I lay on Vladimir's arm, putting my foot on his stomach, and laughed softly. Volodya tried to raise his head to look at my face, why is she laughing. However, I gently was pushing him with my hand in the forehead that not to spy, and I continued to laugh.

"Well, Gina, what are you laughing at," Volodya said, "is something wrong?"

"Everything all right, Volodya," I answered with a happy laugh, "it's just a nervous reaction to intercourse, everything was too sharp, you almost broke my spine off. There still something is beating inside, here, put your hand here." I took his hand and laid it on my stomach. Volodya felt something twitch at hand, as if it was trying to penetrate outside.

"It's my womb, look, it's knocking, she's still wanting you, waiting for you to push her again." I turned sharply, pulled him to me, and we again merged into embraces. However, we were not allowed to continue. At the door knocked the waiter, who brought the ordered products.

I stopped Vladimir, put the dress on my naked body, turned on the light, and went to the door. The waiter rolled a table into the room, on which were bottles of champagne and cognac, grapes, oranges and a box of chocolates lay. Closing the door behind the waiter, I took out two glasses from the sideboard, threw a towel over my arm like a waiter, and, bent in the waist, said, "Eat here, sir."

Vladimir liked this invitation; he laughed, jumped up and flew round the room with me. Then he put me in a chair, poured champagne into our glasses, turned on the player and put on it a large vinyl record, then a slow foxtrot swam around the room. Volodya stood up in front of me and invited me to dance, bowing politely. With glasses of champagne in our hands, sipping a sparkling wine, we stomped in the middle of the room, snuggle each other so tightly that through the dress I could feel his heart beating, his strong fingers walking up and down my back, and his unquenchable desire had risen in front of me, picking up the hem of the dress. Taking the grape along the way and put the wineglasses, we again rushed into the bed and did not let go of each other until complete devastation.

"Well, Gina, you are adorable already," Volodya commented contentedly, stroking my stomach, "you were probably studied with Tolly."

"Do not say anything about him now," I said with a skeptical chuckle, "I could not learn anything with him. He drank all his skill, but with you I want to perform such miracles as I can."

After drinking a little and eating fruit and chocolate, the lovers again began their own games, only this time we came up with such poses that fit us and could withstand our strong bodies. Insensibly, the darkness closed the sky outside the window, and lamps were lit in front of the building's facade. The plate with the foxtrots, under which we were doing our somersaults, was scrolled countless times, but we were not tired.

Finally, I decided that it was already late, and it's time to part. I wanted to get up and go to get dressed, but Vladimir stopped me and said, "Gina, excuse me, with this love games I forgot why I came."

"Are you going to marry me again?" I asked, taking his hand away and getting out of bed, "and you do not tire?"

"Well, what can annoy you?" Volodya was surprised. "Well, I use every opportunity to see you. Now I'm in the commission to check your air corps, I asked the marshal for a day for our meeting. He is a man, he did not say too much, just asked, "A woman?" Well, I said "yes". Tomorrow I should be there."

"You will be there tomorrow, but now it's time for me," I said, collecting things scattered around the room, "I already told you that my fate is connected with Anatoly, we have two children, and I could not even save your son!"

My voice faltered and I brushed off a tear that suddenly ran up. I got a grip and quipped, "And now, Volodya, did you kicked out his wife again? How far is she down your list?"

"I do not kick out them, but they leave me on his own initiative," Vladimir explained sadly and also starting to dress, "they feel, probably, that I do not love them, I think always about you. However, I did not offend them, it's alright. Now what can I do for you? Maybe I transfer Tolly somewhere closer to me. My army service now is in the Moscow region, I am the head of the Center and I can take him to my place."

"And in what capacity will you take him?" I asked skeptically, "he will be the husband of your mistress? He is not able to do anything he is simple office clerk. You do not need him to work, but I do not want to arrange a martial love in front of all your colleagues. Here we met in the middle of the Earth, you owe me nothing and I do not owe too. Now we will be running away, but we would remember this day as a sweet dream, would not we?"

"Yes, it's good for you to talk, you have family, you have everything just like people," Volodya began to scuffle, "but I'm not lucky. When I had met a woman, I thought that we will be all right, but further she turns into a virago, arranges for me an unbearable life, and leaves me. I'm sick of such a life."

"Do not whine, man, you can find a woman for the night," I reasoned, "any woman go with you!"

"She will go, but not far. I have no one like you, therefore life and does not form."

"It's not my own fault," I snapped, wrapping the fruit in the newspaper to take them with me, "it was not necessary to disappear when I was bad. Where were you when I wanted to leave Tolly in nineteen fifty-first year?"

"I fought in Korea, I was not here for two years," Vladimir justified himself.

"Where were you when I came here? We lived in Moscow for four months, I already thought that I would not go to him, but you were not there again!"

Vladimir lowered his head as if regretting the missed opportunities, but objected to my allegations again.

"At that time I was sent to Cuba as the first adviser from the Soviet Union, when Fidel still did not think to be friends with us. I managed to persuade him to accept our help, after that Khrushchev started delivering to the island strategic missiles and Il-28 bombers."

"Hey, I know your work," I said and waved, pulling on stockings and buttoning them on my waistband. "Your colleagues even raised officer's families here, in our garrison when the Caribbean crisis happened, we thought they would evacuate us, but it had not done. Generally, we cannot meet when we need each other, we meet only to make love for a short time, and then we go to the different directions. Do not be offended, Volodya, this is our destiny, we must endure and live on."

With these words, I picked up my coat and came to him. He helped me to put on my coat and, taking the bag, led me to the exit. We went down the stairs in silence, just as silently went out into the street and stood outside in the yard under the flakes of snow, which had just started to fall and covered a ground a little. The ice on the lake in the light of the lanterns seemed blacker, only the drizzle left on him the traces, constantly creeping from place to place like the big snakes.

"You can take a car, Volodya," I said, turning to him, "I'll get home myself, here I'll turn to the right and walk to the end of the street where my house is right by the road. But you go forwards, take care of yourself because the ground is slippery."

Because of my care or because he understood that he will not see me again, Volodya darkened his face and told. "Thanks for everything, Gina, I'll never forget you," but I stopped him.

"Stop it, please, otherwise I will pay. Drive your car and do not worry about anything. Remember, I love you and I will always be happy to see you. Unlike you, I'm not going to change my life and especially your life. I cannot do it because I do not know what end will wait us ahead. Better let it go as it is."

I pecked him on the cheek, ran a hand over the bristle on his cheek and went away. Vladimir covered by his hand a spot on the cheek, to which my hand touched, and stood there looking at me, until I disappeared behind the turn. Then he went to the car and drove his way.

At that time, I stood beyond a bend to the Birch Alley and cried. I was angry with myself for indecision, for fear of change, and for him that he not insisting, he did not make me obey to go after him. My heart was bursting with longing about my beloved, but even more I yearned because of I would have to return to my house, where I was dragging the hateful life full of fails.

His car swept past the night street with a roar, and my soul dropped down frozen by the winter cold, without desires, which flew following my beloved. I did not care, but the vexation for the wrong fate pressed on my breast by the heavy sediment. Thus, I wandered, raking the freshly fallen snow, and thought about nothing until I was near the hole in the fence.

At home, I was joyfully greeted by children who did not notice anything in me that would have distinguished me from the everyday state, and vying to inform me about school news, asking me to tell where I had been and what I brought.

"Where's the father?" I asked my daughter, who was older and calmer than the younger son was. However, a thirteen-year-old schoolgirl-daughter, who already understood a lot in her life, fell silent, pursing her lips and looking away.

"Well, why are you silent, he is drunk lying somewhere around or what else?" I began to ask my daughter.

"No, he came in the afternoon when we just arrived from school, he collected things and strongly scolded that you were not here. Even with the obscene words."

"He went away on business trip, but he scolded with bad words, because he could not find his underpants," continued my daughter. "I do not know where he went; he told me that on order of the regiment commander. Some kind of commission verifies them, they need these things, as he said, the presents," she recalled a new word of her lexicon.

I had fed the children and was going to sleep, rejoicing that my husband was not home. Let him swear, he never knows what and where lies, and I'm like his servant, to give, to bring, to feed. He could not even step without me. Until he was not here, I'll try to recover my senses after a stormy day and calm down. The bottom of my stomach was empty, even cold, but inner thighs was on fire, rubbed by Vladimir for several hours of intercourse. My mood has increased; the life did not seem such unsuccessful as an hour ago. The main thing is that my children love me, I need them, and I can manage my husband.

In the morning, I was awakened by a phone bell. I turned on the light and looked at the alarm clock. It was only half past five in the morning, who needed my Tolly at such a early morning? Do not they know that he is not at home? I reluctantly lifted the receiver of the ringing phone, only to not wake the children, and I heard an unfamiliar voice. The duty officer called to me. He said that my husband, who yesterday went on a business trip, had an accident near Potsdam. He is alive, but he was taken to a hospital in Beelitz. His wife can visit him on Saturday and Sunday from ten to five, thereto goes a suburban train from Berlin.

I lost sleep with the first words of the duty officer. Today is Thursday, till Saturday is still far, I'll go today, they cannot refuse me go to my own husband. I got up, went to the kitchen and checked there, what I could take to my husband, and then I began to cook. Until seven o'clock in the morning, I had prepared everything for my trip and got the children ready for school then fed them and went with them to the school bus. I wanted to go with them to the railway station, and to take the train to Beelitz, but on the way we were met by the Lt. Col. Ostapenko, the son of whom was learning in the same class with my son.

Ostapenko was a deputy commander of regiment for political affairs; he let the children go to the bus, and stayed to talk to me. He went to see me especially to tell me about my husband's condition. He told me that I did not need to go to his hospital because Anatoly had surgery on his skull and he had not yet recovered. Visitors are not allowed to enter to his ward in hospital; my food will not be taken to him, and then what should I do there? "We must wait until he can be visited," the political deputy told me, "I will keep you informed of the matter."

"I want to know how did this happen?" through the tears I asked him, "what did he do, is it his fault that led to accident?"

"No, it's not his fault," the political deputy reassured me. "It was happened when at twilight a local German on a cart went out from the secondary road to the main one and he did not give them to go. The jeep was driven by a young soldier, he began to dodge to the left, sharply turned the steering wheel, and the car glided on wet snow, rolled out of the road and hit the tree. Anatoly was badly hurt by his head, and his face was cut with glass fragments. Eyes, it's known, remained intact."

I returned home in frustration. The fate avenges even for such short moments of happiness that I allow myself with Volodya. I thought that it wants to punish me, destroying the family and taking my husband away. In addition, I thought that with Volodya nothing would happen, because Tolly had suffered instead. In fact, what was the Volodya's fault? Everything was because of me. While I had made love in bed with my lover, my husband was lying near the road in a broken car and was bleeding.

Having imagined this picture, I shivered like from chill. After all, I loved my Tolly, even though we lived almost twenty years, now the love was a calm even love-habit, for which there is no need for loud words and great feelings. You just need to know that your loved one is nearby, at any time, you can find him in your bed at arm's length, and you live together taking care of each other. Now he could die, and I could nothing do to help him.

Yes, of course, I invited disaster for him while thinking about him badly and spending time in the arms of another. My experiences and troubles have receded into the background. The main thing was for the husband to survive. I did not think about that Vladimir offered to marry him, it could not be done for such a price, but I thought that if I were home at that hour, I would get ready Tolly for the road, and he would take a trip calm, and on the way, nothing happened to him. Only I alone was to blame! Tears flowed by themselves. I cried sobbingly, leafing through pages of my grievances and losses, wounds of the passed youth, missed opportunities and my awkward life, but suddenly I stopped.

"If something happens to the children on a slippery road," I thought with concern for their safety, "my heart probably will burst in half while I wait for them from school."

At that time, someone was romping in the doorway, and my children entered the room. The bus with the children was not let out of the garrison by weather conditions, so everybody were let go to their homes after a short wait.

"Mommy, we had not went to school today," the son shouted joyfully from the threshold, "now I'm going to walk outside, we'll make a snowman and play snowballs with the guys!"

"Mom, why are you crying," the more attentive Nelly asked, "something happened?"

"Yes, kids, your dad got yesterday into an accident on the road, his car was crashed," I explained, "now he is in the hospital, nobody is allowed to enter to his room, as soon as possible, I will go to the hospital."

"And I, and I!" Yegor shouted, rejoicing that because of his father's accident it would be possible to go somewhere far, beyond the limits of this small town he had known backwards and forwards.

"What do you rejoice, you fool," sister interrupted him, "the father is sick, he is in the hospital, but it is the joy to him! Think first, and then say!"

"What did I say wrong," Yegor was embarrassed, "I'm not happy. We'll just go to Dad, we'll see him, and he'll be better off."

Then my children sat down on my bed, embraced me and began to cheer me up. Their simple love and compassion restored my lost balance. I sent them to walk and returned to her daily duties. But the obvious connection between my love adventure and my husband's accident was bothering me for a long time.

Over time, the term of military service in Germany of Major Buchenko ended, at the same time, our youngest son had to graduate from school and to continue his studies at the university. I took Yegor to Moscow, where we met with my daughter-student before she went with the construction team to the Saratov region. Three days in Moscow flew by like one hour. While I was visiting my aunts, adult children had remembered their childhood, the best moments of which were connected with Moscow, and said goodbye to childhood forever.

At the Exhibition of Achievements of the National Economy, they visited their favorite expositions, ate pork sausages with buns, read the fresh magazines in the pavilion "Culture" and rode a boat around the fountain sticking out of the lake near the restaurant "Golden Ear". In Sokolniki Park they took a ride on attractions, went to the exhibition, where the American goods sold, walked in the park amidst the greenery and coolness. Finally, they made a two-hour cruise by the Moscow channel on a double-decked pleasure boat. It was especially interesting for them to float along the bridge above the road and watch the cars driving down the highway.

After our meeting Nelly and I put Yegor on a train, in which he went to join to the military school, but we went to Saratov. I stayed there for a week, until my daughter and her group went to the construction site, and then returned to Moscow. I could not immediately leave for Germany to my husband, that day I had to take a ticket for a train that will depart two days later, therefore I got a room at the nearest hotel by name of "Sovetskaya". Entering the room, I found myself in the twilight of the curtained room, in which there were no sounds even from the noisy Leningradsky Prospect. For the first time in my life I stayed alone for two days, and suddenly I was seized by the feeling that I was alone in this universe, my husband was somewhere in Germany, the children had left me, I did not need anyone and I was lost and forsaken.

To dispel somehow my anguish, I took a thick phone book and began to flip pages at random. The hand itself found the right page with the surname "Smirnov". There were four pages with this surname, and a first name "Vladimir" had about four dozen people. Thank God that there was only one with patronymic Alex among them. I picked up the receiver and started to dial by the finger trembling with excitement, hitting one's finger in the wrong number. From the fourth or fifth attempt, I dialed the correct number, and long hooters were heard in the receiver.

"Hello," said a familiar voice in the receiver, "Smirnov is listening."

"Volodya, it's me," I stammered in a tearing voice.

"Gina, ah, Gina," cried Vladimir, "where are you, why are you silent? Are you in Moscow?"

"Yes, I'm," I somehow soothed breathing, "will you come to me?"

"Why do you ask," Vladimir exclaimed admiringly, "say already where you are?"

"I'm at the Sovetskaya Hotel, number three hundred and eight, second floor, to the right along the corridor."

"Well, I'll be in forty minutes, wait for me!" Then Vladimir hung up.

I listened to short beeps and could not understand how I dared to do it. Four years have passed since our meeting at the lake, I already thought that our ways had completely diverged, but I myself called him for some reason. Maybe I'll stay with him forever?

This thought no longer seemed to me as seditious as before. The children grew up and went their own way. My husband was an alcoholic and he remained an alcoholic now, but on top of everything, he lost his masculine strength. I had no doubt that Volodya would ask me again to marry him, and now I will not refuse him. Waiting for my beloved, I cleaned myself up for a hot meeting, took a bath, changed clothes into clean, spread out my bed and lay down for a minute.

I woke up from a loud knock at the door. The blood rushed to my cheeks, and it seemed to me that my heart was beating louder than that man outside the door was. I put on my robe and opened the door. The joyful Vladimir burst into the room, laid fruit and wine to the table, picked me up in an armful and circled the room.

"Oh, well, Volodya, do not do it " I resisted reluctantly, "I'm too massive."

Nevertheless, I hugged him by the neck and pressed to him as tightly as I could. Finally, he set me on the floor and began to take off his clothes. Either my head was spinning from an unexpected meeting or from the pirouettes, I had done, so I sat down in a chair and watched the movements of my lover. Vladimir neatly hung a light summer suit with a shirt in the closet, threw a tie over it, and returned to me.

"Well, hello, my darling," he said gently, laying out the supplies and pouring champagne, "what is the destiny that took your to Moscow?"

"I had sent my children from me, younger, a graduate, went to a military school, elder, a student, went to a construction squad, now I left alone and my train will be only two days later."

"Gina, it's so cool," Volodya laughed, "I'm also on vacation now. My wife and child left for Sochi, and I'm alone too."

I was shocked when I heard about his wife. Hence, he again is not free, and I build my own bright plans. What is the strange thing, a woman for a moment had felt herself free, and immediately brains muddied. Well, who am I to him! He just divorced one wife, here is another wife, and they already have a child. This Volodya is incredible!

I decided not to waste time in vain, since there is no future for us, so at least we could snatch this day. Taking a glass, I went to Volodya. He straightened, also holding a glass in his hand, and looked at me questioningly.

"Let's drink, my dear," I said, "for our brief meeting, which could be longest for us!"

I picked up my glass and touched his glass gently. There was a thin ringing, so piercing, as if moaning at our ungainly love. Tears appeared in my eyes and, I tilted my head over the glass to hide them, and I turned away. I pulled yourself together and sipped the champagne, and then I turned to Volodya. However, he did not notice the internal dissonance of his friend's soul chose a cluster of grapes and already held out to me.

"Gina, have a snack, and if you want for more important to eat, I'll order to the room."

"It's afterwards," I firmly rejected the proposal and by a slight thrust forced him to fall into the chair, "you better think about how you will be pleasuring me now."

Pulling off my robe, I sat down on his knees, spread my legs wider and began to move closer to him. Volodya only managed to put the glass on the table and he immediately grabbed my thighs with strong hands, gently and passionately pulled me to him. From the sweetness of a long forgotten feeling, I even moaned, and Volodya winced.

"I hurt you," he asked in a guilty voice. "I'm sorry, darling, but I'm ready to smear you on me so that there is not even a slit between us."

"Do not be afraid, Volodya," I whispered, kissing him near his ear. "It's all right; I just forgot how wonderful it is. Do it now, I'll help you."

Arousing ever stronger and coming into a state of ecstasy, we forgot about caution and were punished. As soon as satisfaction came and our arms were weakened, the chair under the weight of two heavy bodies fell backwards, and we flew to the floor crying loudly with pleasure and fear.

Having fallen, we fell silent and for some time lay without movement. Stunned with love euphoria we did not feel the bodies and did not feel the pain of the falling. I jumped over Volodya and hit my forehead and knees, and he hit his occiput and rolled over the head to the left of me.

"Genie," he called for me in a weak voice after a minute of silence, "did you not break anything?"

"I did nothing, but did you not break the most important thing?"

"The main thing is in order," Volodya reassured me and jumped to his feet cheerfully, holding out his hand to me.

I rolled onto my back and palpated my head. On my forehead grew a cone and I looked like a mischievous one-horned devil. I took his hand tightly, and he tried to pull me to him, but I decided in my own way. With all my strength that he did not expect from me, I pulled him on myself, and he barely able to group not to crush me with his body, landed gently on me, and we began foolish lovers' game again.

This time there were no injuries. After that, we sang fun songs about pilots, which was known to us from the front, then washed in the bathroom and "slicked down" the wounds received on the love front, then sat down at the table, drank and ate enough, and we went to bed. A powerful passion knocked us out of the rut, took away our strength, so with some of meaningless words we plunged into a shallow, disturbing dream.

I dreamt the field of cornflowers, which Volodya collected for me at the military airfield. I seemed young and free; there were flowers all around, bright sun and clear sky. However, suddenly an airplane appeared in the sky, which flew straight at me. The pilot fired from all the machine guns, and the bullets whistled toward me. The plane was coming closer and closer, and already in the window, I could see the pilot's face. It was Anatoly, who pressed angrily at the trigger, but the bullets flew by me.

"Tolly, mother-fucker," I cried, choking at the sounds of horror, "you aren't able to fly! Now you'll crash a plane! Jump right now! A-ah!"

The plane was getting closer and closer, now it will fall into me, and I wailed a terrible voice, fully stunned with fear, and woke up in a cold sweat. I was shaken by Vladimir, who trying to wake me up.

"Gina, why are you shouting, did you have a nightmare?" he inquired curiously.

"Yes, I saw my husband in the dream, he wanted to kill me."

"Is he so jealous of you that he even pursues in a dream?"

Vladimir laughed, imagining Tolly in the role of Othello.

"Do not laugh, Volodya," I pouted thinking that he laughed at me, "Because I'm deceiving him, after all."

"Come on, Genie," Volodya smiled broadly. "I'm not laughing at you, but above him. He probably has not been sleeping with you for a long time?"

"That's for sure," I agreed with a sigh, "but that does not mean that our marriage is over. He's my husband, you know."

"I know, but I cannot agree. We feel good together, why then you are with him, and I am with others?"

Vladimir looked at me questioningly, as if saying, "Who is to blame?"

"Yes, it's my fault," I agreed sadly, stroking Volodya's breast gently, "I'm such a bad woman, has spoiled life both to you, and to itself."

I could not extrude out the right words with which to explain how I want to connect with him and live together the rest of my life. I remembered Vladimir's words about his wife and child and did not want to force him to abandon them, but with a dying heart, I waited for a signal from him that would let me know he was ready to unite with me.

However, Vladimir did not notice my torment. He embraced me and said, "You are the sweetest woman I've ever met in my life. Yes, really, I'm not exaggerating. I'm fine with all the women, and they do not complain about me, but I do not feel such pleasure as with you."

They are not so sweet for me, there are no such sensations with them, but you are burning up from all sides, you are absolutely fire! Even if I would not want you, no matter, I will want you necessarily! Tell me, what am I going to do without you?"

Here it is! I prepared myself to hear that he would say to stay with him for life, but Vladimir continued, "In an hour my wife will call from Sochi, I need to be at home so that she did not invent unnecessary things, and then I'll come to you for overnight, will not me?"

"So be it," I said in disappointment, but Vladimir did not pay attention to my tone, quickly dressed and left the hotel.

I continued to lie, thinking about my situation. Strange things happen with me. Here I am a free woman, I lie unattended, but no one obtains me, I am not needed anyone. Even the only person in the world, whose love I have carried through all my life, does not want to take me with him.

"My life is in tribulation," I thought somehow distantly, without much regret, "I never get what I want. No one understands me when I need it, and I cannot do anything with myself or with others. I lived like a poor grass, where the wind blew, there I bent over."

I was cunning with myself even in my thoughts, because I was always a strong enough woman. I always suppressed my husband with my mental strength, so he could only do in return to drink the alcohol and to forget everything. The children were also completely in my power, till they were sitting under my wing, I'll see how they behave in "a free swimming". I provided myself with the way of life I was striving for, forcing close people to follow my course. Next to me for a long time, there was no man to whom I could lean and become a weak defenseless woman. I was tired in the life struggle to be an "iron hand" in my house, and needed pity and affection, which no man could give me before and now.

Even now, instead of understanding my beloved, his attempt to start a new married life, I want to be the ruler of his soul, to make him obedient executor of my will. Nowadays I have wanted to change my life, and it means for me that everyone should change with me. If Vladimir does not want, so he immediately have become bad.

Nevertheless, I did not like to consider this side of me, moreover, to discuss it. My infallibility I raised to the rank of the law, and always believed that someone was wrong, but not me. I always had the explanations of my obvious mistakes either by intrigues of enemies, or by unhappy fate. Sometimes I realized that I was the source of my tribulations, but I did not admit it, I cursed fate in everything.

Now I had to go to a frank conversation with a loved one, to open my soul to him, but trying not to put him before a choice, she, or I, but just to confess what I have in my heart. If a loved one is ready for everything, I am his number one now and always will be. If his new family suits him more than I do, then we will part with no regrets. Nevertheless, I had to explain myself, and not get angry with Vladimir, as if he was again unprepared for a meeting with me. Always was like, if he becomes free then I'm busy, and now I'm free, but he's busy. Suddenly I sensed that I was just afraid to get a refusal if I was the first to ask him to come together. The refusal was death to me! It's better not to say anything and run away.

I flipped through the phone book and looked at my watch; it was about six in the evening. I dialed the ticket office number of the Belorussky Railway Station. The voice on the other side explained that I could come to the cashier's office and exchange my ticket for the today train, because there are tickets in it, but I have to be in time for an hour while they keep the ticket reservation. That's good.

"You, Volodya, live with your wife and child, and I'll go to my Tolly!" I thought, going to the station.

I managed to get out before Vladimir arrived, and he ran around the hotel, not understanding where I had gone, why I disappeared at the best moment of our life. Later, already in his declining years, he told me that his wife, already ex-wife, called him at that time and said that she was leaving him with his boss, who resting at the resort with her. Vladimir raced like on wings to let me know about this and ask me to throw this ignominious Tolly and live with him, Vladimir Smirnov, the rest of their lives, but did not find me on the spot.

I was looking out the window at the running trains and recalled how good it was to us together. Everything was simply excellent, but what I lacked when I had decided to spoil everything? After all, it's not his fault that we do not coincide in our love road. I always go ahead, now I ran away ahead of time, but we could spend another day together. I did not even write down the phone number, I did not remember it. Moreover, where am I going now, to whom?

Chapter 5. Fly up to fall

Life has become like a snow slide with springboards, the jumps or life highs had been happening sometimes, but less than it could be, in general, life was rolling down the hill. The mood sometimes changed for the better, especially, when my son came and brought my granddaughter, or I managed to save money for a new purchase, or I won a crossword contest announced in the newspaper "Book Review".

However, the joy was quickly replaced by frustration, irritation or fear when the husband woke up, and it was necessary to watch that he did not do anything unwanted. When we moved from Germany to this big city, standing on the crossroads of many roads, it got even worse, because Anatoly brought his parents, and I had to confront the three Buchenko who understood each other well and stood shoulder to shoulder.

It was still that family! My husband Anatoly by that time was already demobilized, and was a complete alcoholic who reacted only to alcohol, and the surrounding reality was perceived him only as a source of toxic beverage. Senior Buchenko, Yegor, also drank, and alcohol, not finding other weaknesses in his body, completely broke his memory. At first he hardly recognized me, and then completely stopped recognizing not only me, but also his own son, and by the end of his life - his wife Anna, with whom he had lived together for more than half a century.

When my husband's parents just moved to us, some mind was remaining in Yegor's head. In response to my reproach that he had not earned own apartment in his life, the old Cossack was buzzing with a thick bass, «You do not know our customs, you fool. My son is obliged to support us, since we have become old; it's a main rule of life, because I worked all my life to help people, and not to get my wealth. Hey, it's not you who may judge how I worked, I'm an honest man! I never hand out my property, but I did not beg anyone for nothing! If you do not like it, get out of here, I'm living with my son, but you are nobody here."

I was irritated by such conversations. All was good before their arrival. My husband just now was demobilized, he got a good pension, and I had the opportunity to control every his step, because Anatoly stopped going to work after a short work experience as a deliveryman of telegrams. For the first time he got a job immediately after the army in the autumn of the same year in the remote bureau of post office. Literally, a month later, drunken Anatoly lost along the way a pack of telegrams, among which were some important one, because of which he was excluded from work, but with a "decent" formulation "quitted at his own request".

By the spring of the following year, Tolly again got a job to deliver telegrams, now in the nearest bureau of post office, and he was running with telegrams by the apartments directly in our area, but he had worked no more than a month. He had taken a pair of earrings in one of the apartments and he was overtaken by an angry host and severely beaten, and after that, I decided that my husband would no longer have to work; otherwise, I could stay without my husband and his pension.

Therefore, Tolly sat at home, gradually taking over his wife's household duties, he washed clothes, cleaned the apartment, went to the bazaar and to the shopping, took out the garbage, in a word, it became easier to live for me, because the duties were diminished, and the object of control was constantly at arm's length. The fact, that my husband had more free time for vodka did not frighten me, the strict course of the alcohol reception, started in recent years, did not allow liberties from his part. He did not need to look for drinking elsewhere, there was always a sufficient supply of alcohol at home, and he was not strong enough for additional libations.

It was the "golden time" of our old age, but one day the owner of the apartment which the parents of my husband was renting in Derbent, Rafik Ismailov, called us by telephone. He said that Mr. Yegor is no longer able to work as before, when he was walking around the mountain collective farms of Dagestan to do office books for them, but in Derbent city, there was no work for him. He, Rafik, has to feed Yegor and his wife for three months already, and they did not pay for apartment for a whole year.

Rafik was a good guy. As a child, he was friended with my children and was running with them to the sea when our family went on vacation to visit Tolly's parents. After growing up, he had finished studying and had taken the prestigious position, in his opinion, as assistant locomotive driver, and then he came to us to marry my daughter, Helen. When he had been refused, Rafik was not highly upset and soon married to his countrywoman, the same representative of the Diaspora of Turkish Kurds in Dagestan, like himself. Now they have four children, and I sometimes thought that after all it was necessary to give Nelly for Rafik, may be, I could have the grandchildren now. Nelly had no children with her husband, and the son Yegor and granddaughter were far away.

However, besides grandsons we needed to solve something with Tolly's old men. Rafik is not such a person who will bother us to no purpose, if he called; it means that things have reached a critical point. In addition, really, why he must bother with non-native old people, although they lived side by side for more than twenty years. I thought about it, internally afraid of inevitable decision, which the husband will necessarily take. Anatoly, of course, immediately decided to go for his parents, but just in case asked me, "Well, what do you think, Gina, they will not disturb us, will they?" Anatoly spoke with visible subtext, as if to say, "Try to say something against, then you will regret the said!"

However, I was not afraid of such talks. I put my husband several conditions, among which was one important point that he did not have the right to drink with the father; otherwise, everyone will fly from the apartment in different directions. This condition did not upset Anatoly, because his filial feelings were greatly dimmed, and the habit of drinking alone suggested that we should agree.

A week later, Buchenko parents settled in a pencil-like room, which was supposed to be their last berth, but so soon, none of them was going to die. A long, exhausting and bloody struggle began for the mastery of the living space.

Old Yegor constantly needed only two things, a glass of cheap port wine and a pack of smelly cigarettes. From the first day, he began to win back his right to smoke in his room and not to go out to the stairwell, as his son always did, also the right to his glass of port wain at any time, when he desires it. The first condition, that is smoking, I had to agree because the old man was gradually losing his mind and it was riskily him to go out of the apartment, but strangely enough, it was my husband Anatoly, who opposed against the second condition.

"What is the matter with you?" he indignantly asked his father by support of his mother and wife, "do you want to become a complete alcoholic? You are some drunkard and cannot live without wine!"

"No, I'm not!" Yegor tried to justify himself, "Well, you, son, I'm not a wino, I understand everything, but sometimes can I afford a little bit? Well, at least on holidays, eh?"

"On holidays, I'll pour you tumblerful, Dad," his son magnanimously informed the decision, and since then Yegor had not any questions. To drink, to eat, to smoke and sleep he had, but what else is needed to meet old age?

The old age, meanwhile, took its own. Each glass of wine, each cigarette wash away from the Yegor's brain the remnants of consciousness, which was broken into fragments by abuses and awful camp life. For a short time, without the constant movement that filled his body with life force in the mountains of Dagestan, Yegor turned into a complete ruin. He struggled to overcome several dozen small steps from the bed to the kitchen or to the toilet, and the rest of the time, he sat or lay in his room.

With the grandmother, it was more difficult. Old Anna, looking like a soft ball, was angular and uncompromising in character. She immediately appreciated how accurately the son repeats the path of his father, and decided that now he is in such a state, when she can still subordinate it to her influence and become a sovereign mistress of the house. She remembered those blessed times when in Central Asia they lived in their own house and were the respected people, but even better she remembered those bad times when Yegor was imprisoned. Anna always felt uncomfortable in the rooms of other people's houses, where she and her husband rented a room, therefore, having found herself in the cozy three-room apartment of her son, she immediately felt it like the own one. She thought that the alien in this apartment was the daughter-in-law that is I; therefore, she had necessary to show me that the queen in our small kingdom is the mother of Tolly, and not some kind of wife.

I immediately sensed where the danger was coming from, and I prepared myself for a rebuff. However, strangely enough, Anatoly came to help me. His mother had long been a distant relative for him, which should be taken care of, but which brings more disquiet than joy. Therefore, he did not want to change anything in his lifestyle, which was completely under my control, about this he warned his mother after when I complained to my husband about her. There was no scandal, because the look of the half-drunk-half-mad Tolly, her native and only son, who was arguing that he is the master of the house and everyone should obey his wife, was more than convincing for his mother Anna.

"You have twisted my son like the ram's horn, you've hexed him with black magic," she hissed to me, when we were alone in the kitchen, "I'll never forgive you for this. What evil conscience you have, when you have complained to son about his mother! God will punish you for taking my son away from me. And who are you to be here? Orphan Gypsy, bastard, you came from zero to hero!"

These pricks hurt my heart with old and new grievances. Many years have passed, it seemed, everything in my life has been adjusted, my origin and kinship had no longer played any role, but here again they are reminded me of what has already had passed.

One day, a month and a half after the old parents had moved to us, the phone rang in the morning. It was Thursday, my daughter Nelly usually called just at this time. She always wanted to know in advance whether she needed anything to buy for her mother, since she was going to come at the weekend. Thinking that this is my daughter's phone call, I boldly picked up the phone, but immediately I was disturbed by an energetic male voice with such familiar intonations. I almost let go of the trembling hand, heard in the tube, "Gina, hello, how are you, can you talk freely?"

It was the voice of Vladimir Smirnov, such a native and so inappropriate now in my shameful life. While he told me something with amiability, I feverishly thought what he needed from me and how I could politely get rid of him. After all, I was already fifty-three, what kind of love I needed now and what meetings could give me relax when nothing for me would be attractive anymore. However, he did not forget me, although he was married three times, he had a lot of children, scattered them all over the Union, what else does he need?

Meanwhile the irritation somehow changed in my soul to excitement and delight. He did not forget me, he loved me, and I have not forgotten anything, his eyes, his hands, passionate burning embraces, I remember everything and am glad that he called right now, in the most difficult time for me. I need to detach myself from this hell, from all these Buchenko, who was packed in our apartment in such quantity that it seemed they were everywhere.

"Well, Gina, will you come?" continued to insist Vladimir, "I'm here on the highway in the car, you get down, we'll go. I got a room in the hotel in the center, nobody will know you there."

"Wait me, please, I'll be soon." I confirmed my consent, lowering my voice, because Tolly had been moving on the couch, and it was evident that he was going to wake up.

Sure enough, Anatoly waked up and sat down on the couch, he looked at me with a meaningless look and asked, "Where are you go, Gina, who called you?"

"No one called, it was a mistake, but I'll go to the bazaar, we have run out of vegetables, I'm going to the market for the railway men and I'll be back soon, well, maybe, if there will be not anything suitable, I'll go to the Central Market. Do not wait for me, have dinner yourself, with your parents."

"Well, okay, take the bottle, because my bottles are over," Tolly said and again fell asleep.

I went into the kitchen, closed the door on the latch, and looked at myself in the old clouded mirror. Thanks to a thin and tender skin, given me by nature, there was almost no wrinkle on my face. I painted the short gray hair with henna, it did not work very smoothly, but it was similar to the highlighting, the light strands alternated with red and chestnut, the gray hair in this bouquet was almost invisible.

I washed myself up, put on clean linen from old, still German stocks, shaved my armpits and, anointing them with deodorant, left the bathroom. In the corridor, I came face to face with my mother-in-law, who opened the door to the toilet. She looked at me, and something in my face seemed unusual to her.

"Genie, what happened, why are you rushing as if you was poisoned by fumes?" old Anna asked me with curiosity, "Where does you go in this time?"

"Mom, I'm going to the bazaar, I need to be on time until the goods are disassembled."

"He's probably have a good "commodity", if you run and stumble, bitch," my mother-in-law viciously hissed at me, "you think I do not know where women with such an expression of a face are hurrying! Did you already wash in the bathroom, right?"

"You are an old fool, what are you talking about?" I was not so much outraged as surprised by my mother-in-law's insight, "you've got some strange ideas, and you've been probably running around males your whole life, now you measure me by yourself."

My mother-in-law was visibly embarrassed. Either she really had lovers, or she realized her wrong, but Mrs. Anna did not respond to the daring words of her daughter-in-law and disappeared into the toilet. I grunted, to be surprised once again, how the secret thoughts and deeds could accidentally unfold, and hurried to a meeting with Vladimir.

His car was on the other side of the highway. Vladimir, dressed in a civil suit, was as elegant and slender as ever, he saw me and waved his hand. I pretended that it was not for me, because a neighbor from the opposite house was walking towards me. I greeted my neighbor and passed her, briefly showing Volodya that he had go forward after the stop. At that place, bushes grew along the road, so no one will see me.

Sitting in the car, I felt myself in another world, where I had been invited on occasion. I felt such like at my mother's work, at the National Hotel, or when I located with my platoon during the war in Germany at the estates of the barons there, or when my husband and I came to a military sanatorium with luxurious palaces, royal furniture and lush southern nature. It also happened every time when I had met Vladimir, he was close to me, but he came from another world and again hid in it for a long time, and every time it seemed to me, that he is gone forever. Nevertheless, my hero invariably returned, inviting me again to the world of beautiful life, which I always dreamed of and was unworthy of it, as I thought always.

Now, having crossed for half a century, I acutely felt that the whole beauty of life, which only occasionally touched me with its wing, had already flown by, but what was left for me? The always drunk husband, his idiot parents, children who do not want to see his mother, because I live with these monsters, a granddaughter who'll never come to me, it's my lot. Everything is wrong because I had cruelly mistaken in my youth and could not make the right choice.

I kissed Volodya quickly and froze on the seat, once again experiencing the injustice of fate, which did not give me anything that was so close and so accessible. I was a fool, really, what a fool I was! Well, why does understanding come so late when nothing can be returned?

As if in response to my thoughts, Smirnov increased a speed and overtook the truck, and he said not taking his eyes off the truck, "Now I divorced again, Gina, that's how I'm not lucky in life, already the third wife left me!"

"Volodya, well, what do you know about, what is it "not lucky", my dear?" I grinned unhappily, "Your wives are idiots because they leave you, and they do not understand what they have lost."

"No, they are not, they understand everything and are not stupid," Vladimir remarked to me. "The first wife married the secretary of the regional committee, but before that she was fucked by the every man in regional committee while I was in Korea. Now her husband is a secretary of the Central Committee, and she lives in clover. I'm a gray little man for her. The second wife married my boss when he was sent to Vietnam, now he is a marshal, she have everything and even more, she has lost nothing.

"The third wife is already ex-wife," he paused looking for the right word, "she took away my cottage near Moscow, I bought an apartment for her, put a considerable sum on the bank account, and now she do not hurry up to marry, she is fucking with the young guys, why does she need a husband?"

I missed a rough swearing word by my ears, paused, thinking about the situation with my beloved, but I did not find the right words. I did not feel sorry for him, so beautiful and strong, he did not need my pity. There is nothing to moan, that he is not lucky, it was his choice to marry them. He could choose someone like me and live with her all his life.

Vladimir seemed to hear my thoughts, and he said thoughtfully, "I have not met in my life another person like you, Gina. Really, no one woman is like you for me! You see how you turned my life upside down, I'm spinning, twisting, but I cannot just stand up straight. But you do not think about, I do not blame you, it's our destiny."

He interrupted the conversation, guiding the car to the parking behind the fountain near the central hotel. We got out of the car, Vladimir took the keys and we went to the hotel. As we walked through the lobby, the receptionist looked at us with condemnation. She was liked to this elderly military man, even if he's retired. After looking at his passport, that he was divorced with his wife, and lived in Moscow, she pictured herself that she could have a romance with him, but now some kind of housewife in a completely domestic garb came with him. Such the catch fell off the hook!

In the luxury room, which I had known since his last visit, everything was already on the table in the front room, as always at their meetings, champagne, cognac, chocolate sweets and grapes. In addition to this, next to the table lay a large watermelon, and in the corner stood a large vase of flowers.

I heavily sat into an armchair near the table and wept softly. I felt sorry for myself, a fat and old woman, who was transferred into a fairy tale for a moment but soon she will be expelled out. I took to sob louder, so Vladimir, busied in another room, came in and asked, "Gina, well, what is it, every time you start with do not cry, please! Everything will be fine, you know, we always do it well with you!"

"I'm not crying about that, darling," I said trembling with my voice. "For six years I have not cried before this meeting, I have no time to cry at home, I have to struggle, I need to be strong and cruel, but not to cry. Here I have relaxed, and my tears flow themselves. You wait, now we'll have a little drink, and everything will pass."

"That's right," Volodya rejoiced, pouring champagne into our glasses, "it will be so much more fun. I've already retired for health reasons four years ago. Now I have no one to drink with, just on Victory Day we meet with colleagues, we are sitting and drinking together, talking and remembering the war, that's all. At other times I'm lonely, but I do not drink alone."

"Yes, for which I love you, that you do not drink," I said, almost calming down, "but you better pour me some cognac; I do not want to swallow these bubbles."

After drinking, we began to remember the friends of the war era, tell each other who, where and how lives at present, and we remembered our love in wartime. I suddenly laughed.

"What's so funny about it," Vladimir was insulted. "We loved each other so much, everything could be good for us, but you're laughing at this!"

"Come on, Volodya, I'm not laughing at this," said I and continued, "Remember, you took me to ride on your plane? It seems like you flew to the reconnaissance and took me with."

"Well, I remember that it was after the May holidays, when the Nazis' planes attacked our airfield, we had to fight and I even knocked out one of them, and you sat and trembled from behind."

"'No, I did not tremble, I even screamed to you from which side the enemies. It turns out that everything is so clearly visible in the air; the air is transparent and increases all the objects like the lens. On the ground surface, everything looks like a photograph, but in colors, therefore it's easier to make out where is the aim. However, I laughed because I remembered how you dropped me off at the end of the strip, so that no one could see that I was in the cockpit. Otherwise, you would not see some stars on epaulets if someone found out it."

"Then the bombing started," I continued, laughing. "You flew away, well; I crawled in the thick grass along the fence to my photo-lab. Much bombs was flung on the airfield at once! I was lying next to runway and afraid that the bomb will fall on me. Around me, it's rumbled everything, and I had beaten my hips by the ground, which threw me so high. You will be laughing, but I crapped my pants because of the fear. I did not tell you then, I was hesitated, but now it does not matter, it's been a long time ago. Well now, the bombs are bursting, and I cannot crawl away, therefore I took off the panties and wiped myself with grass. Imagine, all around me was so dirty and smelly, even the fear went away and it became fun, like now. I spat on the bombing, threw the panties in the bushes, and ran to the photo-lab. I washed there, changed my underwear, and calmed down, but every time when I thought about it, I longed to laugh."

Volodya looked at me carefully, guessing the fresh young features of me in that old time; he imagined the situation and began to laugh too.

"Well, you're having fun now," I sulked, "that's why I did not want to tell you then, and now I did not have to."

"Do not be offended, Gina," Volodya answered, laughing. "I do it from the heart; I love you in any kind. If I were there at that moment, I would have washed you to the white."

Then we fell silent, imagining how he would wash me. From such a piquancy of the situation, we felt again young, healthy, and strong, we were attracted to each other, as before. Volodya stood up, took my heavy body for the armpits, lifted me from the chair to my feet and led me to the bed.

"Yes, you are strong," I muttered, cuddling him, "you lifted me like a fuzz, but I'm so fat, do not look at me, I'm shy."

Nevertheless, Vladimir, it seems, did not care how I look like. He was remembering me young, so I stayed the same for him as I was at that time. Yes, I had already the fattened swollen breast by the size of G or more, it was spread over me like two half-flat balls, the hips that he moved apart were soft as if completely without muscles. Nevertheless, the skin was still gentle to the touch, which made him always be delighted, no women had such a delicate skin, about this he could be convinced from personal experience. Most importantly, he knew what I was like in bed! I was strong and gentle and brought him to ecstasy in two shakes. I remained the same mobile now, in my fifty.

We had made love three or four times then fell asleep for half an hour, but suddenly woke up together, as if on command. Although I had not exited from the love bliss, I cautiously hinted to Volodya that it was time for me, they were waiting for me at home, but he stopped me with a gesture, jumped off the bed, pulled on his panties and went into the next room. Returning with a bouquet of flowers from which water dripped, he fell on one knee by the bed and proclaimed, "Gina, finally, give me your hand and heart, marry me!"

I gasped and covered my face with a blanket. I waited for this turn, but I did not expect that everything would be like last time, his wife left, and he asked to marry him, and what did I do? Nothing, as before, I'm ready to refuse him. This fairy tale is not for me, because I cannot fit into this luxurious life with my fatty ass. I must go to Moscow and set among fashionable ladies, but I had not at most half of teeth already, only front teeth have remained. No, no and NO! Volodya will find a couple this time, as before, he will not remain without wife, and I have such a tail at home that I cannot throw it off, but I'm one who can live with them, the other will not be able to cope them.

While I was thinking, Vladimir regarded the long pause as hesitation and decided to push me.

"Gina, how can I live without you further, you rip my soul, come on, agree. In Moscow I'll buy you what do you want, gold, diamonds, we'll go to the rest to Czechoslovakia, Germany, Bulgaria, I have the car, my apartment is five-roomed on Lenin Avenue with the most convenient layout. We'll buy a country house, I have enough money for this, I have a personal pension two thousand rubles, like your Tolly has for a year. Well, come on, agree, and come with me!"

The mention of Tolly was very inopportune. I remembered that it was time to go home and to buy vegetables on the way; it's good that just near the hotel was a tram line toward the railway market. It's time to go. Vladimir looked at me and at the lack of my reaction to his words, and did not know what to do. He could not use his last chance to persuade this stubborn gypsy woman. Now she, as always, will leave, and could we meet later, it is already unknown.

"Well, go! Dammit!," he said rudely, turning away and brushing off the uninvited tear.

"Do not be so rude, Volodya, it was all so good for us," I chided him. "You must understand, I'm not worthy of you. Find yourself a good woman without claims, so she will love you like me, then you will be happy at last."

"Ah, it already was in my life," Vladimir began to get angry. "At first everyone loves, everything is good, and then, it turns out, they need nothing but money. However, what kind of person are you? I'm offering you everything that you do not have, but you refuse!"

"I'm spoiled, Volodya," I answered sadly. "I do not have anything good, and I do not need anything, it's my live, and I'll live to death in this way. You do not take me home, I'll go myself, and you will not come any more, leave me alone and do not put salt on my wound. We have different ways, good-bye."

The monotonous routine of our small nursing home was pulling further. I tried to line up my day so that as rarely as possible to intersect with the elderly, each woman was preparing meal for her couple, doing this at different times, and we ate out in turn, without interfering with each other. Outwardly, everything seems to have passed decently, but secretly the struggle for supremacy in the house did not stop for a minute. Again and again, Anna repeated attempts to strengthen her influence on her son in order to bring down the pride from her daughter-in-law. At the same time, she did not miss the chance to prick me harder, emphasizing that they, Buchenko, are the united family, but I, a foreigner, have clings to her son, and I have rights neither to Tolly nor to an apartment.

"Shut up, you, the old freeloader!" I answered indignantly, usually lowering my voice so that Anatoly did not hear. "You never were a smart woman, otherwise you would have your living space in Derbent, somewhere near the coast of the sea, and Yegor would receive an increased pension as a victim of repression. However, you just sat at home and were not interested in anything; you waited that anybody will bring something for you and put it in your mouth. You are the cuckoo!"

"And you, Genie, what do you have done in your life?" Mrs. Anna went on to contend, "You sat all your life behind the back of your husband, but you reproach me! He is absolutely drunkard; you consider it as your achievement in a life?"

"You can see your Yegor, Tolly is just a chip off the old block," I triumphed evilly, "it's his hereditary, but I saved my husband from prison, he served in army whole his time and retired with Colonel pension, why he drinks, you can ask him, but I limit him as I can, and I can say that I had saved his life."

"Look at her, what a benefactress she is!" came the turn to resent old Anna, "he served in army himself, he earned a pension himself, he got the apartment himself, that means it's everything ours, the Buchenko family, and you are here the freeloader!"

"You will not reign here, Mrs. Anna," I said angrily and calmly. "Your time has passed, command your husband if you can, but my husband is Anatoly, as I tell him, so he will do to you. I agreed that he would bring you to our house, and you are here, but I will tell him tomorrow something other, and he will take you to a nursing home, you will live in a state house. If you begin to speak again, I will tell him, and he will kill you everybody."

Suddenly a knock sounded in the corridor, and then shuffling steps were heard. We were frozen in fright, because Tolly came out with a knife in one hand and the pliers in the other one. Anna was struck by the coincidence of my words with the appearance of her armed son; she backed into a corner and pressed herself against the wall. Anatoly went up to her, raised his hand with a knife and showed a finger, on which a violet hematoma swelled. His mother, neither alive nor dead, looked in horror at her son, preparing for the worst.

"Mother, you see how I have been clutched by pliers," Tolly commented actively the appearance of a bruise on his hand, "I wanted to fix the handle on the window, I had clamp the screw with my knife, and turned the nut by this pliers. Well, the pliers broke off and grabbed of the finger. It hurts, ma!"

"Well, you're my little one, come here, I'll regret you," his mother said, she pressed him to her and looked triumphantly at her daughter-in-law, "it's Gina's fault, she made you work that she is wrong, bastard!"

"Mother, what are you talking about? I said you, that you do not touch Gina, I will not let you!" Anatoly said with furious either from the pain, or from the words of his mother. "She's my housewife; you'll do what she says. You will not talk badly about her, but if she complains, I'll give you a merry life! And you, Gina, watch it, do not offend my mother, I do not let you too behave outrageously!"

In addition, in support of his words, he shook by pliers near his mother's face, and he pointed by knife at his wife. Old Anna abated, slid down the wall to the chair, but did not bowed her head and looked at her daughter-in-law with triumph. This round was not lost, the forces for further struggle remained. Let's see, somehow it will be further!

I was surprised by the impulse of my husband and decided that his mother's words led him to such a state. Therefore, I need to provoke my mother-in-law more often, so she would be looking for protection at her son, and he would not like it, then his peace will be broken, and the mother will be to blame. She will have to answer. However, it is the bad fact that he was waving a knife. Moreover, if not the pliers, but the knife would break and pierce him, what should I do? Merely I need to stop his work about the house. To do this I can hire neighbors from the opposite door or wait until my son Yegor will come to us on vacation.

Thus, we lived like in trench war. This depressed me most. There was short spurt and the sortie, somehow verbal shelling, but we did not reach hand-to-hand fighting. The presence of Tolly's old parents filled the house with ill will and malice, directed against me; they poisoned my existence, made me nervous and upset, and loosened my already weak nerves. I already hated my husband's parents so much, I wished them every misfortunes, moreover, sometimes I wanted to grab someone of them in my hands, which had not lost its strength, and to crush them at all. I needed a way out of the situation to get out of this accumulated stress.

This way out came to me by itself without preparation, but like if I ordered it. One evening in the autumn, when for the first time on the TV showed a TV series entitled "Seventeen Moments of Spring", in my room there was Tolly, his mother and I, only old Yegor stayed in his room, occasionally reminding about himself with a heavy cough, which was choked the sound of the TV. Film just came to an episode when the all-Union well-known scout Stirlitz celebrated the Day of the Red Army. He drank a glass of vodka, took a potato baked in charcoal, and was leading a song in silent.

This moment excited Anatoly. He laughed sarcastically and said, "Look mother, he is not a scout because he drinks vodka, it's forbidden for him. However, we can drink. Gina, prepare me something in the kitchen, I'll have supper."

He did not care that his wife also watched the movie with great interest, that she was not indifferent to Tikhonov as an actor, most important for him was that she silently got up and went to the kitchen to fulfill his order. Sighing with regret, I went to the kitchen, thinking, "Nothing, I will look through the series tomorrow in repetition." Still being impressed by the more than convincing game of my favorite actor, I turned the corner, going out into the corridor, when I suddenly collided in the twilight with a dark, huge figure. It was the father-in-law, who had grabbed me with bony hands to avoid falling, but I was so disgusted with the old-smell of his body and the smelly shag that I had cried out and had shoved him away from me with all my forces.

The son and the wife of Yegor hurried to my cry and the noise of a falling bony body. What they saw in the dim light of the old light bulb, when I had lit the light in the corridor, was like the usual fall of an old man when he stumbled or could not find support with his hands, but this time, under his back of the head, which fell on the corner of the refrigerator, spread dark pool of blood. From the stench of fresh blood I could not breathe, my stomach had hurt. I rushed to the toilet, and long, painfully vomited. When it was a bit easier, I got out of the toilet and saw that my mother-in-law with my husband are frozen and numb, and they stood near Yegor doing nothing.

I rushed to the kitchen, grabbed a dishtowel and returned to Yegor. The blood had flowed out of him so much that it touched the feet of his wife and son, and I had to join them to get close to his head. "Tolly, Mrs. Anna, you do not stand without moving," I cried to my relatives while bandaging the father-in-law with a towel, "wake up, please, call to ambulance, let them send a doctor. Tell them that he had fallen, it's a head trauma, and he lost much blood."

The ambulance arrived quickly. To the arrival of the doctor, Tolly and his mother had already dragged Yegor to bed, and I was finishing wipe blood on the floor. In my opinion, the doctor was too young, somewhere over thirty, but in the ambulance, he had worked for seven years. Doctor had seen different things, and this case was not seen remarkable to him. The feeble drunkard old man, who had no muscle left to move normally, fell in the corridor and hit his head on the refrigerator. No crime is here.

The doctor asked Anna whether such cases had happened with the old man before and, having received an answer that this had happened many times, but God had saved, not like now, he decided that there was nothing criminal to search here, it's a typical mischance. Moreover, after giving first aid, bandaging and several injections against tetanus, from infection, calming and anesthetizing, old Yegor recovered and looked at the one or at the other, but he was silent and did not move.

Old Yegor Buchenko was gone in the middle of autumn. The autumn season in our city corresponded to the mood for the funeral, small tedious rains filled everything around, the clay on the roadside becomes mild and flows down by a fat layer along the asphalt under the feet of passers-by and under the wheels of cars, the withered leaves that have not fallen to the ground, was hanging like wet scraps of cloth, moistening the ground with water, even when it did not drip from the sky. The dampness was around you, the dampness was inside you. The soul is wet, as if from tears, but not salty, and some tasteless and damp, there are no passions, no desires, no grievances, no gratitude, only widespread dampness. I do not want to trudge along the soggy earth among the graves, getting wet while the deceased will be buried; this way is not for me.

Therefore, I stayed at home, I did not go to the cemetery under the pretext of an aggravated illness, and the liver bothered me permanently, since I had been ill with malaria during the young years in the war, so it caused no objection and condemnation. Only my daughter Nelly, a simple fat woman with a small round face, could assume that I did not go to the cemetery because of the accumulated hatred and resentment of my father-in-law. She was sorry for and understanding me now because grandfather was unpleasant to her too, but both my daughter and the others saw only the tip of the iceberg of passions that raged in my soul.

I closed the door with a key, infixed a chain, and went into the kitchen to drink boiled water from the jar, which was always stood ready, because we could not drink raw water from a city water pipe because it's like drinking from a puddle on the road. I remembered how in the North area where my husband was in military service, in the spring we had been taken water directly from a huge puddle of melted snow on the roadway opposite the house. It was not only difficult, but also dangerous to walk in the spring to the source, the some fountain, that bubbled up in the rock halfway to the river. The path spattered with water, which spilled out of the buckets, quite steeply descended to the river and under the rays of the spring sun guttered by bare, mirror-like ice, turning the hike to fetch water into an acrobatic etude.

I mechanically rubbed the right thigh, which hit then, twenty years ago, and the resentment due to the awkward life again clouded consciousness with a muddy wave. This fool, such I mentally called my husband without tenderness and warmth, but without hatred, because everything passed and burned out, this fool could serve in Moscow that time, where my mother had a room in a communal apartment, and instead we wandered about the garrisons, and now we live here in this disgusting, dirty city!

After drinking more water, I saw a curl of brown sediment on the bottom of the jar and thought that the water in that long-ago puddle was clearer than here. Having deep breath I walked along a narrow corridor to a large room, stroking along the way the corner of the refrigerator with chipped piece of enamel, and I thought that it's needed to tint it. Thought was some vague, not necessary, in the sense that it is unlikely that anyone in this house will do such a job, and what for? Looking at the floor next to the fridge, I imagined old Yegor, who was lying in a pool of his own blood.

Old Yegor was raw-boned at the end of his life, although he ate so much as if the threw his food in a deep. However, he was never fat, unlike his son Tolly, who in his best years looked like a fed-up dolphin, either from the smoothness of his skin, or from a weak not-male shape. Creaker was always bony, and his character - prickly too, and his convictions were just as angular, painfully beating on those, whom he did not like or disclaimed. This side of the character of old Yegor I explored well on my own experience for more than thirty years of living together with his son. He did not love me, and I paid him the same price.

"Who is buried now?" I asked maliciously with a short, sarcastic laugh, and immediately stopped, looking around, whether not anyone saw, did not hear. No one must notice my joy, because somebody could guess who helped this creaker to get directly to the corner of the refrigerator.

I opened the window in the big room, where the coffin with the body was standing on the table until recently, went into my room and lay down on the bed. Having a little pause, I took an unsolved crossword puzzle, which I cut from the newspaper "Book Review", read next task and fell into thought. Then I put down the newspaper, turned my gaze to the window behind which the sound of the engine of the departing hearse could be heard, and smiled with satisfaction. So, this nasty old man was gone from our world, he was my headache for many years, but in recent years, when they had moved with his wife to our apartment, he was a real obsession driving me crazy, because I hated him so much.

I did not know how it was happened when I helped the old man find the only position on the corner of the corridor, where on the one side was the kitchen, and on the other was the refrigerator near the wall, so that he bumped his head directly into the sharp edge of the refrigerator with his considerable growth. There was no calculation, only chance and luck, this time they were on my side, and in my heart, I secretly rejoiced, not allowing myself even in a closed room without witnesses to rejoice openly, how everything went smoothly. I even wanted someone to guess how cleverly I had deluded everybody, and then I could say openly, "This is to you that my life failed, per all my failures, for the fact that you did not live a life like mine!"

Before the inner gaze, one after another, pictures of the insults inflicted on me in life arose, and the image of a father-in-law who could have been nice, interesting and charming to someone, but he had been behaving to me like a pig. From the first day, since the wedding, when Yegor came from the Japanese war to Moscow, he arrived without a gift, he did not appreciate the merits of his son future wife, but also tried to dissuade his son, he said, she is not a pair for you, the Cossack of the Black Sea troops, this Moscow goose. Most recently, he was tromping in the corridor of the apartment, which we had been waiting for so many years with my husband, expectorated under my feet with nicotine from the terribly smelly cigarettes "Pamir", and in response to my remarks he barked insolently with a thick bass, because he could not speak normally because of deafness, "You are not Lady, pick it up, lick it with your tongue, I deserve it!".

"You deserved it from me, old goat, that's it!" I thought with satisfaction and was going to addict to my favorite pastime guessing prize crosswords from a newspaper, which I had been buying for a dozens of years, when the doorbell rang. Only my daughter Nelly had such jingling, it means they did not let me enjoy my triumph as I wanted, they already buried the old devil, and I had to open the door.

"Mom! You made me wait so long!" she said, "I'm cold and I want to go to the toilet."

My daughter, a big, fat woman of thirty years old, on whose round face the scornful look was frozen, was a distorted copy of her mother. The amorphous, weak character was combined in her with pathological offensiveness to everyone and everything, but she, like me, hated this city, and just considered everyone around below her position, so she neglected to communicate with others partly from contempt for them, partly because of fear to do or to say something wrong.

Leaving the toilet, Nelly came to the kitchen, but seeing a disapproving expression on my face, muttered, "Well, all right, already began!" and went into the bathroom to wash her hands. I loved my daughter, but a lot of flaws prevented me from feeling affection for my creature. I remembered her six years old; it was a real angel. A modestly fat, round girl with lively dark eyes and timid character was extremely quiet, especially unlike her brother Yegor, who terrorized everyone with his indefatigability for the most unthinkable and daring acts, if one can say this about a three-year-old child.

However, Nelly was different. She could spend hours in the kitchen, where I cooked food, not doing anything, but carefully watching what and how I did. Then she suddenly made an exact observation about what she saw, and this put me in a dead end, I could not understand what such a baby could understand in the kitchen affairs? On the other hand, maybe she did not understand, but said it somehow by accident? The girl seemed to me clever, but in a life, it did not need for her. Really, it is true, to be clever with the complete absence of determination and vital energy became for Nelly an irresistible wall between her and real life, which she did not overcome either in her youth or in adulthood. She could understand everything, but was not able to change anything, this was a real tragedy, which depressed her will and created a monstrous perversion in her mind.

However, everyday affairs distracted me from internal digging, so Nelly liked to come to me, she felt in me a soul mate and, most importantly, she thought that I was more offended by my life than she was. The latter circumstance to some extent consoled her and raised her in her own eyes.

"Where's the father, did he come?" I asked. Of the tension of my voice, Nelly realized that she could not tell the truth, but she still decided to tell me to make her mother nervous and feel more comfortable from that.

"He went out on The Rock River Station, said he would be later," the daughter answered and smiled knowingly. I already turned blue from anger.

"Well, he's a pain, did it even on such a day. Although, what are his days now?" I was already boiling, like a kettle on the stove.

My husband Anatoly has long been an alcoholic, he was not the forced one, which suffered from his inability to resist the urge to drink, but he was conscious, convinced drunkard. He believed that there is no better cause in life than drinking alcohol, and never be. So he drank with an excuse and without it, with drinking companions and alone, everything that gets caught, he was drinking our money, own health and the remnants of his mind.

He did not vandalize, did not paint the town red, did not drink steeply on a grand scale, he silently filled himself with a poisonous liquid until strength and reason would have left his body. As the body becomes accustomed to alcohol, Anatoly developed a persistent reaction of the chronic alcoholic, when after taking a small dose of wine or vodka, a brief disconnect of consciousness and motor functions was happening, then he had a quick recovery and could add more. Thus, it was repeated until there came a moment when he could be dragged to the side and allowed to lie down until sobering.

However, his drinking was not only at home, but also at work, on a fishing trip, in restaurants, in the market at the kiosk, on the road in the train compartment, with random fellow travelers and without them. In general, Anatoly did not have the desire to abandon the addiction, but on the contrary, he used in principle every opportunity to pour in himself anything, if only to knock him off. Time to time, this let him down. Sometimes he was not in time to get home from the service because his consciousness was clouded by the vodka, and strength left him, then he had been falling where he was without safety, breaking his knees, elbows, face and, most sadly, his skull, exacerbating the infirmity of an already weak brain.

Many times in the ten years, which we had lived in this city, neighbors was coming to me and reported maliciously that Colonel Buchenko was lying in a puddle next the sidewalk near the neighboring house. I don't know how many times the young guys from our micro district had brought the lifeless body of the pensioner Uncle Tolly, but they grew up before our very eyes and saw how their old neighbor wallowed in the dust and mud, they pitied him and helped him to get home. Later, when they became older, they themselves gave him vodka because of pity for the old drunkard, or because of a desire to laugh when he starts to cut down, or from a misunderstanding, that alcoholism is an indisputable disease that had led him in such a condition today, but tomorrow they could turn into alcoholics too.

I prepared for the worst. The worst in this situation, I thought, was terribly messy pants and a cloak and the need to go and take it so far from here, there were five trolley bus stops to The Rock River Station. The second variant was in general unacceptable, because pulling me out of the house from some time was not an easy task, and often was useless. The constant psychosis and stress that visited me in life with this bibber rewarded my body with a large bouquet of various allergies and phobias, and the climax did not pass unnoticed, easing the bones for a few milligrams of calcium and loosening the joints on the arms and legs so that the former athlete, which I was in yang years, could hardly put on my shoes and walk a few steps to the bazaar around the corner of the neighboring house and come back.

However, under the well-known Parkinson's Law, the worst variant was even worse than I could imagine. Tolly returned sober because he had to give the last money that he found in his pocket to the undertakers who did not want to carry the coffin from the car to the grave, arguing that it was their business to dig and bury, and let the loaders carry the coffin. Adequate money made kinder the souls of the servants of death, but what lacked for Anatoly's soul, it was difficult to convey in simple words.

Coming out of trolleybus on The Rock River Station, he completely forgot that there was no money in his pocket, but here they sold a cheap and pretty safe, natural port wine on tap. Anatoly's soul was eager to the cask of wine, but there was not a single bastard who would pour a glass of wine to him, to veteran of two wars, the World War II and the Perennial World War against the devil's water. He won in the first war because he was Soviet and his cause was right, but in the second war, he was losing hopelessly, although he had a much larger army of alcoholics, drunkards, drinkers and just sometimes drinking men and women. Probably, the enemy was much more numerous and insidious than all the armies of all countries of the world combined. May be, the enemy had never a shortage of the weapon, alcohol was streamed like the river at all times, even when it was forbidden, and it won not because of its strong pressing and forcing the opposite side to fight, by no means, because the whole innumerable army of drunkards did not resist and surrendered at the mercy of the drunken Victorious.

Anatoly's brain, accustomed to the poison, demanded to drink, stimulating weakened muscles to move toward the kiosk with wine, gave him aggression against those who obstructed him. He asked the local drunks to splash at least a glass of wine into his soul, he beseeched them and tried to get money in debt from nearby old women, who sold the fried sunflower seeds, and from passersby at the bus stop, but it's useless, because everybody knew him here, and there was nothing to say more.

Exhausted by the absence of the main nutrient, Anatoly's brain gave a short command, "Attack!" and he pounced with his fists to the bull with the red face, who threw to him disdainful "Fuck off, bibber". This man made a lot of money in the bazaar on the last tomatoes, even much more than in the midst of harvesting. He poured already not first glass into his broad throat and with good reason believed that his fest would not spoil this goat from the trash box.

However, Anatoly did not understand this, as well as other things around him, because his brain perceived only gurgling, more precisely, when it gurgled in his throat. Nor he knew that he had reached the dreadful stage when man is not guided by consciousness or instincts, but only reflexes, mostly conditioned, which had been developed by a long-standing habit of alcohol.

Now the main reflex demanded at any cost to receive his dose of drink, deal did not work out, the situation became tense, any negative signal from the outside only increased aggression, therefore Tolly rushed to the red-faced man. He screamed, squealed, bit the man's hands, tried to break his mouth with the fingernails and to tear out his eyes, he kicked him, in short, he was a real nightmare for this man. The first fear, which arose in man under the impression of such a breakthrough he did not expect from the shabby old man, quickly passed. He threw Anatoly to the ground in two blows and continued to beat him anywhere.

Sellers, who drank nearby, immediately sobered up and quickly dragged the red-faced man away, which was angry that this old man had spoiled such a good day. The old colonel was brought to the trolley bus and was shoved in it out of harm's way, and he went home in shock because of what had happened. Nevertheless, the shock quickly passed, because the brain continued to demand recharge, giving strength and pulling out of the depths of the subconscious some forgotten associations, suitable for search of options to get the alcohol. Among the options the main and only thing was to go home, to take money, to buy two bottles at the store in their house, no, three bottles (two now, one to hide), to come home and drink, drink, drink! You drink slowly, losing consciousness from the kaif and returning to this world, but it thing, the bottle, stands in front of you, does not get anywhere; you can pour in and drink! This is real life!

"Damn it, this virago is here", may be, he thought of me in such manner! But I was frightened by the kind of my husband and the expression of his eyes, in which there was such hatred for everybody around him that I did not consider it possible to object to him when Tolly, repeating only one word in every way, "Scums. Scums... Scums!", climbed into the cupboard, where we kept money for household. He did find no money there, because I regularly hided them in other place not to give the husband another reason to pull money, not so much because of vodka, but because he will take and lose it.

Anatoly straightened at the side of the cupboard, silently looked at me with insane eyes, and clever daughter Nelly rushed to the hall and brought her purse. Everyone was saved. Tolly left, but I was shocked by this moment and silently took money from a secluded place, returned the debt to my daughter and retired to my room, not forgetting to say, "Feed him, as he comes, everything was prepared for the wake in the kitchen."

I could not lay down long enough to bring thoughts in order, of course. An hour later came neighbors who were preparing food for the funeral, together with Nelly they began to lay the table. Almost immediately, Eustace came after them, an unclear old man from the next entrance, who had never visited our apartment, but at meetings on the street, he showed such respect to Anatoly, as if he was either his son or his subordinate or the drinking companion. However, I was not seen him notably drunk, although he worked as a loader in a military deli, and you know what contingent it is.

However, the movement of my thoughts was interrupted by the cheerful voice of Eustace. "Mrs. Eugenia, I am truly sorry for your loss," he began quietly. "I did not know Yegor very well, but I think it was a good man, let him rest in peace."

He turned to the others and greeted the whole honest company, and at the same time asked, "But where is the master of the house? I saw him run home from the trolleybus."

By perplexity on the faces of the women bustling around the table, I realized that they were also interested, where Anatoly is, and I said unwillingly, "He will come now, he went to buy cigarettes," and after a pause I added, "And vodka."

The women exchanged understanding glances, and this immediately angered me, I knew that they condemned me for my husband's drunkenness. "Why, I ask you?" I thought, "He drinks, he does not want to refuse it, but I'm to blame!" In the depths of my soul, I could admit that they were right in that I not only did not want to cure him, but I also specifically worked out this order of life to keep him on a vodka's leash, pulling it by and letting it go so that he was always under control. Lately, he drank at home, and if somewhere he broke off a course in public, it was not often, once or twice a year it was possible to survive.

Another thing was worse. I kept him at the level of constant "incomplete drinking", so he was permanently irritable and easily put into screaming, he was quarrelling with marketers in shops and on the market and with anybody in transport, sometimes he was beaten for it. For a short time, the irritation was removed when he took the dose I had measured for him, but it was coming back again, because I did not allow him to add more and more, until his consciousness would be turned off.

At such a life, a moment would come sooner or later, when he would have left home and somewhere, without company, alone would have drunk to unconsciousness. Then someone had found him lying on the roadside in the dust, or in a puddle, or in the snow, often broken from a simple fall, sometimes with serious injuries, but, thank God, there never were any fractures, except for a beaten brain, because Tolly always landed down to the head. However, I could not consider it as a serious trauma. He had no brain in his youth, but now he had drunk the remnants of it.

See, how could these women know something about this? Stupid chickens, they lived with their husbands, next to them they felt comfortable. Their husbands are dragging into the house everything, they accumulated wealth, provided for the family, collected children and grandchildren around themselves, but we had an ordinary pension, the children scattered in all directions, my daughter has no children, and I have not yet seen my granddaughter from the youngest son. We had neither the car, nor the dacha, nor the pitiful patch of land in the horticultural cooperative, in a word, we had the only title that he is the colonel, in fact there was neither family welfare, nor family harmony, and never was, but anyway we would be lived, no matter how disgusting it is!

I called for my daughter, "Nelly, go and get him home," I whispered, and when she left, I said loudly to those who were in the room and the neighbors who were coming in. "Now Anatoly will come, and we will sit down."

"Tell me, Mrs. Eugenia, why had Yegor died?" blurted out Eustace by the heart simplicity. The women shushed at him, thinking that the question would offend me, but on the contrary, I replied with visible satisfaction, "It was bad with his legs, he's stumbled. There, in the corridor he had hit his head to the fridge by the temple directly.

Standing in the corridor Mrs. Maria, the neighbor opposite, immediately recoiled from the refrigerator. "What a horror, he was at home and did not go out anywhere, but he was not saved anyway," she whispered to her husband, "how is this possible?"

"Anything can happen, "I answered, hearing her voice, "he fell several times, but God protected, he was alright, but this time he had fallen to death. This led him to such finish."

I would continue this exciting topic, but Mrs. Anna, Yegor's wife and Anatoly's mother, a small, round, elderly woman appeared from the door of the next room. She looked at the crowd in the corridor with hostility and told to me, "Eugenia, why do not you invite guests, you see, they are crowding in the corridor, it's closely here."

"Anatoly is absent," I answered coldly, "He will come and we'll sit down."

"God bless him, he is not who dead now," the matron joked severely. "Come along, good people, sit down and eat, what God sent, remember my husband Yegor, God rest his soul. Before he died, he did not suffer for a long time, God took him to Heaven,"

Mrs. Anna's voice faltered, but she restrained herself and did not cry, then turned and shuffled into the toilet.

The guests hurried to occupy seats around the table, which stood in the living room right in the middle of the room. On one side of the table, one could sit on a sofa bed, from all the others - on chairs and stools. There were enough seats, but the hosts did not sit down, they served the guests. The first funeral toast was said for the repose of the soul that he rest in peace, but we was not in time to drink, because Anatoly had appeared.

To say that he was surprised, this is not to say anything. It seems that he did not understand what a hell such a meeting is, the events of today have completely brought his dying brain to be broken, and he had to take vodka inward because the soul thirsted. Tolly stared blankly at those sitting at the table, while they shouted greetings, condolences, invitations to the table. Gradually, not seeing the reaction from his side, everybody had been silent, and a puzzled silence had hung.

Anatoly as if awakening from stupor defused the situation.

"Let's remember my father," he said in a husky voice because of parched throat, taking vodka from the string bag, "May he rest in peace! Eternal memory!"

"May he rest in peace! Eternal memory!" the guests echoed with an unsettled chorus and overturned the first glass. Then everything went on as usual, as on every Russian booze. After a few glasses of vodka, those, who respected the customs and did not consider drunkenness their main occupation, left the table, the remaining people almost forgot about the purpose of their arrival and devoted themselves to their favorite occupation with skill and understanding, they needed to get drunk today in order to have something to recall tomorrow.

Unfortunately, not now! Anatoly as the most important person in our home always made the rules when he got drunk. Now was exactly the same moment, when everything was coincided, due to the experience of this day alcohol immediately sucked through the walls of the empty stomach directly into the blood, and the blood had brought the alcohol straight into his head. The guests gathered around Tolly did not become closer and more familiar due to the adopted vodka; on the contrary, he did not understand why they were sitting here, fuck off!

The last words he was already shouting out loudly, but his tongue was poorly obeyed, so in the general hubbub his grumbling was not perceived adequately to the meaning of what he said.

"Yes, Tolly," the neighbors rejoiced, they were flattered by his attention to them, "everything is fine, your wife was done everything very well, she respects his father, evidently, and loves you."

The apparent inconsistency of the thought expressed by the guests, with personal perception collapsed his brain, in his mind the wife was the main enemy, whom he hated but depended on entirely, and he hated her even more because he feared her and was weak to resist. The irritation from the violated intimacy of communication with the main subject of adoring his life - with the vodka increased sharply, and he shouted in a loud voice. "Come on, fuck off from here, why did you come here to eat my vodka?" he did not address to anyone personally, but he shouted with a howl, barely moving his tongue, "bastards, go from here!"

The guests were initially frightened, but when they recovered, they became excited, especially the elderly males, the fathers of families whose wives helped to cook on the table. They were against such behavior, if you are drunk or not drunk; you have to be polite, if you are not polite, then you get a blow to the face.

The situation was calmed down by Eustace. He told Anatoly, "Well, what are you worried about, Anatoly, now everyone will go, and we'll help you."

He together with me took Tolly to the kitchen and I gave him more vodka, and Tolly passed out for a while, then took next glass and died again, then come to life again, in a word, he was in the sweet world of dope.

As I could, I reassured the guests, explaining in a nutshell that Anatoly was having a hard time surviving the death of his father, he is tired now, but he will have rested, everything will be fine, you do not have to be offended, it's not a life or death matter. With the vodka, such explanations were accepted, people ate, drank, and then they added more vodka, and again, and ones more, in short without him the people had sat for an hour and a half and went home pleased, almost forgetting this incident.

I was sitting in the kitchen and was looking at my daughter, who wiped plates, and on the disheveled head of my unconscious husband, which lay on the table, and then I was drinking a half-warmed tea from muddy tap water and was thinking about my own.

Georgiy Ulchenko

Mentally, I was sorting out the milestones of my life; again and again, I was leafed over the pages of fate with the registrations of the life's failures that had haunted me for almost sixty years.

Now when I have lived most of my life, I had been knowing one thing, there is happiness and misfortune in everybody's life, and each of them are distributed evenly, you need only to be able to put up with misfortune, turning it into good for yourself, then you can enjoy those crumbs of happiness that are scattered anywhere and do not always make themselves felt.

"Nelly, how is your father there?" I asked my daughter quietly.

"I had dragged him to the sofa, he's asleep already," the daughter answered with carefree voice. It also seemed true happiness to her the small breaks between drunken scandals, hospitals, in which was treated took turns her father and mother, and her fights against her own husband. "Tell me what's new in the Book Review."

"You know, they printed a new prize crossword," I said. "Let's try to solve it now while you're here, because they gave only ten days for some reason, not two weeks as usual."

For a second it seemed to me that there was no old Yegor, there was no funeral, there were not the last ten years, and we were happy again and just now got an apartment. However, behind the wall, the old Yegor's widow began to cough, and I was covered again by a muddy wave, I began to feel sick because of what had happened, and most importantly, how it had happened. In spite of my hatred of this whole tribe, I considered myself a decent woman, worthy of every respect, and somewhere even sublime.

"Although not, we'll be making a crossword puzzle later, you go to a grandmother and find out how she is there; all the same they lived together for more than fifty years." I offered my daughter make, in my opinion, a generous gesture although I would not be able to console my mother-in-law for any money.

My mother-in-law, Mrs. Anna Buchenko, in pre-revolutionary times came from a well-to-do family, and she early learned her superiority in wealth before others, as well as she felt the respectful attitude of her surrounding because of prosperity too. Now she could not get out of the sense of self-importance in half a century after all their wealth was swept away by the rampant proletariat. She was a small, plump woman, round and soft in every places, for which her husband Yegor loved her, but an iron rod sat inside her, she had a strong spirit that did not allow Anna to bend because of difficulties of life before and now, when she lost part of her life with the death of her husband.

"Grandma, how are you feeling?" asked Nelly, entering the room, which was narrow and long like a school pencil-box.

This room, like the whole apartment, was, in fact, a complete misunderstanding. When moving from Germany to this city, my husband and I had been waiting for the queue for an apartment, and we had been renting a corner in a private house in a working village from a lonely woman who worked in the management of the plant. Her parents died when she was only seventeen, and she provided herself with a comfortable existence, renting out rooms in her big house.

We lived in the rent rooms for about two years, until it was the queue to get our housing. However, in that time the fate again had made its turning and brings us a new test. Anatoly was proposed in the housing commission to choose from two places for life; in one place was the large "Stalin" apartment downtown with high ceilings, but it had only two rooms. Although the area of this two-room apartment exceeded in one and a half times area of a three-room apartment in new buildings, Anatoly refused. He chose the second option, this apartment in a military town on the outskirts of the city.

"Well, it was wrong option," shuddered me, "A murrain on you! He did not consult and did not talk with me, immediately took and agreed to move into this squalor."

The living area of this three-room apartment was like a small two-room apartment! The slag-block walls did not retain heat into it, so in short winters I froze in an apartment in any corner of it, except for the room where old Anna was sitting now.

In my room, the sun appeared only for a few minutes at the end of a summer day, when the sun went around the house and had time to glance through the window before disappearing behind the opposite house. The corners of the room was always damp and dark, the blurred fuzzy shadows of the trees, swaying outside the window, were walking by the walls; the shadows resembled the figures of people in waved dresses. At the wall, behind the books, which Nelly brought for years and for which there was not enough room in the cupboards, an elusive grig had been settling in last month. His monotonous song blurred the sounds of the night and made them strangely unrecognizable; this made me even more irritated. Over time, my temper became the same as this room; it became oppressed, uncertain, hypochondriac. The old phobias, which had passed in childhood, and those of them, which was accumulated in the process of life struggle, were added by new one, if I may say, someone on the top or bottom floor drilled the ceiling or floor trying to get to my room, then someone included in the basement a machine and its vibration threatened to destroy the whole house.

The son who sometimes came to see me on vacation did not hear anything, although I woke him up at night and forced him to listen during the day, he only laughed at my fears, though gently and without malice that I could not take offense at my insensible child. My son, unlike me and everyone else in our apartment, believed that both nature and life gave him enough to live happily and not suffer because of the neighbors having something more and better than he had. Although my son's optimism was incomprehensible to me, but it was I, who brought him up and gave him all of myself. I knew him both in moments of desperation and in moments of triumph, and I realized that he was not like us, and most important was that he does not want to be as we are. So, after seventeen he had been leaving me for learning and had still kept away from us, passing military service on the peripheries of an immense Union. Nevertheless, in this apartment my son also did not feel very well, so he had been spending whole days somewhere in the city, coming only to the night.

I listened to the intonation of the daughter and mother-in-law, whose voices were mumbling behind the wall, but I did not hear anything threatening for me, so I again plunged into half-sleep, remembering those short moments of happiness that had fallen to my share so rarely.

"Mom, I'm leaving, it's time," Nelly shouted from the corridor.

I suddenly became uncomfortable, as if my daughter was leaving me forever, and I asked, "Perhaps you will stay, why are you going home in the night?"

"No, I'll go through the center," answered daughter, "I need to look into 'Youth market', they promised to bring tulle. They work up to ten."

The occasion was clearly far-fetched; Helen found a reason not to stay in a house where there was still a smell of funerals and misfortune. Her father suddenly snorted in his sleep and turned over on the couch.

"All right, I'll go, otherwise I'll wake dad, you'll have to be cared for," Nelly said sympathetically, she kissed me on the cheek and went to the stairwell. I was standing at the door and listening to the descent of daughter down the stairs, and then I had heard the slam of the door of the porch and returned to the room.

"What's the matter, Gina, does Nelly went home already?" asked my husband in a very sober voice. He had already digested his dose of alcohol and was ready to receive a new one, but it was not urgent, so Anatoly was in good spirits and wanted to share this with his wife.

"Tolly, will you eat?" I asked instead of an answer. "I'll go to bed, I'm tired today."

"Do not worry, Gina, I'll find something to eat. You can go to rest, I want to read something, give me a book."

A rare case, when Anatoly could think more or less, I could not to lose, so I decided to use it. "Tolly, did you see how your father stained the mattress when he was dying?" I asked as sympathetically as I could. "I asked for a neighbor to bring a new mattress by car and gave him money, but the old one must be taken out now in the trash site, because it stinks, and your mother would not sleep in such stench."

Anatoly raised his eyebrows in amazement to show the hard work of his thought, but he could not think of anything specific.

"Listen, when did my father die?" he asked me cautiously, fearing to provoke my anger. He completely was not remembering the very event of death. However, I was calm, because I was solving my problem.

"Tolly, Dad died yesterday, today he was buried, you buried him yourself," I answered, strictly articulating the words. It was noticeable as in the extinct brain of an old drunkard some impulses break through with every my word, and he had remembered something about I said.

"There were some other people here, who they are?" he asked just in case, in the hope of hearing that he had been behaving well and had not offend anyone.

"Tolly, people were at a funeral feast, they have already left," I continued to articulate word after word. "Now you'll get up, take the mattress and take it to the trash site. Is it good?" I raised my voice at the last word.

Anatoly felt a threat in this intonation of his wife and with reel and nagging, began to put on old faded sports pants, in which he walked in home. He found the mattress in the mother's room, she looked at him frightenedly and did not recognized in him her little Tolly, who was so tender with his mother, always, listened to her, but now he is a real monster.

"This is her job," she made her usual conclusion about me; "she made him as he is."

At this time, Anatoly grabbed the mattress in his arms; backing away, he went to the door of the room.

"Tolly, you have seen off his father," she asked or just confirmed the fact. "Is there a place for me in the cemetery? Soon it'll be time for me."

Mother spoke with a tear in her voice, deafly as if for herself, but something in her tone for Tolly, who did not understand the meaning of what was said, suddenly brought him something native and familiar, loved since childhood.

"Ma, do not cry, do not rush there, nobody expect us there," Tolly replied the wrong thing, but got to the very point, because old Anna guessed how her husband died and did not want to repeat his fate.

While Anatoly was taking out the mattress, I collected from the pans what kind of food remained from the funeral feast, put out a bottle of port wine and went to look for a book for my husband. Surprisingly, for all his degradation Tolly still loved reading books, at least he kept the book in his hands and from time to time specified from me or his daughter some details that were not clear to him from the life of the characters. He read books in such rare moments, as now, when his soul and body were in balance with the volume and degree of drunk alcohol, and he had nothing to do in home.

I must say that I determined the tasks for my husband once and forever. The list included washing and ironing clothes, washing the floors, taking out the garbage, picking the groats before cooking and other similar activities, as well as the most responsible - going to the bazaar. Earlier, in prosperous time, it was his autonomous hike through the whole city from our outskirts to the Central Market, but now he walked under my supervision to the nearest market beyond the corner of the neighboring house. For all that, it was a risk, but I endured it because even in his condition Tolly knew better than my about the quality of potatoes, vegetables and fruits, and he could bargain not conceding to the most zealous sellers.

Tolly returned quickly, he always knew that his wife, when giving him responsible tasks, was able to express her gratitude appropriately. It has been so since I realized that my husband's illness is endless, and I had no other way out but to manage its current, so that it would benefit the family, that is, me, neither the daughter nor the son was not counted. Therefore, my son visited the "family nest" rarely, and the daughter, having gone to live with her husband, came to me alone but with husband infrequently. Nelly came to me only when I promised her "to give something", in good times, it was the deficit food from the buffet of the office of her father, and after his retirement, it was cash donatives from his colonel's pension, which was considerable by the standards of civilian life.

"Gina, leave me a book on the sofa, because I'll have dinner," Tolly said energetically, heading from the toilet to the kitchen.

"Wash your hands and take the bread," I ordered my husband. "What is the father, such is the daughter, both are sloven, when they are pissing, they do not want to wash their hands, assholes," I thought without spite and laid to bed. It was already late, and the day was unusually troublesome, so, despite my usual vigils for midnight with a book or crossword, I felt asleep quickly even not turned off the desk lamp on my bedside table.

Georgiy Ulchenko

Chapter 6. Living people with dead souls

People, according to the simplicity of their soul, have believed that life is the existence of intelligent human beings, more or less similar to us, and they guess that life as a phenomenon have the same meaning as the lives of one single individual. However, scientists argue that life is just a way of existence of protein bodies, and whether they have intelligence or not it has absolutely no significance. A tree with blossoms and leaves, a green grass on the lawn, a bumblebee, which is humming on the bright flower, the playing puppies of a domestic dog and an infusoria under the magnifying glass of a microscope, all this is a life that lives and develops. It conquers both grief and adversity, the machinations of cruel bearers of mind, and the own failures of the weak man, because each of the livings is mortal, but the life is eternal.

Before the winter I had time to rest after the funeral and was already accustomed to the fact that on the way from the room to the kitchen I was not meeting old Yegor, I did not have to give way to him in fear, to listen to his curses and damnation, to wipe the floor after his spitting and to choke on the fumes of smelly cigarettes.

Life got lighter tones, there appeared the energy in my movements again, and I forced my husband, holding him on the "low heating", to spend some repairs in the apartment, although in the winter it caused serious inconvenience. It is good that the neighbor opposite, accustomed to using our considerable subscription to the magazines, which were the most popular literary magazines of that time, did not refuse when necessary to move the cabinets and couches from place to place. By spring, the floor was mostly painted with brown oil paint, and the window bindings were somehow smeared with white-blue paint in half with age-old dust, which no one thought of washing off. As a result, the most glasses were covered with the colored stains almost a quarter, because Tolly's trembling hands did not allow him to lead the brush more accurately/

One day, taking out the garbage to the trash site Anatoly stopped at the corner of the house to smoke. I did not allow him to smoke at home, because only his deceased father could smoke without leaving the room, so Tolly always mixed business with pleasure and was accompanying his occasional exits out of home with cigarette breaks. Unexpectedly, something cold and wet poked into his leg, it was a small dog of the breed named a miniature pinscher and had hair on his body less than the hair on the head of a new recruit. The little dog was trembling and whimpering, it got settled to Tolly's boot to somehow escape the damp dank wind and puddles of icy water underfoot. Anatolia was accustomed to the local climate, winter was seemed him up soft, in the middle of February there was sometimes snow, more often it rained, sometimes the sun was shining, it warmed not very much, but so steady that the weather seemed him really vernal.

"But why this dog," thought Tolly, "is like a non-native, it is warm in the street, but she is cold."

He glanced around in search of the owners of the dog and even went beyond a far corner to the neighboring yard, but found no one who could claim the right to be the owner of this insignificant shaking thing. However, the dog kept following him, touching his legs, it jumped trying to reach and lick Tolly's hand, and there was nothing for him to do but bring it home.

Before opening the door, Anatoly hesitated, he thought about what would be with his wife, when she would have seen this dog, but he could not assess the consequences because of such an unconventional combination of circumstances. The strangeness of happening was caused by the living being, which was never been in their house, except for a week-long stay in Polar region of a shepherd puppy who fled to the street during a big party with numerous guests on the occasion of the Day of the Soviet Army. Anatoly decided that such a small dog will not be an obstacle and he entered the room to his wife.

"What? What had you brought, Tolly?" I asked stuttering from surprise and indignation.

My reaction seemed to Anatoly even stranger than the presence of the dog. However, suddenly I thought that it was the lost soul of the old Yegor, who came to me with the dog to remind me of himself constantly. I was frightened and already decided to order my husband to throw this misfortune out of the house, but a small black creature suddenly began to spin around my legs, desperately wagging its short tail and barking furiously.

"Shut up, you, button!" I said sternly, and these words made an unexpected action on the dog, it felt silent, pressed her tail and began to roll to me in a sideways manner.

"Look, Tolly, she is trained," I said with interest because I liked this obedience, it was in my spirit. Clearly, it was not part of Yegor; otherwise, the dog would not be so submissive.

"Your name will be the Button," I said her, "and now you go to the bathroom to wash your legs."

Here we had another surprise; The Button itself jumped into the tub, lifted her hind leg and waited for her to be washed.

"It seems that the hosts taught her," I decided, "but where did you get it, Tolly, maybe the owners was there?"

Tolly explained that the owners were not, he was looking for them, but I had severely ordered him, "When you go out into the street, look at the ads, maybe someone will look for them, but for now let her live with us."

Eventually, we agreed on that. The place for the Button was taken in the hallway near the cupboard for shoes, on which an old tube receiver stood, which had served Anatoly a broadcasting point, when he was still cared what was happening in the world.

Our apartment seemed to come to life. The Button ran from room to room, fondled all the inhabitants indiscriminately, and it was unifying us, who had forgotten, what normal communication is. Even the strained relations that existed between old Anna and me, not only softened, but also became quite human and unnecessarily did not strain us.

The Button loved to run after a small tennis ball. She clattered by the claws on the floor boards, slipping and falling on her side at the sharp turns, but jumped up and continued to run until she grabbed the ball with sharp teeth. Then she returned with a triumphant look of her funny muzzle and gave me the ball, so that everything would be repeated from the beginning. When she played too long, the Button began to bark loudly, but then immediately noticed in time, and she licked at me with guilt, because she immediately rated me as the leader of our little bevy.

The small dog reassured my soul, and I began to think about my life, which seemed to me a long prison term, although it was not a real imprisonment, but something like a voluntary imprisonment in a madhouse. Collecting on life different adversities and failures, I could not understand why I did not experience the fate of some generations of Soviet people who disappeared in the imprisonment or stayed there for long periods. I reasoned in such manner, that probably every wave of repression had a certain direction, when only a small part of the "accused" was destroyed, but the most of the repressed, who was represented consistently rich and kulaks, deviators and factionalists, military experts and cosmopolitans, doctors and others, regularly supplemented the countless hordes of the workers for nothing. If we take into account that the fate of the "accused" was shared by their families, friends, acquaintances and colleagues, it becomes clear that in this way a continuous flow of workers to the construction sites of socialism was created, otherwise they could not be lured into those places voluntarily.

However, who had fallen under the hot proletarian hand during the war against the enemies of the people, for example, as Nick my brother, carried alone their own cross and did not add their loved ones into the hellish maelstrom. Perhaps they had not fallen into the high-priority "List" of manpower or did not belong to the category, which is intended for recruitment, which would have been mobilized by the Chekist. They was something like additional burden for the "competent authorities", so they suffered themselves, but their near relatives were not touched until the next "List" came up, according to which they could become a free labor force.

"They could have to imprison me," I thought, stroking the bare abdomen of the dog. "Many times they could remember my brother, my father and grandfather, but somehow it did not happen. Perhaps, philosophers are right, life goes in strips, sometimes it is good stripe, but sometimes it is the bad strip. Damn this life, why the bad stripes are so wide, but the good ones are narrow at all?"

I threw the ball on the floor, and when the Button clawed the ball and ran away, sounded the doorbell. The postman came and brought a telegram from my son. He wrote that he got a vacation and would be from the Far East with his wife and daughter in a day, I needed to get ready urgently. The news was just wonderful. I felt that a good stripe lately had expanded too much. Pah! So as not to jinx it. I have not yet seen my granddaughter Alice; therefore, I was happy with the good news and anticipated the meeting with the impatience.

A day later my son called and said that on weather conditions their vehicle has landed to Perm instead of Moscow, so he will stay on the road for another day if he can get out of the Perm airport. They were able to reach our town not through Moscow, and they gave a detour of thousand kilometers, but they had come before nightfall. I met the dear guests myself, fed them, and placed them for the night as I could not have imagined, I had laid my son and daughter-in-law on my bed, next to her granddaughter on the camp-cot, and I laid down on the couch with my husband, which had not happened for ten years. True, I spent there only one night, and for the second one sent him to his mother to the sofa next to her bed.

I was filled with a joyful mood. The son, named after his grandfather Yegor, noticed for himself that her mother was unusually alive and in an elevated state of mind, and without due modesty attributed this state to the fact of his arrival to the parents' house.

The son stayed with us not too long, it was necessary to prepare for examinations for the Academy, and the relationship of the daughter-in-law with her mother-in-law strained him by hidden hostility. Once again, I was convinced that this hen is not a pair to my son. She is stupid, she does not read books, she does not solve crosswords, and she did not even think about cooking for them during vacation, that I had to stand by the stove. Where he took this hen?

Only for Tolly these nuances were invisible, he quickly became friends with his granddaughter, therefore he came to life and began less often to drink, he seemed refreshed and began to think better.

One day he brought his son to his parents' room, where his mother was half-sitting on the bed experiencing the death of her husband, he showed Yegor a glass standing on the cupboard. The glass, covered with a dry crust of bread, was empty.

"Look, son," Anatoly told his son in the most confidential tone, "we poured our grandfather to his wake, and he came and drank. The glass was full, and no one saw how dad came in, my mother was here all the time, but he came in and drank imperceptibly."

The foggy brain of Anatoly hardly perceived this unusual phenomenon, he was sincerely affected by the fact that even after death his father did not leave his favorite drink, he returned and drank, and Yegor Jr. thought in his own way.

"Probably the vodka was dried up," he decided. "It's a long time ago, or maybe he drank it and forgot about this, an old drunkard."

Yegor did not have respect for his father. He could not forgive him for his weakness for alcohol, or rather, he would forgive him for weakness, but he could not forgive the fact that he put the attachment to vodka above any other human attachments.

I correctly linked the changes in my husband with the appearance of my granddaughter and decided, by all means, to leave her at our house before the son's arrival to Academia in Moscow. However, this his bitch-wife did not want to stay with us in no case, and Yegor himself did not want to leave his daughter with us. Departure was already approaching, but I still could not persuade my son. He only agreed that he would accept the help of his mother if he had difficulties on arrival in Moscow. After their departure our apartment was emptied, Anatoly bowed his head and spent most of the time in alcoholic forgetfulness, and I in hard entered the familiar rut.

When Yegor Jr. was still in our home, I had a talk with my son about the old life and his paternal grandmother and grandfather, whom he knew well, and about my parents, about whom he knew almost nothing, about my youth, then the conversation turned into an evening of memories of my military youth. Son looked at me, I was telling briskly, in detail, in colors, with expressive intonations, and he probably thought in surprise that the best time of my life was the war.

In my personal misfortunes, I never forgot about my relatives, especially about my son Yegor, whom I saw rarely, missed him and was always glad of his rare visits. Since my son enrolled in the academy, I did my best to help him with anything, and when he asked me to shelter his wife and daughter while he was in the training camp of the academy before starting studies, I was happy to agree. Somehow I will survive the sullen character of the daughter-in-law, her blatant illiteracy, inability to support the conversation, because in our house there will be this small, smart creature, my son's daughter, my granddaughter.

The daughter-in-law had stayed with us for a month and went to Moscow, it was clear that my son had some disagreements in his family, and she could not afford to leave Yegor alone for a long time. This option suited me even more, because the granddaughter stayed with us until February, when the son could come for the winter holidays, anyway, now the granddaughter's life charge lit up everything around. Alice and the Button were rushing around after the ball, and the dog was stricken that she had a competitor, who took the ball, and attention its owners, but she never touched the baby, on the contrary, the girl tormented the dog, hugged and teased it. Peace and harmony have come in our family, but maybe it was only a respite?

I did not cherish any illusions about my husband, because I knew that alcohol in him overcame his love for his wife in due time, prohibited him from going on a trip to the women, repulsed the desire to meet friends, and this idyllic moment of love for my granddaughter will pass. But I wanted let this happen as late as possible, at least lasting until February, while his granddaughter was at home, and then in the spring, maybe something will change, I tried to deceive myself, not believing in my fairy tale.

With care for the granddaughter I had no enough time for crossword puzzles and reading, therefore I often entrusted my husband to take a walk with granddaughter, seeing that he was not going to run to the store with her, but was honestly walking for as long as he should, and after that he would come home and then get drunk, although he did this less often than usual. When I remained alone without my granddaughter and my husband, even the squeak of the bed of my mother-in-law who was tossing and turning behind the wall, did not irritate me, but acted reassuringly, because everything went as I had determined, and I did not have to strain my nerves because of Tolly, in addition, the granddaughter brought only joy into the house.

However, February was not slow to appear in all its winter beauty. This beauty was formidable and simply dirty, because the fierce winds carried the soil from the surrounding fields by the air, blew it into all the cracks, the dirt was carrying into the house with legs and in the folds of clothes. Frost at this time was so strong that the temperature had fallen below twenty degrees below zero and with the wind and dust, which was flogging the face with sharp gusts like wave of a whip the weather was generally incredible. We tried not to go out, and little Alice was not allowed to go out for a walk, but anyway, there was a draught in this accursed apartment, when the cold air moved from every corner, she had been caught a cold and was sitting at home with the shrouded neck examining pictures in children's books and in illustrated magazines.

Someone rang the doorbell.

"Whom does it carry in such a bad weather?" I was surprised and hurried up to open the door. Behind the door stood my son Yegor with a small bag in his hand, everything was covered in the soil, his face was red, but nose was white apparently frostbitten.

"Mom, I've come for a vacation," he said by lips, unruly due to the frost. "Have you not received the telegram?"

"Eh!" I said in surprise trying to figure out why there was no telegram, either the son lied, or the mail did not work, but I could not decide, which version is preference, and said: "Well, come in." It seemed to Yegor that the reception was match the weather, it was same cold and gloomy, but the true reason for my displeasure was not his arrival without a telegram, but the fact that the family idyll ended. This became clear right now, because I did not like to beat around the bush.

"Did you come for Alice?' I asked in displeasure, without looking at my son.

"Well, yes, we agreed on it before the holidays," the son replied, taking off and shaking off his coat, and meanwhile he was trying to understand what made his mother so upset, "you said me that you are old, it's hard for you to care little granddaughter, what is wrong in my words?"

I went into the room and crouched on the couch where Anatoly was sleeping, my eyes, contrary to custom, was filled with tears. For twenty years, Yegor did not see his mother tears, since I buried my mother.

"Ma, do not cry now, I'm not leaving today because I'll stay for ten days, you'll get used to it," my son reassured me.

"Don't care, son, I'm all right, but it's happened suddenly," I answered wearily, "but Alice is ill now, she has a sore throat."

Alice was hiding from the Button in my room at this time; she had heard the voices and had peered out cautiously.

"Daddy, Daddy has arrived," she screamed loud, but the voice had been lost and turned into a wheeze, and she was coughing, standing in front of her father.

Yegor raised his daughter in his arms, kissed her and carried her following the mother to the kitchen.

At the kitchen, we talked about the weather, about Alice's illness, about the son's progress in the Academy, about his sister, and finally reached his father.

"Your father became different on himself, as Alice appeared here," I said. "He plays with her, reads to her, goes for a walk, drinks less," I whispered, as if Alice could not hear this, sitting on her father's lap.

"Grandpa is good, he bought me a new ball," Alice climbed into the conversation, "we're playing together with the Button."

When hearing its name, from the corner a small pinscher dog appeared without a tail, black as pitch, with such short hair and a bare belly that it seemed to Yegor inappropriate in such a cold time.

"What kind of phenomenon is this?" he asked, surprised that, finally, some living creature appeared in the mother's house, "Mom, before now you could not stand dogs, where did you get it?"

I told the story of the appearance of the Button in our apartment, and Yegor acutely felt the impending old age in his parents, in which even to live together do not save us from loneliness. It was necessary to appear a dog right now so that it could violate all these rules and taboos, which for many years regulated the life in the parents' house, and along with it, the granddaughter settled here, with her spontaneity breaking the ice in relations between adults. Now he will take away Alice and deprive his mother of the last joy in life.

"Umm, what a bad luck," Yegor summed up his observations aloud. "I thought that Alice would be a burden to you, but you made friends with her, you became a real family."

"Yes, Yegor, son, she is as glorious as you once were," I said happily, "but she's much calmer, more judicious, she does not run like crazy and have not still broken anything, it's a very tidy girl, I love her!"

I gladly repeated the ending of the phrase and emphasized her care to personal hygiene. "We always talk with her about it," I continued, "she is interested in it and I explain her everything, she wants to know. She is clever baby and always wash her hands. On the contrary, you never asked me anything, you tried to find out it without myself. You ran around with the same wankers as you were, but she is a little girl and is always with us, she's open-minded and open-hearted, and with grandfather they are two friends at all."

"But my wife and I missed her," the son said, and began to talk to her, "Your mother and I missed your, but it is obtained that you're unwell."

Son was looking at me and saw that I in displeasure pursed my lips and turned away because he seemed to accuse me of the fact that his daughter was ill.

"Well, nothing," he continued and tried to put the conversation on a neutral subject, "you'll get well again, and in summer you'll go to a kindergarten in Moscow, like any children."

"Yeah, right now, in the kindergarten there are all the sicknesses," mother inserted her word, "at me you were sitting at home, but was still sick, and if I would have put you in kindergarten, I do not know what would have happened to you now."

Thus, the evening passed in conversation, then it was time to pack Alice to sleep, at that time Anatoly woke up, and he was very happy to see his son again, but he did not talk much, because he had supper with a good portion of wine and fell asleep again. My son and I stayed in the kitchen, and as usual, the conversation about the modern affairs had smoothly

Georgiy Ulchenko

turned into my monologue about my past.

At night, I had rose from my husband's couch and looked into my room. Son slept on my bed, stretching his arms at the seams, like a soldier in the close order. He snuffled quietly, and his chest under the blanket was moving almost imperceptibly. Opposite him, my granddaughter Alice slept curled up at the window on the folding bed. Between beds on the floor laid a children's book, which he probably read for her before going to bed.

The idyllic picture touched me so that for a second I imagined how we together live like a big family, everyone is healthy and happy, but right now I had heard in the kitchen the slaps of Tolly's bare feet, in addition, mother-in-law was tossing and turning behind the wall, and the idyll was scattered without a trace. "She hinder me," I thought about my mother-in-law, thought for the first time as concrete, as if I had already drawn up a plan for her removal from my life, but then I dismissed this idea as incompatible with the little oasis of family happiness that I had now in my room.

They say that one misfortune in life entails an even greater misfortune, and those mistakes that we make ourselves lead to even more sad consequences than the greatest misfortune. I was already convinced in this by the bitter experience of my own life, and it seemed to me that I had the most difficult fate among all people, because every worst thing was for me, only I made any mistakes, while others lived in clover and laughed at my suffering.

I wanted a bright stripe that came into our life, not to end, but circumstances would be compelled us to return to the old path, in which there is no light, no warmth, no hope. If the son will take away my granddaughter, this shaky happiness, in which I was for the last few months, will break into small pieces, then I will be alone again, Tolly will stupefy again, and he will drink in dirty way, the resentment and the hatred will be reigning in our home. I could not wait nothing good, because everything will only get worse after that.

"Maybe, something will change for the better, because hope is still alive, tomorrow everything can be different," I thought so, getting comfortable on a hard sofa. While the life is continuing, my tribulations is not ending, but on the other hand, life is good in itself; to walk, to breath, and to see everything around, as well as to hear the sounds of the world and to feel the heat and the cold, all these things are the moments of life and its colors, it's a gift of fate for such unhappy and deprived persons as I am.

Now, when my life has already turned into old age, I otherwise assessed everything happened to me in those days of the war. I would have made love with Volodya and would not be the prude with him; at least, I would be having something to remember. Because I had not too much pleasure with this Tolly. He did not have the male strength for me after his numerous women, and then the booze took away the remaining strength; therefore, I was a widow of the living husband. During the war, there were so many males around me, each would be yours, just beckon him. Nevertheless, I could not give up my honor and had remained untouched during the war, because I had been yearning painfully per my Volodya.

At that wartime, my organism, which had been undercut of the trials, lost its defensive powers, and for the first time in my life, I fell seriously ill. Being billeted near the marshes, which abounded in Byelorussia, I caught a cold initially and then contracted malaria. The acute crisis were shot down by doctors in the medical battalion, and I was recovering already in my photo laboratory and was subjected exhausting attacks of fever repeatedly. A young organism was hardened in sports training and competition and it overcame the disease, but for the memory of illness for life, I received chronic inflammation of the liver with all sorts of phobias, allergies and other misfortunes associated to it and inherited by my children.

When my son vacation was ending, the weather gradually calmed down, but Alice's illness did not pass. Yegor did not dare to take her with him, because in Moscow was even colder then here, around the city was sunny, dry and frosty, but within the capital there was special kind of climate, which was cloudy, chilly and dank, in short, unhealthy. To my immense joy, Yegor decided not to drag Alice with him while she was ill. Currently, she remained with us almost till the end of summer, and we will be together the whole half-year! This outcome suited me very much.

Yegor did not consult his wife about his daughter, it worried me, but I did not attach much importance to this, it was not a big deal for me, it was their business and I will not interfere. However, for myself I noted that my son and his wife do not live very well, because, in response to my attempts to start talking about his family life, Yegor kept silent or translated the conversation to another subject, and for the whole time he was here, his wife never called him on the phone. However, the joy due to the granddaughter, who remains with us, was so great that I did not want to think about anything bad things. The bright stripe continued, and it was great.

Meanwhile, Yegor came back to the Academy, and the days similar to each other like two drops of water were passing, its grayness was illumined by the barking of the Button and the chirping of Alice. After a certain time, the son had taken away his daughter to his house, and everything returned to the custom rut.

One day, as usual, I was laying in my room and sorting out the events of my ridiculous life. Yes, there have been successful moments for me too, when I could take my drunkard to my hands, let us say, when we were in

Georgiy Ulchenko

Germany. Frankly speaking, he did not stop drinking, but in general, I was able to perform the program. The bedroom set was purchased, its wardrobes and beds were standing all over the apartment in each room, the sideboard is full of porcelain and crystal, around us, there were the carpets that were given us by the queue in the military shop, and now the moth had almost killed these carpets. It seemed, I managed to do something thereat, but then, already here, in this southern dusty city, when the menopause and the diseases came, it became much more difficult. There were many problems with the apartment, and Tolly had quickly turned into an old ruin, in a word, not everything was so simple.

Unexpectedly the phone rang. I flinched and looked at the phone by a hateful gaze, because I did not like it when he was calling. It used to be associated with the military service of my husband, who was called at any time of day and night, but now some hooligans had been calling and saying that they got the wrong number, though they called in the night and obviously, they had no reasons to call. From time to time the neighbors called to say me that Tolly was lying again near the stop of the trolleybus in such a state that it was disgusting to approach him. However, in this moment, the phone kept ringing, and I rose from the bed and wandered to the console mirror, at which stood this ringing monster.

"Hello, who is this?" I began the conversation, "speak, please, I'm listening to you."

"Mom, it's me, hello," after a pause, the son Yegor answered, «are you alright, is everything normal?"

The son was clearly upset, otherwise, he would simply say "hello", as always, but would not ask if everything is normal.

"Yegor, why are you calling, do you need something?" I did not want to go around the bush and I asked my son directly, "how can I help you?"

"Mom, I will divorce from my wife," Yegor said directly too. "We do not live together anymore; I had left her and rented an apartment. I do not know what you think about it, but you do not have to persuade me to come back. I will not live with her."

"I will not try to persuade you," I answered without a second thought, "I knew that it would not be like this for a long time, but I do not understand why you thought so long."

"I did not think, I felt sorry for my daughter, I had been trying to somehow reinforce our marriage," Yegor explained. There was a note of tension in his voice; it was evident that he could not easily talk about it. He was silent for a while.

"And now," he went on more calmly, "it became clear to me that I cannot change her, let her try to live alone, she thinks that someone will rush at her. While she was living with me, the males swirled around her, and when I left, all of them turned away from her at once."

"Whom do you talk about?" I asked, "Did she have a lot of lovers?"

"There are not lovers, they have no idea about love," Yegor answered sadly, "yes, I heard about some fancy men, I do not know exactly, it's her business, I do not care anyway. Only I am sorry of Alice," he repeated again.

I also regretted that Alice would no longer be in our house, but the son was much more darling.

I sighed and advised my son, "You do not really worry about it; your alimony will give them the opportunity to live comfortably. But how will you live alone, will you not become a drunkard like your father?" I asked the most painful question.

"Come on, mother, I do not look like my father, you know," Yegor answered calmly, feeling the support of his mother. It was difficult to start this conversation, to report the main thing, and when it was done, the rest went by itself.

"I have the intelligence not to drink in vain and without measure," he continued, "I know the main thing that distinguishes me from my father."

"Well, what is it that distinguishes a son from his father?" I asked with a mockery in my voice, because I felt sorry for my husband, whom my own son does not respect and does not want to be like him.

"Ma, when I was only fourteen, we were in Germany then," he began to tell me his life experience, "then you were with Nelly in Saratov, father came home with a bottle and sat down to drink it in the kitchen absolutely alone. I was surprised, after all, I already had some drinking experience, and I was drinking in the company with my friends always for some reason, for fun and rest, but here he was alone like an owl and was drinking with himself without any reason, just to get drunk. I ask him, why you drink alone, in this case there is no joy but only muck. This is what he answered me, it's you, boy, still young, you do not understand high joy. There is nothing better thing than to drink vodka, and what about why I drink alone, because there is no one who interferes, I will get more vodka. Well, that's what impressed me so much that I had remembered his words for life. Here we are different, he drinks because he likes it, but on the contrary I obliged to drink for the company, but I never like it."

Son's monologue left in my soul an ambivalent feeling. On the one hand, it's good that the son will not go on the disastrous path of his father and will not turn into a lost drunkard. On the other hand, he sees too clearly everything, what I have tried to hide from children for years, and maybe knows about the role I played in my husband's failed life. I looked around, as if cowering under condemning glances, but there was no one in the room, except Anatoly, who slept on the sofa.

Somehow, I ended the conversation with my son, threw the phone in irritation, and went into the kitchen. On the way, I clung to the edge of the

Georgiy Ulchenko

gap in the floorboards by my slipper and nearly fell for my full height. Thank God, I was able to reach the wall and, bumping not so badly by my head, slid to the floor. The annoyance gripped me again, and I was especially angry about Tolly. While he was able to think more or less, he kept order in the house. He was repairing something, was dyeing the floors regularly, and was nailing down any shelves and hangers; in short, the minimum things necessary for life were within his power. Now he lay like a log, ate, drank, slept and crapped. It is necessary to give him overclocking and to compel him fill up the cracks between the floorboards and paint the floors, before he will become completely stupid. No sooner said than done. I calculated what this process would lead to, because the main expense item here, as usual in recent years, is to buy booze. The reserve of money that I constantly kept in home, I hided from place to place, that will allow me to do repairs and to save money for a rainy day.

I waited until my husband woke up from sleep, put himself in some sort of order, and sat down at his table in the kitchen, where he was going to have dinner. He ate a little. On the table was a dessert plate with a handful of buckwheat porridge and a piece of boiled meat, beside it lay a bundle of green onions and a slice of black bread, neatly peeled from the crust. The bottle of port wine was already uncorked; a faceted glass was poured to the brim.

As soon as Tolly reached out and wanted to take the glass, I put my palm on the neck of the wine glass and pulled it towards me. He looked at me with surprise and tried to understand what was happening.

"What do you want, Gina, take your hand off," he mumbled, already realizing that his peace of mind was coming to an end, but still hoping that this gesture of his wife was just an accident, "let me eat, then you'll pester me."

"Wait, Tolly," I called him, as in the good old days, "I need to talk you while you're sane."

"I always sane," Tolly began to irritate because of the delay, "come on, and tell me, what's necessary."

"Well, did you see the cracks in the floor in the big room?" I have started to agitate the husband, "they are very deep and wide, you have to fill cracks by something, and then paint the floors."

"What kind of flooring, Gina?" Tolly worried, because such work was no longer possible to him, "I can't, we do not even have putty, and the paint from the last repair have dried up. Moreover, I had given my brushes the neighbor, but he had not returned brushes back until now."

"Do not worry, Tolly, I'll bring everything to need." I felt that my husband's resistance was small, and it was falling every minute while the craving for a drink increased, "we need the paints, the brushes, the diluent, I'll buy everything at the department store, and to seal the cracks we have a plasticine, two packs of it remained from Alice."

The mention of his beloved granddaughter completely deprived Anatoly of the strength to resist, so he suggested with unexpected enthusiasm, "Well, come on, I'll paint the flooring everywhere, and then the windows. Is it good?"

I began to doubt, rightly believing that Tolly could not match such a volume of work, but then decided that the main thing was to set a goal, which should be striven for, but if it did not work out, it would not be a problem; we would not get any worse from this. The main thing is to get involved in the struggle, as the great Lenin said, and I will help my husband to cope.

Oddly enough, the work captured Tolly, and he diligently was pushing the plasticine into the crevices between the withered floorboards, then he painted it, crawling by the floor in old sports pants, in which his son was engaged in physical culture in the military school. I tried to stay out of his sight, but strictly watched the working process. I divided in my mind the whole process into temporary pieces and always appeared in that time, when something went wrong or when the body of Tolly required to recharge.

I was spending the rest of the time in my usual works, alternating the solving of prize crosswords and the reading books and magazines with reflections on the fast flowing life and with memories of the past days. The black and white TV set, which my son bought for my birthday fifteen years ago, already worked very badly The antenna was room, and the television center was located on the opposite side of the house, the picture jumped and doubled, besides the channel switch was badly contoured, covering the image with dark and light stripes.

Watch this was impossible, so I, unlike most of the Soviet people, for whom the TV has long become a member of the family, lived in a world without hot news and intrusive TV communication. I knew from my unfortunate life that randomness was more often bad than good; therefore, I was not in a hurry to find out news, rightly believing that the lack of news is the good news in itself. The best thing for me was memories, when I was fingering the moments of my life, trying to guess where I did something wrong, why everything got upside down.

I was determining the moments of life when everything could be turned to one hundred and eighty degrees, I tried to imagine how life would have walked if there had not been next misfortune or misstep both from my side and from the side of my husband.

I regretted that my son did not become what I expected him to be. While he was studying at a military school, I vainly tried to make hint to my husband, who categorically forbade me to go into his military affairs that he would talk with his superiors in Moscow about the future location of our son's service. Still sitting in the aviation headquarters of the military district Lieutenant-Colonel Anatoly Buchenko could do much. In theory. However, in practice, he adhered to the patriarchal-communist idea of equality of opportunity in the Soviet Union and the need for everyone to self-punch his or her way in life. Consequently, his son had to go through all the stages of officer growth anywhere his Motherland would send him.

The company commander had been become the Motherland for the cadet Buchenko Yegor there, commander had been the petty officer in the penalty battalion, and he did not like the proud and unyielding descendant of the Cossack family. Well, Yegor did not understand many military stupidities, always stood up for his cadet friends, he could not stand the commander's impudence and rudeness and answered the same, because of which he regularly received the most painful punishment by the deprivation of leave into city. Nevertheless, he did not lose heart and did not give up, he never bended his head to the commander, therefore, long before the graduation he was planned for the Pacific Fleet.

I had sensed that my son would go to serve in far edge, and I repeatedly got into conversation with my husband about finding the place for my son next by home, but Anatoly was inexorable. He was proud, that without any help, he went through his military life, and he wished the same fate for his son. In the end, let him serve, and then we'll see what comes out of him, then we would have decided how could we help him.

Frankly speaking, I had my own reasons to keep my son near me. If he would live with us in the apartment, then he could help me to guide the drinking husband, he would look for a father lying in a puddle somewhere in the town, and when I would want to teach Tolly as not to drink, then my son would protect me from possible rebuff. Even if the son did not live with us in the same apartment, but somewhere nearby, then I could always come to him to guest or to rest from the heavy daily struggle.

Who will tell me, how will I go to the Far East? I did not come to my hometown Moscow ever since we were transferred from Germany, but it was near our town, and what could I say about seven thousand kilometers to the Far East, it would take a week by train, what was just impossible to endure, or half a day by plane, on which I had never flown. I would never get there, it's better not to think about it. However, my son was sent to the very south to the shore of the Pacific Ocean and he got stuck there. Moreover, this asshole Tolly did not help him, he thought only about himself, and he was not a good father. If my children knew all that I had suffered from him during all the years of our life together, they would have hated him. But I was a good mother and saved my children from the abomination of the drunken life of their father, I believed in that they had grown with love and trust to their father, forgetting that the truth itself sooner or later emerges outward.

Therefore, Yegor said, that for a long time he knew that his father was a drunkard, but Nelly was silent although she knew everything, because she is older than her brother is. Of course, because of this, the children abandoned me; I had thought so while my husband tapping by his knees and elbows to the floor painted the floor with a brush. At first Yegor did not want to stay with me for anything and went to the military school, where, as he believed, he had all the chances to overcome the entrance examinations and to stay away from mother's guardianship.

And then the daughter, whom we had terminated the study at the university in Saratov to get extra square meters in the new apartment and was forced to live with us, went to live in the hostel of the enterprise, when my husband brought his parents from the Caucasus. Evidently, the longer my life lasted, the less joy I had from it. The children left my house, I had hoped that they would help me to build a life with them, but they lived each own life and only visited me sometimes, but once again they will not come, not to see their father's drunken face! I cannot say that I did not try to solve my family problem by civilized methods. One day, when it was already unbearable to endure this life, I decided to talk with my husband, trying to part with him in an amicable way. As usual, after a drunken spree, I made my claims to my husband, scolded him properly, and when he already thought that this was enough and the conversation was ended, I continued, "Well, Tolly, how much longer do I have to fight with you?" I strained my voice even more, although I already spoke with enough heightened tones, and my husband, immediately sensing something amiss, began to be worried. "It's time to solve something. I know you will not give up your vodka, so stay with her alone, I'm already tired, this life has bothered me. The children have walked out, your parents will be with you, and we could divorce, change the apartment and live separately."

"What are you saying, Gina? You decided to leave me?" Anatoly was indignant, because he did not imagine that he could be a hindrance to someone close to him, especially his wife. "How can I be alone, did you think? What can I do with my parents without you, we have lived together for a long, and after all, I love you, and you, Gina?"

Tolly's indignation was asleep, giving way to lethargy and pity for himself beloved. He began whining; complaining about life and asking me to change my decision, but seeing that I was standing unshakable on my decision, immediately went crazy and with foam at the mouth attacked me. "You're a bitch, you've got yourself a lover, you're leaving own husband for him," he yelled, grabbing me by the breasts.

I just got up from the chair and shoved him, as I could do from a young age. I pushed him by my hands hard into his chest, causing Tolly to be jumped over the sofa and to be flew into the wall. The luxurious fleece of the "Roses" carpet softened the blow, but it was still tangible. He moved his body to the edge of the sofa, sat down, dangling his legs, and without raising his eyes, began to mumble by deafly voice, "Do not you think that I'll let you go. We lived with you, and we will live. Nevertheless, if you want to leave, then you will not get an apartment. I will not give you to change an apartment. If you'll insist, I'll go to the cantonment service of the district and return the apartment back to the state, but you do not get anything. If you'll leave, I'll kill you with a knife."

Then Anatoly suddenly fell to his knees, crawled up to me, grabbed my legs and began to wail, "To whom did you exchange me, damned woman? Come back, I'll forgive you everything, do not throw me alone, I will be lost without you! Stay home, I will do everything that you say. I'll throw the drinking, I promise, but do not leave me!"

I was taken aback by this pressure. For a long time I did not see in my husband the signs of life's passions, he was some sort of sun-dried fish, he was always indifferent to everything and could only shout at the playing Button when she began to bark, and even then, he shouted without excitement, completely indifferently. Now there was such pressure, such passion! Well, I ceded to him in that time, and now I'm reaping the fruits of my indecisiveness.

About this I thought, listening to the scrape of the brush behind the wall. Secretly, I did not admit even to myself that my decision to divorce and leave him was not final and strong, but only one more way to influence my husband. Otherwise, I would stand adamantly and, after all, would insist on my own. Then a new, unknown and frightening life would have begun. However, such life frightened me much more than this familiar and obvious drunkard. I could manage them, I even achieved some success in this path, for example, as now with this repair, but what I could do with my own lonely life, I did not know. I had not worked from the end of the war, and my pension was too low to provide my life. Yes, in secret, I wanted to save everything, as it is, so everything remained as before. There's no one to blame, and there's no reason for it, when everything goes according to plan, and then we would see. I didn't want to think farther, because we are not ageless. Now it was possible to repay debt to his mother for my years that were ruined by her son.

"She will suffer from me," I thought. "He will know what it's like to live with such a monster, he'll be even worse than his father."

The shocks of the soul gradually subsided, and the monotonous the days passed one after the other as usual. I continued to wage a grueling struggle both against my husband's drunkenness, and against the attempts of a decrepit mother-in-law to intercept my influence on her son. In the rare breaks between the combats, I still dreamed that over time, my youngest son Yegor will move closer to us, and his new wife would not prevent me to be next to my son.

Then there came a spring, amicable and sunny, which we had not had in a long time. Yegor came to us; he spent in our home for a few days after he had finished settling his affairs with admission to the adjuncture at the military university. He told us about a beautiful view, which revealed from the windows of airplane to the gardens, that surrounded our city on the other side of the river. While the plane circled above the gardens, performing the approach to landing, in the porthole was seen a sea of flowering trees, covered with white, pink, blue and yellow flowers. It seemed that the plane was flying over clouds of flowers!

My soul did not respond this comparison either by the uplifting of the spirit or by the pacification, because in the half-light of the room, most of the day hidden from the sun, the spring spirit was not smelled. Nevertheless, I envied my son, who for a young cause can still genuinely admire by the simple natural things. One thing, with which I could agree, that the spring had some sort of magical power that set in motion feelings and desires, seemingly already asleep for all time, awakened new, previously hidden vitality, even refreshed the memory and cleared the brain. Even my husband Anatoly in this spring waked up for a while from sleep, freshened, became less likely to drink, took up some additional household chores, in short, was completely different.

Then, unfortunately, my son Yegor appeared. One day, the son and father were going to go down the ravine, where the railway was passing along the bottom, to collect in the bushes a young wild garlic, which probably was brought there from the surrounding garden plots. While walking, they talked about how grandfather had died. Yegor Jr., was not even informed about his death, and later I did not talk him about it, and he could not talk to his grandmother Yegor, but there was no one else to ask. Outdoors, the curtain in father's mind slightly lowered, he talked reasonably, remembered all about how they lived, and Yegor asked him to tell how his grandfather died.

Father began to tell his son how it was. He struggled hard to come into the storerooms of his memory through the tangle of damaged nerve cells, gradually building a logical chain of events. No matter how difficult it was, he got to that point, when I left the room where we were watching television, and then everybody heard a yell and the fall of grandfather's body. When father of the younger Yegor and his grandmother had run out into the corridor, the old Yegor was already lying in a pool of blood, and I was standing on the other side of the old man and turned on the light in the corridor.

Anatoly stopped talking and fell silent. It seemed to him strange that at the same time with his father in the corridor was his wife, and then he had fallen. Maybe, she helped him to fall when she left the room. How did she do it? Just she pushed, and he died? Too simple, though, it's possible. Tolly

Georgiy Ulchenko

hardly remembered the details, and now he began to worry due to sudden insight, so the thoughts mingled, revealing just the one, which as a sharp blade tormented his mind, "She killed him!"

The father and the son terminated to pick the wild garlic and hurried home, or rather, the father was hurrying, but the son walked behind him, to watch him on the railway and crossing the highway. At home, my husband already had seriously excited by his discovery, and he immediately came into my room.

Yegor did not hear what we were talking about behind closed door, voices were hearing at high tones, but this was not new to Yegor, because my husband and I abused regularly, desperately and for any reason. Recently, when the reasons and occasion for quarrels noticeably was decreased, we swore less often, but life did not stop, did it?

Anatoly was bouncing of furious, and was rushing back and forth, then waved his hand and went to the kitchen, where he had a bottle of port wine. Half an hour later he was already deadly drunk, lying on the table with his head and sleeping. Yegor picked up his father under his armpits and dragged him to the sofa. He awoke for a moment and looked for me with dull eyes and not finding me, he shook his fist to the emptiness and said, "Bitch, you killed my father, bastard!"

Yegor put his father on the couch, and he immediately snored. The son went to my room, closed the door tightly and looked at me. However, I lay on the bed as if nothing had happened and read the magazine.

"Mother, what you were with father not sharing here?" asked the son.

"Nothing, everything is fine, "I answered indifferently, "it's all because he have not drunk enough today, because when he have not done it, he imagine all the nightmares. Was he already drunk?"

"How do you know?" son was surprised by my insight, "I put him on the sofa."

"I do not need to know nothing," I replied unconcernedly, "everything is as usual. Today he have not drunk enough, then tomorrow he'll drink more, he cannot find the golden mean, because of this he always roughhouse. Maybe, he could be sent for compulsory treatment, do you think? Do you know how this may be done?"

"This may be done simply, but would you like to do it?"

"What is mean 'but', look at him, he would have slaughtered everyone here before you know it. When he drinks in the kitchen, I'm afraid to come there. Once, he threw himself at me with a knife, no less!"

"Well, listen," the son began to explain, "You first need to tell the police that he is rioting. He will be taken to the prison, and then they will do an expertise and make a decision that he is a chronic alcoholic, and he must be sent for compulsory treatment. Then the case will be referred to the court, and the court decides whether to send it for treatment or not.

"And what, it is impossible without militia in any way?"

"It is possible without the police, but there is a snag here. If you want to do this, the doctor can diagnose him, but the father must go to the doctor by himself, and then he must go to the treatment by himself too. That is, he must do this voluntarily, but with the police it mean forcibly."

I laughed skeptical at the low chances to assess of voluntary treatment, "You see, I can be done nothing with him. Let him drink, even let him will fill his maw fully, damn it!"

I took the book and began to read again. Yegor paused, assessing whether to ask additional questions, but he decided not telling something, because I was out of humor and did not want to speak. Well, that's my business. A couple of days later he was already traveling back to the Far East, leaving his parents with their disassembly.

I saw my husband's condition, who directly accused me of killing his father, and could not concentrate in any way to master the situation. To explain him that it happened by accident was pointless, to admit in something was even more stupid, to stand on the fact that nothing was happened would be led to further increase suspicions up to his full confidence.

There were few options and everyone was the losing one. I had the last argument, which Anatoly always applied himself, and it was an alcohol. I decided that only the wine could drown out my husband suspicions, and most importantly, it would erase gradually from his memory any mention of my role in the death of his father.

The stores of alcohol in the house came to an end, it was necessary to replenish them urgently. I did it and took the wine stronger to intoxicate husband quicker and more effective. In addition, for three days of drinking Tolly already did not remember where it all started. He communicated with me in short breaks from one drunken oblivion to another as if nothing had happened. He could not remember the thought that dawned on him, and he did not want to. Without these nonsenses, it was calmer and easier to live.

One thing prevented me to rule him, because the disconnected brain could not properly control the body, and Tolly several times fell to the floor, clinging his foot to the rug or the other leg, and one day he had hit with his hip so much, that his leg became blue, swollen and did not allow him to walk alone. I hardly was lifting my husband out of bed to take him to the toilet or eat in the kitchen, my back and hands suffered too, because after each transition I had to rub my hands for a long time and to stay in bed while the pain in my back would pass.

Georgiy Ulchenko

Chapter 7. On the way of madness

Meanwhile, life gradually was taking away my years from me. Winter, summer, autumn, and spring, every season flashed before my eyes, and it seemed me that the Earth received acceleration and was spinning ten times faster. The most difficult for me was to survive the day from morning till night because every day seemed like an eternity. Filled with empty everyday affairs and petty events, the unchanging and identical days of my life were indistinguishable, so the very next day I could not say definitely about anything, was it yesterday, a month ago, or even several years ago.

Whatever it was, the day ended, and I suddenly found out that another month had passed and soon a new year would come, and then, perhaps, something will change, suddenly in life there will be some interest, the gray routine will be replaced by holidays. I loved to dream about to go out somewhere, taking my husband with me, who would suddenly wake up from a drunken madness, and we together would do some useful work, which could be doing by the old people. After all, we still had the strength, sixty-five is not a deep old age, and we would still be able to make small additions to our pension without too much effort. For example, they had wrote in the newspaper that somewhere in the forests near Arkhangelsk elderly people were being recruited to collect mushrooms. They would live in the forest dwelling and would have a food, so they would just pick up the mushrooms to the barrel throughout the summer, is it really so difficult?

Anything is good, but we have one snag, because Tolly could not be hauled anywhere. He was the very bad worker. He was not be able to take out the garbage as it should be, because sometimes he could unload it somewhere before the entrance, and then people had come and complain. No, it is necessary to sit at home and dream about a trip, it's still better than somewhere along the way to lose a husband and with him to lose his pension. Colonel, who won the war against Nazi, had relatively large pension, therefore everyone in our family had enough to live, and it remained else to give something my daughter, and to add some money once in two or three years for my youngest son, who was solving his personal affairs and could not fit in life.

I received a small pension, a little more than minimum one due to the fact that I, too, was a participant in the war. What could I do if I did not have husband's pension? I was already thinking about to do some kind of entrepreneurial activity, like these co-ops, who were bred around with the beginning of perestroika. I would buy myself some kind of "Snickers" or "Mars" on the wholesale market and sat on a busy trail near the trolleybus ring, eventually, I would earn myself five-ten rubles a day. Good addition to my pension!

However, everything rested again on the fact that I needed to look after Tolly. He, the scoundrel, though dulled himself over the years, but he had animal reflexes and he always wanted to slip away somewhere, it happened that he stole money and ran for a bottle, in other time, he just went to smoke, but then had run away in an unknown direction. I also remembered such a case, when he, wearing slippers and torn tricot, was found in the noshery on the other side of the highway, you see, he wanted to drink a glass of wine. This was with me, with my vigilance and knowledge of all his habits, but if I would leave him under the care of someone else, then it needed to wait for trouble.

One day in late spring, I asked my neighbor, an elderly woman of my age, to look after my household, husband and mother-in-law who was already approaching ninety years. The neighbor, by the way, never believed me that my husband could not be kept in my hands so that he did not drink. She always liked Tolly. She saw him rarely, so she did not see him in very drunk kind, and when he was returning home dressed decently, with a noble gray hair in a Cossack forelock, lean and slender, she always thought that this Frau from Germany was very lucky, that she have a good husband. She always thought, what does she want from him, is she equal to him? She lived herself without husband half a lifetime, would you have known what it means to grow old alone!

We agreed with a neighbor that she would stay with my relatives for an hour while I was driving to a library, which was in the nearby quarter one mile from the house. I needed to get the missed issue of the magazine "The Change", which for some reason the postman did not bring to me last month and the continuation of the detective-love novel of the foreign author was printed in it. In short, it was necessary to fill the gap before the next issue of the magazine would be brought.

I turned relatively quickly as I promised. I went forth and back by courtyards, the library did not hold me long because the staff was kind and mobile in it. However, at home everything was the opposite.

On the porch of the entrance, I met my frightened neighbor, who did not even have time to get dressed; she jumped out as she was, although it was still cool outside.

"Dear, what happened to Tolly?" I asked her with worry, "why did you leave them alone, his mother may wake up, and she will open the gas suddenly?"

"Do not think that they will do something bad to themselves," neighbor interrupted me indignantly, "do you want to know what they had been going to do with me?"

"What was happened, why you ran away from them?"

"Do not you know your hubby?" the neighbor said continuing to boil. "His mother left the room saw me in the kitchen and without a word speaking rushed to her son and woke him. What did she say to him, I do not know, but he burst into the kitchen with a hammer in his hands, waved at me over my head, and almost killed me kept shouting that I am a thief, he expelled me away, and I had to run out of harm's way. Well, I'm standing here and waiting for you that they do not run away from home, these psychos. You have been right, Eugenia, forgive me, I never believed you that your husband becomes such a beast when he is drunk, he comprehend nothing!"

"Well, nothing, neighbor, everything will pass, you just do not tell anyone what you saw, it's not necessary, okay?" I said and confidently looked into the neighbor's eyes. I saw there that the whole house would know today about this case, and why a house but the whole neighborhood would!

"Yes, it was a wrong decision to call out you, forgive me, please, you'd better go home or you'll catch a cold," I said and hurried home after carrying out the next-door neighbor.

Nevertheless, at home, strangely enough, everything was calm. Tolly was asleep, the furniture was standing still, there were no broken dishes, the floor with the ceiling did not change. I went into mother-in-law's room. She was sitting on the bed, leaning her hands on the mattress and looking stupidly at the wall in front of her. Long years of sitting lifestyle did their job, Mrs. Anna became heavy and swelled, with growth less than one and a half meters she weighed more than two hundred and twenty five pounds.

"Mom, what happened to you, why did you expel the neighbor?" I asked cautiously, trying not to raise my voice very much.

"Are you talking about that terrible woman who wanted to rob us?" indifferent asked my mother-in-law, barely turning her head in my direction.

I could not stand such a disregard for myself.

"You mind telling me what you think about yourselves, Mrs. Anna?" I turned into the scream, "I left a woman here for you not to do anything, but you made a scandal, you almost killed the neighbor and expelled her out, now the whole city will be discussing it for a month!"

"Well, what else have we done?" old Anna replied with a grin, "Something seemed to Tolly when he was sleeping, and he was naughty a little. Now ask him and he will not remember. So you do not make any noise, otherwise he will wake up and it is not known, what he will think this time."

"You, you ..." I gasped for such insolence, "you still mock me, and you threaten me? You know that you will not live for a long time, you will follow your Yegor!"

I was dumbfounded by my confession that I tried to hide even from myself. However, let her be afraid, it is even more interesting, now the advantage would certainly be on my side, and this ugly old woman would no longer spoil my nerves with her presence.

However, Mrs. Anna did not seem to understand the meaning of my words. She silently looked into the wall, and when, after a long pause, I turned to go, quietly said, "Your neighbor said that I ordered Tolly to kick her out, didn't she?"

There was contempt in her voice, she spoke legibly and clear and not at all worried.

"I will say Tolly, and he will strike you with a hammer on the head," she said and straighten out, looking me straight in the eyes, "Do not threaten me, Gina, you better worry about yourself."

I was frightened of this change in my mother-in-law, I was excited not so much the words spoken by her that affected me, but the tone, in which I felt superiority and knowledge of something that was beyond my power. Control of the situation went away from me again, and the consequences of this will be unpredictable. It was necessary to do something urgently, so as not to lose face completely.

"But you will not have time to do anything," I found, "while you're running to Tolly and explain to him what you need, I will do with you anything I want."

Having already mastered myself and calmed down, I continued, "I advise you to stay out of my sight when you leave the room. As soon as I see you in the corridor or in the kitchen, at any moment I can do with you what I did with your old husband. You'll go to the other world to meet him."

The old woman looked at me and realized that I was not joking. If I said, then I'll do it.

Apparently, she thought that this Gina the bitch had ruined her Yegor, it was then necessary to say the doctor that she did it, but now what to do. Nobody can say to the police, because nothing has happened yet, but Tolly will not believe her, he forbade his mother to complain about her daughter-in-law.

Anna's face felled, she sniffed and began to fear and feel sorry for herself. Years did not allow her to fight at full strength, and God did not give her to die in natural way, evidently, she would still have to suffer.

Now, when I won a convincing victory, I calmly left the room shutting the door tightly. Let them know who the hostess is in the house. Everything had to be the way I said, and if someone would contradict it then payback would wait for her. Like for Yegor. Everyone will go after him!

I walked past the sleeping husband, picked up the hammer lying next to the sofa, tried it on his head, as if I wanted to hit, smiled silently at my inner thoughts and went to my room to hide the hammer in the corner behind the cupboard where was the stocks of cereals, canned food, flour and sugar. He would not look for him here, he could not understand. Let now the mother-in-law will invent up any other variant with other tool. It will be necessary to hide chisels and screwdrivers to reduce the risk of using them. There are still knives in the kitchen, but if you would hide them, how would you prepare food?

No, another method is needed to avoid the influence of the mother on the son, it's probably easier not to let them meet at all, this will be a guarantee against such troubles as it was with a neighbor recently. Lately, Tolly increasingly came to his mother's room, what would he do there? Several times, as if by accident, I looked into the room where they had gathered, well, and what I saw there, they were sitting like two chumps, and did not talk to each other, they just sat and were silent. Maybe they were communicating in a telepathic way, and they did not need words, they passed their thoughts to each other. Then they didn't need to assemble, because thoughts can be transmitted to any distance anywhere. Probably, their thoughts are so short that they do not fly far.

All these questions bored my agitated brain, and I could not calm down for a long, but in my head, there was yet no consistent strategy of behavior towards my household members. I delved in my memory remembering the well-known variants that brought positive results in the struggle for power in the house, but similar remedies did not come to my mind.

However, with the old woman it was necessary to decide something. Now son Yegor with his new wife had finally settled in Ukraine, he was teaching in the military school in Kiev, maybe I would be able to invite him here. The Soviet Union has collapsed; Ukraine is already an independent state abroad, why should the son live abroad from his mother? Certainly, grandmother takes a place that had to be given to her grandson. It means that the grandmother was superfluous.

As if in response to my thoughts, I heard the door of Anna's room opened, and she shuffled into the toilet. I cautiously rose from the bed, so it did not creak, and with the gait of a carnivorous beast crept to the corner in the corridor and froze in anticipation. I heard a sound of draining water, and the old woman was coming back. "Well, bitch, you cannot wash your hands," I just had thought about it, and my mother-in-law already stood in front of my nose.

"Oh, fuck! Get it now!" I breathed out and shoved the old woman to the chest. However, either the previous thought about unwashed hands did not allow me to concentrate, or my mother-in-law was lower than I expected, but the push came out more sluggish, as if tangentially. The old woman backed away on her tremble legs and did not fall backwards, but only hit against the opposite wall. Leaning against the wall and breathing heavily, she looked at me with horror.

"Gina, what are you doing to me, you fool," she exhaled out, barely breathing, "You can kill me like that!"

"Because I want to kill you, old witch," I nodded in the affirmative, "I promised you that you will not live for a long, you'll follow Yegor!"

"How so, Gina? It's not humanly, you cannot do this, I'll tell the police about you!

I listened to whether my husband had woken up, and laughed evilly to the face of my mother-in-law.

"I just do what I promised. There is no place for you in this house. Better, of course, that you'll die your own death, but if it does not work out, then I will help you to die."

"But you are not a God to control my life," Anna said when recovered from the shock. "Tolly will wake up, and I'll tell him everything, he will not forgive you for this!"

"Your Tolly is half corpse now, how can he deal with me," I answered with a smile of superiority, "but if you'll complain on me, then you just speed up your end, you know me. You can live, for now."

With these words, I pushed out my mother-in-law off my way and went to the kitchen. There I suddenly felt a chill and felt sick, as if I had taken a smell of the fresh blood.

"Why I do it like some kind of beast," I thought. "It's a sin to wish a death to person, and even greater sin is to kill him. It was happened accidentally with old Yegor, why should I dirty my hands of this old woman?"

I sat in the kitchen trying to figure out what would prevail in me the natural purity of thoughts and the fear of sin or the desire to get rid of an annoying relative. Gradually I had calmed down and solved, let will be as is, and the life will prompt what to do. It's for the best, that the mother-in-law was very scared. Now she would look around ten times before leaving the room. I just needed not let Tolly go to his mother so that she will not say unnecessary things. How to do it, I know well, from this day it is necessary to increase the dose, then the husband will have no time to communicate with his mother, he will just drink and sleep, I should do one necessary thing to choose the proportions correctly in order not to harm myself and, in general, not to overdo it. Everything is good in moderation. Today the measure was this to fill Tolly with alcohol so that he was passing by the door to the mother's room and he did not have a desire to come in. To make it so that my mother-in-law did not appear in the kitchen when her son was there, I took care of it when I scared the old woman by my threats.

After putting my husband to sleep after another binge, marked by an obviously increased amount of wine, which only pleased Tolly, I went shopping. Well, how much time did a cheerful elderly woman need to get around the grocery, wine-vodka and dairy stores and to go to the market around the corner of the house? It'll only take a minute, but when I returned there was an ambulance near the porch, and on the threshold of the entrance I met a neighbor from the opposite apartment who asked me, "What happened here, Mrs. Eugenia? Who needed the ambulance?"

I gasped at the premonition and did not notice how I flew up to the second floor, burst into the apartment and stopped in confusion. The doctors were right in front of the entrance; they surrounded someone in a large room. Well, why I told 'someone'? Certainly, it was Tolly, who was crawling in the middle of the room with foam at his mouth, and he was howling by insane voice.

Somehow, the doctors managed to seat him on a chair, although, according to their confession, it was not easy to do it. In the frail body of the old colonel, under the influence of the delirium tremens, some powerful forces had arisen, he was scolding and was fighting back, was biting the hands of his opponents and was cussing out, in a word, he resisted so that three healthy men could hardly cope with it. Nevertheless, the iron grip of strong hands and a timely injection brought him to life. He looked around the audience with a stupefied look and found familiar faces of his mother and wife, and then he calmed down and pitifully asked to let him go.

An ambulance doctor, probably a shift supervisor, briefly interrogated me and the patient's mother to clarify the diagnosis 'the delirium tremens', and after confirming my assumptions, he suggested that I send my husband to the psychiatric ward of the district military hospital, to which Tolly was attached and which was five minutes from home.

While I was thinking, it's good for me or bad, Tolly at the level of the instinct of self-preservation immediately reacted to the signal about the threat to him from the doctors. He again was growling like an animal, was shouting that he would not go anywhere, and then he rushed to the nearest paramedic and sank his teeth into his hand. They tore him off together with a hard disengagement of teeth of a tablespoon. The shift supervisor gave him one more injection, after which Tolly fell silent, and they put him on the sofa.

When everyone calmed down, the doctor suggested, "Mrs. Eugenia, now your husband will sleep for twenty minutes. During this time, we will take him to the hospital and will arrange him as a chronic alcoholic with the delirium tremens, and we will leave him there until full recovery. They will put him in order, relieve the fever, and try to get him out of alcohol dependence, and then you can talk about treatment for alcoholism. We just need your consent, and the rest we will do ourselves.

I even got dizzy from what he said. For the first time in many years, it became possible at least for a few days to free myself from constant dependence, to get out of prison to freedom. Yes, it was not I, who was the supervisor of my husband, but he kept me in the jail. I was like a chain dog that runs around the yard and barks uselessly, but now freedom is shining on the horizon, but who knows what the true price of freedom is?

"Tell me, doctor," I asked cautiously, "they will treat my husband in the hospital now. Will they treat him for alcoholism too? Or not?"

"Of course, not, because alcoholism is treated in a special clinic, they do not have such a department in the hospital. Well, for you it will be easy. Write an application addressed to the head of the hospital, and already on this basis, they will send him to the clinic."

From what the doctor said, I nearly felt sick. After all, if Tolly would find out that I sent him to a psychiatric hospital, and then wrote to force him into compulsory treatment, then he will return home and surely kill me. There is only one hope left.

"Will he not drink after the treatment?" I asked, not believing myself. "Well, when he will be treating in the clinic, will they had him to turn away from alcohol forever?"

The doctor looked at me inquisitively, shook his head and replied, "Of the one hundred and fifty alcoholics after the treatment only one drunkard ceases to drink. The rest almost immediately begin to drink, someone can refrain from drinking for one year or two, but they also cannot stand it. Treatment is ineffective. Well, at least you can relax from such performances."

He nodded toward Tolly, who was lying on the sofa with head down and arms outstretched, and snuffled in his sleep. Foam did not come from his mouth, but his face was cyanotic, unhealthy, through the light gray hair, there was an erythema on the scalp, and the inflated vein pulsed around his neck. I wanted to help my husband roll over, but the doctor stopped me.

"Let him lie down for the time being. When there will be vomiting, you cannot help him if he is lying on his back. In this position, he will dirty the blanket, and you just will wash it, but your husband will remain alive. Well, what do you have decided about hospital?"

"No, I will not let my son go to the madhouse," old Anna intervened in the conversation, "you are a bitch, you decided to put Tolly in custody?"

"What are you talking about, Mom," I said politely, but emphatically, "if he gets worse, what will we do then?"

"I will not let him go, that's all," my mother-in-law said, "you just want get rid of him!"

"Well, Ladies, you will decide among yourselves, but it's time for me to go," said the doctor, shaking his head. "Here is a certificate, everything is written here, you can cause the ambulance directly from the military hospital, you will just read a diagnosis to them, and they will decide whom to send."

The doctor sat down at the table, wrote a few words on the letterhead, left the paper on the table and went out with the brigade. I was realizing that the last hope to change the situation went out, but I was afraid of the consequences of such a step.

Tolly was drinking not under compulsion, but because he wanted it. If I would stand in his way, he would be able to sweep me off the face of the earth as a hindrance, because I had seen how he dragged strong men, and he'll cope me in two ticks.

The doctors left, and then old Anna hid in her room. I sat down wearily at the table and began to read the diagnosis, which the doctor wrote in certificate. His handwriting was illegible, like by every doctor, and I had read with difficulties something like 'alcoholic degeneration with psychopathic symptoms in stage III.' Especially I was amazed by the word 'degeneration'.

In my distant childhood, they always called mentally retarded and worthless children as degenerates, but here it concerned my husband. Can it be true, that everything has gone too far? I didn't know what kind of stage was this, the third one. Is it the initial stage or is it already final? Moreover, what I could expect from this degenerate now when he would wake up?

At the same time, I was seized with anger at this nasty old woman mother-in-law, who did not allow my husband to be sent for treatment. I did not remember already that I hesitated with the decision, that I was scared to become the judge of my husband, I remembered only one thing, and this bitch prevented me at the most crucial moment, perhaps when my future fate was being decided.

I jumped from my chair and ran around the room.

"Well, what can I do," I thought, trying to calm myself down, "now I just call the hospital and send him to the treatment, but why me? He will know everything, they will tell him that I took him to the hospital, but can they cure him? Hardly. When he will return, then my life will end. Moreover, this bitch will tell him about the conversation I had with the doctor, and then not anyone can say what will be. Well, I'll give her a bashing she not to snoop for me!"

With this thought, I rushed into room of my mother-in-law, engrossed with spiteful determination to do everything for this one, I could not find more offensive words to name my mother-in-law, I'll do for "this nobody" that she fell silent forever. Furious, I grabbed my terrified mother-in-law by the neck and began to shake it like a pear. The old woman's head was dangling from side to side, some hoarse sounds could be heard from the throat, and there was no fear in the eyes, only deadly longing.

I pulled the old woman's head closer to my face and hissed with superiority in her voice, "Now, Mrs. Anna, do I have the right to speak in this house or do you still think that I'm nobody here? Alternatively, do you want to drive me out of my house so that I do not disturb you and your son? Now I'll choke you, right here, and I won't ask your name, then we'll see who's in charge here!"

Shouting it all in my mother-in-law's face, I squeezed my fingers harder and harder, she could no longer breathe, her face turned blue, her eyes rolled out of her orbits and covered with a shroud like, as the person was already unconscious. Suddenly my attention was distracted by sounds coming from the next room. I loosened my grip and listened. So it was done, Tolly was vomited and he did it right on the bedspread, what a pig he is!

I threw the old woman to the bed and rushed into the hall. The picture was depressing. Tolly floundered in a puddle of vomit, trying to raise his head and crawl away. From this, he only rubbed the vile puddle along the veil, the carpet and the sofa. I gasped at the sharp stench, which at once filled the room, but overpowered myself, grabbed my husband by the armpits and pulled him with a jerk off the couch to the floor. Then I ran to the bathroom, wet a rag, took a scoop and a bucket, and on the way back I looked into the room of my mother-in-law. She was alive and had already climbed onto the bed, and now she was lying and rubbing her neck, on which the blue marks from my fingers appeared.

Well, she's alive now, it's okay, I didn't care about her. I tidied up the husband's sofa and around him, took off his shirt and singlet, wiped him from all sides and took the dirty rags to wash it. While I was washing, Tolly moved away from the stress caused by the fever and the vomit, but he could not get to his legs, but only got on all fours and crawled into the kitchen. The speed he could creep was insignificant, and by the time he when he crawled out around the corner, I had already rinsed the washing and carried it into the balcony to dry.

At the sight of creeping Tolly, I involuntarily got into the laughter. "The degenerate, well, what will you take from him," I thought. I laughed louder and louder and could not stop. The events of this day had severely struck for my nerves, and now with laughter this nervous tension was gradually leaving me.

Tolly heard my laughter and stopped in bewilderment, but he could not lift his head to see my face. He propped his face on his hand, leaning his elbow on the floor, and looked at me sideways, trying to understand why I was so much fun when he could not even stand on his feet. I laughed even louder and more desperately, looking at his upturned face with meaningless eyes that could not stop and concentrate on me.

From an inconvenient posture Tolly's hand fell, he collapsed to the floor and rolled under the hanger. I could not laugh any more, watching the tortures of my husband, I could just sob, and gradually my sobs turned into crying. I had beaten in hysterics, involuntarily sinking to the floor next to my husband, hugged him by the shoulders, pressed my face to her bare back and began to sob in a loud voice. I howled and screamed from yearning, from my own weakness and inability to change anything in this madhouse.

Under my weight, Anatoly initially suffered, subconsciously sympathizing with his wife, and then could not stand, turned, trying to get free of my weight. My mind was racked by the flood of emotions, so my husband's attempt to throw me off caused a new outburst of anger. I stopped crying and began to beat him with my fists on the back, on the head, on the sides, wherever I got, and the terrified Tolly screamed by the changed voice. I woke from a stupor, released my husband and sat down next to him breathing hardly.

"Well, why I have this trouble?" I asked not addressing anyone specifically, "you, everybody, have bored me to death, assholes, when will you die at last?"

"Both you and your mother torment me," I said directly to my husband, "each of you wants to lead me to the grave, but what will happen to you, do you thought about it? You are nobody and nothing without me, you cannot wipe your ass by yourself!"

Mentioning shit, I remembered that I was going to hang his underwear, and on the way back grab my husband and take him to the bathroom. So I did. I could do it easily with his underwear, but I was not able to drag my husband into the bathroom, I was weakened from the stress, and Tolly was absolutely none, could hardly move. I had to call for help to my mother-in-law.

She left the room, neither alive nor dead, but when she saw her son lying on the floor of the bathroom under his hanging underwear, she immediately turned to her daughter-in-law and shouted, "What did you make to my son again? You do not calm down; you want to bring everyone to the other world!"

"Come on, Mom, stop shouting," I said wearily, "help me to drag Tolly into the bathroom, he got dirty from all sides," I added, feeling the new nasty smell coming from my husband.

An hour later, when Tolly had been washed and changed clothes, and he was already sleeping soundly, I put myself in order and went into my mother-in-law's room.

"Anna, excuse me," I said, "that I did this to you, but you must understand me, because you had made me do. For the future, remember that you do not need to touch me, do not tell me anything, do not meddle with your proposals, then I will not touch you either. Do you agree?"

I spoke calmly and confidently, looking straight into my mother-in-law's eyes. She involuntarily shivered under this look, which did not bode well, and she had to agree.

"Besides, I do not want you to talk to my husband in my absence. If you want to communicate, you are welcome, but only when I hear what you are talking about."

"What do you think of yourself, you are like a warder in a prison?" The mother-in-law resented to such excessive demands. "He's my son, and we'll talk about anything and anywhere, and you could not forbid us to see each other."

"Mom, I do not forbid you to see each other," I continued as coolly as I could, "but you must not blurt out anything extra in the conversation, which will make Tolly to be worrying. You can see what he is, the doctor diagnosed a delirium tremens, and this is a kind of insanity. He can also do something bad for you, if you turn up at his arm, and you had called the doctor not in vain."

"He's ill, but what did you have wanted to do with me?" the mother-in-law has offended, "you don't seem to drink, but that means that you wanted to kill me wittingly?"

"Well, what did I want to do, and then I did;" I responded evasively, "now it does not matter. You know that you live in this world too long, it's time for you. And I'm happy to help you to go to the other world."

"What the bitch you are, Gina," the old woman was surprised. "How can you kill me, and your conscience will not gobble up you?"

"Nobody kills you, Mom," I answered with affectedly, "it seemed to you. Moreover, the fact that you have bruises on your neck, it's because of your son. He have started to provoke me this today and have led me to be ready to kill you. I repeat you once again, do not push me to extremes, and you will be fine. Have agreed?"

I made a move, as if I wanted to get close to my mother-in-law. She recoiled to the wall and nodded vigorously, agreeing to the demands of the daughter-in-law. She watched with horror my arms because they are so thick and fat along the entire length, may be they seem weak, but the hands give out strength, they are so sinewy and bony, if I'll grab, you will not escape.

"Well, it's good, Mom, that we understand each other, you can live while, but I'll make sure that such misfortune will never happen with Tolly."

I nodded to my mother-in-law with a meaningful look, which caused even greater fear in her mind, and left the room. I checked whether my husband was okay, but he was lying, covered with a blanket, that I saw only his face pale and haggard, with pointed features. "Like a corpse," I thought and decided to check if my husband was dead really.

I touched his forehead with my hand it was icy and wet. My hand slid under the blanket, skin around his chest was also cold, but my hand felt a heartbeat, equal and strong, like a perfectly healthy person had.

"Wow!" I said in anger, "anyone would have already suffered three heart attacks from this booze, but he does not care. His heart is healthy; he will live long with it like a grandmother, about hundred years."

From my touch, Anatoly opened his eyes, led them to the left, to the right, and then, finding me, calmed down, and fell asleep again. I went to my room, sat down on the bed, picked up the newspaper "Book Review", opened it on the page with a crossword puzzle, and tried to guess the next word, but nothing was coming to mind.

I thought about the events of the past day. I drove them away one by one until I caught the thought about from which everything began. I needed that the husband did not meet with his mother, for this I applied a method already tested in the past; I increased the dose of the alcohol to the point when he switched to the regime of complete alcoholic amnesia. He slept, ate, drank so much to go back to sleep, then he woke up again and drank, after which everything was repeated again.

Yes, now I could not wait from him any household chores, after this dose of alcohol his condition was very sluggish, his hangover forced him to undergo treatment, but after new dose of alcohol the mood did not rise, he just wanted to sleep, and nothing more. It happened when he got the calculated dose, but when I left home, for sure, he was taking too much, and this led to a fever. Therefore, I need to monitor the dose, and then there will be no need to protect him from communicating with his mother, it will simply be impossible to communicate with him.

I had laid my thoughts and conclusions on the shelves of my tired brain and fell asleep, forgetting to turn off the light and undress. I did not dream anything this night; I did not hear the husband walking in the next room, because he also slept through the night without ever reaching for a glass. I did not hear how my mother-in-law rolled over her bed in the next room, because events of that day did not allow her to sleep peacefully. In addition, I did not react to the normally annoying sounds of the night, the hooters of cars, the knocking on doors in the entrance, the cries of drunken men, the sirens of police cars and the rumble of a passing train.

I slept soundly and calmly, because I decided to go with my husband through every steps of his madness, but not to let him jump off the hook, on which I had held him firmly in recent years. Previously, he looked like a man, he did some work around the house and could go out into the street or go to the market to carry heavy weights, but now he had only one benefit, his pension, which was many times bigger than my pension or my daughter's salary. The homeland still loved with its army, and many veterans have a good pension, so I could sleep peacefully, when the pension come regularly. Money is money, without them it's no life!

The next morning, after revising my achievements, I was satisfied with the current alignment of forces. On the one side, there was an old intimidated woman who was approaching the nineteeth anniversary. Of course, she retained a clear mind and a serious character to this day, but this is more a disadvantage than a virtue, because she saw everything, understood everything correctly, and could not change something. I could say with certainty that her time was over.

On the other side, there was I, Eugenia, old woman, full of strength and energy in my seventy years. Clearly, I'm not young, I have not been healthy for a long time, but I can still twist everybody in this apartment into a sheep's horn. What, in fact, I now did, I brought order in the relationship with my mother-in-law and completely put my husband on a short alcoholic leash.

Finally, my husband Anatoly was in the middle of this layout of the force vectors, He was unconscious, simply and easily driven by a pre-calculated portion of wine. Now it had no practical use, but it was enough for me that he just did not interfere with my life and did not interfere me to deal with my daughter, when he always met her with his drunken squeals, and did not interfere me to talk with my son, although it was occasionally, but I wanted to talk without interference, at last, I wanted that he did not stop me from simply lying down and indulging in memories or dreams of a better life, since I did not have a happiness in real life.

Just now, my son called and said that he would come in a week that I needed to prepare. I started to fuss, began to estimate how to meet my son better, how much I had accumulated in my stash to give to my children, so as not to offend my younger son, and Nelly got enough. I had to go to the savings bank, get my husband's pension, after that I had to stock up the food for a week, because for longer than one week Yegor could not be together with his parents. Well, thanks for that!

A week later, the son came, kissed his mother, came to his grandmother to greet her, went into the room to his father, who only smiled at the familiar face in a half asleep and said, "Ah, little Yegor has arrived," and continued to snore.

After supper, having disassembled the things and having laid out gifts, the son as usual sat down near my bed to talk with me. We spoke freely, at ease jumping from one subject to another, not particularly loading each other with details. The son continued to serve in the Ukrainian army all at the same teaching position, but simultaneously moonlighted in a private company, he already got money, and this means he does not need my help. It's also good, the money will be save for me, and I could win something

Georgiy Ulchenko

for myself.

"What do you think, Yegor, can you fix this TV set?," I asked cautiously, pointing to an antediluvian black and white "box", standing in a corner on the unreliable legs. "The screen is big, but it almost stopped showing something. I asked my neighbor to help, but he did not manage, he says that everything was fallen off from it because of old age and he did not know where the spare parts to buy. A TV wizard did not even take money for the call, said that this TV set is older than a quarter of a century, so long they do not live!"

Yegor inspected the TV, reluctantly turned the power, twisted the handle of the channel switching drum, peered to the back of the printed circuit board from which someone had removed the protective cover a long time ago, and said, "No, Mom, it's really time to send it to the trash. Come on, I'll buy a new TV tomorrow, you will have a birthday present," he suggested.

For me, his proposal did not come as a surprise, because I knew my son, as I knew that he had a generous soul, and he would give to his mother everything he had. I did not need his money; the main thing was that he said it. I sat back on the pillow with satisfaction and told him, "It's good that you think to buy a new TV, I'll give you money tomorrow. In addition, be quiet, I do not need your money, I've saved money to buy the TV set. You will go with Nelly, she know, where the good shops are, buy a new import one, so that it does not break."

Soon, my son and I went to bed, and next morning Yegor and his sister went to the city center to a new store where every walls were covered with TV sets. They chose a good Japanese device, almost half the cost of which Yegor added to my money, and took home by taxi. However, it turned out that the indoor antenna, by which our Soviet semi-broken TV set was taking programs, in the decimeter range, where the most interesting programs were located, was weak for the "Jap". Yegor had to go through the whole city to the radio market and to take a Polish antenna, about which he heard a lot of good things, and he installed it on the balcony. After wandering around the nearby construction site and finding a wooden beam of the right length, Yegor set it on the railing of the balcony so that the antenna peered around the corner of the wall to the other side of the house. The telecentre was on the other side of the house, and without such cunning, the antenna would not catch the signal. Finally, in the late afternoon everything turned out well. Yegor set up the programs, and a "nationwide" viewing of the color broadcasting had begun which the "local population" could see only on a visit to neighbors, and then could see only me, because the rest part of the family did not go out of the apartment.

Yegor invited his grandmother to see a movie, too. She looked at me with apprehension and settled herself on a chair closer to the exit from the room. In addition, when loud voices and music from the TV had woken Tolly, he joined the audience, marveling at the quality of the picture and the bright colors. He did not ask where the TV came from, because it was clear to him, Yegor arrived and bought the device. The idea was simple, without tricks, and mainly, correct. I had been able to spend money on TV set and did not receive questions from Tolly, for example, why did I spend money on unnecessary things, and not on vodka, and the like. Everyone was in high spirits, because the opportunity to diversify leisure time, at least for the time of Yegor's stay, was a gift for everyone among the gray weekdays.

Then everyone went to his or her night shelters. Anatoly had supped and had drunk the glass of wine I had poured, and then fell to bed, and Yegor took his grandmother to her room and stayed with her for a few minutes. After a pause and settling herself more comfortably, old Anna complained to Yegor, "You see, Yegor, my grandson, how long have I been living, I have no forces anymore, it's hard for me to look after myself, I cannot leave the house, and I think it's time to die, but God does not give me the death."

"Well, what do you talking about, my grandmother," - answered Yegor airily, "you can live while alive, why do you hurry what is preordained? You have some years to a hundred years, live it and you will be the great long-liver."

"Ah, grandson, to live is not to set records," the old woman waved her arm. The fat in the decrepit skin rushed around the bones, wrapping it around, then the other way, and calmed down only when the old woman dropped her hand. This movement seemed him like a sign of deep old age, and he felt sorry for the old woman.

"Grandmother, they are not offending you here," he said. "They give you something to eat and to drink, they do not drive you out of the house, and you're dressed and shod. Well, what else do you need in old age? Live all together, communicate, no one interferes you to live, well, stretch your live for a century, and then we'll see."

"No, I probably cannot reach this age," sighed the old woman, remembering the threats of the daughter-in-law. "Do not think of me bad, when you will remember me."

"Of course, granny, I will remember, but now you must live."

Yegor caught a tone of the fatality in the words of the grandmother, but did not go into the details of local life, and did not want doing it. He knew that with such a selection of characters and destinies, their joint existence was not easy.

He noticed this every time he came to the parents' house and listened to the mothers' complaints about his father and the grandmother, but tried not to delve into the point, because during the week he could not figure it all,

Georgiy Ulchenko

but to stir the anthill and to run away it was not in his rules.

Nevertheless, the next day he still decided to talk with me.

"Listen to me, Mom, something is worried my grandmother about," he began from afar, "she is feeling blue for some reason, maybe he misses his grandfather."

"Nothing is that she miss him," I said skeptically, "they'll meet soon. Everything with her is normal, she is excruciated from idleness."

I spoke confidently, smoothly, it was clear that the answer to this question was deliberate in advance. However, Yegor did not hear the caring notes in my voice.

"She's quite old, you must regret her. She complains that she live in the world too long, it's time to rest, but God does not take her."

"What am I to help her, Lord Jesus Christ?" I retorted aggressively, "although who knows..."

In this time, I uncertainly waved my fingers through the air, as if figuring out how I could help. Yegor interpreted this gesture in his own way.

"You can be more kind to her, may be, you could watch the TV together in your room, because the grandmother sits in her room and completely stop moving."

"Yes, who forbids her," I said, "let her look, but she just does not want, she is such a person, everything is wrong for her. I was wrong for her all my life, I was wrong in relations with her son, and I was wrong when brought up my children. In general, it's her life and she would receive from it full measure."

The strange ending of my tirade touched Yegor; he did not understood what an old woman of almost a hundred years old should receive? Her very life today is a complete punishment, and what was in her young years, it's time to understand, forgive and forget.

"Yes, it's good for you to say, forgive her," I objected with resentment, "If you would have lived with them for at least six months, you would have understood what an inferno is it."

"Well, inferno or not inferno, but it was only you who chose such a life for yourself," he reasonably besieged me.

Then it was my turn to contradict my son.

"Well, son, how can you talk to your mother like that? I did not choose anything here, I always obeyed the circumstances, and everyone decided something for me. Now you dictate to me how to live with a grandmother. Now I know how to make it with them," I concluded sharply and paused meaningfully.

"Well, mother, you've become quite nervous," Yegor said. He did not understand my excitement. "Maybe I'm wrong about something, I'm sorry; I will not get into your business. I took the tickets for the day after tomorrow, I'll be about to leave you on the sly."

"Ah, so quickly, is it really a week had gone? I worried, either regretting the imminent separation or rejoicing of it. "Would you stay for another week because watermelons and melons will go soon, you would take these berries to your home. May be, you would move to our city, you can also serve in the Russian army, but you would live next door, everything would be more fun."

"Well, we also have melons and watermelons, Ukraine is not the Far East," answered the son, "but I'm not going to move here, at least while I'm serving. I took the oath of allegiance to Ukraine, now I will not serve in any other country." He paused and then continued, switching the conversation to another thing, "You better tell me what gift Nelly wants for her birthday? Maybe I should give her money, because I will not be at her birthday?"

"Yes, Yegor, you'll go to visit her tomorrow, in Saturday, she will be at home, and you'll agree there. Then you'll give my greetings for her husband."

Soon my son went to his home, but I was bothered by our conversation about his grandmother. I could not understand in any way, whether he suspects me of something concerning his grandmother or this is an accidental coincidence. Maybe, she told him something that he should not know about, but then our conversation could be dissimilar, not so peaceful. Nevertheless, old Anna complains that the Lord does not give her the death, so I needed to help her. That decided me!

I was not need to hurry with this, because nobody was pushing me, but to frolic while old Anna bent her head down of fear, and hubby was not recovered from drinking, I was not averse. I could not make out whether it was a game with my mother-in-law, or I became such an animal, which liked killing, or it was just a game, that is, it was happened not for real. The reality and the alleged actions mingled in my mind.

Sometimes it seemed to me that I had already done this, but I could not remember when my mother-in-law had been buried. Then I gingerly peered through the door to her room, and I was convinced that she was sitting in her place. Trying to understand myself, I became to dive in a paranoid state deeper and deeper. I could even express my secret thoughts loudly, because there was no one to catch me on it. At home, where every witnesses was incapacitated, nobody could touch me, but in public place, when the dead home environment had changed to live street, I suddenly changed, was sensible, reasoned and did not talk with myself.

Coming home, I again fell into a stupor, but not immediately and gradually, sometimes even noticing for myself how my perception of the surrounding reality was changing, and was frightened of it. There lived two entities in me, one of them was the "good me" as I defined it, and the other on the contrary was the "bad me".

At first, everything was clear with the "good me". This my side was dissuading me from unworthy actions, that is, I should not berate my mother-in-law, should not get my husband drunk, should not harm anyone including my mother-in-law. After the skirmishes with my mother-in-law, the "good me" made me worry about what I had done, even forced me to apologize to my mother-in-law, who was incredibly surprised at this moment. It was happening, when I poured wine to my husband measuring the right dose, at that time the "good me" always yanked out my hand, because of this I did not add to the desired level or overfilled, and sometimes I overturned the bottle, using "working liquid" for nothing.

"Bad me" was not much different in methods, but required me to do everything on the contrary. To strangle old Anna, to get my husband drunk to death, to make my daughter serve me for the rest of her life, such the modest desires the "bad me" possessed. I did not have to wait for special sophistication from the "bad me", so in time I refused her services, but the "good me", on the contrary, was in my struggle a more useful ally.

The "good me" was seeing how I suffered and invented ways to get rid of my mother-in-law, then this my side began to tell me what and how to do. The help that came from the unexpected side was very useful. At this stage, split was passed, and I realized that the remorse in my struggle was an unnecessary luxury, which I got rid of on time. It was necessary to stop being afraid of myself, to be afraid of problems with my mind, not to watch my words and actions. It was a simple status, I was right about everything, but if anyone doubts, he is wrong always. It's time to move on to real actions. The "old trout" was doomed.

I noticed that there are people active and energetic, who all day long are busy, they are working, are doing things, are organizing and leading people. I was not such a person. Starting some business, for a while I was full of desire to implement it, and then I gradually was cooling and forgetting about my desire. I just loved to think everything over and to plan spending days on the bed and mentally going through all the stages of the upcoming case.

This time, it was as always. No matter how strong the desire to get rid of the mother-in-law was, the fear of punishment and the unpredictable consequences of the planned actions hampered my initiative, but in my thoughts, I never left this case without attention. Every free minute, and there were more than enough of them during the day, I mentally went back to how I would do THIS, I did not named the deliverance from mother-in-law as a murder, but mentally dubbed it as THIS.

"First of all," I reflected, lying on the bed and holding a newspaper that I could not begin to read, "everything should look true, as if an old hag died by natural death. No traces of crime of the fact that I was involved in

THIS should not remain. What did it mean no traces? What traces can there be? "

I got up from the bed excitedly, left the room, and went to the kitchen, looking around to find places where there might be some traces left. However, nothing in the familiar apartment opened up to me its new sides; I could not understand what traces I could leave when THIS would happened. Till I did not understand such an important thing, I was not able to take any action.

Passing the corridor, I threw a fleeting glance at the refrigerator. Around the handle on the white surface of the enamel was a fuzzy dirty spot, stained by unwashed hands. Here it is fingerprints! They should not be in any case; otherwise, they would immediately catch me. Where could I leave the prints? May be, it was necessary to put the question in another way, was there such a place in this house where my prints was absent?

I took a rag from under the bath and started to wipe the refrigerator. Gradually the stain was succumbing, especially when I added the paste for washing enamel. Satisfied the fact that the tracks can be removed easily, I continued to find every new spots on the white enamel and to wipe them off. When I got to the bottom of fridge, I suddenly stopped when saw the flaky paint near the refrigerator's leg. Yes, it was the same angle, on which old Yegor had fallen, I meant, had fallen with my help.

That time, I did not think about any covering the traces, and nobody had thought that I did it. How many years have passed since the old fart died? It's almost fifteen already. Where are the doctors now, who came that time? How many times over this time, an ambulance was called, and I did not watch none of them again. Hence, no one would compare the case of old Yegor with THIS case, which I would do.

How events happened at that time? I mechanically was rubbing the non-existent stain on the fridge and was remembering. I vividly imagined my husband, he was foolishly laughing at Stirlitz, who celebrated his Soviet holiday in underground, among the Nazi. This really hurt me, because he laughed at my favorite actor Tikhonov, but it hurt me much more when Tolly ordered me to cook dinner, although I watched the movie, too.

When I left the room, I was annoyed and angered, and I could not release these feelings outside me, they overwhelmed me and forced me to make abrupt movements. I walked with an elastic, impetuous step, and when I collided face to face with Yegor, I could neither back down nor miss him in a narrow corridor. Somehow or other, my heavy body would pushed him out of the way by my mass, and he would have fallen anyway, but the accumulated irritation and indignation, caused by the tactlessness of my husband, suddenly poured out on his father and I shoved him with all my strength.

How I shoved my father-in-law, I did not remember, but this moment was the most important and decisive. I remembered only the choking smell of fumes from his cheap tobacco and the specific smell of the old man.

"This terrible smell, it was coming from his breast," I thought, "because he's taller than me and I had just stuck my head in his chest, lower than his face. My mother-in-law is below me, as I am below the father-in-law. Thus, I cannot shove it so that she gets on the refrigerator."

Further, coming back again and again to the time I was coming out from the corner, I began to recall details that are even more significant. When I buried my nose in his chest, Yegor yelled with surprise with his bass, "Well, you muff, where you are going!"

I strained and shoved him from me. Yes, I pushed him namely in the stomach, lower the chest, so he bended in half, and his head got exactly there where it should be. If he had fallen by the full growth, he would certainly have missed, and nothing would have happened, but he did not miss and died. Occasion helped me, but now there should not be any eventualities when I would do THIS.

What significant things I had also remembered about that day? The time, which elapsed from the moment when everyone heard the screams and the rumble to the moment when everyone was come. I remembered that I had got around old Yegor, turn on the light, and just then old Anna appeared first. My position relative to the lying body was completely unrelated to what really happened, that is, it was not about me, he fell himself. There were witnesses that I have nothing to do with him.

I liked this conclusion and repeated it aloud, "I have nothing to do with him, and he himself fell!"

Repeating the phrase I liked, I patted the refrigerator and went to wash the rag. It seemed that everything was right. To do THIS and not to leave any traces, it was necessary to catch the mother-in-law so that she took the necessary position in the apartment space with relation to me and to the place where she was supposed to fall. After she would fall, I needed to take a completely different location, somewhere far away from my mother-in-law, so that the witnesses could establish it, but who would be the witnesses?

Here there was a snag again. Of the witnesses, there were only a dog Button and my husband Anatoly. Both are wordless creatures. It's true, the Button could bark and bite, but what my husband would do, I did not know. After all, sometimes some human traits woke up in him; he could talk with me by a couple of meaningful phrases, regularly read books and came to watch TV. What would he say to the doctors when they come for his mother?

However, I can do without witnesses. Tolly would sleep, and I would entice old Anna to his room and would beat her head against the sideboard. For her small growth, this is the most suitable option. In addition, the pedantic Germans tried hard to strengthen the legs of the sideboard and added a crossbeam, the corner of which happily protruded outward.

"I need to aim here," I decided, and then thought how I could lead my mother-in-law hither, if she was afraid to leave the room. She was sitting all day behind the closed door, and came out only when I went to bed after dinner, or when Tolly was in the kitchen late at night and early in the morning. No, she would not go itself; I need to come up with something that is natural and attractive not to cause suspicion.

Finally, the moment when THIS would happen was important. Must be not dark, but in gray, so that the twilight concealed the outlines of people and objects and hid my movements. In addition, twilight comes in the evening, when everyone was tired after a hard day of the old person, relaxed and lost their vigilance before going to bed. In the twilight, I could still discern the layout of the furniture in the room and the silhouettes of people, but in the dark, I would definitely miss my aim. Actually, I agreed to wait this moment. It's one thing to dream and even to plan THIS, but different thing was to do THIS, which could make me headaches for life.

I was able to wait. Quite recently, I alone with myself celebrated the golden wedding with my Tolly. No one congratulated me, but no one knew about it. The certificate of marriage was lying somewhere among the papers in the dresser cupboard, it was impossible to find anything. Children about the fact of registering their parents' marriage had the most general idea, no one showed them a certificate, but they did not ask.

I remembered well that the moment of marriage was joyful, but for half a century there was so much bitterness mixed with it, that I did not want to remember it. Moreover, my joy was mixed with a large share of doubts, which I fence out from me as best I could. Even when I came to the registrar's office, I felt that I was making an irreparable mistake. My Volodya stood before my eyes, when Tolly got taxi to me, when I signed in the modest office of the district registry office, and when we were sitting at the head of the table in the restaurant. Volodya image did not leave me, when we went to bed with Tolly, for the first time we did it openly in the mother's room, who on the wedding night of the young couple went to a cousin.

Thus, I met fifty years date of our marriage with Anatoly. I had forces and mind, there was some kind of prosperity in the house, but there is no happiness. Old age crept imperceptibly, now my happiness is to get rid of my hated mother-in-law, no matter what it would cost me. I just needed to wait a little, not years and decades, but quite a bit. Psychologically, I was not yet ready to do THIS myself, of my own free will, by my own hands.

But here's the trouble, I did not see the possibility to pull out old Anna from the room, I did not imagine what would make my mother-in-law to go out of her room into her son's room, where she had been a year before, because she did not walk there.

However, why I thought that she did not walk, if she exactly walked, and not one time. I liked this idea. I looked at the schedule of TV programs and found out that about seven pm the next episode of the film "My Second Mom" began.

I hastily had supper and fed my husband, and then I put him to sleep, turned on the TV and went to the room of my mother-in-law.

"Mrs. Anna, why are you sitting here in the dark?" I asked in a friendly voice, turning on the light.

"What do you want," muttered her mother-in-law, squinting at the light. "Nobody was inviting you here."

"I just remembered that Yegor Jr., when he left, told me to watch TV together. I'm still waiting, but you do not come. Well, I decided to invite you to watch TV."

My mother-in-law could not understand anything from the surprise. "Where did this bitch so learned to pretend," she thought, "she smiles and affectionately talks. Oh, she makes the bed gently, but there'll be rigidly to sleep." No, old Anna could not be confused by friendly words, she expected a dirty trick, but could not find an explanation from where to expect it, but the mention of her beloved grandson completely confused her.

"Well, if Yegor wanted to, and then let's go," she groaned, standing up from the bed.

I was studying the mother-in-law in the bright light of a chandelier, which was rarely lit here; mostly I used a table lamp. Anna's little face remained round and smooth, despite her advanced years. However, the figure was terrible. The influxes of fat all over the body, which with difficulty held by sagging flabby skin, shook and wagged with each movement; the width of the mother-in-law was almost the same as in height. Obesity and weakened muscles did not allow her to walk at a normal pace, Mrs. Anna walked like a duck, swaying from side to side, not leaning forward, as people usually do when walking, but leaning back to balance the weight of the voluminous abdomen.

My mother-in-law approached the door, not noticing that I carefully followed her by my gaze, she squeezed through the door not directly, nor sideways, but somehow half-turned, turned on the spot and reached to my room. Her son was asleep, the TV was already beginning the overture to the film, and I was pushing a chair from behind, so that my mother-in-law could sit comfortably.

We watched the movie in mutual silence. What my mother-in-law thought was not of interest to me, I was waiting for the right moment. Several times I got up, saying something like, "I go for a drink," and came back again. Before the last film frames had to end, when the final accords of music played, I quietly got up again, went out into the corridor and froze in the half-light, waiting for Mrs. Anna to come out.

Already the voice of the announcer announced when tomorrow they will show the next series again, and I heard the shuffling of slippers of mother-in-law. After waiting a moment, I took a step towards her and found myself face to face with my mother-in-law. To the left and to the right of me there were walls of the corridor, it was impossible to avoid me; old Anna could not move back, because she could not keep her balance, so she took two steps by inertia and froze with bent head, expecting the worst.

Her ears were plugged up from excitement, and like through the cotton she could hear my voice, "Mrs. Anna, what happened, already the film is over. But I did not see the end, what a pity."

My voice was cheerful, and my mother-in-law looked up in surprise. I did not have a smile on my face, and my eyes looked angry and menacing. The old woman was scared, she already regretted that she caught the bait of her daughter-in-law and agreed to leave her refuge. However, nothing happened this time.

I took a step towards my mother-in-law, lifted my arms bent at the elbows to the level of her breasts, as if trying to measure, then I walked around her and mentally with my eyes traced the line from her head to the leg of the sideboard.

I chuckled with satisfying and said, "Good night, Mother, do not forget, tomorrow at the same time will be the next episode."

Then I went to my room, and the old woman stood still for about five minutes near the door and could not understand what it was now. Presentiments told her that all this was not for the good, but the fact that she was watching the film with the daughter-in-law and moreover, this film itself with sentimental notes, brought her into a blissful mood. Such a diversity in her life had not been for a long time. "Let it be so," Mrs. Anna decided, "whatever she does to me, it does not give a damn, I has lived so much that it's not terrible to die, but to live like this, looking directly into the eyes of this thick-lipped fool, and every day watching a color TV, is a real life. As they say, see Rome and die! "

Then the old woman came to her room. Opening the door, she squinted at the bright light, because no one turned off the light when leaving. She automatically turned away from the rays beating in the face and saw the lighted corner of the fridge, near the foot of which the paint was broken. Mrs. Anna was numb with a terrible guess, "She also wants to finish me, like Yegor. She already tries on. Although, why she does it from another side? I think, it will not work in such manner." Embarrassed old woman went to bed. She lay without sleeping for a long time, but suddenly she saw Yegor in her dream. He entered the room noiselessly, not the way he had been stumbling the last few years, but with young and resilient motion, only his face was as old as hers was. He sat opposite her on the clamshell. He slept on it erenow, but Anna remembered exactly that the clamshell was removed immediately after his death.

"Well, Anna, my baby, I've got tired of waiting," Yegor began, stroking her hair gently, "I'm bored without you, I'm lonely. I called for my son, but he did not answer me."

"It is too early for him to go to us," Anna said resolutely to her husband, "but you can take me away even now. I'm also lonely without you, nothing pleases me, it's time for me to see you, but God does not give."

"You could ask Genie, she will help," Yegor suggested with meaning and disappeared.

Old Anna woke up and heard that her daughter-in-law was shouting in her sleep by the strange voice. "She have probably seen a bad dream again," she thought.

It's the end of the night, and everything became gray outside the window. It was too early to get up, but she will not be able to sleep, Anna knew this for sure. She waked up in the same way from time to time for about twenty years, when Yegor and she had come here, and she thought, lying on the bed, about her life. It made her laugh, because if she, during only one minute, would think about one year, then it would take more than an hour and a half! However, she had time until the morning, probably, three hours no less.

Then she began to remember how Yegor had looked in a dream. She remembered exactly that he was even older than when he died. After all, he was only seventy-nine then, he was still quite young, but in her dream, he had looked like she, just as old and wrinkled.

"I don't understand it, is it really he is getting older in the other world?" Anna thought, "Or it was just a dream? In fact, he precisely called for me; it means that the dream is a truth too. Why did he call for me? In the other side, if I would call for him, could he come back from the other world?" She grinned as if admitting all the stupidity of superstitions associated with dreams. Her soul got calm, yesterday's fears disappeared with the rays of the morning sun, and Mrs. Anna quietly fell asleep again.

This night in my room, I woke up, choking on my own cry. I saw in my dream the old Yegor, who accused me of all mortal sins, but he was some strange, youngish man like half a century ago, and what he did, I did not remember. Looking at the shining dawn outside the window, I remembered this dream again, trying to understand why this ghost came to me, but fell asleep again without the result.

I slept almost before dinner, and when I woke up, I completely forgot everything that was at night. I was again surrounded by enemies, my body was old, sick and battered, my thoughts, which was swirling in my head, was bad and even worse. I was ready to break anyone who would stay on my way, but no one came across. Tolly slept peacefully, having already taken a second dose, and his mother, out of harm's way, was not walking out her room.

To calm down a bit, I decided to go for a walk. This was also an uncommon case, because I had long been hesitant to leave the house without extreme need and exactly when I choose a certain time. In this case, I just was about to went outside, not checking whether my husband was asleep, what the grandmother was doing, whether all the cutting and stabbing items had been removed. Something was happening to me, but this new state did not bother me.

I got out of the entrance and went behind the houses along the highway to the exit from the city. To my right, there were the fields, in the distance the gardens could be seen, and workers on the left side of the road swarmed in the new building site. I walked slowly forward for half an hour, until I got to the suburban train stop. I sat down on the bench, as if waiting for my train, and silently, completely thoughtlessly watching what was happening around.

The children ran through the railway crossing, probably returning from school. The crow somewhere found a walnut and threw it from a great height, trying to split the shell. Homeless climbed into the trash can, and the cleaning lady drove him out. Now was coming the train, I need to decide something with my life...

I looked at the approaching train, estimated the distance to the rails and went to meet the train. The train slowed down, got out of the bend directly to the platform, and at that moment, the locomotive driver noticed an elderly woman who was walking directly to the wheels.

"Anna Karenina, fuck off, where are you going, bitch!" he shouted, turning the handle of the brakes sharply, "hey, mates, there hold her, do not let her on the rails!"

The guys who talked next to the bench did not hear the driver's call, but they noticed how the strange old woman went directly to the train, and rushed after her. The most deft and fastest of them managed to grab me by the blouse when the train was just two steps away. He jerked me on the run and fell to the ground, pulling me after him. When I had fell on him, he only gave a cry under the weight of my body.

Guys running to us lifted me up, joked about sex and about who wanted to rape whom, but the guy just was rubbing his elbow, which bruised in the fall. Over them the locomotive driver, who managed to stop his train just in this place, swore and shouted, "Hey, you, hand her over to the police, so that she'll not be wandering anywhere! Either, it is better to call a psychiatric hospital; a madhouse is waiting her for a long time!"

The driver continued to shout, already moving the train, but I sat on the ground among the guys around me and did not understand how did I get here, who were the young people around me, why is this blockhead shouting over my head? Nevertheless, after hearing serious words about the madhouse and the psychiatric hospital, I realized that it's bad for me. That is the result of my life; I lived with a psycho all my life and became myself like him.

With the help of the guys, I got to my feet and having said goodbye to them walked home. The walk was wonderful. Shattered knees and palms was sick, my head ached from a sharp jolt when I had fallen, the outward things before my eyes was some unstable and shaky, as if houses, trees, poles and passing cars were bent by a nonexistent wind. I didn't know, why did I go so far? I could not answer this question, but gradually, remembering the events of the previous day, I concluded that my mother-in-law was to blame for this state of mine. Yesterday I had to endure such a nervous test when I activated my plan, but I could not stand it and had broken. I decided that all this was due to nerves, so I went on the way to the pharmacy to buy a sedative.

At home, everything was quiet, as if I had not gone away. Only the dog Button jumped joyfully, inviting the hostess to walk outer, because the dog's patience is short. I had to go out again, but this time the dog did not allow me to doze, the Button was running around the yard with barking, stopping for a minute to do their own business, and then came back to me, jumping and rolling over in the air, then again run around a circle. On the bench between the porches sat my old acquaintances-neighbors who invited me to sit with them and talk. I approached and greeted them, but did not sit down.

"You, Gina, are never sitting with us, you are not talking, what's wrong?" asked me the most brisk old woman who knew me since we were moved into this house.

"It happened, girls, I'm busy now" I answered evasively, without going into details, "there's no time for me to sit with you."

"Well, you are busy of course, how I can forget," the neighbor remarked, resentful of such disdain, "but why Mrs. Anna does not come out, she used to like to sit with us."

"Yes, she is the bad interlocutor now," I laughed and asked my neighbor, "Well, tell me, how old are you?"

"Surely, older than you are," neighbor evaded the answer, feeling my dirty trick, but I insisted, and then she said, "well, I'm eighty-four already, but what?"

"But so that Mrs. Anna is more than ninety-three," I answered triumphantly, "she's a centenarian. Where should she take the strength to come out into the street?

It's good that she is able to take care of herself, otherwise it would be a disaster."

"Yes, old age is not joy, age is a serious matter," the old women said, nodding their heads knowingly. After listening to them for a minute, I shouted to the Button to go home, and proudly walked into the entrance. I knew that now behind my back these old women briskly condemned me, they say that this Frau appreciated them very cheaply, but who is she herself, why is she better than they are?

"I'm not better, but unhappy," I thought as I climbed the stairs, "they think I would not like to sit with them and to chat about that or about this?" Of course, I would gladly exchange news, discuss the last series of my favorite TV series, would wash the bones for everyone whomever I could hook. But how can you leave this restless tribe, who knows, what'll they make in next time?"

When approaching the porch, I already noticed the silhouette of my husband in the kitchen window, so I immediately came home, and I was just in time. Tolly stood in underpants and in a singlet near the gas stove and he was striking a match sharply on the box. I shoved him away from the stove so much; that he flopped into a chair and hit his head against the wall, and I immediately turned off the gas already was turned on. I was horrified catching the smell of accumulated gas in the air, quickly opened the window and ran into the room to ventilate there too.

The draft pulled out gas in an instant, and I returned to the kitchen to take the matches away from my husband. He had nothing in his hands, but his fingers were black with ashes, and burnt matches lay around him. I was relieved to take my breath and sank my back into the chair at the exit from the kitchen. Since Tolly quit smoking, there was always a matchbox on the windowsill near the stove, in which we stacked the burned matches after the burner was ignited. Thus, the cinder did not crumble around, and we could save new matches, using the burned matches again. Fortunately, drunk Tolly did not understand that he had taken the box with the burnt matches; otherwise, everything would have burned a clear flame now.

Such a loss of vigilance was unacceptable. I realized that I could not relax further. The procedure for using gas should be as follows, I myself will turn on one burner on the stove in the morning, after which everyone could use the fire, but no one would have the right to turn off the gas. I turned on and off the extra burners myself, and in the evening, when everyone ate, drank tea and went to bed, I turned off the gas myself, and not only on the stove, but on the pipe, and hid the key away from the sin.

At last, I needed to finish off old Anna, when it was not too late. What meant words "not too late", I imagined not very clear, but the second sign for today could be the last for me. Till nothing would have happened to me, I will have to escort these two for the final journey. Everything was already prepared to do THIS. I just need to practice a couple of times, that's all.

Georgiy Ulchenko

Chapter 8. The desperate assassin

Twilight was falling, the series «My Second Mother" began again, but old Anna did not appear. I looked out of the room. Husband read, lying on the sofa. The incident in the kitchen, oddly enough, brought him to life, and I commanded him, "Bring your mother to watch TV here."

We mutely watched TV again, and I went out of the room two or three times as it was many years ago, when old Yegor had died, and again Mrs. Anna and I met at the exit from the big room. I firmly took the old woman by the shoulders and, setting leg forward like a real fighter, abruptly lowered her to the floor near the corner of the cupboard. Mrs. Anna shook up with all her wide body, she did not feel pain and did not immediately understand what had happened to her, but I straightened out and said loudly, "Oh, Tolly, mom have fallen!"

He sat up on the sofa, staring in surprise at the strange scene, his mother was lying on the floor near the door, and his wife was standing next to the sideboard as if she had nothing to do with it. Indeed, if I had pushed my mother-in-law, I should have stood in the doorway, and she was from the opposite side. Therefore, he was sitting with a meaningless expression on his face, but I began to raise the old woman, and she screamed, waving her arms, "Son, she is it, why you did not see? This is she, snake in the grass!"

Mother's voice caused Tolly to be annoyed.

"Well, what are you, mother, always coming up about my wife, what do you want from her! Look, Gina lifts you up, she tries hard, probably, it is harder to do alone, but I cannot help her, because it's hard for me to stand on my feet. Do not shout to me now, otherwise I will drub you too."

The mother-in-law was silent overwhelmed by the reaction of her son. She mutely stood up with my help, glanced at me with hatred and disappeared into her room.

Pleased with the successful completion of a difficult day, I went to my room. Everything indicates that my plan is correct, and I am ready to fulfill THIS. However, there remained just one invisible barrier, which I had not yet been able to cross, because when you drew a picture of what you had planned to do, everything might look harmless and smooth. Otherwise I could imagine that one wrong move can lead me to prison, it is, at all, was for me at the level of a heart attack. No, I needed to wait, when the moment comes, I myself will feel that it has come.

Thus, we continued to watch our favorite series in the evenings. Occasionally I frightened the mother-in-law, being in her way after the end of the film, but did nothing. I even liked that I was not alone, that there was someone to discuss interesting episodes, there was a listener to whom you could express your thought about the heroes of the film, well, and everything was like in a movie theater. The mother-in-law was surprised at the change in the daughter-in-law, but she kept silent more and more sometimes inserting her word into the approval of the plot or the artist. She did not believe in positive change, and this respite given to her by fate could have ended from day to day. Mrs. Anna was just going to the cinema, without thinking about what else this gypsy scum would come up with tomorrow. Life went on, and these were not the worst days of her life.

At night, she heard a cry in the next room again. I screamed in my sleep, and my mother-in-law liked it. «Let her suffer," she thought, «her heavy sins put pressure on her, and she is howling. Lord, he sees everything, he will not give me offense, and he may be rein in Gina so as she not torment me."

After nights filled with nightmares, I couldn't come to my senses for a long time, for whole morning I had to gather my strength that to leave the room. I didn't want to see anyone, the world around me was some kind of ghostly, my body didn't listen well, and there was rising a blind irritation in my soul. It was turning out that I had no power over myself, these dreams would take the last my forces, but I still needed to do THIS.

Suddenly it dawned on me. Probably, fate protected me from the last step, not to cross the border, beyond which I would cease to be myself. However, why someone had to decide over me? I was able to understand what needed to be done and how, I know what the possible consequences of my actions are, and most importantly, I want to cross THIS line in order to test myself and to find out what I was capable of.

Having made a decision, I calmed down. I liked that I was once again embraced by the joyful rise of vital forces, there confidence appeared in my movements, and there balance and composure in my soul. As they say, everything has its time, but now it's time for the mother-in-law. From that day I did not have any nightmares, everything was clear, all relationships were clarified, and all pawns were placed on the board. I no longer trembled at the mention of how to do THIS. I decided that the Lord chose me to be his hand. Since he does not want to be polluted about an old woman, I'm ready to do it for him.

I had understood what my destination in life was. It was not for nothing that I suffered so much and endured, that I suffered enough with my husband and his relatives. The atonement had to come to give relief to my soul, tormented by a hard and ineffectual struggle. One had already received his atonement, but it happened so fleetingly, by chance, that I could not even truly appreciate and enjoy this moment. Now was the time of my triumph. I would execute God's judgment here on earth, without leaving my apartment.

The feeling of my greatness and equality to God overwhelmed me and was ready to spill out. I was no longer afraid that someone would notice something in me that would give out my intentions. I was above suspicion, for my mission was as high as that of the Lord. I felt like an athlete before the start, the muscles are tense, attention is exacerbated, and the body is concentrated on achieving the goal. It remained to sound the starting shot, and THIS will happen.

One of these days, as usual, everyone gathered in my room to watch a movie. Even Tolly came, son of a bitch, although he for a long time was not interested in this. I laid down on the bed more comfortably not to waste my energy, and began to watch movies. Nevertheless, the tension of the day made itself felt, and I dozed off. When I woke up, the series was already completed, and the mother-in-law was not in the room.

In desperation that I had missed such an opportune moment, I jumped out of bed and resolutely went to look for my victim. A light was on in the bathroom, water flowed. I looked into the crack and saw the mother-in-law who was washing herself in the bath, pouring water from a bowl. The water pressure in the water pipes at such a time of day was not enough to wash under the shower, so we always took water into the bowl. Such were the conditions of our life, but to struggle with them in order to try changing them somehow, it was not peculiar to me and to any of my relatives. However, the fact that the mother-in-law, as if nothing had happened, washes her, when I overslept my chance, it did not fit in my head.

I jerked the door on myself, jumped into the bathroom and shouted, "I'll kill you, bitch!" Mother-in-law dropped the bowl with surprise, and I grabbed it and hit her on the head with all my might. Mrs. Anna staggered, but remained standing on her feet, and then I raised an almost empty bowl and, pouring water over the walls, put it on my mother-in-law's head. She rolled her eyes under her forehead, turned pale and began slowly, leaning on the edges of the bath with her hands, to sink to her bottom, but I continued to hit her with the bowl again and again, as if nailing by a large hammer.

When the bowl was banged on the edge of the bath, I set it down and looked at my mother-in-law. That was left of the old woman floated in her own blood and brains, and her head without the top of her skull rolled over her shoulder. The water poured around, the stifling smell of blood and the ugly picture of the torn body made me shiver. I was gripped by animal fear through what I had done, and I wrapped my hands around my head, squeezed my hair so that they began to tear off from my head, and screamed in pain and despair.

I woke up because I screamed in a dream, and my husband and mother-in-law shook me for arms and legs so that I would wake up. It was just a dream. I shook my head, driving away the terrible vision, and looked around. Everyone was watching a movie that was not over yet, but frightened by my cries, started to leave.

«Okay, you can watch your movie," I said grudgingly, trying to see their reaction in the dark, «I had a dream, it has already passed."

"Yes, Gina," the husband agreed, "you began often to cry in a dream lately, you don't give me sleep. You are sick, or what?"

"Everything is normal, probably, it's stuffy in my room, how they heat it, as if it is already winter, but I'm afraid to air it, because it could blow me."

«You can ventilated it before bedtime," the mother-in-law timidly advised, «then you can breathe easier all night long. I know it."

«We'll see what's what," I replied businesslike, stopping the conversation on this topic, «what did I miss there while I slept?"

«Nothing interesting," Tolly shrugged. «Her daughter came to mother, and her groom met another. Mom tells her that you cannot marry him, but she balks."

«Everything is as always, the same things," I concluded, «let's see through to the end."

Then the movie show was held in mutual silence. After that, the movie was over, I was left alone and began to relive my dream. I thought that it was a warning came from heaven. It was impossible to do anything today but what the day is today? Oh, yes, tomorrow will be Nelly's birthday; I could give her a good gift!

I got up, opened the cupboard door, rummaged on the second shelf from the bottom, closer to the right wall, and took out the money set aside for the household. What is happened? One third of the month remained to the day, when I'll get a pension money, but the money was almost not spent. It is unclear, why I saved so much. I looked into my notes, which I had been writing since I knew that abundance in my house was not expected, and I had to count every penny in order somehow to maintain the well-being of my family. From the records I saw that we ate almost nothing this month, and in the past, too, especially at the end. I thought, recalling the events of the month, but could not understand why it happened. Well, okay, I could not eat because I was not up to that, but what did the others eat? Tolly was not in such a state to cook for himself, but what did the old hag eat?

I went to the kitchen, looked around the pots, peeked into the fridge and opened the freezer. Empty, it's very empty! Everything was eaten by bark beetles, but I did not detect. Tomorrow I'll have to carry full bags from the store. I took out a bag of breadcrumbs from a shelf that I had dried for a rainy day, took a glass of water and began to soak the rusk. The remains of my teeth could not even bite off the rusk, not something to chew. While it was soaking, I could suck some bread, it was also food.

I ate a little bit of a black rusk with water and went to the room. I was afraid to fall asleep again so that this terrible dream would not be repeated, so I took the first available magazine and began to read the story of some trendy author. It is clear that he was trendy, because he wrote detectives. These authors are as many as the dirt. Everyone author imagines that he has penetrated into the soul of a criminal and can decompose his psychology and put it to the different shelves, but if he would have tried to kill, I suppose, he could not because he don't have the guts!

However, this novel was reading easily, the author did not indulge with special frills, but he wrote in clear, intelligible language, explaining the details so that reader would not have to think out for the author what he or she wanted to say or do. I liked the heroes of the novel, especially the old duchess, who was pursued by an unknown criminal, killing all her relatives.

Carried away by reading, I did not notice how the small pointer on the clock passed after midnight. It remained to read some five or six pages, because I specially glanced at the end of issue to make sure that there would be no continuation. The end of the story I liked the most. It turns out that the duchess herself killed all her relatives, but they could not catch her. Such a cunning beast! It is clear, that from her I could take an example, but not watch scary dreams with some unreal content.

Could I, a woman of severe rules and good parenting, be able to break up a person's head to death? Of course not, because I was afraid of blood, and I had no such experience. I don't even know where to hit to kill. The heart is somewhere here, but it's not necessary to beat it, but to cut it with a knife, it's some kind of nonsense, and when you beat to the head, what kind of power do you need for the brain to fly out! No, it's not for me.

The sly duchess was able to furnish everything so that her victims themselves fell into the placed snares. However, it was so long ago, when many of today's methods of investigating crimes were simply unknown, even before Sherlock Holmes and Nat Pinkerton. Today, such things do not pass.

For example, the duchess lured his old cousin to the cellar with wine. He got very drunk and did not notice that someone opened taps in all barrels. He floundered in a sea of wine, lost his strength and choked. Then someone poured wine down the drain, and everyone thought that the cousin is just an old drunk who died by the drunkenness. Well, where my wineries were, where the barrels of wine were? I didn't know how it is possible, for the sake of some goat to let out so much valuable drink in the sewage system, this is big money after all!

Next case, closer to the subject. Her cousin wants to take possession of the duchess's husband, and she came up with a trap for her with such

Georgiy Ulchenko

thoroughness, spent so much money that duchess could just give her husband away, and don't bother much. She lured them both to a hotel on the ocean islands, paid a trip there for them, accommodation, meals; they were entertained there at her expense. Then they took a boat ride to the ocean, and the boat sank, and just then, the shark ate them, one by one. However, a boat is a yacht; it's worth a million dollars, why there were such expenses?

However, there wrote one relatively simple way to get rid of the annoying relative. The duchess refrigerated her nephew-hooligan in the freezer room along with her meat supplies. It's unknown, why did he come into this chamber? Because she sent him a note as if from his lover, who arranged for him a secret meeting in the freezer. Maybe, he wanted her so much that he froze his genitals and himself to the death at one. No, this was not a simple way. This freezer was expensive, but where could we find it? Only the oligarchs have such a freezer, but what ordinary people must do?

Nothing of this suited me. It is necessary to adhere to a previously developed plan, but not to spend time, because I have already matured for a decisive step, I just needed to get rid of the fears and took a step towards my release.

According to the established tradition, in recent years I did not go to my daughter, did not make any exceptions for her holidays, including her birthday. It was impossible to leave these imbeciles unattended, so I sat as attached to the house, my daughter came to me, and together we celebrated all our holidays. Now, when the circumstances could fundamentally change in the near future, I decided that nothing would happen if I'll leave them food and drinking for my husband, turn off the gas and go to my daughter for a couple of hours.

The road takes only fifteen minutes by the bus. I was surprised looking at the environs, flying outside the window. I remembered very well that there were some household yards, garages, small factories, but now everything was different. Now in their place stood new high-rise buildings, well-groomed courtyards around them were green, everywhere there was the free place and the purity.

«These people are knowing what a beautiful life is," I thought and envied the tenants of these houses, «on the contrary, we got a shit apartment during the Soviet regime, and we remained to live in shit having no well-kept yard, no roads, and no greenery."

They say that one colonel commanded the construction of our community, he was the head of the construction department and he had sold all the new pipes to the third party, for this money, he built a house outside the city, but for us he had buried the old tubes into the ground. This goat lived happily after this case, and he was not punished for his crime, but we had suffered all this time. As the autumn comes, so they begin to tear off the asphalt from the roads, searching for leaky pipes, and then they buried them somehow, trampled down it a little, but asphalt was gone. The rain will slightly dampen the earth, and the inhabitants of the community float in clay until the sun comes out."

"Life has changed all around," I thought further, "the normal people began to live better, they get so much work that they can afford to buy a car and change their apartment to a new one. Look at them, they were dressed up and soigne, and did not in a hurry, someone rested and others went to work. Unfortunately, we cannot do anything because we are the old farts. It's good, that my husband is getting a decent pension, I have already saved up for a new fridge, but this cannot change my life."

When I remembered the refrigerator, I began to drive away the thought about my mother-in-law. I came to my daughter after a long break, life seemed me fine and I didn't want to bother myself with even extra thoughts. I had a first day off, which I deserved for a long time.

In high spirits, I walked into the staircase of the skyscraper, where my daughter and her husband lived, and saw a familiar picture, shabby walls, rubbish all around, the elevator is painted with incomprehensible foreign words, among which our words were only obscene, a dim light of the bulb barely allowed to figure out the numbers on the buttons of the floors. Nothing has changed in their house, and in their apartment, probably, was the same mess.

Crossing the threshold of the apartment, I was made sure that years had no power over these lazy people. I was met by Mitchell, Nelly's husband. He was dressed in the same old, faded and sagging sweatpants, like my husband, and a shirt, which had been washed so many times. Mitchell hugged me with a big smile and happily spoke with his illegible patter, "hello, Mom, you are on time. Nelly is already setting the table, I'm going to fry the mushrooms now, and then we will sit at the table. Get your slippers and go through."

I put my feet into the old slippers, which I remembered from old times, and went to the kitchen. The layout of their one-room apartment was good. In addition to the large room, the kitchen was about fifteen to seventeen, they even made a large hallway, partitioning kitchen by the curtain. In the kitchen itself, one corner was filled with books, which had been dragged by both bookworms during their life together, and the other corner, on the opposite side near the balcony, was equipped with shelves with pickles, jams and other conservations. Here and there, there were some rags, open books, cans with uneaten conservation, plates, pans and other utensils, and in the middle of the kitchen near the stove my daughter cooked dishes, wiping the sweat from her forehead.

It smelled good. I did not approve of my daughter for laxity, but I paid tribute to her culinary abilities. She was lazy to cook, but for the sake of cooking some dish according to the found recipe, she could stand at the stove all day.

«Hello, daughter," I greeted her quietly, and she shuddered in surprise and almost let out the pan she was about to carry to the room.

"Mom, you already arrived, you scared me so much. You always sneaking up like a spy! Have Mitchell met you?"

«No, I got here myself, Nelly, because there are just two steps to get from a stop," I waved my hand and fumbled in the bag I brought with me. "You have a present from me, hide it, and let Mitchell not know how much money you have."

«But he doesn't care, mom, he knows how to do without money," the daughter said scornfully of her husband, «Well, let's go to the room, otherwise the roast will cool."

Leaving the room, we almost ran into Mitchell, who was in a hurry to pick up mushrooms, the tempting spirit of which had already spread throughout the apartment.

We had sat well. I especially liked the variety of dishes, each of which I tested. There were no delicacies from the store on the table, all the dishes were cooked from vegetables, mushrooms, berries and fruits, skillfully prepared by my daughter and her husband, and from the meat was just some cheap sausage, which remained untouched. I especially liked the little blue ones, smothered by my daughter according to some special recipe from the female calendar, which I myself gave her, and I forgot.

«I often cook vegetables," the daughter explained, satisfied with praise, «because we live on the outskirts. In the mornings, Mitchell runs to the neighboring fields. He brings home eggplants, cabbage, radishes, and other, so I don't have to go to the market. In addition, the woods behind the Armenian Church is full of mushrooms, all this on the table is from there. Whole summer and autumn he was bringing something every day, he even manages to extract mushrooms from under the snow in winter."

Nelly loved to eat and didn't exhaust herself with diets, therefore she had overtook me by weight long ago. She also was liked to drink, while her husband and I strained the dry wine from our glasses, she drank a bottle of port wine and her face was reddened either from mother's praises or from drunk wine. She animatedly explained to me what and how she prepared for today's table, but I thought that with such a pace in drinking she could follow in her father's footsteps.

Meanwhile, Mitchell had eaten mushrooms a little and had overcome his glass of dry wine, and he became noticeably drunk, his gaze became distracted, inattentive. He sat with the ladies a little more and lay down to sleep on the sofa. I significantly exchanged glances with my daughter, and she only shrugged. In order not to interfere with her husband, Nelly led her mother to the balcony and continued the conversation.

"You see how my husband has weakened," she complained with annoyance, «well, he is just like our father, but he does not drink all the time, very rarely mostly at home, a little bit, but you see what is the effect." «Well, he doesn't look like a drunk," I said, «and it's unimportant that he is weak. The main thing that he not keen on these potions, then the habit will not be. Since he cannot drink, you would not give him to drink, and he'll not drink at all."

«You see, his friends with their wives come to us, we sit here, have a drink, talk about books and about movies, play chess," the daughter explained her thought, «everything is grandly noble, and then he suddenly has a kick and is ready. I feel uncomfortable to people because of him. Although they relate to this with understanding, they do not condemn him and continue to come to us; they try to pour to him not too much."

«Here, you see, he is a simple worker, and what a smart one he is, he doesn't drink, he reads books and plays chess with friends," I approved of my son-in-law, «although he doesn't bring much money, but you don't die of hunger, he'll bring food for no money. You must take care of him; you have no children, who will look after you when I die."

I said the last words with a noticeable tear in my voice.

"Well, mom, you okay, do not start you song again," the daughter got angry, "I always told you that you shouldn't look after me, I've been an adult for a long time. Do not tell me about no children, because the Lord did not give, you know."

The sad topic had to silence us and to transfer the conversation to another topic. Daughter said, "Mom, you brought me too much money, it's more than a father's pension."

"Nothing, daughter, let it remains for your fiftieth anniversary, who knows what else will be in two years?" I always thought far in advance. "Did Yegor leave you something when he went home?"

«Yes, he gave me three hundred dollars," the daughter quickened, «and why do I need dollars? I asked him to transfer to rubles, I want to save the money and buy myself a decent overcoat with a fur collar."

I mentally thanked my son for the gift for my daughter and said aloud, "You have enough money for the overcoat if you add it up to my money. I saw in the military shop some nice overcoats at two thousand new rubles. Let's come to see."

We agreed about meeting, and I began to get ready for the road. I didn't want to spoil my good mood, because I knew that if I'll begin to teach my daughter, poking her nose at a mess in the house, then everything would surely end in a quarrel. I was guesting; it's time to come home! My daughter, whatever she was, will remain like this; she could not be remade by talking to her, although, when she lived with us, she could have learned from her mother how to live. In other matters, what she could learn from me, I had broken my life, transformed it to nothing! I am not the role model for my daughter, let her go by own way.

I was satisfied that I spent such a good time, and everything ended quietly and calmly, I was returning home. Already on the way to the entrance, the postman stopped me.

"Mrs. Eugenia, "she said with respect because she had known me for many years, and with her every visit with a pension money, letter or the money transfer, I definitely gave her some money, "They recalculated the pension payout and added to you as a war veteran. In truth, it was already a long time ago, but they could not recalculate, so, you have a good amount for six months, they decided to give immediately, not to wait for the pension money to be sent."

"It's good that I met you, thank you," I thanked the postman, «give me the money and I'll run away, my family wait for me, but I was in my daughter's home at the other end of the city," I could not stand it and boasted. Taking the money, I signed the distribution list, left a few small bills to the postman and hurried to the entrance.

It was getting dark outside, and at the entrance where the light did not turn on, it was completely dark. I stumbled by my feet on some stones and boards, which were left by the plumbers, who carried out the repair of the heat supply yesterday.

«What kind of asshole broke everything and threw it here," I thought out of habit, «tell me, who was this crazy man that invented such idiot thing that the heating pipe would pass right under the threshold of the entrance?

The basement is full of pipes, but it's not enough for them, and they put pipes here too."

Cursing everybody and everything, I got up to my floor and automatically pressed the bell button. Then I realized that I had called for no one, because no one in this apartment could come out to open the door for me, so, rummaging through the string bag that served me as a handbag, I found the keys and opened the door. In the corridor, where everything was familiar to the smallest detail, the outlines of objects could hardly be guessed in a gloom.

I threw the package on the shelf of a shoe cabinet built by Tolly in immemorial times, and with rapid steps went to my room. In the dark, I did not notice my mother-in-law who came out to meet me, because she, taking the advantage of my absence, decided to watch TV herself. Frightened by the bell, she hurried, as she could, to hide in her room, but did not have time and flew straight at me.

In surprise, I screamed, feeling the closeness of some kind of soft, shapeless mass that was submerged right in my stomach. I did not even have time to slow down my moving, as the old woman, trying to hold me by her hands, was pushed off from my belly and she fell back, by her head right on the corner of the cupboard. The mother-in-law's body covered with fat fell almost inaudibly, but the sound of the broken head on the protruding leg of the cupboard, similar to the crack of a bursting ripe watermelon, sounded loud in the dark, and then the mother-in-law screamed in pain, and I echoed with scream after her.

If someone told me that I would cry while sitting above the body of my mother-in-law, I immediately spat on his face. Father-in-law Yegor was disgusting to me, and his wife Anna was disgusting. I hated both, because I considered them the focus of evil that was in my life. They spoiled to me the last thing I could hope for, a quiet happy old age. Now, when I had a real opportunity to get even with my mother-in-law, this ridiculous incident had occurred.

I knelt before the bleeding mother-in-law and sobbed out loud, throwing my resentment with tears at the fact that I myself could not do this. Tolly stood next to me, and he was surprised to observe this picture. In the twilight, when he woke up, he could not make out who was lying there near the sideboard, and about what his wife was crying. The latter fact especially excited him, because I rarely cried at all and expressed my adversity with anger at the offenders, and did not waste my tears in vain. However, there is so much noise because of what?

Anatoly walked around behind me, turned on the light and immediately saw his mother, who was jerking in death-dying convulsions in a pool of her own blood.

"Gina, what is happened with she?" he asked shyly, "why is she lying there? Why blood is here? You, take it away, otherwise we all get a mess."

The words of this degenerate brought me back to reality. I or not I, but I did it, and everything happened, as I wanted. Besides, it turns out that the deed is done, and I have nothing to do with it. All by itself turned out. Alibi!

"Tolly, look, your mother fell," I interrupted my sobs and said almost calmly, "I just arrived from Nelly's home, and here she lies. Didn't you drop her?"

"How could I do?" Anatoly reasonably objected. He was not able to drop someone, because he was barely able to stand on his feet, "I was asleep, and you were screaming here, well, I woke up. You could cry quieter, a lot of noise is from you."

Then he went to the toilet with a disgruntled look. In perplexity, I sat on the backside, stretched my legs and folded my hands on my knees. "What a horror," I told, "his mother is dying, but this idiot thinks about sleeping," I talked to myself, swaying back and forth and watching the blood seep through the gaps between the floorboards. "Of course, he cannot help me.

Where is he now? What should I do?"

I somehow turned around, got on my knees and crawled to the phone. Typing number, I confusedly explained what had happened, and when they understood me, I put the phone down carefully and rose on my legs. At this time, in the corridor there was the shuffling of men's slippers. He entered the room, saw his mother and asked, "Mom, what are you doing here? There is enough space in your room, why do you want to live here? Gina, why is she silent? What is this, blood? I said you to remove it!"

He uttered the last words with noticeable irritation, his hands trembled, he tried to attach them somewhere, but they moved on their own, palpating his clothes, scratching the skin on his face, neck, and head and making him difficult to go forward. He tried to step to the other way from the mother's leg, but his left arm turned back, which made jerk up his right leg. He stumbled on her leg and balanced for two or three seconds, as if choosing where to fall, and then crashed in the middle of the room. He landed as if after a jump, at first he waved his hands, his legs flew up, and then he fell from his own height, spraining his hand and hitting his thigh and head. Tolly gave a cry in a low voice, tried to get up, and lost consciousness.

I threw up my hands in amazement. She was already lying under the sideboard, now he had flown. Well, just some kind of general catastrophe! Then the doorbell rang, and the ambulance team entered the door, because I forgot to close. In the bright light of the chandelier, the picture that the medics found here amazed even them.

"Look, it seems like the global tree felling," one of them, apparently, the chief, professionally joked and began to give orders, "Sally, examine him with Nickolas, and Peter with me will deal with the old woman."

The chief checked the pulse, and with their assistant, they lifted the head of the mother-in-law, from which blood had already ceased to flow, and only slightly trickled, from the wound on the back of the head. He took a bag with a bandage out of his bag and began to bandage the victim's head, finding out in passing what had happened here.

"How many time an old woman lies here, why she had fallen, who is she for you?" he asked me.

"This is my mother-in-law, but I was not here when she fell, I have been at the daughter," I answered without hesitation, "when I came she already lay, blood was flowing. I called an ambulance. You arrived quickly, thank you."

"Because we were here nearby, there the man from the second floor fell out, got drunk and fell," the sociable doctor explained, and then asked, "Why is there not enough blood although she has been lying for a long time?"

"Mr. Basil, look, what the floor is like here," Nickolas said, who had already pulled Tolly on the sofa, he drew his attention to the essential circumstance, "there are slots with a finger width here, all the blood went out there."

"Yes, you are right," said Mr. Basil, raising Mrs. Anna along with Peter, a young student, "hostess, where can I put your mother? You see, the blood will still go, it will stain everything."

"Well, this is as a conspiracy," "I thought with displeasure, "why they talk about to soil and to stain, first Tolly, now this doctor. What is soiled, this can be washed, but life cannot be returned! "

"And I will put a towel," I said out loud, "carry her in her room and put her on the bed."

The mother-in-law lay on a bed with a bluish-white face, merging with the color of a towel put under the head. While the doctors were adjusting a dropper with saline, Mr. Basil asked me about my husband, why he was lying on the floor in an unconscious state. He got drunk or what else was?

"He often falls, he doesn't hold well on his legs," I explained, "he is weak. Now he wanted to get around his mother, caught her leg, and fell. Only now he fell not as usual, but sideways, probably, he broke his leg."

"Exactly, he did it and have lost consciousness," Sally confirmed, "Mr. Basil, there is a steel plate under the skin on the left side of the skull above the temporal lobe, possibly the effects of an old head injury. How old is this plate?" she asked me.

"When he crashed in a car," I confirmed, "it was in the year sixty-second or sixty-third."

"Thirty years have passed, it was supposed to grow into the base tightly," Sally continued to explain, "And when he was struck, this plate was peeled off and shifted, now part of the hole in the skull is covered only with skin, and in another place where the plate went, there is an extensive hematoma. Nevertheless, the blood has already stopped; there is no danger of internal hemorrhage.

"What about the thigh, is it intact?" Mr. Basil specified, passing the needle to Sally so that she launches a drip into a vein.

"Strangely enough, there is no fracture," Sally comforted, "only a wide bruise along the entire length of the thigh and dislocation of the tibia. Nikolai was fixed the dislocation, patient didn't make a sound, and the bruise should be treated with compresses and trituration," she said for me.

"Well, let's think about what to do with the old woman," Mr. Basil spoke reluctantly, addressing not so much the brigade as to me.

"What will the mistress say," Nickolas carelessly prompted, "if we'll take her to the hospital, perhaps she won't reach the hospital. She lost a lot of blood, besides she was about eighty years old, right?"

"Well, you are wrong, young man," I said modestly, "under eighty it's me, and she's already ninety-three. Why to carry her here and there? Let her die here, at home, and bury her from here is more convenient, so as not to go to morgues."

"Why do you, woman, bury your mother-in-law before her time," Mr. Basil asked suspiciously, "she still could come through."

"Well, then take her with you," I got angry, "you will help her to climb!"

"Come on, don't be angry," the doctor hurried to reassure; "her chances are slim. If she doesn't wake up to tomorrow, she will not survive. So get ready. And one more thing. I'll leave a certificate about your mother-in-law's illness; when she dies, do not forget to call an ambulance and show this certificate to the doctors. Then they will write you a medical report about death. Without this certificate, you will have problems. If God willing, she will wake up until tomorrow, then immediately call the brigade; let them take her to the hospital."

The team began to gather on the way out. Meanwhile, the doctor gave me instructions on how to care for patients, what medicines to buy, in what sequence to give them, advised a couple of folk remedies to speed up the resolution of a hip injury, once again felt the old woman's pulse, shook his head and left.

When I was left, alone I changed the towel under my mother-in-law's head, wiped her blood near the sideboard, carried it to the bathroom and went to see my husband. He had already recovered and lay on his back, moaning in pain.

"Gina, my leg hurts," he complained to me, "take pity on me, please."

"Why I have to take pity on you," I replied sadly, "You fell down yourself, so, lie down and do not whine. I'll go to the pharmacy now to buy the ointment for you. I will grease you and everything will pass, but nothing will help your mother any more, soon she will die."

"Why should she die?" he said, "She was going to live hundred years old, and now suddenly dying."

"Don't you remember how she fell?" I asked him in bewilderment, "You stumbled over her and fell down too."

"How I fell I did not forget, but how she did it, I do not remember," Tolly answered indifferently, "but what kind of men were here, what they have come for?"

"There were doctors here, they wanted to take you to the hospital, but I didn't let them do it."

"That's right, Gina," my husband frightened and approved my decision, "I don't want not to go to the hospital, you will cure me. Well, come on, go to the pharmacy, I'll wait for you."

He leaned back on the pillow. His eyes immediately became sluggish and rolled under his forehead, after a minute he was already snoring.

I bought everything that the doctor ordered to take in a pharmacy, took a sedative for myself, picked up three bottles of wine in the store and returned home. Then I slowly made dinner, drank tea, went to my room and returned to the kitchen, delaying the moment when I would have to visit my mother-in-law. What if she had already died or, but worse, suddenly recovered? What then I could do with it?

So, I moved back and forth around the apartment, but suddenly stopped at the door of my mother-in-law's room. "Why should I cry?" as if it dawned on me. I did everything myself, I intercepted the mother-in-law in the right place, I shoved her as it was intended, the only thing was that everything was done so unexpectedly that I did not even have time to figure it out. And if I had time? Could I then do THIS? Now I had no answer, but what happened was just one hundred percent consistent with the plan. Therefore, there is nothing to cry, but just to record to myself a second life in this house, which I took away from my offenders.

I confidently pushed the door away from me and went into the room of the mother-in-law. Mrs. Anna lay still not moving and not regaining consciousness, nothing in her appearance suggested that she would be able to return to this world. Then the phone rang. I went into the big room and picked up the phone. It was daughter, who called to know how I had got home.

"Nelly, there is such a trouble, and I don't know how to tell you right on your birthday!" I answered excitedly, delaying the moment of a direct conversation.

"What had happened with you again," the daughter snapped irritably, who had tired of our old-men problems, "either my father got drunk again and hit his head or ran away from home?"

"No, daughter, even worse," I decided to tell everything, "while I was at you, your grandmother fell and smashed her head against the leg of the cupboard, lost a lot of blood, now she is unconscious, probably, she could die before morning."

"Well, things are going from bad to worse," the daughter caught her breath and continued to interrogate her mother, "did father drop her or she herself fell?"

"No, your father was asleep when I found her," I replied being honest, "and he also did not almost give up his soul to God."

"What wrong with him?" the daughter was surprised at how true the Russian proverb was, when trouble came you must open the gate, and she asked mother with hope in her voice, "does he die too?"

"Nelly, what do you say, you must cross yourself," I was frightened of the daughter's evil eye; "he just caught on the mother's leg and fell. He scored his muscles on the thigh, now he cannot walk. Tell me, please, can you come to me now? I cannot cope with this hospital alone."

"Yes, of course, Mom, now I will come home only to warn Mitchell and then I will go to you."

My daughter did not have a phone line at home, so I could not call her, and the daughter called me from the pay phone in the street. Under the Soviet regime, neither she nor her hubby could get the telephone, and now they continued to live without a telephone also.

This fact always got me angry with my daughter, because in such cases as today I needed her help, but how can I call her? "Well, nothing, she will come and I will tell her everything!" I thought, "Let her think about it! There are other times now; you can get the phone very easy, just pay. They save money! She wants to buy a coat for herself, but she has no money to hold a phone. It's impossible; you have to think about your mother!"

While I was waiting for my daughter to come, I managed to feed my husband right in the bed so as not to take him to the kitchen. I gave him a glass of wine to smooth out the today stress, but Tolly did not adopt everything, drank half a cup and refused. It seemed strange to me, because the husband could drink this muck from any position, whether he was healthy or ill, it didn't make any difference at all, but now I had such a discomfiture. "Probably he hit his head hard," I decided, and began to lay my husband more comfortably on his side to put a compress on his leg. Straightening his head on a pillow, I felt something soft like jelly under the skin instead of a solid skull.

"My Lord, this part of the brain is naked," I was frightened and told him, "How are you going to sleep now? If you lie down on the other side, then you'll crush a brain."

I was worried about the safety of the thing, which he didn't need for a long time. Tolly himself reminded me of this.

"Gina, do not worry, I had a plate there. When I crashed, they didn't put it on me right away, I went for a whole month, and nothing was not crushed."

"Yes, you can't crush anything there, everything is shriveled," I responded to my husband's tone, "your brain is scrambled, and now even more so. Why did you not finish the wine, I ask you?"

"I don't want it, I have eaten already and do not want anymore," the husband explained, obviously mixing up his favorite drink and simple food.

"Well, God be with you," I agreed, "I can't help you now. If you do not drink wine, it means that your situation is absolutely bad."

"Ah, it's fine," Tolly said and waved his hand wincing at the pain, when I put gauze with mustard patches on his leg, "the main thing is that everyone is alive and well."

"Of course, this is especially true of your mother."

"What about my mother, what are you haven't shared again," my husband became angry, obviously forgetting again, what had happened to her mother.

"Do not worry, Tolly, try to sleep," I reassured him, "I'll go see her."

A bright light was still burning in the room of the mother-in-law, but I did not dare to turn it off and light a desk lamp. It seemed to me that any eyes were watching me; they see everything and know every step I take. If I turn off the light, then the owner of these eyes will come here, and it is unknown what will happen then.

I quietly left the room, not closing the door behind me, and sat in the kitchen waiting for my daughter. I could cope with my wounded alone, but I could not be left alone with the dying mother-in-law. Who knows when she will die, and I did not intend to sit all night near the mother-in-law. Besides, these eyes that follow me are not good. When Nelly will come, I could hide behind her wide ass let her cover me up. And here she is!

Before the bell rang, out of nowhere a Button popped out, which with fear all this time was hiding in my room and did not crawl out of it until it felt the arrival of the younger hostess. Nelly never got tired of playing with her favorite dog, so the grateful Button showed her a special canine love and devotion.

Having called, Nelly just in case immediately pushed the door open, and contrary to the usual thing, the door gave way, because I left the door open again after the doctors left. The Button with a loud barking rushed at her feet began to bounce and to spin, and then it ran away and, returning, brought a tennis ball, with which it was always played.

"Well, okay, Button, will play after that, it's not up to you now," Nelly dismissed the proposition, what made the dog extremely surprised, "Mom, have you already walked with the Button?"

"Oh, no, I didn't have time, when I came; I'm whirling among these all-time along," I pointedly moved my hand around me, "go to the walk while I set tea."

After returning from a walk and having washed the dog's legs, Nelly came into the room of her grandmother through a door that remained open. Old Anna as if sensing her arrival suddenly opened her eyes, groaned indistinct, took a deep breath once, another time, then her chest fell off, and Nelly heard a prolonged exhalation. Her grandmother's facial features suddenly sharpened, deepening appeared under her eyes, although her eyes were still open.

"Grannie, what's happened?" Nelly said and took a step towards the bed, she before had never seen the very moment of death, "do you need something? Tell me and I'll bring. Mom, hey, mom, come here, what's with grandma?"

So she screamed until I came running and stopped her.

"Your grannie have stopped her torment," I announced solemnly, and if Nelly hadn't been so scared, she would surely have heard triumphant notes in my voice.

I walked over to my mother-in-law, leaned over her, listening to her breath, and then took her hand to feel the pulse. The hand was cold and lifeless; the pulse could not be felt. I released her hand, closed her eyelids with my palm and walked over to my daughter. She stood neither alive nor dead, and only laid her eyes on me then on grandmother and back.

Finally, she decided to ask, "Mom, what was there, how did it happen?"

"Who knows," I answered carelessly, "I come in and saw that she lies, and there is blood all around her, and this her son, instead to help her, also flew through her. What a nasty family!"

"Well, we are also from this family," objected my daughter.

"Don't count me among them," I retorted my daughter, "They never considered me their own, even though I would live with Tolly for more than a hundred years. Everyone considered me a lower race! Let them consider now in the other world, but I would still live more."

It seemed to me, that I was engaged in controversy not with my daughter, but with someone from the other world. Nelly had been noticing my skirmishes with her grandmother, but did not attach much importance to this, something was happening in any family, she also quarreled with my, but then she always put up with me, but now there was specific passion here. The "King Lear" and Shakespeare are resting here! Probably, they had divided her father between each other all their life, but never could divide; now he is at the mercy of his wife for personal use. Although there is no use, just one burden!

Nelly called the ambulance, briefly explaining what the matter was. The same team arrived, so there were no problems with the formalities. Mr. Basil wrote a death report and left, and Nelly went to her husband's house to help him with the organization of the funeral.

I called the neighbor opposite, she knew women in our house who help with the dead. They were not long in coming. Half an hour later everyone gathered, washed and dressed Mrs. Anna to her last journey. Then they laid body in a large room on the table between the cupboard and the sofa, on which Tolly slept, they read the necessary prayers and left. I was left alone with a dead mother-in-law and a half-dead husband.

I was afraid to sleep in the presence of the deceased, so I went to my room and lay down to read, leaving the door ajar. I flipped through the pages, not really delving into their content, and listened to the sounds in the next room. The silence was so shrill that I heard the crackling of the incandescent filament in the lamp and the rustling of cockroaches behind the wallpaper, which did not fit to the wall. Gradually, I dozed off and fell asleep.

In the morning the daughter came here, she looked tired due to the sleepless night.

"Where is Mitchell? I asked.

"I went to the funeral office," Nelly said shortly and went to the kitchen to set tea.

"What about money?"

"Then we will discuss it, this will not run away from you," the daughter said with a meaningful expression on her face, so I considered it my duty to find out what she was thinking about.

"Why are you so angry, daughter," I asked gently, "did you not get enough sleep?"

"Ah, what a dream, all night was nightmares!"

"It happens when such stress is," I shook my head as if I know it and continued to ask, "well, what you saw in a dream?"

"I saw everything!" cut off my daughter and reluctantly continued, "My grandmother tormented me all night with her own conversations."

"What did they talk about?" this burst out of me eagerly, "Don't wait too long, speak! They slandered about me, I suppose."

"Exactly, Mom, about you," the daughter turned to the window to catch her breath, which intercepted from the sharp conversation, "she says that you pushed her and she fell and broke. It's true?"

My daughter turned to my face and looked into my eyes with curiosity. She had nothing against such a maternal act, but the fact that I decided to do THIS raised me in her eyes.

"No, it is not. Don't think so, daughter, how can I do?" I tiredly dismissed the accusation, "I repeat you, when I arrived, and she have already lain in the blood. I don't know how did it happen, either she fell by herself or your father help her, only The Lord knows. Why are you had believed grandma immediately? You had thought badly about your mother, isn't ashamed to you?"

"I didn't think anything," the daughter said with disappointed, "it was so, as it was, I didn't see it. I am not going to accuse you; you never know what is in a dream happen."

"Well, come on, wash your hands and sit down to have tea," I took off the boiling kettle and began pouring out the tea.

"This is an old whore", I thought about my mother-in-law, "she talk with my children about me, I need to dig her deeper so that she will not walk over the forbidden path."

While drinking tea, Anatoly woke up. He tried to get up, but he felt the pain in his hip and fell back on the pillow and began to call me. I fed him, but yesterday's story repeated, he drank half a glass of wine and did not get more. Noticing the repetition of this surprising fact, I together with my daughter took my husband to the toilet and back, and hurried to share my observations with my daughter.

My elder daughter Helen was smart, when it did not concern her own life. She read a lot, had an unfinished university education in theoretical physics and a full course of commodity research at a trade college, so she easily and naturally judged such abstruse things that I could not understand. She also merely judged the father's illness, he was an alcoholic, and had no willpower; he could stop if he would want. She was supporting this error in me, and I agreed with her. Nevertheless, the degradation of the consciousness of her father, she connected very faithfully with the destructive effect of alcohol, which was taken too often and in unlimited amounts during his life. This fact that he began to refuse alcohol, in her opinion, indicated only one thing, he reached the drinking limit!

However, this conclusion was unclear to me. I could not believe that there is such a limit of alcoholic degeneration, after which the brain no longer responds to an alcoholic stimulus. In fact, the twilight of consciousness, condensed during this period, interrupted many of the pathways of internal and external stimuli including alcohol; it ceases to be an irritant. I couldn't grasp such a difficult situation at once, time would have to pass, but for now I had to think about the upcoming funeral and funeral wake.

"We will not invite anyone specifically," I explained to my daughter, "but surely the old women who were sitting on the bench with her would come. So go to the store now, buy a drink and something for a snack, and here I'll cook meat and a side dish. Take my wallet, the money is there, take to the cemetery a couple of hundred rubles. Give money to the local workers to carry the coffin. About Mitchell, I will repay him myself."

Nelly and her husband came at the same time with the guys from the funeral team. They brought a modest coffin, decorated on the outside with black thick paper and inside with white material trimmed with laces and bows, on headboards lay a cushion and ribbon areola.

Mitchell brought stools on which they placed a coffin near the table. The elder of the funeral team had commanded to his workers, "Take it on three-four, and took!"

Three-four, and they raised the corpse, carried it above the table, and carefully laid it in a coffin. The elder placed an areola on the old woman's forehead, folded her hands over the chest and covered her legs.

"Now you say goodbye," he continued to command, moving away from the coffin. However, no one approached the coffin everyone remained in place. He paused for a second, but he accustomed to everything in his work, so he gave the last command without stopping, "Carrying". Then everyone, except me and my husband went following the coffin to the porch of the entrance. There already gathered old women and old men, who learned about the death of Mrs. Anna. Seeing that no one invited them to take part in the funeral, they moved aside, and the car with the coffin and the funeral team, with Nelly and Mitchell moved off toward the cemetery.

I was in the kitchen and did not even look out the window. It is enough, that now I have to cook for the mob of guests. Nevertheless, I did it quickly, in just a couple of hours, and by the time, my daughter arrived; everything was ready and placed on the table where the deceased had just lay.

I was tired and wiping sweat from my forehead asked my daughter, "Where are these, her friends?"

"They are sitting on the benches, like birds on a bough, tweeting something," the daughter answered lively, "probably, they are commemorating grandmother."

"Well, invite them at last," I suggested, "do not waste time, otherwise they will disperse and then will be speaking ill of me that I made no the funeral wake."

The very same people gathered again, around the table who commemorated old Yegor fifteen years ago, however, there were five times less of them, and they were already old and ramshackle. They sat quietly, spoke in low tones, drank a little, and ate a little. I kept my husband out of harm's way in the room that his mother had left free, and did not sit at the table, occasionally bringing from the kitchen additional dishes.

The conversation somehow turned to the fact, why Mrs. Anna died. The old women who cleaned the deceased, vying with each other, began to explain the details of the injury, which led to a quick death. They said, that legs of old Anna were probably already poorly held her, so she fell down, and so successfully that she died right away, didn't even suffer at all, because she was unconscious.

"Now I remember," Eustace, who was completely old, mumbled, "Yegor was buried in that day. I remember that he also fell at his head, that's why he died."

Silence fell over the table. At first, they thought about the vicissitudes of fate, which gives a husband and wife similar death, and then suddenly a guess was born that something is unclean here! Having exchanged glances, the guests were ashamed of their thoughts, they say, we drink here, we eat, but what thoughts we had? After drinking the last glass, guests quickly dispersed.

Nelly accompanied the guests. She saw the expressions on the faces of the old women and their shyly hidden eyes; this seemed to her a bad sign. She came into my room, stood a bit, waiting for me to pay attention to her, and said, "They guess."

I studied the daughter, who was always prone to panic, and immediately dispelled her doubts.

"Don't take it into your head," I said with disdain, "these old people today or tomorrow will go for eternal peace, so they imagine something like a hell machinations, I suppose, they remembered how Yegor died. Let them think they want but it was so as I told you, and nothing else. Do you believe me?"

In addition, I looked at my daughter searchingly. She was embarrassed under the gaze and hurried to answer, "Well, mom, of course, believe. In addition, that I told you about my dream, it's all nonsense, sleep is not reality, and it is counted nothing."

"It's good that you understand me correctly," I spoke with some deep hint that contradicted the previous words, but the shocked daughter didn't know what to think, "it was just an accident. If you would live to such years, you will have legs like stilts, and then you will learn what it means to fall. Now you go home, I'm tired, I need to rest."

"I'll wash the dishes," daughter offered me her help.

"Nothing to do, tomorrow I'll do this somehow, go, please, it's already late."

My daughter left, but I sat in the kitchen at the table, filled with dirty dishes, and thought. It turns out that no one needed to see anything to think of you badly. For what, I tried to do that there were no witnesses and no traces, it's ridiculous, indeed. In fact, anyone could come up with any nasty things about you, and for this, he does not need any traces or witnesses. Moreover, if I had killed my mother-in-law with an ax, what would they say then? No, let everybody go far away. Now began a new life, in which there are no longer those old people who was poisoning my existence.

Chapter 9. The end of the road

In my new life, everything remained the same gray and dull. In vain, I hoped that with the departure of my mother-in-law something would change. Actually, in order to change my life, I had to change myself, but how will I do it in old age? There is neither strength, nor desire to change anything, whether will you change a lot when such a load as the sick husband, hung on you? All my strength had been spent on first raising him to his feet, and then watching him daily and hourly, that no accident would have happened. My hopes for change were in vain, and all the efforts were empty. Now I could not even go out the house for more than half an hour. Previously, it was possible to hope that the mother-in-law will take care of her son, but now there was no living soul I could rely on.

Meanwhile, Tolly's disease progressed. He stopped drinking wine, just did not take it in his mouth, that's all. He did not like the taste of this a drink that didn't get hit in his head. On the contrary, he preferred hot tea, which warmed his sore bones, and sweet juice, and indeed, his tastes changed so that I had to change his diet radically. Various "Snickers", "Mars", caramel and cakes appeared on the table, but meat and potatoes had to be excluded. Well, at least he ate porridges, if they were well flavored with sugar, otherwise I would have gone broke a long time ago, after all, a kilogram of candy costs twice as much as a liter of wine, and he ate it twice as fast as he drank. Well, when I could go shopping?

It saved me that my daughter called me and brought everything needed for her father. Nevertheless, this was not an option. From the controlled alcohol consumption, Anatoly turned to uncontrollable devouring of everything that stood in front of his sight. I could cover completely any of his wishes with wine, especially, since he had not so many desires, but now the process is out of control. I had wanted to limit my husband to eating sweets less, but he was becoming furious and clutched a knife. Although he was weak, I was afraid of an accidental injury, and that when I slept, Anatoly could sneak up unnoticed in my room and kill me. I had to prop up the door to the room from the inside with a chair, but at night, I listened with horror as my husband scratched near the door and called for me to go out.

My dream that my son will move to live with me, when his grandmother had gone, did not come true like my other dreams. He came to visit as usual in the summer, brought gifts. I noticed that well-being came from him, wages were raised in the army, and a good money was added from the part-time civil job, in a word, he had money, why did he need a mother with his father. Thank God, he did not forget us, at least, and came again.

I used the arrival of my son to solve some of my own problems. Recently, some laminated floors were advertised on TV, and I decided that my son would cover floor while he will be here. Yegor bought newspapers with ads, found who was selling laminated floors. Yegor never saw laminated floors, in Kiev they were an exclusive wonder, accessible only to bandits and oligarchs. Nevertheless, his mother wants, and that's it! He had to go to the warehouse, to buy as much as it needed for the apartment, and to cover cracked floorboards.

The work was near ending. Yegor has already covered the entire floor with imported planks, cutting them along the perimeter of the walls and attaching one to the other with the glue. In the corridor, he had to paint the joints with paint so that the water that often flowed to the floor from the damp refrigerator did not spoil the whole floor.

While Yegor fumbled with paint, shuffling footsteps were heard, and his father appeared in the corridor. He walked, barely dragging his feet, entered into fresh paint and left marks all over the floor. Yegor could not tolerate such a mockery of his labor.

"Father," he called out to him, "you could raise your legs not to do stains!"

"Yes, of course," his father answered indifferently and went to the toilet and back to his sofa, leaving a strip of tracks.

Yegor wiped the traces of his father's feet with a solvent, painted the joints again, and wanted to finish the work, when his father reappeared. Ignoring the paint, he moved his legs, erasing paint from the joints and carrying it to the kitchen.

"Well, don't you see where you are going?" Yegor got angry, "I told you to lift your legs!"

"Don't talk to me, pup," the father answered evilly and continued to walk, bypassing Yegor, who was sitting on the floor.

"Well, what do you need here again?" the son asked, "Tell me, please, I'll bring it."

"It's not of your business," his father said rudely once again, continuing to step over the corridor, "I know without you what I need."

Then Yegor could not stand it, jumped to his feet, grabbed his father's armpit, shook off his slippers and carried him into the room. The father, feeling the iron grip that impeded him in his free walk, began to twitch and to shout, "Hey, you, asshole, let me go, you're asshole!" He yelled in such manner until Yegor laid him on the sofa.

"Lie here, do not shout," Yegor ordered him, puffing both from heaviness and anger, "if you will try to get out again, I will tie you to the sofa!"

The father looked at his son with fright, not recognizing him, but the words he spoke, father understood correctly. Two hours passed until everything was done, the paint grabbed slightly, and it was covered with plastic wrap. All this time, the father did not appear in the corridor, only occasionally approached the door, looked at his son, hiding behind the cant, and in his eyes Yegor read hatred and fear. Yegor, in turn, did not recognize his father; it was some kind of anthropoid primate, without any signs of mind.

"How are you live here with this crazy?" He asked me, "He does not understand anything."

"That's when you remembered about your mother," I condemned him, "but where you used to be before, because your father did not immediately become like this but gradually. You could keep him from this disease; could treat him, or something else. But now you ask me!"

"You could know that now he does not drink already," I continued to pour out my intimate things to my son, "it turned him away from drinking, alcohol does not act on him. Moreover, his brain have completely been scrambled. Nevertheless, this is still nothing, because he had not been distinguished before by special brain, the other is worse. He eats in a terrible way, without ceasing. All the money goes to feed him, he eats everything, as much as he gets. It would be better to drink him vodka, all the same would be cheaper."

"Well, you exaggerate, Mom," Yegor laughed. "Look at him; he is thin as a starving man. It is not noticeable that he ate so much."

"You could observe how he eats," I advised, "and then see how often he goes to the toilet. Everything he eats goes down the toilet, it does not bring pleasure, but the money is spent."

"Mom, have you consulted with the doctors?" the son inquired, out of habit, transferring the mother's complaints into a practical plane, "there are such drugs that establish the intestines, improve digestion, the food is more fully absorbed and the appetite decreases. Give him the medicine, and you'll see, the process is normalizing. There is one of two things, either he will continue to eat, but will get fat, or he will stop eating and will remain as thin as ever. But the expense will decrease."

I was surprised how easy he solved the problem over which I had fought for half a year already. The polyclinic was next from us through two houses, therefore, without wasting time, I ran to the family doctor. It was a middle-aged man, he came to our home periodically to see how Anatoly was feeling, and he treated me with respect, always gave me serious and practical advice.

Everything turned out exactly as Yegor explained. The imported drug was expensive, but its effect was instant and amazingly effective. I had to

Georgiy Ulchenko

experiment a lot to put the medicine into my husband, because he didn't want to take the pills. I came up with it, dissolving the drug in the juice that Tolly was drinking before the meal, and everything went smoothly. Even before Yegor left, his father stopped walking back and forth like a shuttle. He came, ate and drank what was put on the table, and returned to bed. He started to go to the toilet once a day or even every other day.

I was glad about this. That's my son whom I lacked all this time. He arrived for only ten days, but had already laid the floors, his father was put in order, his antenna had been standing on the balcony for a year, and the new TV set showed. He had hands of real male, and his mind is strong, not drunk. Now I decided at any cost to persuade my son to return to the parental home. However, how to start a conversation? What could I suggest him that he would agree?

Meanwhile, time had come for Yegor to leave. He already bought a return ticket and collected things for the trip not to forget anything. I was spinning around him, making some empty talk and trying to catch his mood, but I was afraid even to hint about my desire, because I knew that I would receive a refusal. Finally, Yegor was tired of these voiceless scenes, and sitting down on the sofa, he asked me, "Mom, do you want something? Well, tell me straight, since when have you have become so shy?"

Really, I felt ashamed that I was afraid to talk with my son about such simple things. If he does not want, then let him go, I have also Nelly the daughter.

"Yegor, you see that there are two of us left, your father and I" I began with a description of the general situation, "but he's completely nothing, it's difficult for me to look after him, and there's nobody to help."

"You have Nelly, don't you?" retorted Yegor.

"She has her own family, she lives separately and is not going to move to us, what help is from her. She doesn't even have a phone to call her when it needed!"

"This is good, that she has her own family, so it should be. Moreover, what do you suggest specifically? Maybe you would hire the housemaid or the nurse?"

I was scared even by the very thought that there would be a stranger in the house and would see all this misery in which I had to exist, and I hurried to refuse.

"No, I do not want anyone, there is enough of us here, but if you would come back here, to your home, to your parents, then we would cope with any troubles."

I froze, waiting for my son to answer, but he shook his head, paused and, with a sigh, answered me.

"Mom, you know that I'm still in the army. I am a colonel, and I can go on retirement only from the age of fifty, therefore I cannot be demobilized earlier than in five years. This is if everything is fine, but I don't have my own apartment yet, I'm standing in queue pretty close, but every year they giving less and less apartments. Last year, the Kiev garrison was given more than six hundred apartments and for the first half of this year only twenty. Suppose that in the second half of the year, they always give more than in the first, but more than three hundred apartments are unlikely to give. So, I need to wait for my apartment for other four or five years."

"Why do you need an apartment in Kiev," I started fussing, "come here, this one will be yours."

"Wrong thinking," remarked Yegor, "at the Soviet regime, such persons as a grandfather could afford not to receive an apartment from the state, but now a three-room apartment in Kiev costs twenty-five to thirty thousand dollars. Could I give someone my money, or are they unnecessary to us?"

"I do not understand in dollars; tell me, how much is it in new rubles?" I asked.

"Well, multiply by six at the current rate; you get one hundred fifty to one hundred eighty thousand rubles."

"This is real money," I exclaimed with admiration, "and I have never seen so much. What will you do with this sum?"

"What are you talking about, mother?" Yegor stopped me, "I have nothing. First, I need to obtain an apartment, and then we'll see. Therefore, I am explaining to you, you can't count on me before I leave the army."

I became sad, but quickly calmed down. I didn't expect that the son would immediately agree, and it would not be necessary to return to this conversation soon. Nevertheless, just in case, I decided to strain the situation that my son thought all the time that I needed help.

"You know, Yegor, the father does not drink anymore, in his condition he no longer needs it."

"What kind of condition does he have?" Yegor pretended to be surprised, because he already noticed that his father was not drunk anymore, "where this condition was before this? Look, may be, your life could have passed in another way."

"Oh, don't tell me," I picked up his playful tone, "but earlier he had a more different condition, the drunk one. Besides jokes. On day, I called the doctor, I do not remember why; probably he fell, as always. Well, the doctor decided to take him to the hospital. So the father started hysteria, he screamed, cursed, spat at the orderlies, scratched everybody until they gave him a prick. As a result, the doctor diagnosed him, something like the degenerate. He said that I needed to put your father in a mental hospital. I did not agree then, but now I regret it."

"And now what the problem is?" Yegor asked, "He is quiet, calm, more asleep, and do not disturb you."

"No, you just don't know him," in a low voice so that the husband wouldn't hear I explained to my son, "he is out of his mind, he can take a knife and follow me. If he would slaughters me what will be? Of course, I can cope with him, I shove him that it will fly upside down, and what if he prevails? I can't sleep at night: he is scraping all the way near the door, he is calling for me. What does he want? Therefore, I lock the door by the mop. Maybe you will go to a social office and learn how to put him in a nursing home?"

"Do not worry, mother, I'll go to the store now and buy a lock for your door," Yegor did not take my words seriously. The danger coming from his father he considered illusory, then he said me, "but about the nursing home you need to think carefully. Their system is this, you give them your pensioner and his pension goes to this institution to support him, but when he dies, his pension goes to the government, and you cannot take his pension."

"No, this does not suit me," I said thoughtfully, "but you can pass him to a madhouse, because the doctor offered to take him away, and now he is not in better condition."

"When did it happen then it was necessary to take him," the son snapped, "but now there is no reason for that. Well, you'll call the doctors, and what do you tell them? Because he follows you with a knife or something else? Who will believe you? The father already cannot deliver a spoonful to the mouth, how can he follow you with the knife? Do not make people laugh, and do not count on me, I can pick you up when I get an apartment, but only if you are alone. Now take care of your husband, because you have lived with him all your life, he is the closest relative for you, and then the rest are. Carry your cross and do not complain."

"Oh, how are you speaking to your mother," I was offended; "I already can't complain you! And to whom will I tell about everything?"

"Tell Nelly, she will probably be interested."

"She is just not interested in. She came to me every week, and she sees everything, but just like you, she does not want to talk about her father."

From this point, the talk of Yegor's return to the parent abode ceased. He set the lock, checked it for strength, and transferred all the knives to my room, except one, whose blade tip was round, and then he announced to me, "Now you are armed, and your father has no weapon. So, if something happens to him, it means you did it."

I glanced at my son, checking whether he said that seriously, maybe he suspects something, but he smiled at his joke, obviously not hinting at anything. He did not even ask how his grandmother died, his sister told him about it. He was not here when his grandmother and grandfather was buried. He knows nothing, and he could never know.

I already wanted my son to go home sooner. If could he begin to guess something? Tomorrow he would go to her sister again, and what if she blurts out something for him? No, it is better for him to be now somewhere far away from here, until everything would be forgotten.

I shuddered at the phone call that rang in the evening. The daughter was calling me.

"Mom, we agreed to meet with Yegor tomorrow, but now Mitchell fell ill. The doctor said that it's the flu, and Mitchell had managed to get it in mid-summer. He also said that in the summer, this infection is especially dangerous; therefore, it is necessary to limit contacts. Tell Yegor that the tomorrow meeting is canceled, and I'll see him off alone."

"That's good," I replied, "that is, it is not good that Mitchell fell ill, but it's good that Yegor will not get infected. It'll be better, if you do not come too, because you could bring us an infection. Call tomorrow at two o'clock, say goodbye, and he will go."

I was pleased with the conversation with my daughter. Everything was arranged to cease unnecessary conversations and not to arise the suspicions. Yegor will go to his place, forget about what I told him, and I will stay on my own to solve my problems, and let no one doubt, I will solve them. If only strength and health was enough.

Yegor left safely, and I again plunged into a monotonous and purposeless existence. For days, there was no one to exchange a word with me, no one spoke to me, and no one needed me. Occasionally the daughter Helen was appeared in our stagnant swamp, she had dispersed the melancholy like a duckweed on the water, bothered everyone, and even her father recognized her and rejoiced at her arrival. Then she left, and for a long time, I calmed down, getting used to my unhurried existence.

Anatoly did not especially bother me, obeying the established for him order. It was a route between the points marked by three "S", to sleep - to scoff - to shit. He by himself was getting up from the sofa, was walking to the kitchen, was slowly eating his portion, was coming back and was going to bed again. I made small portions for him. First, due to the abundant food Tolly could eruct and could choke. Secondly, the frequent feelings of hunger tied him to one route, and he did not have time to go anywhere else, because it used to happen that he went out the door until I did not see him, but he could not return. He stood somewhere around the corner until I had detected his absence, or something worse, someone leaded him into the house. Now I could not worry about it.

At another time, the route could change, instead of the kitchen, he went to the toilet, did his cases, and went to bed. Sometimes, malfunctions occurred in his regularity, when Tolly having slept did not have time to reach the toilet and did his cases into the pantaloons that he did not take off day or night. In this instance, I had to wash my husband, wash dirty clothes, but such cases did not bother me so much because they rarely fell out and marked by no regularity.

With this kind of life, I had a lot of free time to take care of myself. I hired a worker who made cosmetic repairs in my room, she whitewashed the ceilings, re-glued the wallpaper, painted the door and the windows, washed the glass. It became fresh and cozy in my room, and I wanted to live and enjoy. Now I could lie on the bed with my favorite newspaper, solving a crossword puzzle, or read a detective stories and a love novel with tearful content. In addition, I had time to remember my life cases.

However, my life was falling into decline, and the mighty organism, tempered in youth by playing sports, through years of trials was destroyed by diseases and senility. While I was sitting in a voluntary-compulsory imprisonment near my husband, because of the lack of movement and fresh air, dizziness began to appear, my legs became weak and painful of the weather. I had only hope of my arms, which could still to wrap this degenerate in a bow, but they also was paining when I had to drag Anatoly onto the sofa, because he had been falling recently more and more often.

I was afraid that one day my husband would fall and would not get up. No, I was not afraid that he would die; such case would mean complete liberation. I was afraid that Tolly would be broken by the paralysis, and that would be much worse than a drunken husband or an imbecile husband. To be a nurse by the patient's bed and to know that he would never get back on his feet, and you'll have to carry him on yourself for the rest of your life and to clean up the shit under him, it was beyond my strength. Therefore, I prayed that the Lord would give me the strength to endure the nowadays life and to punish my torturer with a sudden death.

As usual, this week my daughter came. We sat and talked in the kitchen, drinking tea with jam and biscuits. I have already ceased to complain to my daughter about my life, so the conversation was about all sorts of things, especially I worried about the prize crossword, for which the newspaper editor raised the reward in three times. My daughter and I were far from economic theories, did not hold foreign currency in our hands and did not understand words such as inflation, default, and indexation. For us, raising the reward was simply manna from heaven, which fell directly into our hands, but in fact, because of the inflation caused by the default last year, the editor only now was able to raise reward, approaching the level of encouragement of their active readers, which existed before.

The stimulus was significant, so we both tried our best, and by the time of our meeting, I had only one word I didn't not guess. Together, we had to complete this successfully developing thing and to send a response long before the end of the deadline. We reviewed all the exercise books that I had been writing for many years. In each exercise book were words that began with one of the letters of the alphabet, and in opposite column was the interpretation of their meaning. In my exercise books, I put words that I met in crossword puzzles, and the meanings of which I did not know. To find the right word in this multi-volume explanatory dictionary it was necessary to work hard, but we were ready to go this way from beginning to end.

Now good luck smiled at us. Nelly, who was looking through the exercise books quickly and not particularly attentively, drew attention to the coincidence of the word description with the task of the crossword. Then she again reread the newspaper and the word description, counted the letters in the word, looked at the letters in the intersecting words, and loudly announced to me, "Here it is, I found it, look here!"

We checked once again that the chosen word correctly became in the cells assigned to it, after which I entered the word into the crossword with my own hand. Now it remained to cut it out, seal it in an envelope and send the letter to the editor. So we did. Nelly put the envelope in the outer pocket of her bag and began to pack up. My daughter and I said goodbye, and she went home.

I began to come out the house little by little and walk with my dog Button first in the courtyard, then in the wasteland behind the neighboring houses, at last I began to walk next the gas station that was built on the other side of the highway up to the railway and further to the garden sites. The autumn weather cleared up, it was dry and warm, red and yellow leaves carpeted the road. The ball, for which the Button was chasing, was hiding under the leaves, but she found him by smell, ridiculously sunk her nose under the leaves and, growling, and got it by teeth. Often, on the run, she made a sharp turn, frantically turning over legs and trying to cling to the ground, but the treacherous leaves was slipped of her claws, and the dog flew head over heels, screaming, wailing, and scaring the crows around.

I found that such old age suits me, but one more question remained unresolved. The next year, my son will be fifty, and he must resign from the army. It was necessary to prepare the base for his returning to the mother. Anew, the question arose about the "weak element", as this rough woman of the Georgian type said on TV. Tolly was not the member of my rosy plans for a quiet old age under the supervision of my son Yegor and his wife Catherine, who was only once at our home, but left me with a favorable impression. I knew that she took good care of my son, but now I firmly decided that the daughter-in-law could take care of me too.

There had come a year of 2000, which everyone has been waiting for. But it turned out that even in such a simple matter as calculating calendar dates, we were again deceived, neither the twenty-first century, nor the third millennium did not start from the first of January, we had to wait for the next year. Someone was expecting natural disasters, other waited the beginning of the apocalypse, someone wanted to meet good luck, and

Georgiy Ulchenko

somewhere anyone intensively spent billions of dollars to solve the problem with the two thousandth year in computers. In some countries, they spat on the calendar and simply celebrated a round date, and the most cunning ones stretched the holiday for a whole year, right up to the real coming of the next century and millennium.

Reading newspapers and magazines, looking at funny colors on the TV screen, I could not understand why everyone fussed so much, who needed it? In my life, nothing has changed, everything was, as before in life of my neighbors and acquaintances, this 2000th year brought no changes, and so why is this alarm? Most likely, everyone simply soothed itself with vain hopes that life would turn out to be more interesting and diverse, and there was not, and could not be any practical benefit from such a pandemonium. Moreover, the calendar was also an invention of people, and they did with it what they want. In hoary antiquity, our country had about five thousand years of our own history from the creation of the world, then someone decided to count from the birth of Christ, but the East and the West of the Europe had different initial conditions that began to coincide only with the beginning of the newest history. Moreover, what about those people who still had their different calendar, for example, Buddhists, Islamists. For them, this is not the offensive of the twenty-first century, but just another passing weekday, not even a new year.

In captivity of monotonous everyday life and in the complete absence of weekends and holidays, I was annoyed by everything that reminded me that somewhere there was a joyful, carefree and happy life. However, sometimes circumstances in that world brought me the joy. The son said that he finally got an apartment after ten years of waiting, now they are doing everything to repair the half-finished housing, and they will move to the new apartment in the spring. The news was not only joyful; it was big and significant due to its remote consequences.

Firstly, I was glad for my son, because it was true happiness for the military man to get his own apartment after many years of wandering around the garrisons. I remembered very well how much hope my husband and I had while waiting for an apartment, how we rejoiced when we received it, and how I lived in this apartment over the years. It's good, if my son received a beautiful apartment in a good area, but it could be such as happened to his father, who had taken this semi-finished product.

Secondly, I did not care, what apartment the son had got, since he must move in with me in order to live the rest of the days together, in peace and harmony. They would sell the apartment there, and would live here, and some money could remain in case. Moreover, It will be possible to take a garden plot not far from us, on the other side of the railway, and to buy a car and a garage for it. We could have everything like other people have. I could be possible to go out into the courtyard with my head held high, that the neighbors understood, I'm fine!

Thirdly, now it is not necessary for a son to serve until the full fifty years. From the army, he received everything the army owed him; it was meaningless to continue the military service. Let him retire for health reasons and move in to me. From my side, I'll be getting ready for his arrival, to free up a place in the apartment. The only thing that stopped me for now is a good pension of my husband, which I would not want to lose. I was choosing the options for a long time, how I would get rid of my husband and continue to use his pension, but nothing practical things came to my mind. Madhouse, nursing home, hospital, every such an option was either temporary or took money from me, but wanted to kill two birds with one stone, but so far nothing worked. Even in my thoughts I avoided the word "to kill", I thought that I needed to do THIS, as it was with his mother. After all, everything went then without a hitch, thanks to proper preparation in advance, and I started getting ready to do THIS.

I had plenty of time to think about the order of action. The husband was completely subordinated to animal existence at the level of weakly smoldering instincts. Most of the day he spent in a dream, and during a brief wakefulness, he either took food or defecated. I looked at my husband sleeping on the couch, then at the dog sleeping in the corridor on the litter, and I could hardly restrain the hysterical laughter. Their behavior was so similar that the old dog Button seemed more human than Anatoly residing in human form. With the dog, at least it was possible to play, but there was no benefit from Tolly. Although, there was no harm too, by and large.

Therefore, I spent minimum time to service the needs of this zoo. I cooked them the same food, because the Button was more than eighteen years old, and she was used to eating with us, figuratively speaking, from one plate. I laid out the dishes for them at a certain time, regardless of whether they wanted to eat now, and when they would get hungry, they could find something to eat without my help, not complaining that the food was cold and not tasty. I think so, if you are hungry, you would eat it, otherwise you will stay hungry, but whether it is tasty or tasteless, these are nuances, and I do not pay attention to it.

Thus, having prepared a meal and putting the dishes on the shelf, I had the opportunity to go shopping or just take a walk, also I could lie down to rest or to read at my leisure. I had enough free time to relax, including watching all the TV shows, although their quantity was constantly growing. I liked how in one American TV series a wife puts a lover in such a way that he kills her husband, and she remains beyond suspicion. Yes, I could arrange everything in such a way for me, but I have no lover. I wondered where Vladimir was now.

Remembering my faithful admirer, whom I had not met for twenty years, I decided to find him without fail. I have not decided yet exactly

Georgiy Ulchenko

how to use him, but my plan gradually developed and acquired new details and feature. I did not know where I could find Smirnov and how to call him. How? Well, at least I could promise him myself until the end of days, however, I was skeptical about my chances at my eighth decade. On the other hand, come up with something else, for example, just ask to render me a service for an old friendship. May be, he will not refuse me.

Then I went to the opposite house, where the long-term colleague of Anatoly Marat Khabibullin lived, he was obliged to Tolly because my husband did it so that his friend could receive a full pension when the army was reduced forty years ago. Marat spent almost ten years waiting for an apartment and received it in the same neighborhood literally one year before us, but he was grateful to Got that he had everything necessary for life, and especially to an old friend, a companion and a savior, Anatoly for a well-fed and secured old age.

Marat was older than my husband was, but he retained both his sanity and strength in order to work the land with his wife in the country house and get good harvests of vegetables and fruits. Four of his sons settled around him in the neighboring houses, changing their apartments to the area closer to their father, and his only daughter and her husband with many grandchildren lived in the parents' house.

I was lucky. When I was about to go inside his porch, the old but neat "Lada" auto drove up to the entrance of the house, from which Marat scrambled out.

"Marat, hi, where did you come from?" I exclaimed with envy, thinking that this old small person, who reached only the captain rank, had everything, but my Tolly is a real Colonel, who had only "I have went to the dacha and brought some canned foods, all sorts of potatoes and pickles," Marat answered in detail, unloading the brought bags and sacks onto the porch, "do you come to my wife?"

"No, Marat, I come to you," I modestly dropped my eyes, and he looked at me in surprise.

"What do you want from me?" he asked.

"Remember, you were a mechanic of the plane of the division commander when we were in the town of Davlekanovo before going to the front? Did you meet Smirnov after the war? You always gathered for meetings of veterans, you went to Moscow, at least while Brezhnev was alive. Have you met Smirnov there?"

"Yes, Volodya owes me his life," Marat replied proudly. "During the attack on Berlin, he also flew on my plane, and we had sent them straight from the highway. Therefore, when he had been landing it was a pipeline, which had broken through the engine fairing, and the fuel spread all over the fuselage. In this moment, this crazy Volodya got out of the plane, of course, lit a cigarette right under the plane. I knocked the lighter out of his hands, grabbed him and dragged away from the plane. He fought back, barely knocked my tooth out, but when he found out why I did it, he apologized for a long time, thanked me, and then always said that I saved his life."

"I don't know why you and Tolly never went to meetings, because you have always been invited," continued Marat, finishing unloading products and closing the car.

"As if you don't know why," I shamed him, "where he could go. Without him I was not needed anybody."

"In vain you think so, Smirnov always asked about you," Marat slyly looked at me, "I don't know what you had with him, but Volodya was very pained that you didn't come to the meeting of veterans."

"And what did you do there, I suppose, you just drank vodka, what else are you guys able to do?" I caught him to lead to the main issue.

"Well, don't say so, Gina, not everyone are like yours hubby," Marat objected with regret. "It's a pity that Tolly became drunkard, he's a good man. At the meeting, we have told about ourselves, who is who, swapped addresses in order to report when other fellow soldiers was found, or who needed help. This is a big deal! Volodya helped me when I needed to get a dacha. I was refused, because I was dismissed as a captain, and that time, you see, the colonels did not receive it. I went through the whole war from the first to the last day, I was fired back in the sixtieth, how many years had passed, but I was not allowed to get a piece of land. I wrote to Smirnov, who was already a deputy in the Supreme Soviet, a big man. Well, he had helped me; they gave me the land at once."

"Yes, Vladimir doesn't forget his friends," I sighed, "and how can we help him? You probably do not know now whether he is alive or not. You are the same age, aren't you?"

"Rather, we were," Marat shook his head, waving his hand in frustration, "our commander has died, and he is not with us for fifteen years old already. Just on the fortieth anniversary of the victory, we gathered, well, they announced to us a minute of silence, and they called him among the list of the names. Later I talked to my comrades, it turns out, he divorced his wife about five years before that, something didn't work on his family front, and he began to drink too much vodka. They tried to cure him, helped him with what they could, but he said one thing, there is no happiness in life, why do I need such a life! Then there was one heart attack, then the other, and he was gone. Such things are happen. What a male he was, all women was for him, but his family life, it turns out, was bad."

I was perplexedly looking at Marat and could not gathered my thoughts. It turns out that I was right when I did not want to be married to Volodya. All men are the same, they can make love with vodka better than with

Georgiy Ulchenko

women, but it does not add them health. My Lord, what kind of love we had, it seemed that he would live forever so that I could hope for a better life, but he had already died long ago. And why! From vodka! The image of a loved one immediately faded in my eyes. He is a drunkard too, although he pretended to be such an athlete and the sturdy, what did he lack in life, that he had been so addicted to vodka!

I hurriedly said goodbye to Marat, who remained at a loss as to why did this Gina come? I went to my house and felt what he was thinking about me now. Like, she let her husband to be a drunkard and walked here, as if she did nothing with it. After the early dismissal from the army, he had boozed very much, but his wife pulled him out of this drinking, very shook him and put him on his feet, for which he was grateful to her for the rest of his life. This woman, he thought, did not care for anything, as if it was not her husband who drank whole life, but someone other, and she was taking it calmly. Maybe she pretended that she did not care. Who will understand these women? The veteran having traced Eugenia hided around the corner, he spat being upset and continued to bring supplies into his housing.

In upset feelings, I slowly approached the entrance. It turns out that Vladimir, who had was so firmly established in my plans, had long since died, and all this time I thought of him like living one. Who knows, is Tolly crazy or am I? The bones of my beloved have already decayed, but I still count on his help. I was angry with Vladimir, who again left me at the right moment, but as soon as I went into the darkness of the entrance, a stifled sob escaped from my throat, and tears began to flow. I felt sorry for my beloved, but I felt even sorrier for myself, it was the lamentation over my ridiculous fate and a complaint to God about his unfair attitude towards me.

I realized that Volodya had become a drunkard when I refused to marry him finally. Exactly, it was when I turned fifty-three, and he was almost sixty, it was needed to decide something both to him and to me. However, I turned everything in my own way, and here's the result, Tolly, who was inanimate for a long, was still existing, but Volodya, who loved the life and was a strong and clever man, has long died.

I was always influenced the fate of my loved ones, I had brought only grief. It was not for nothing that my son Yegor ran away from home far away from me right after school, because he did not want to get under bad influence. In addition, my daughter Helen eventually realized that she would not have life if she remained under the wing of her mother. It's true that she understood this not immediately, therefore she still suffered next to me, but then she went to the community, and only then got married. Unfortunately, my husband Anatoly had nowhere to run, and I could not get away from him, so my evil destiny crushed him.

Although, which side to look from. How much blood did this drunkard spoil me, but he still alive, and God did not take him, and the devil did not mill him. However, such good person like Vladimir is long gone.

It was time to decide everything. Tolly was my misfortune for more than half a century, and this world had to be cleansed from him, since it would not do this for now, I had to help it. Last week, our dog Button died, and I saw in this event a sign that the decision was correct.

I felt tired after the events of today, somehow I managed to get my husband to eat, and I went to my room to rest. On the way, the telephone call stopped me. It was my daughter.

"Mom, how are you?" she stunned me in a high loud voice, "why for so long you didn't take the phone, what happened?"

"Nothing happened," I muttered in displeasure, "why you are all about the bad and the worse? You better say me; do you have a free day this week to go to the Military Commissariat?"

"Well, if necessary, I ask for the leave warrant at work," the daughter replied without hesitation, "and what do you need in the Military Commissariat, something for the father?"

"Well, all of you are thinking about your father," I said offended, "but who will think of me?"

"Okay, mom, I think about you all the time, and now I call to find out how do you do?"

"Well, daughter, that is good that you are next to me," I had a change of heart, "there is something to take care of. You will go to the Military Commissariat and find out how much I will have pension payments if I switch to my husband's pension when he will die."

"So what, he is so bad that it's time to get ready," she smarted, but immediately recovered, "I ask you, did he become worse?"

"Well, nothing is not worse, but we need to prepare now," I said philosophically and continued, "if they give half of his pension, as I heard, then I will have twice as much as now, but if less, then I do not know why to do this."

"Okay, mom, I will do everything," the daughter reassured, "tell me what to bring to you when I arrive?"

"Do not carry anything, daughter, I have everything," I answered, "you will better do what I ask, then come to me."

I hung up the set and imagined how my daughter stood at a loss in the telephone booth, wondering over her motherly words, until another caller started knocking on the door, pushing her out into the street. Nelly was amazed that her mother was so sure of her father's near death. She recalled about how her grandmother died, and much earlier, about three months before that, when nothing said about the approach of her death, her mother subtly hinted that the grandmother would soon end. That is exactly what she said, "the end will come soon". Then it came. Now she was preparing to replace her pension to father's one, although he is still alive and quite animate for his bestial state. Thus, she was preparing the end for him.

The guess that came to mind, made Nelly hasten the pace. She ran up to the fifth floor, not waiting for the elevator, and disappeared behind the door of the apartment. She trembled greatly. What a hell, how did grandfather and grandmother die? Both of them fell and smashed their heads, and that is why they died. Maybe, nobody had fallen! She hit them on the head with a stick and laid them on the floor, saying that he or she had fallen himself. It's just the horror!

Nelly needed to do something to calm down. She was not sorry her father not a bit. In early childhood, she loved him more than her mother, and communicated closely with him in her girlhood and even in her youth. They was fishing together sitting on the shore all day long and taking care of the sick mother when she was taken to the hospital for another operation, and she even discussed her affairs with him, although she never received any advice from him or specific assistance.

Everything changed when she moved with us to a new apartment, because of which she dropped out of her studies at Saratov University and transferred to this city. Not only that in order to get an extra room, she left the university she loved, but she also had been become clear that her father was a real drunkard. What trouble it brought her, she first learned when she brought her friend, also a student and a modest young man, to the house. They wanted to be together, but then her father intervened in this process like an accident. At dinner for the sake of a guest, when everyone drank wine, the father, as usual, quickly became drunk and began to push the unhappy young man out of the house. He swore obscenely, calling out both him and his whole family by the worst words just because of this guy dared to get close to his daughter, and he was so diverged that everyone understood that a little more, and he would beat young man.

While I was calming my husband, Nelly quickly gathered her friend and led him out the door. There they parted out coldly, because the guy was from a good family, his father was an example for him in everything, and here is such a terrible drunk! How was it possible in such circumstances to acquaint parents with each other? How should she live on? After all, if you had to deal with alcoholic, not anybody knew what is on his mind, would he suddenly put a knife into your back, how he threatened, who needs such a final?

So the roads of young people went their separate ways, and Nelly didn't bring home any other guys, you see, what could be the development of the love affair if you don't meet your parents with him? Therefore, every potential suitors passed by her, but her father was becoming worse and more intolerable. The end of her suffering came when her father's parents arrived. Nelly had to leave her room to the old people and to move into her mother's room, but, having become accustomed to her separate room, she no longer wanted to live in the barracks, as she called the common sleeping room of her boarding school, where she was studying. She had to go to the community precisely because of her father; she always remembered this fact and did not forgive him until now. From now, she was no longer interested in the old drunkard at all; he was no longer her father, because he had never been a real father. Her mother hid the fact that he had drunk vodka along his life, she told children fairy tales about him that the children could respect him, but they saw him occasionally, and mostly in drunk.

Well, it was his queue. Nelly has calmed down and tried to determine whether she condemns her mother or not? No, there was only pity in the soul. To live half a century in this madhouse and to keep similarity to human form, it was her life feat. Only a strong hatred could motivate the mother to remove from her path one by one all those who brought her the most disappointments in life. But pity was mixed with contempt for the mother as a criminal, and with the respect for willpower, which everyone must have for such cases, and which Nelly did not have, and confusion, because she could not, and the perplexity because she could not and did not want to believe in this conjecture in the deep of her heart.

Nelly dismissed dark thoughts, and felt relieved. What kind of nonsense came to her mind, probably, the father did her, being drunk, so her head is not doing well, since she can think such things about her mother. My daughter loved her mother, felt a kindred spirit in me and always shared with me her joys and sorrows, and I helped her as much as I could.

Especially Nelly was grateful for my support, when she had to go to the community and to get settled in a new place. I gave her something from the furniture and regularly threw money to her in secret from my husband, who was unhappy with her departure. Now, when the difficult times of change were almost over, Nelly remembered with gratitude that it was the mother's help that allowed her and Mitchell survive, he had no works because his plant stood without production orders, and she could not get a job when her bookstore was closed.

Probably, her mother could not do this, it's just a coincidence, Nelly made such a conclusion and calmed down completely. Moreover, the conscience will not torment her even when her father would leave us, hitting his head on some hard object. This would be just a matter of chance, because he was unsteady on his legs and could fall at any moment.

I couldn't imagine, which seditious thoughts were now coming into daughter's head. I thought that my actions were secret, and if anyone has questions, it is not for me, I have nothing to do with it. Everyone dies in his own way, but there are similar cases, I think if the living conditions are the same, then the death must be similar. The most important thing for me was

Georgiy Ulchenko

to decide now how much more profitable for me would be one of the options, either continue to suffer with him, to feed him, to care for and to wait for a natural death, receive his whole pension, or let him get out of the way, and I would use half of his pension, which would then become my own. What will be more profitable, that I will do? Of course, a significant advantage would have the second option if my son could move in with me, but it's better to rely on your own piece of bread than on someone's support, even if you have your own children.

Nelly came to us three days later, on Saturday, without calling by telephone in advance, which immediately made me nervous. Probably, the daughter did not want to report bad news by phone. We went to the kitchen, sat at the table and began to talk.

"Mom, everything turns out to be different from what you thought," in the course of the conversation, the daughter went over to what disturbed both of us, "you do not just change to the pension of my father, because they may give you a pension for the loss of a breadwinner. Either you have your own pension or you choose the pension of the husband."

"Do not tell me how I will do it," I calmly cut her off, "tell me how much money I will have when I'll change it?"

"In the pension department I was told that you can get forty percent of his pension."

I silently moved on my lips, remembering the amount for which I signed by power of attorney at the savings bank, and asked my daughter, "count me, how much it will be forty percent of seven thousand?"

"Two thousand and eight hundred."

"Yeah, these marauders plunder our money," I drawled, disappointed with the calculations, "there will be only for one thousand and one hundred rubles more, but what will they do with the rest, I suppose, they will divide it among themselves?"

"Okay, mom," my daughter reasoned, "no one will share anything, they just stop paying because of the death, that's all."

After what she said, there stood a tense silence in the air. The word "death" sounded such out of place as the mention of the rope in the house of the hanged man. The daughter was embarrassed, and without looking at me, she backed away, muttering something like, "Well, bye, mother, I'll come back later." At the exit from the kitchen, she abruptly turned to go to the door, but in front of her, out of nowhere, a father appeared, who was walking into the kitchen for dinner. Cumbersome and awkward fat Nelly tried to deviate, but still hurt her father, who turned around and flew face down towards the fridge.

Embarrassed by the words of my daughter, I did not look at her when she left, but I was attracted by the sound from the corridor. I turned around and saw a mute scene, due to which I felt cold in my heart. My husband,

Anatoly, lay face down next the corner of the refrigerator, and his daughter stood above him, neither alive nor dead.

"Mom, how could it happen, I didn't want to," Nelly squeezed out of herself and choked on sobs. I quickly approached her, put an arm around her shoulders and led her to my room. Returning, I found the same picture, but the body of my husband, as it seemed to me, took some other position. I stood over him and waited for something, suddenly I saw him moved the hand and tried to crawl away, but he failed, and froze again. Bending over my husband, I tried to examine his wound, but did not find any openings or blood. It seems that he just hit his head on the floor, but such a fall was usual for him, therefore it was no reason for concern.

The peculiarity was in fact that usually, after such a fall, Anatoly quickly recovered, but now he was lying and did not get up, only sometimes he twitched his hands, as if trying to crawl. Just in case, I called an ambulance and began to calm Nelly down, but my daughter didn't react to my words, but only sobbed more and more. Then I spread her hands, with which she covered her face, and with all my might, I slapped the daughter in the face, so that her head reclined back, then moved forth and stopped. A strong blow shook Nelly, she stopped crying, and a trickle of blood ran down her lip and chin.

"Look, you are bleeding, go to the bathroom to wash your face," I commanded.

"I will not go, there he is... he is lying there... I am afraid," the daughter again began herself to cry, but I approached her in a threatening manner. Nelly shied away from me, but I did not touch her.

"Blood is yours, but not his!" I explained, clearly sharing the words, "Nothing terrible happened to him. Now the ambulance will arrive, the doctors will confirm this."

"Why did you call the ambulance?" daughter continued to wail, "They will see that I killed him and will take me to prison. Tell them that I did nothing, please, I did not want to. Will you tell them?"

"Daughter, calm down, I tell you that nothing happened to him," I was surprisingly calm, and, looking at me, the daughter also began to calm down, "he just fell in the corridor, as he often did. The "ambulance" is needed to determine whether he has any injury, or some vital organs are injured."

I did not consider the head of my husband a vital organ. However, if he stops walking by yourself, then I would be dead. To look after the paralytic for the rest of my life, I will not survive this.

"Walk away, daughter, wash up, tidy yourself up and go home," I sent out my unfortunate daughter, pushing her to the door, "and don't think about something bad, it happens to your father sometimes, he often falls."

Nelly cautiously walked around her father, looked at him, then looked at me smiling timidly and said, "He doesn't even have blood, probably you are right. And I'll go, bye."

Nelly quietly closed the door behind her, leaving me alone with my husband. I turned on the light in the toilet, opened the door wide, then went into the empty room where Tolly's parents had lived, and turned on the light there, as a result it became rather light in the corridor. I put on my glasses, squatted next to my husband and began to examine his head.

On Anatoly's head, the whitish skin shone through the thinning gray hair, on which I saw a trace from the impact of his head of the door about the fridge. Against the background of the skin, which was ruddy with blood from an uncomfortable posture and quickly acquired a bluish tint, I could barely make out the thickened scar, and I touched it with my finger. The skin under my finger suddenly fell inside the skull, and I realized that the blow hit directly to the open brain.

Tolly suddenly moaned, as if he felt a touch, he tried to turn his head, but I grabbed his head with both hands and pressed it to the floor. Then, feeling how his neck weakened, I put his scar close the edge of the door and several times with all my strength, I hit my husband's head on the edge of the fridge. With each blow, my strength seemed to grow, and I delivered the last blow with some kind of desperate frenzy.

Tolly moved his body only after the first blow, but then he calmed down and did not move any more until I let go of his head. The head hit the floor, and then a bell rang at the door. I shuddered in surprise, but did not lose my composure. I straighten up slowly, adjusted my crumpled clothes, smoothed hair, checked my hands for blood, and hurried to open the door.

The ambulance crew was familiar to me. They repeatedly came to my call, when Tolly fell again, or they pricked me with medication, when the pressure increased; and there was such a case, when they even saved me from poisoning, because I allowed myself to eat a piece of the dried meat, which was left from Tolly's yesterday breakfast.

The doctors immediately examined the head of the husband, felt a hole in the skull, and muttered something among themselves, and then the elder told me, «Woman, do you understand that we cannot help him with anything"?

"What do you say, everything is so bad, doctor?" I looked at the young, but already grated doctor, as if saying, "Do not hang me noodles on my ears, and speak straight."

"You see, he is already old, he hit his head, he can't take care of himself, and he needs help. If we get him to the hospital, then the service personnel will require payment, they will force you to buy medicines in their pharmacy, it doesn't matter, whether you need them or not. It is endless expense, but whether he will survive due to that treatment, no one will give a guarantee. He is at home now, its own walls help him; let him lies quietly, maybe he will wakes from a stupor and then survive. After all, there is nothing to treat, in fact. Here it is a bruise, may be, a concussion of the brain was, probably, there are hemorrhages that need to be operated on, but I do not see it, infections and inflammations are also possible. Pain shock from the blow will pass. He just needs a calm. He will lie in his own home and everything will pass, but I don't know, he will pass forward or he will pass away, to be honest. Well, what is your decision?"

"It's not necessary to decide anything, everything has been decided long ago," I said with double overtones, "help me just to put him here in this room," and I pointed to the door of the room of my husband's parents.

The young guys deftly picked up the old man, one of them got him under the arms, other by the legs, and they quickly put him on the bed. In appearance, nothing testified to the injury inflicted on him, he lay calmly, breathed evenly, his face turned pale, and the scar from the blow barely turned blue over his left temple.

The doctors spent a few more minutes at home, one of them wrote the medical certificate, other gave Anatoly the supporting injection of vitamins and dimedrol, rest of them just rested, rejoicing of the free time, and when they left, I turned off the lighting and quietly went to bed.

At night, I had dreamed Tolly's parents. They excitedly thanked me and forgave me all the sins against them, including against their son. The dream was light, joyful, common tender emotion reigned in it, and I woke up with tears of joy in my eyes and in a good mood. However, reality brought me back to the world of sadness and bad luck. Behind the wall, my husband moaned loudly, so I hurried to see him.

Anatoly was still in the same position in which the orderlies left him yesterday. He did not regain consciousness, but still, from time to time, he cried out loudly from the pain that was produced by the blue-brown scar over his left temple. I approached the headboard and saw that yesterday's barely noticeable scar was darkened, and under it in the depths of the skull, something was pulsing, inflating the skin in the form of a hemisphere the size of a small ball, by which was once played the Button. Tolly shouted to the beat of the pulsations. I liked my work, and I pressed a swollen ball with my palm, which caused Tolly to scream, to bend at the waist and to push his legs to the stomach. I quickly withdrew my hand, and he stopped screaming, relaxed and sprawled on the bed like a dead man.

At this time, the daughter came. She immediately went to her father, who was lying unconscious, but he looked the same as usual, except for the swollen bumps above the temple. Nelly stood for a while by the bed, then walked around the room to and fro, but for some reason she was afraid to leave the room. She was uncomfortable with what she had done to her father, but if she knew what I had done after she left, she would faint at all. Now she saw only the consequences of her clumsy actions, this terrible bubble, which swelled on his head, and a yellowish-pale face, on which the seal of death was already visible.

I entered and saw what was happening with my daughter, so I sternly shouted at her, "Well, why are you feeling blue? God willing, he will die soon and will not torment us. See what's going on with him? If he will survive, he will not rise to its feet; who will take out the shit from under him!"

"Mom, I didn't want to," again, like yesterday, my daughter began to cry, and I felt sorry for this stupid fat woman, after all, she's my daughter.

I hugged her and pressed her to me, then I gave her to cry plenty, and when my daughter calmed down a bit, I took her to my room and began to inspire, "You must understand, Nelly that everyone dies sooner or later in this life.

The best thing is when a person dies on time. For an old man, the time is right when he loses the strength to walk on his own, to drink and eat and to relieve himself. If he continues to live in such a helpless status, he becomes a burden to his relatives. Moreover, by the time he finally dies, no one loves him for a long time, rather, he is hated for inconvenience and suffering. No one wants to be a burden for his or her relatives, but everyone clings to life, as if it can still bring them joy. But you saw it yourself that more often, old people converted to animal condition when they do not understand that their life is unwanted in this world."

"What am I talking about animal state," I continued. "You remember that the Button died of old age, but until the last moment she could walk by herself and was in a clear mind. Even when her legs were damaged just before her death, she had looked at me as if she apologized for the inconvenience. This is animal, but the old man who has lost his mind does not become an animal, he remains a man who is devoid of mind. I do not know anything worse in the world than this bestial state, and I do not want to reach such a condition, although I love the life very much. Whatever you think, but to help the "former" person to move into a different world is a noble cause. Don't you think so?"

Having finished the monologue, I straight looked in to the eyes of my daughter, but she still stood with her mouth open, shocked by what I said. She realized that I had built a whole system of my own values, and I put them into practice within the limits I can reach. Therefore, she also understood that I did this with her grandfather and grandmother. Well, with her father, she did it herself. As old Newton said, the apple doesn't fall far from the tree!

Nelly gradually came to her senses and began to help me. Together we washed the clothes, cooked dinner and sat down to eat. My husband lay quiet, did not bother us, we just came to him sometimes to make sure that he had not yet died. I asked my daughter to call an ambulance, because the swollen bump on the skull had already become a purple-burgundy and had spread over half of the head.

The ambulance doctor, after reading the medical report of his colleagues, spun around Anatoly and began to negotiate so as not to take the patient to the hospital.

"Mrs. Eugenia, you understand that," the doctor convinced me politely but persistently, "two options are possible here, and both will be fatal. If he stays here, hematoma, gradually expanding, will cause paralysis and rapid death within twenty-four hours. If we take him to the hospital, then he will die on or during the way, or after the operation. Choose the option."

I listened to the doctor and thought that history repeats over again according to the same scenario. Nobody wants to be engaged in old men, nobody cares that they could live another five years, and they let them die. Now I did not mind the doctor. Everyone is right in his own way, the rightness of the doctor is not to bring the corpse to the hospital, and my rightness is to bring to the logical end the case my daughter had begun. The doctor gave twenty-four hours to solve my question. Well, I could wait a day because I had waited more time.

The ambulance left and we continued drinking tea. We rested, and it was a well-deserved rest. We enjoyed a strong fragrant of tea, which had not brewed in this house for a long time, and we became more closely related than ever to each other than before. After talking about everything, about three hours later we parted. My daughter went home, and I went into the room and made sure that my husband was still in the same position, and then I went to take a nap.

I did not see dreams again, so I slept a long time and woke up only towards evening, when the fast winter sun was already hiding behind the horizon. My mood was upbeat. I cheerfully got up, went to the kitchen and saw the dinner that my husband had not eaten last evening. Already a day had passed, as he did not eat, and I decided to try to feed Tolly. Having collected what was left fresher, I brought dinner to the room where the patient was lying.

The husband was still lying on his back, did not move, and breathed slightly. He did not regain consciousness, so I decided to revive it myself. I patted my husband's cheeks, then sprinkled him with water, pulled a hand a couple of times, but he did not move and did not even flinch. Then I wet his lips so that he drank a little, but there was no response. It didn't make sense to feed him in this condition, so I took the food back to the kitchen and threw it into the trash.

I sighed sitting down on a chair. I did not know what to do. For the first time in a long life, I didn't need to take care of anyone. My husband has not died yet, but he was doomed, and there was no longer a living soul next to

Georgiy Ulchenko

me. I went back to my room, lay down on the bed and picked up a book, but could not read a single line. Thoughts in my head were mixed up, became confused, but suddenly I clearly understood, I had to call Yegor so that he would say goodbye to his father while he was still alive. However, how to say goodbye, if he was still alive? We would wait at least until tomorrow, when it would be clear.

The silence in the apartment, which I always lacked, became annoying me first time. No one walked, the floorboard did not creak anywhere, and the door did not slam. I was frightened that I became deaf, and began to listen attentively to the outer sounds, then I heard that ordinary city life was continuing outside, someone walked above my head in a neighbor's apartment, and someone knocked the door at the entrance, thank my Lord, I was not deaf. Everything is good, it will take a little time, and I will be able to enjoy life fully. Of course, not like, it was in my youth, but every age has its charms. Remembering episodes from a past life, when it was possible to radically change my life, I no longer cursed fate, did not scold myself, did not blame anyone, but only sighed inwardly; regretting that life had passed, but I still didn't saw good and happiness. Maybe now, when my son would move to me, I could feel calm and happy.

The next day, before calling my son, I went into the room to visit Anatoly. He was lying in the same position, but his breathing became heavy and intermittent, the skin on his head turned yellow and taut, only a dark maroon tubercle remained from the blood convexity. My husband's eyes were still closed, and his open mouth was frantically catching air.

"Yegor," I said, when my son on the other side of the wire picked up the phone, "your father fell a week ago and hit his head. At first, the doctors did not say anything bad, but today he had a blood lump on his head, and, probably, he will die soon."

"Mother, why are you always exaggerating so much?" the son asked skeptically, not really believing in my story. Usually he was not informed when somebody was dying in our family, but now for some reason I called him in advance. "You will better call me when he dies, then I will come at once. If you want me to be released from the service to look after the sick father, then send me a certified telegram that the father is in serious condition."

"Well, you do not believe me, but why?" I was offended, "I speak the truth."

"Where the sister is?"

"She is at her home, promised to call tomorrow."

"So, everything is not so bad," the son summed up, ending the conversation, "in general, we will agree in this way, if the father dies, you call me at any time, okay?"

"Perfectly," I replied, genuinely surprised by my son's reaction, and hung up.

Meanwhile, events were developing in the fastest way, somewhere after midnight a phone call rang in Yegor's apartment in Kiev, and I called him. After talking with me, Yegor told his wife that his father had already died, and he needed to go to his mother for his father's funeral.

Yegor managed to get home only late in the evening. Nelly and I were at home, and on the table in the big room the father's corpse lay, he dressed in a blue uniform of the colonel of the Air Force. After a quick supper, everyone gathered in my room to discuss the upcoming funeral.

My daughter and I did not show any signs of sadness, which could correspond to the moment, and it seemed strange to my son. The very kind of the corpse was unpleasant to him, and the fact that it was once his father caused sad thoughts in him. The absurd life of an absurd person, and the same ridiculous end. Surely, in all this, it was some regularity, but he did not want to think about the causes and effects.

Trying to find in the faces of their relatives a response to their sad thoughts, Yegor repeatedly tried to transfer the conversation to the fact how his father died, what his last moments were, what his mother and sister felt at those moments, but we spoke about tomorrow's concerns, were practical and even delved into small insignificant details. I had already prepared a part of the money, and Yegor should have added the rest, to do everything like people do.

Finally, everything was solved, and Yegor came out. In the room where his father was lying, it was gloomy, he smelled of wax and burning candles that were at his head. Yegor opened the window to ventilate the room and went to his father. Peering in the wrong light of the oscillating fire into the features of the once native person, he was recognizing him and did not recognizing. There were concave eye sockets, an yellow-matt complexion with appearing cadaveric spots, disappeared sclerotic veins on the nose and cheeks, a pointed nose turned from duck to aquiline, everything was unfamiliar. His father in whole life was soaked with alcohol to such an extent that wine flowed in half with vodka in his veins, and from him a mile away was filled with smell of booze, but now Yegor felt only the suffocating smell of a decaying body, which could not erode even the fresh, frosty air.

The night was long and nervous. Yegor arrived in military uniform and did not change clothes, but it was almost cold outside on the cold apartment, so he could not even take off his coat for a minute. He went into the room where his father lay, then returned to the kitchen, once again made tea or coffee and endlessly scrolled in his mind episodes of his father's life, which the son had lived with him for almost fifty years of life.

After an hour and a half, he was joined by a sister, who also could not sleep next to the deceased. They were stayed awake and talked about everything, trying to bypass the thorny topics of their life, so as not to heat up the situation.

They were not as close as one would expect from a brother and sister. His sister left home to boarding school when she was fourteen years old, and since then they have met only occasionally during her brother's short visits to their mother. In their youth, most of their conversations "about life" had ended in quarrels, because the elder sister, in the indefatigable care of the younger brother, tried to impose her views on him, lectured him and, in general, tried to show him own seniority in everything. However, Yegor, who was really the youngest in the family and, accordingly, had the least rights and trust, could not tolerate such a situation because he had felt himself like a male from the age of twelve years old. He could hardly tolerate his mother's moral speeches and was often wrangled to her, but he couldn't bear it at all when his sister taught him, so skirmishes and conflicts constantly occurred between them. The sister immediately fled to complain to the mother, so the hostility between brother and sister grew over the years.

Their relationship began to change for the better when they had lived a most of life, and it became obvious that there was no junior Yegor, but was a mature man who had obvious advantages over the husbands of his mother and sister. He knew how to do a lot with his own hands, was smart, educated and continued to study for further growth in the army. In addition, since he was an officer, Yegor was no longer a madcap and a chatterbox, as they had previously considered him, but he had acquired such traits as responsibility and balance. No matter how much they argued with him, Yegor quietly listened to everyone, and then put everything in its places by two or three words and removed all their doubts and problems.

Yegor's sister could trust him problems with her husband and inconsistent relationship with her mother, without fear of hurt or contempt, and in response to trust he was delicate, did not disturb her with helpful advice, but did not spare the warm words to support the spirit of his sister in all life situations. Therefore, it established between them that they were frank among themselves, but did not overstep the limits of delicacy and tried not to burden each other with their worries.

Sitting on that night in the kitchen, Yegor and Helen told each other how they lived in recent years, recalled everything that happened to their family, and when they lived together, and when they broke up. Often, Yegor had changed the subject to his father, to his vice, which destroyed their family well-being and put an imprint on their entire life, and Nelly was just assenting him, remembering more and more details, which unknown to her brother, but put a pain in her heart.

In fact, the youth of his sister for such a short time, while she looked fresh and attractive, was spoiled by their father, and then he did it with the rest of her life, when in a drunken stupor he lectured her and expelled every of her potential suitors. She married a forty years old worker only at maturity, being a fat thirty-year-old woman, and she didn't consider him equal to her in origin, intelligence and subtlety of feelings.

Yegor listened to his sister and understood that her fate was shaped like a mother, with the only difference that it contained much less bright events and big feelings, but, on the other hand, there was much less shit. In general, a gray and miserable existence, no lofty aspirations, no fulfillment of desires, and perhaps, she never had the real desires. But Yegor was in no hurry to feel sorry for his sister, because, contrary to her complaints, she did not look like an unhappy victim, on the contrary, she was full of healthy optimism and vigorously used those crumbs of the charms of life that were available to her.

Only one thing was not clear for him, why did she avoid details in talking about the reasons for her father's death and his last minutes. Mother didn't speak much either, and Yegor stopped altogether raising this topic. He read a medical report about death prepared for tomorrow, which said something about traumatic brain injury and cerebral hemorrhage, and began to examine his father's skull, trying to find traces of the injury. However, it was impossible to discern anything in the twilight because of the blue-brown dead spots that were visible through the skin. The only sign that could have been taken as a mark of the blow was a diagonal scar above the temple in the square of the scars from the old operation, which his father got after the accident in the car.

Having overcome his disgust, Yegor touched this trace with his finger, but his finger suddenly fell into the inside of his cranial bone. From surprise, Yegor pulled back his finger and swore out loudly. His sister came to his voice, and his brother, in order to defuse the awkwardness, had to compose something like his interest in his father's hair, unlike his baldhead, his father had thick, though gray, hair until his death. The sister accepted his humorous tone, and the rest of the night, they spoke in a friendly and cordial tone.

The next morning, Yegor, along with his sister, went to the city center and settled all the formalities with the registration of the death and the organization of the funeral. Delighted with his military deportment and colonel's epaulettes, the lady in the funeral office helped him in all matters, so the funeral was appointed in the middle of the same day. When they went outside, it remained about three hours before the funeral. Nelly called me to arrange a funeral wake of pre-prepared products, while they went to the military commander's office with a death certificate, so that the commandant would give them a guard of honor and an orchestra for the military man of this rank, and then they went to the military enlistment office to take care of the mother's pension.

Georgiy Ulchenko

All these institutions were in different parts of the city, so the brother and sister arrived at the house at the same time as the hearse. Two hefty heaver carried the coffin and loaded it into the bus. Yegor, Nelly, and four local elders, who knew Anatoly for at least the last quarter century, sat there. When the coffin was being carried out, Yegor noticed that I was still dressed at home clothes, and wanted to hurry me so that I would rather dress, but I silently went into my room and closed the door behind me. Well, to be sure! He even jaw dropped from such a turn of affairs. It is necessary to live for half a century together, so as not to even go to the cemetery to bury her own husband. Whatever he was, nevertheless, he was a husband!

While they were driving, Yegor could not calm down from indignation, but he did not want to discuss this with his sister. No, he will not be able to forgive his mother that she did not spend her husband at the grave on his last journey. What the hell did she live with him for all these years while he was drinking to the complete degradation and loss of a human face? Was it profitable or for some other reason? Maybe she was pouring him so that he would not interfere with her in doing some kind of business. These thoughts swarmed in my son's head, but he could not get an answer to them, so he became angry even more.

At the cemetery, the bus stopped near the grave. It was necessary to walk from the road through a narrow passage in a low fence, along a mound of raw clay, which the excavators took out from the grave. A guard of honor from three cadets of a local military school led by an ensign and an orchestra with a trombone, a drum and a flute from two ensigns and a soldier met us far away from the graves in order not to get dirty their shoes. While the old men were pulling the coffin out of the bus, the orchestra began to play a funeral march, and Yegor suddenly was sorrowed that he was burying his father, who never was a friend or elder companion for him. Nevertheless, the son, for the first time in his life, was proud of his father, who went through the war, served in Air Force his whole life in the army and became a colonel, as he did.

His lips trembled, and he already intended to let a tear, but one of the old men, when they carried the coffin through the passage in the fence, stumbled and missed the coffin from his hands. The rest of the old men, as best they could, kept the coffin all three, but the weight was unbearable for their weak hands. The coffin touched the ground, and Yegor in one jump turned out to be in the place of the outgoing carrier. Together, they somehow scrambled up the slippery clay, sticking to the soles of their feet with weights of ten pounds, and set the coffin on a stretcher made by the diggers. In the distance, the orchestra played and played Chopin, the sound of music was blown away by the young spring breeze, but the old people were pleased that military honors were giving to their deceased comrade.

A senior of group of cemetery workers invited everyone to the coffin to say goodbye to the deceased. The daughter bent over her father, kissed him, and laid flowers in the coffin. Then Yegor approached his father, but he could not overcome himself and kiss him. He wordlessly shook father's hands and walked away from the grave. After him, the old people said goodbye to Anatoly, the workers covered the coffin with a lid, grabbed it with two nails and skillfully lowered the coffin into the grave. Yegor picked up a piece of clay and was about to throw it on the lid of the coffin, when suddenly a discordant gun salvo of three rifle made him shudder, and he ducked and dropped the clay from his hands.

"Damn," he cursed softly and looked around. Nobody paid attention to him. The old men in high spirits listened to two more volleys, threw the clay into the grave and came into the bus. The orchestra and the guard of honor turned around and went to the commandant's truck stayed not far away.

Yegor took a handkerchief from his pocket and began to wipe the clay on his hand. "Commander," turning to the colonel, the senior digger said with politeness that especially was not inherent to him, "If you wish, we can put up a fence now and attach the monument in a month, or let it remain so, and you will make it yourself?"

"Here no one will deal with this himself," Yegor explained his position to the worker, "do everything you need now because I pay you. How much money?"

"It'll be enough one hundred fifty rubles, we will also write the name on the monument, until you strengthen the photo, and we will drink for the repose of your father."

"Well, drink for my health too," Yegor said, payed them two hundred rubles and went with his sister to the bus.

At home, there were three neighboring women, whom Yegor did not know; they set the table. He put the old men at the table and went into my room. I was reclining on pillows as if I was dozing. My face was painful, there were black circles under my eyes, and the skin on my face had a grayish tint. In order not to wake me, Yegor softly opened the door and was about to leave, when I suddenly opened my eyes and said, "Oh, Yegor, you have already arrived, but I was already tired of this funeral, I decided to lie down."

Yegor, who had a feverish state after two sleepless nights and sadness over the death of his father, could understand me, but he was irritated about why I did not go to see off my husband.

"Mother, why are you lying here? Some women are working with food about the table, everybody have already come for the funeral wake. At least, will you come to them or no? Whose husband he was, yours or them?"

I looked attentively at my son and realized that he was annoyed very much, but I was not interested in the reason for his irritation. From now, I was free until the end of my life, and no whipster, even if he is my son, can dictate to me what to do.

"These women, as you say, were mistresses of your father, and they hated me. Let them celebrate now without me, but you and Nelly go to the table and stay with them because he was your father. Do not teach me, I know what I do, without any advisers."

I paused and turned to the wall, and Yegor shrugged his shoulders and returned to the table. Some strangers sat around him, spoke good words about Anatoly, poured, drank, and poured once more. Yegor's tired body quickly gave up under the influence of alcohol, and he felt good and comfortable. He forgot about the strange behavior of his mother, forgot about the fact that recently the late father was lying on this table, and he sat at the table with everyone until the last person left. After that, the same women quickly cleaned everything from the table, washed the dishes and were gone too. In the kitchen remained brother and sister.

"Nelly, why didn't the mother go to bury her father and didn't go to the guests?" Yegor asked the sister.

"Do you care?" not very politely the sister asked in response.

"Of course, I want to know it," said Yegor in her tone, beginning to get angry, "It is looking somehow strange, and is not it?"

"What can these people say?" Nelly smiled contemptuously, "you don't know how we lived here, you served in the Army somewhere far away, but I was here with my father and mother, and I know everything."

"Well, we know who was and where was, I ask you why does this have to do with the funeral wake?"

"Because this have to do with!" Nelly also began to heat up, "did you see that old fuckin in a green dress from the material for officers' uniforms? She sat at the table across from you."

"I have seen, so what?"

"So it is the fact that our father, when we had moved here, contacted her and made love with her, he drank vodka and walked with her, and then came to our mother and said that he would bring a new wife, and let our mother go to the hell."

"That's how! Tell me, why did I not know anything like that? You could tell me about this case!"

"May be, you forget where you have been," sister said me sarcastic, "I could not write about this in a letter and could not tell by phone. We survived these dirty times somehow, but the mother has not yet forgiven this bitch, so mother leaved the guests because this whore was sitting at the table."

"My God, you've all gotten mad with anguish," exclaimed the drunk

Yegor with a joyful voice, "because you had to beg her to take our father away from us, and there would not be so many troubles, but you fought against her! You were mistaken a little!"

"Now you can laugh at us, but then we were not laughing." Nelly sat down on a chair and shed a tear. Then she blew her nose and continued, "He was driving us out of the apartment into the street every day, he got drunk like a pig and made a scandal for us, drove us out and throws our things out, as if completely lost his mind. Well, okay, if he would do this to the mother, because she is his wife, but why me? After all, he could not divorce his daughter! Disgusting man, he is scum! I will never forgive him!"

"Such memories you have here," said Yegor thoughtfully, hugging his sister by the shoulders, "okay, calm down, it's a thing of the past. In the end, you expelled him to the next world, but not he."

He felt as Nelly shuddered after his words, and he asked, "What happened, Nelly? What's wrong again?"

"How do you know that?" sister asked in a stifled whisper, "Tell me, did my mother say to you about this? I asked her not to tell anyone, but she had already begun to ring every bell!"

"Hey, what are you talking about?" Yegor said, he was upset, looking at his sister who was losing control of herself more and more, "what could my mother say to me? What else I do not know, explain to me?"

Nelly looked at him with wide eyes, in which he clearly could see fear and remorse, and she could not utter any word. She understood that she had said too much, but she could not return her words. Then she gathered her courage and told her brother everything, both about how grandmother and grandfather died, and how she herself was the culprit in the death of her father. Yegor listened to his sister and mentally thanked God for the fact that he had saved him from living together with this damned little family. No wonder he served in the Army all his life far from their home and did not even try to get close to him.

"Okay, sister, do not worry," Yegor sympathetically stroked her head, "anything can happen in life, I cannot judge you. If to ponder, no one is to blame, this is such a place here. Let me better take the mother with me so that neither you nor her will fear each other. It is never known what would come you to mind."

"Oh, here you also think that I am guilty," my sister whimpered again, "but I didn't want to, it just happened."

"I do not think so, and no one here think anything. You do not do anything, it is happening besides your will. Now, put yourself in order, so that the mother did not notice anything, and I will go and talk to her about the move to me."

I did not sleep already when Yegor entered the room. I read a magazine, and again, this slashed his soul as if by the knife. Indeed, do mother really have nothing left for his father? Nevertheless, there were also young years, joys and love. Children were being born here. Well, what is the result? That one is in the coffin under the ground, and this one is reading a book on the bed! Well, these persons are still not clear what they are!

"Mother, I come to you with such an offer," Yegor began uncertainly, doubting whether he was doing correctly, "let us sell the apartment, and you will move to live with me. We have a separate room for you, Katya does not mind, she suggested such an option herself. Either you can generally live separately in a three-room apartment in nearest town. We could come to you once a week and no one would disturb anyone. Come on, decide it!"

"Yegor, you do not think what you say," I said to be indignant. "I waited for so many years that you, finally, will move to live with me, we will be together in the same house, but you are going to move me somewhere. No, I will not sell my apartment! For so many years, I have been waiting for myself to be the chatelaine in my house, I have gone through all the obstacles, and now you are proposing to drop everything and go there, I do not know where. No, this will not be, and you do not urge me. At least let me live in my pleasure in my old age."

"Mom, you need to know that I will not move here for anything, and you do not count on it here. What will you do here alone I do not know. In my town, we would live together, because you are my mother, and my Catherine will care the house. If we sell the apartment, then we will have enough money to buy a car, and we will be riding where we will want."

"Oh, that's why you need my apartment, "I said in response to the words of my son, "you want to sell not an apartment, but you want to exchange me for a car. Have you thought about such a case if I will not put up with my daughter-in-law? Where do you move me, may be, to the dump? No, I will not go with you, and do not think about it! And if you don't want to move to my house, then you can get out of here even now."

"You misinterpreted our conversation," Yegor said in anger, "but no matter, I will go right now. Someday you will comprehend me and will regret about your words, but it could be late. Goodbye, mother!"

Then he left the room, slamming the door so that the plaster fell. Yegor quickly gathered his case, got dressed, said goodbye to his sister and left. The city met him with a light drizzle, but Yegor was only glad that in mid-February, the winds did not walk with twenty degrees of frost, and during the day, weather was rather warm albeit with a rain.

He got to the train station quickly and bought the train tickets; he has two hours to wait for its arrival. There, at the end of the road, he was already awaited by his beloved wife, military service, part-time job, petty household chores, in a word, all that he loved and appreciated. In everyday affairs and concerns that filled his days from morning to evening, the events on the day of his father's funeral quickly erased from memory, then the grudge against me disappeared little by little, and a couple of years later, Nelly and I began to call him. Further, the daughter was talking with him without me, because my mind began to weaken, either from old age, or from the tribulation, which I experienced.

One day in the summer, my turn came to go through THIS. I was dying now, and it seemed to me that I heard my daughter was calling her son and was screaming into the phone in an agitated voice, "Yegor, our mother is dying, she fell in the kitchen and hit her head on the corner of the gas stove. Now she is very sick, the doctor said that she would not last even two days. I do not know what to do. Come soon!"

Yegor listened to his sister and was silent. The events of that February day, when his father was buried, and his sister, who told him how his father died, surfaced in front of his eyes. Now his mother went in this road. Who next?

"Yegor, can you hear me?" Nelly continued to shout, guessing the reason for his silence, "Why are you silent? You think it's me? No, I did not do it, you must understand that she did it herself, I was not even at home."

In my fading consciousness, the events of my life flashed one after another, and I could no longer understand whom I was, what was wrong with me, and why Nelly was refusing what she did to me? After all, I am grateful to her for the fact that she stopped my earthly tribulations, and I can fly to God. He will take me to him, because I was both his victim and his punishing right hand, and I had did his work for him, but at all, I was not a blind providence. I could decide myself whom to punish, and whom to pardon. My Lord, forgive me, and let my children not follow my path!

Printed in Great Britain
by Amazon